FUEL FROM WATER

Energy Independence With Hydrogen

Sixth Revised Edition

by

Michael A. Peavey

Merit, Inc.
Box 694
Louisville, KY 40201

ISBN 0-945516-04-5

POTASSIUM HYDROXIDE SODIUM HYDROXIDE
STAINLESS STEEL ELECTRODES

POSITIVE ELECTRODE = OXYGEN
        NEGATIVE = HYDROGEN

Pg 25

Tennessee State University sponsored **hydrogen race car** shown at the Bonneville Salt Flats. Car was raced at this location from 1991 to 1994. It currently holds the official world's record at 102mph for 1 mile in alternate fuel class. Timed at 108 for 1/4 mile. Engine: 1990 Nissan 2400 with a modified Lamborgini Kit body. Dr. Cliff Rickets supervised the project. Pictured in front of the car are chief mechanic Terry Young and engineering student Dave Tompkins

FUEL FROM WATER

Sixth Revised Edition, Copyright (c) 1995 by Merit, Inc. **All rights reserved.** No portion of this text may be repoduced in whole or in part without the specific written permission of Merit, Inc. Published by Merit, Inc., P.O. Box 694, Louisville, KY 40201 Designed by Michael Peavey. Printed in the United States of America. L.C. Number 88-188956. **ISBN 0-945516-04-5**

NOTICE

"I believe that water will one day be employed as a fuel, that hydrogen and oxygen will constitute it, used singly or together, will furnish an inexhaustible source of heat and light..."

Jules Verne,
Mysterious Island

CONTENTS

Chapter 1: INTRODUCTION

1 2

Chapter 2: ELECTROLYSIS

Chemical Reactions Producing Hydrogen   **14**
Electrolysis   **18**
- Water Splitting --- 18
- Separators -- 21
- Measures of Efficiency --- 21
- Energy Requirements -- 19
- Voltage vs Temperature --- 19
- Cost of Electrolysis --- 25

Electrolyser Design   **25**
- Adding the Electrolyte --- 28
- Output -- 28

High Pressure Cell   **28**
Solid Polymer Electrolyte   **29**
Cell Connections   **32**
- Advantages of Parallel Electrolysers Compared to Series ------------------------ 32
- Disadvantages of Parallel Electrolysers Compared to Series -------------------- 32
- Advantages of Series Electrolysers Compared to Parallel ------------------------ 32
- Disadvantages of Series Electrolysers Compared to Parallel -------------------- 36

Commercial Electrolysers   **36**
High Pressure Electrolysis   **40**
High Temperature Electrolysers   **40**
- Increased Performance --- 40
- Materials --- 41
- Modes of Operation -- 41
- Costs --- 43

Photovoltaic Powered Electrolysis   **46**
- Hydrogen as an Energy Carrier --- 46
- From Sunlight to Hydrogen --- 47
- Solar Hydrogen Aircraft --- 49
- Costs of Solar Electrolysis --- 49
- Wind Power --- 51

Chapter 3: CHEMICAL HYDROGEN PRODUCTION

Electrochemical Reactions Producing Hydrogen   **5 2**

Photovoltaic Processes   **5 3**
- Solar Electric Hydrogen --- 53
- Photoelectrodes -- 53
- Electrolysis of Hydrogen Sulfide --------------------------------------- 54
- Texas Instruments Solar Energy System ------------------------------- 55
- Summary --- 55

Biological Sources   **5 5**
- Plants as a Carbon Source -- 55
- Biological Production of Hydrogen --------------------------------------- 55
- Summary --- 56

Direct Thermal Water Splitting   **5 7**
- Solar Thermal Energy -- 57
- Solar Thermal Collectors --- 59

Thermochemical Cycles   **6 2**
- Isothermal Steps -- 62
- Efficiency --- 63
- Costs --- 63
- Demonstration Plants -- 64
- The Nitric Oxide Process --- 67
- Summary --- 67

Chapter 4: FUEL FROM TRASH

Steam Reforming of Coal   **6 8**
Thermodynamic Cost --- 68
Thermodynamic Concepts --- 69
Maximum Useful Work Available from a Synthetic Fuel ------------------- 70
Thermodynamic Cost of Synthesis Gas Production ---------------------- 71
Thermodynamic Cost of Hydrogen Production ------------------------- 72
Thermodynamic Cost of Methane Production ------------------------- 73
Summary --- 75

Steam Reforming of Biomass   **7 5**

Oxydation of Hydrocarbons   **7 6**

Pyrolysis of Hydrocarbons   **7 6**

Chapter 5: STORING HYDROGEN

Perspective   **78**

Pressurized Gas   **79**
Low Pressure Stationary Storage -- 79
High Pressure Storage on a Vehicle ------------------------------------- 83

Liquid Hydrogen   **8 7**
- Comparisons --- 87
- Liquefaction Plants --- 87
- Magnetocaloric Effect --- 92
- Cryogenic Tanks -- 92
- Ortho to Para Conversion --- 94
- Using Liquid Hydrogen as a Coolant ---------------------------------- 94
- Liquid Hydrogen as an Aviation Fuel ---------------------------------- 94
- Cryogenic Auto Fuel -- 98
- Recovering Refrigeration Energy -------------------------------------- 108

- Railroads --- 108

Hydride Energy Storage   **110**
- Using Heat to Store Hydrogen ------------------------------------- 110
- Heat Exchange Fluid -- 112
- Types of Hydride --- 112
- Hydride Packing -- 116
- Contamination -- 116
- Heat Exchange Systems with Magnesium Hydride -------------------- 118
- Heat Exchange Systems with Iron-Titanium Hydride --------------- 118
- A Hydride Tank Design -- 120
- 1975 Pontiac --- 121
- 1977 Cadillac Seville -- 121
- Dodge Omni --- 121
- Hydride on the Racetrack --- 124
- Hydrogen Tractor --- 125
- The Riverside Bus -- 130
- Mercedes Benz Van --- 134

Storing Hydrogen in Carbon   **139**
Formate Salts as a Storage Media   **141**
Microsphere Storage   **141**
Evaluating Hydrogen Storage Systems   **142**
On-Board Hydrogen Generation   **120**
- Hydrogen from Gasoline --- 142
- Hydrogen from Methanol -- 144
- Hydrogen from Iron -- 144

Chapter 6: ENGINE MODIFICATIONS

Benefits and Problems of Using Hydrogen   **146**
- General Considerations --- 146
- Preignition and Flashback -- 147
- Efficiency of Combustion --- 147
- Emissions -- 147
- Wider Range of Combustion -- 149
- Summary -- 149

History of Hydrogen Conversion Projects   **149**
Modern Conversion Projects   **150**
- Diesel Conversion in China --------------------------------------- 150
- Billings Postal Jeep --- 150
- Diesel Conversion in India --------------------------------------- 152
- Hydrogen Mining Vehicle -- 152

Fuel Mixing   **152**
- External Fuel Mixing --- 154
- Internal Fuel Mixing --- 154
- Equivalency Ratio -- 157
- Engine Governing --- 158
- Methods of Reducing Preignition ---------------------------------- 158
- The Musashi Liquid Hydrogen Diesel ------------------------------- 161
- The A.H.A. "Smart Plug" -- 161

Compression Ratio   **163**
- Spark Ignition Engines --- 163
- Diesel Engines --- 163

Fuel Dilution   **164**
- Sources of Pollution --- 164
- Water Induction -- 166

● Exhaust Temperature and Combustion Efficiency ------------------------------ 166
● Cryogenic Cooling --- 167
● Exhaust Gas Recirculation --167
Ignition Timing   **169**
● Spark Advance -- 169
● Spark Gap -- 169
● Avoiding Cross Induction --- 169
● The Ignition Sequence -- 171
Hydrogen as a Supplemental Fuel   **171**
● Diesel and Hydrogen --171
● Mixing Hydrogen and Gasoline -- 173
● Selective Use of Hydrogen or Gasoline --------------------------------------- 174
● Precision Spark Ignition -- 178
Continuous Flow Engines   **181**

Chapter 7: ELECTRICITY FROM HYDROGEN

Hydrogen vs Electric Power   **183**
The Hydride Battery   **184**
Fuel Cells   **185**
● Reactions --- 185
● Materials --- 187
● Solid Electrolyte -- 188
● Automotive Applications -- 188
● Stationary Power Generation --- 190

Chapter 8: STATIONARY APPLICATIONS

On-Site Power Generation   **200**
● The Energy Carrier -- 200
● Hydrogen vs Natural Gas -- 200
Harness Hydride   **201**
● Heating and Cooling -- 201
● Complex Hydride Energy Systems (CHES) Project --------------------------- 202
● Power from Hydride --- 202
Aphoid Burners   **202**
Open Air Burners   **204**
● How a Burner Works -- 204
● Hydrogen vs Natural Gas -- 204
● Burner Port Sizing --205
● Appliance Regulators --205
Catalytic Burners   **205**
● Flame Assisted -- 205
● Flameless Combustion -- 206
● Lighting -- 209
● Water Production -- 209
The Hydrogen Homestead   **209**
● The Hydrogen Delivery System -- 212
● Hydrogen Production -- 212
● Cooking and Nitrous Oxide Formation -- 214
● The Lorenzen Homestead --- 215
● Determining the Needed Hydrogen Production Capacity ---------------------- 215
● Conclusions --- 215

Chapter 9: SAFETY

Venting 216
Safety-Related Properties of Hydrogen 216
- Density and Specific Gravity --216
- Diffusivity -- 216
- Heat Energy --- 219
- Explosion Energy --219
- Flammability Limits and Optimum Mix ------------------------------------ 219
- Ignition Temperature --- 220
- Ignition Energy -- 220
- Flame Luminosity and Temperature ----------------------------------- 220
- Flame Speed --220
Embrittlement 220
Regulations 222
Summary 223

Chapter 10: THE HYDROGEN ECONOMY

Fuel Use Trends 224
- The Unmet Challenge -- 224
- The Technology Trap -- 224
- From Carbon to Hydrogen --- 225
- The Future of Coal --- 225
Utilization Efficiency of Hydrogen 225
Air Transportation 229
Production Costs 229
Pipelines 231
Underground Storage 232
Environmental Costs 232
The Last Word 236
Sources of Information 237
Sources of Equipment 237
Bibliography 238
References Cited in Alphabetical Order 243
Index 247

LIST OF EXHIBITS

1. Kipp Generator for Making Hydrogen -- 16
2. Collecting Hydrogen "Over Water" --- 17
3. Hydrogen-Oxygen Electrolyser -- 20
4. Electrolyser Polarization --- 23
5. Temperature vs Voltage -- 23
6. Cell Crossection --- 24
7. System Schematic -- 24
8. Cell in Operation -- 26
9. Six Cells Connected in Series --- 27
10. High Temperature Electrolyser "Sandwich" -- 30
11. Solid Electrolyte Cell -- 31
12. Crossection of S.P.E. Cell and Joint Detail -- 31
13. Electrolyser Cell Connections (Series and Parallel) ------------------------------- 33
14. Design Performance of Four-Cell Unit -- 34
15. Electrolyte Circulation in a Four-Cell Parallel Unit ------------------------------ 35
16. A Module of S.P.E. Cells -- 37
17. Lurgi Parallel Electrolyser --- 38
18. Stuart Series Electrolyser -- 39
19. Cell Voltage-Current Density in Conventional
    and Advanced Electrolysis -- 42
20. Cost of Electrolytic Hydrogen -- 44
21. Cost Comparison of Electrolysis and Natural Gas -------------------------------- 44
22. Cost Comparison of Electrolysis and Electricity --------------------------------- 45
23. Solar Cell Performance and Light Intensity ------------------------------------- 48
24. PV Cell Performance --- 48
25. Electrolyser Performance Summary --- 50
26. Estimated Cost of Residential Hydrogen --- 51
27. Biological Sources of Hydrogen -- 57
28. Water Dissociation at Various Temperatures ------------------------------------ 58
29. Sun Motor --- 60
30. Large-Scale Sun Motors --- 61
31. Hydrogen Production Costs --- 64
32. Heat of Formation of Various Substances --------------------------------------- 70
33. Enthalpy and Free Energy Change at 25°C --------------------------------------- 71
34. Availability Loss for Carbon Conversion to Synthesis Gas ---------------------- 72
35. Availability Loss for Carbon Conversion to Hydrogen -------------------------- 73
36. Availability Loss for Carbon Conversion to Methane -------------------------- 74
37. Availability Loss for Synthetic Fuels -- 75
38. Annual U.S. Waste Production --- 77
39. Energy Content of Common Fuels --- 80

40. Energy Density of Various Fuels -- 81
41. Comparison of Fuel Storage Methods -- 82
42. Hydrogen Gas Fuel System -- 85
43. Engine Compartment of Postal Jeep --- 86
44. Hydrogen Olds -- 88
45. Characteristics of Fuel Systems --- 89
46. Properties of Liquefied Gasses --- 90
47. Flow Sheet for Liquid Hydrogen Plant ------------------------------------- 91
48. Typical Liquid Hydrogen Plant Specifications -------------------------------- 93
49. Liquid Hydrogen Storage Dewars --- 95
50. Liquid Hydrogen Dewar Specifications --------------------------------------- 96
51. Liquid Hydrogen Storage Losses due to Ortho-Para Conversion -------------- 97
52. Hypersonic Aircraft --- 99
53. Aircraft With Alternative Fuels -- 99
54. Alternative Fuels in Long-Range, High-Payload Aircraft ----------------------- 100
55. Alternative Fuels in Short-Range, Low-Payload Aircraft ----------------------- 100
56. Liquid Hydrogen Fuel System --- 102
57. Flow Control Wiring Diagram -- 102
58. Liquid Hydrogen-Powered Buick --- 103
59. Liquid Hydrogen Storage and Filling Apparatus ----------------------------- 103
60. Liquid Hydrogen Pump --- 104
61. Crossection of Liquid Hydrogen Tank Showing Fuel Pump ------------------- 106
62. Musashi-7 at Expo '86 -- 107
63. Liquid Hydrogen Tank and Pump for BMW Experimental Car --------------- 107
64. Liquid Hydrogen Fueled Vehicles --- 109
65. Composition-Pressure Isotherms --- 111
66. Thermal Capacities of Selected Materials -------------------------------------- 111
67, 68 & 69. Pressure-Hydrogen Content Isotherms ----------------------------- 113
70. Properties of Metal Hydrides --- 115
71. Comparison of Hydrides --- 115
72 & 73. Iron-Titanium Hydride --- 117
74. Hydride Heating Using Engine Exhaust -- 119
75. Hydride Heating Using Engine Coolant --- 119
76. Tube Bundle Hydride Tank -- 120
77. Water Heated and Cooled Hydride (1977 Cadillac) --------------------------- 122
78. Dual Fuel Dodge Omni --- 123
79. Crossection of Dodge Omni --- 123
80. Hydride Tank with Internal Heat Exchanger ---------------------------------- 126
81. Hydrogen Tractor Specifications -- 126
82. Metal Hydride Bed of Tractor, Interior View --------------------------------- 127
83. Jacobsen Hydrogen Tractor Fuel System -------------------------------------- 128
84. Hydrogen and Bed Temperature for Air-Cooled Cell Refueling -------------- 129
85. Bed Pressure and Temperature During Typical Running Cycle --------------- 129
86. Billings Hydrogen City Bus -- 131
87. Schematic of Hydrogen Bus --- 131
88. Schematic of Billings Riverside Bus -- 132
89. Hydrogen Powered Bus --- 135
90. Details of Mercedes-Benz Hydrogen Van -------------------------------------- 136
91. Hydride Container Tested in Mercedes-Benz Van ----------------------------- 137
92. Performance of Iron Titanium Hydride Vessel -------------------------------- 137
93. Details of the Mercedes-Benz with
     Gasoline and Hydrogen Operation --- 138
94. Test Data for Experimental Hydride Vehicle ---------------------------------- 139
95. Volumetric and Mass Densities for Different Storage Alternatives ------------ 140
96. On-Board Fuel Reforming System --- 143
97. Fuel Reforming Reactor -- 143
98. Volume of Hydrogen from Methanol -- 145

99. Influence of Combustion Method on Engine Power ---------------------------- 148
100. Thermal Efficiencies of Gasoline and Hydrogen ----------------------------- 151
101. Hydride Tank Mounted on Vehicle --- 153
102. Hydrogen Converted Dodge Omni Engine ------------------------------------- 155
103. Hydrogen Intake Ports --- 156
104. External Hydrogen-Air Mixing and Water Induction System ------------------ 159
105. Crossection of Combustion Chamber
     Showing Internal Hydrogen-Air Mixing ----------------------------------- 160
106. Exhaust Manifold Variations -- 162
107. Thermal Efficiency of Hydrogen --- 162
108. Hot Surface Igniter -- 165
109. Impco Gas Mixer -- 165
110. Temperature of Exhaust Gasses --- 168
111. Power vs. Speed for Full Throttle --- 168
112. Brake Thermal Efficiency vs. Engine Power at Full Throttle ------------------ 168
113. Lean Best Torque Setting -- 170
114. Spark Advance at Various Fuel Mixtures ------------------------------------- 170
115 & 116. Diesel Smoke Production with Supplemental Hydrogen Fuel ---------- 172
117. Diesel Smoke Production with Various Injection Advances -------------------- 172
118. BMW 745i Experimental Vehicle -- 175
119. Engine Compartment of Hydrogen BMW 745i ------------------------------- 176
120. Intake Manifold of BMW 745i -- 177
121. Computerized Engine Control System for BMW 745i ------------------------- 177
122. Diagram of the Engine Control System Microprocessor -------------------- 179
123. Operation Principal of the Motronic Computer ------------------------------ 179
124. History of Hydrogen Converted Engine Experiments ------------------------- 182
125. Comparison of Hydrogen and Electric Cars --------------------------------- 184
126. Schematic of a Hydrogen-Oxygen Fuel Cell --------------------------------- 186
127. Experimental Solid Electrolyte Fuel Cell Crossection ----------------------- 189
128. Electrical Circuit Diagram of Fuel Cell and Battery Powered Car ----------- 191
129. Load Sharing of Combined Fuel Cell and Battery System --------------------- 192
130. Schematic Diagram of Hydrogen-Air Fuel Cell Automobile ------------------ 193
131. Fuel Cell Stack with Eight Modules -- 195
132. Fuel Cell Module with 48 Electrodes --- 196
133. Elenco Fuel Cell Electrode --- 196
134. Voltage vs. Current of a 24-Cell Module at 65°C (149°F) -------------------- 197
135. Voltage vs. Time of a 24-Cell Module at 65°C (149°F) ----------------------- 197
136. Experimental Iron-Based Combined Electrolyser/Fuel Cell ------------------ 198
137. Voltage-Current of Experimental Electrolyser and Fuel Cell ---------------- 199
138. Comparison of Heat Storage Systems -- 203
139. Principal Parts of a Typical Atmospheric Burner ----------------------------- 203
140. Billings High Temperature Flame-Assisted Catalytic Burner ----------------- 207
141. Hydrogen Flame Stove Top --- 208
142. Nitrous Oxides from Hydrogen and Natural Gas at Maximum Combustion -- 210
143. Water Production form Combustion of Various Fuels ------------------------- 210
144. Hydrogen Delivery System for the Hydrogen Homestead --------------------- 211
145. Hydride Vessel Specifications -- 213
146. Computer Data System --- 213
147. Catalytic Safety Burner for Escaping Gas ------------------------------------ 217
148. Safety Related Properties of Hydrogen --------------------------------------- 218
149. Ignition Temperature of Various Fuels --------------------------------------- 221
150. American Regulations for Distributing Hydrogen ----------------------------- 221
151. Fuel Use Trends -- 226
152. Fossil Fuel Use Projections --- 227
153. Hydrogen Research Goals --- 228
154. Utilization Efficiency of Hydrogen and Fossil Fuels ------------------------- 230
155. Estimates of Fossil Fuel Damage --- 233
156. Effective Cost of Synthetic Fuels -- 235

11

Chapter 1:
INTRODUCTION

HYDROGEN has been called by Peter Hoffmann the "forever fuel", in his book by that title. When hydrogen is burned water vapor is the main product. Hydrogen can also be made from water in an endless fuel-water cycle. Despite long standing difficulties, the problem of finding an efficient way to split water is gradually being solved.

The advantages of hydrogen over other fuels will be covered throughout this book but can be summarized as follows.

- Hydrogen can be made endlessly from water.
- There are widely varying methods of production.
- Combustion produces low levels of pollutants in the form of *nitrous oxides* , but these be virtually eliminated by various combustion control methods.
- Hydrogen has the most energy *per unit weight* of any fuel: about three times that of gasoline.
- Hydrogen can be transported safely in pipelines.
- Hydrogen is nontoxic.
- Hydrogen dissipates rapidly in air. This minimizes explosion hazards.

Hydrogen also has some disadvantages, but when compared to the benefits of this clean burning fuel, hydrogen is still a major contender as an alternative fuel.

- Hydrogen has a higher range of flammability when mixed with air, compared with other fuels. This means that it will burn at lower concentrations.
- The storage technology is complex when compared to liquid fuels and other gaseous fuels.
- Its low liquefaction temperature, -253°C (-423°F), requires a large energy input for the refrigeration process.
- Hydrogen has a low energy content *on a volume basis:* about one-third that of gasoline. Storage devices tend to be bulky.
- High flame velocity and low ignition energy give hydrogen an advantage in engine performance but present special safety problems. There are also other safety
        advantages so that, in general, hydrogen is no more dangerous than other fuels.

This book will explain the general sources and uses of hydrogen as a fuel. An overview of some experimental technology and proposals for expanded use of hydrogen in the economy will be given. More specifically, this book describes:

- The principles of constructing a simple electrolyser.
- The principles behind converting internal combustion engines to hydrogen fuel.
- The safe use of hydrogen fuel in all its primary applications.
- The results of current research on hydrogen use, storage and its production by electrolysis.

Hydrogen makes up 90% of the atoms in the universe. It is abundant in interstellar space with an average of about one hydrogen atom per cubic centimeter. However, on earth, the gas constitutes about 0.2% of the atmosphere.

In 1776 the British chemist Henry Cavendish discovered hydrogen by dissolving metals in dilute acids. He also found that when hydrogen is burned it produces water. Later on, hydrogen was named by the French chemist Antoine Lavoisier in 1783 from the Greek words meaning "water producer".

Hydrogen can also be produced by passing an electric current through water. This separates the hydrogen from the oxygen in the water molecule in a process called *electrolysis*.

Unlike outer space, hydrogen on earth is chemically combined with other elements such as oxygen, forming water. Water, however, is not the only source of hydrogen. A class of compounds called *hydrocarbons* combine hydrogen with carbon. It requires energy to separate hydrogen from the carbon in hydrocarbons or the oxygen in water. Energy is released as heat when hydrogen combines with oxygen during combustion. Burning hydrogen in a device known as a *fuel cell* can produce an electric current. In this way, the combustion of hydrogen gas can provide electricity as well as heat energy.

The units of measurement used in this book are in the metric (kilogram, meter, second) system. English units are given in parentheses. Names in parentheses, such as

Numbers in parentheses, such as **150p23** refer to sources listed in "References Cited" section at the end of the book. The first number cooresponds to the title of the source. The second number is the page number of the citation in that source.

Chapter 2:
ELECTROLYSIS

CHEMICAL REACTIONS PRODUCING HYDROGEN

ABOUT *one billion cubic meters* (35,000,000,000 cubic feet) of hydrogen is produced in the United States yearly. This does not include amounts used in ammonia, methanol, synthesis gas, and petroleum refining.

The most common method of producing hydrogen is to remove it from hydrocarbons such as methane, gasoline, fuel oil, and crude oil. A hydrocarbon molecule, in the presence of a nickel catalyst and 700 to $1,000^oC$ (1,290 to $1,800^oF$) steam, is split into carbon oxides and hydrogen gasses. The oxygen in the water combines with the carbon in the fuel to release the hydrogen. **200**

For propane (C_3H_9):

$$C_3H_9 + 3H_2O \text{-----}> 3CO + 7.5H_2.$$

The product gasses can be processed further at 350^oC (660^oF).

$$3CO + 3H_2O \text{-----}> 3CO_2 + 3H_2.$$

An iron oxide catalyst is generally used for this process.
Pure carbon in the form of coal or coke can be reacted with water.

$$C + 2H_2O \text{-----}> CO_2 + 2H_2.$$

The carbon dioxide can be absorbed by a solution of monethylamine and water, leaving the hydrogen behind.

In the U.S. and many parts of the world coal is more plentiful than natural gas so that the cost of producing hydrogen by this method is the lowest cost alternative. Hydrogen can be produced at the energy equivalent of $0.04 per liter ($0.15 per gallon) of gasoline. This excludes distribution, retail costs, and tax credits which could still leave hydrogen competitive with gasoline. Billings Energy Corporation plans to adapt a housing subdivision to burning hydrogen from a small decentralized coal gasification plant.

Less common methods of hydrogen production include using high temperatures to dissociate (split) the ammonia molecule.

14

$$2NH_3 \text{ -----> } N_2 + 3H_2.$$

This yields only small amounts of hydrogen but is convenient for lab use. A similar process is used to "reform" liquid hydrocarbon fuels on-board a vehicle to supply hydrogen to the engine. This process is described in a later chapter.

Electrolysis gives hydrogen of high purity, in excess of 99.9%, but is relatively expensive.

$$2H_2O \text{ -----> } 2H_2 + O_2.$$

With continual research, the costs of water splitting are gradually declining. Electrolysis, however, is the most convenient way for the individual do-it-yourselfer to produce hydrogen in significant quantities.

Small amounts of hydrogen for laboratory use can be produced by reacting metals with acids. Acids are compounds which contain hydrogen. The reaction proceeds as follows.

Metal + Acid -----> Metal compound + Hydrogen gas.

The metal displaces the hydrogen in the acid. **Exhibit 1** shows an laboratory apparatus for making hydrogen from metals and acids. The reaction of zinc with sulfuric acid will produce hydrogen and zinc sulfate (a combination of zinc, sulfur, and oxygen). Zinc also reacts with hydrochloric acid to produce zinc chloride and hydrogen.

$$Zn + 2HCl \text{ -----> } ZnCl_2 + H_2.$$

Iron reacts, in a similar manner, with sulfuric acid.

$$Fe + H_2SO_4 \text{ -----> } FeSO_4 + H_2.$$

Sulfuric acid or hydrochloric acid can be mixed with water to any levil of dilution. Pour the acid *slowly* into the water. **Do not pour the water into the acid.** Dilute acids act vigorously with zinc to produce hydrogen. Pure acid and zinc react more slowly than dilute acid. Small amounts of copper sulfate can be added to the solution to increase the reaction rate.

Hydrogen can be purified by passing it through a sodium hydroxide solution. Water vapor can be removed by passing the gas through silica gel or concentrated sulfuric acid.

Exhibit 2 shows how hydrogen is collected "over water" in bottles. This prevents the hydrogen from flowing back into the reaction bottle. An apparatus like this, or a commercially available one-way valve *(check valve),* is used anywhere it is desirable for the gas to flow in only one direction.

The following metals will replace hydrogen in dilute sulfuric, hydrochloric, or many other common acids.

- Potassium (K)
- Sodium (Na)
- Calcium (Ca)
- Magnesium (Mg)
- Aluminum (Al)
- Zinc (Zn)
- Iron (Fe)
- Lead (Pb)

Sodium reacts with water according to the reaction:

$$2Na + 2H_2O \text{ -----> } 2NaOH + H_2.$$

1. Kipp Generator for Making Hydrogen

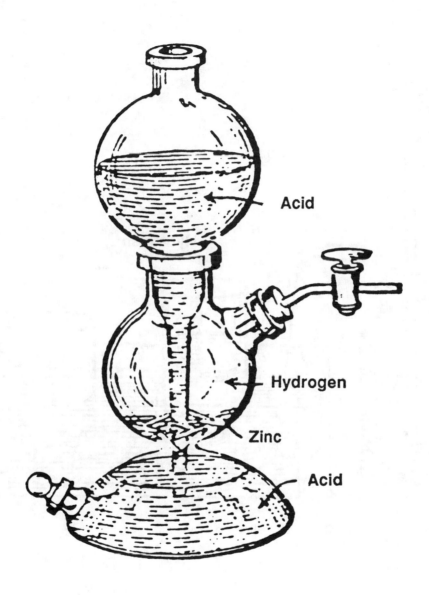

Acid

Hydrogen

Zinc

Acid

2. Collecting Hydrogen "Over Water"

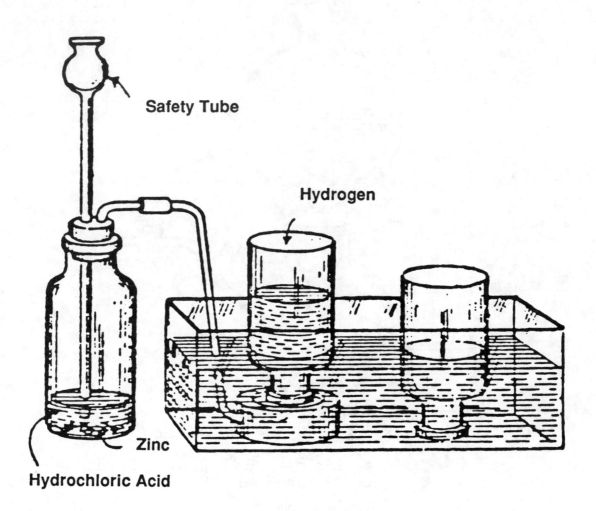

Safety Tube

Hydrogen

Zinc

Hydrochloric Acid

Sodium and calcium metals react violently with water to produce heat and to release one hydrogen atom from the water and combine with the other atom to form a *hydroxide*. With sodium the reaction is:

$$2Na + 2H_2O \longrightarrow H_2 + 2NaOH.$$

Sodium + Water $\longrightarrow$ Hydrogen gas + Sodium Hydroxide.

We write H_2 instead of H because hydrogen atoms, like oxygen atoms, usually travel in pairs forming hydrogen (H_2) and oxygen (O_2) molecules.

Potassium reacts even more vigorously with water. The reaction may produce enough heat to ignite the hydrogen. Hydrogen and potassium hydroxide are formed.

Each of the elements in the above list reacts with only *half* the water. The other half is liberated. Sodium hydroxide and potassium hydroxide readily dissolve in water forming a clear solution. Calcium hydroxide remains undissolved in a milky suspension in the water.

Sodium hydroxide, water and aluminum may be further reacted to form more hydrogen. 55 square centimeters (cm^2) of aluminum reacted to produce one liter of hydrogen per minute. One square foot (ft^2) of aluminum produces 0.6 cubic feet (ft^3) of hydrogen per minute. A 1 cm (0.25 in) thick plate lasts about 24 hours. It requires about 12.5% more surface area for zinc than for aluminum.

Alkali solutions of aluminum or silicone also react with water.

$$2Al + 2NaOH + 6H_2O \longrightarrow 2NaAl(OH)_4 + 3H_2.$$

$$Si + 4NaOH \longrightarrow Na_4SiO4 + 2H_2.$$

Calcium hydride can produce a large volume of hydrogen, but is expensive.

$$CaH_2 + 2H_2O \longrightarrow Ca(OH)_2 + 2H_2.$$

1 kilogram (1 kg) of CaH_2 produces 1 cubic meter (1 m^3) of hydrogen. 1 lb. yields about 16 ft^3. Sodium borohydrate produces still larger amounts of hydrogen but is even more expensive.

$$NaBH_4 + 4H_2O \longrightarrow NaB(OH)_4 + 4H_2.$$

Exhibit 1 shows a laboratory device that delivers a continuous supply of hydrogen from the reactants. The weight of the acid in the container pressurizes the hydrogen in the middle container. As hydrogen is drawn off, the pressure is reduced in the container and the acid level in the lower chamber rises and comes into contact with them metal. More gas is generated, thereby increasing the gas pressure and forcing the acid level down. This action governs the rate of hydrogen production and prevents hydrogen production when not needed.

ELECTROLYSIS

Water Splitting

Electrolysis is a process of producing hydrogen and oxygen from electricity and water. Two hydrogen atoms and one oxygen atom are electrically attracted in a molecule of water: H_2O. When an electric current passes through water the chemical bond breaks down. The result is: two positively charged hydrogen atoms (positive ions) and one negatively charged oxygen ion (a negative ion).

If two oppositely charged electrodes are inserted into the water and a current is passed between them, the negative oxygen ions migrate to the positive electrode (the anode) while the positively charged hydrogen ions are attracted to the negative electrode (the cathode).

Direct current applied to water results in the following reaction:

$$2H_2O \longrightarrow 2H_2 + O_2.$$

Half as much oxygen as hydrogen is produced. Electrons are transfered from the anode to the cathode.

The electrical resistance of pure water is high: 100 ohm/cm (254 ohm/in). This resistance may be lowered chemically by applying one or all of the following:

- 700 to 1,000°C (1,290 to 1,800°F) heat.
- A salt like sodium chloride
- An acid such as sulfuric acid, or
- A base such as potassium hydroxide.

Salts tend to corrode electrode metals. Platinum and phosporic acid can be used together but this is expensive. Potassium hydroxide (KOH) with nickle-iron (stainless steel) electrodes provides the best compromise between performance and cost.

The reaction for an alkaline electrolyte (like KOH) at the cathode is.

$$4 \text{ electrons} + 4H_2O \longrightarrow 4O^{2-} + 8H^+.$$
$$4O^{2-} + 8H^+ \longrightarrow 4OH^- + 4H^+.$$
$$4 \text{ electrons } 4H^+ + \longrightarrow 2H_2.$$

Four water molecules are decomposed into eight positively charged hydrogen ions ($8H+$) and four negatively charged oxygen ions ($4O_2-$). Each oxygen ion attatches to one hydrogen ion to form four hydroxyl ions ($4OH^-$). Four hydrogen ions remain. Each of them combine with four electrons emitted at the cathode to form four complete hydrogen atoms. Since hydrogen atoms combine in pairs the four hydrogen atoms combine into two hydrogen molecules (H_2). The four negatively charged hydroxyl ions are attracted to the positive electrode. The electrolyte allows the ions to be drawn to the anode by increasing the conductivity of the water.

The reaction for an alkaline electrolyte (like KOH) at the anode is as follows.

$$4OH^- \longrightarrow O_2 + 2H_2O + 4 \text{ electrons}.$$

Four hydroxyl ions give up four electrons to form a molecule of oxygen gas (O_2) and two molecules of water. The four electrons enter the anode and complete the electrical circuit outside the electrolyser.

The anode reaction is an *oxydation reaction* - free electrons are produced. The reaction at the cathode is a *reduction reaction* - free electrons are absorbed. The flow of ions is depicted in **Exhibit 3**.

The reaction for an acid electrolyte such as sulfuric acid (H_2SO_4) at the cathode is:

$$4 \text{ electrons} + 4H^+ \longrightarrow 2H_2.$$

The reaction for an acid electrolyte such as sulfuric acid (H_2SO_4) at the anode is:

$$2H_2O \longrightarrow O_2 + 4H^+ + 4 \text{ electrons}.$$

19

3. Hydrogen-Oxygen Electrolyser

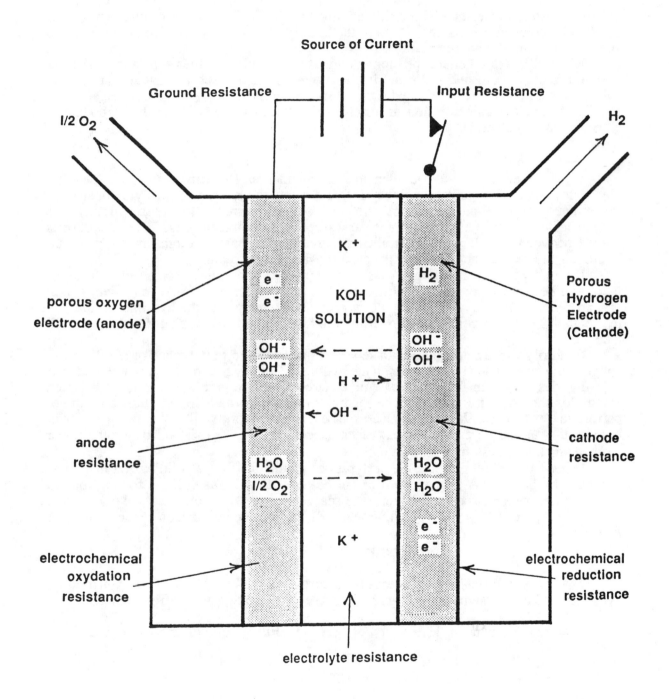

Alkaline electrolytes are less corrosive to electrode material than acids. According to G.A. Crawford, alkaline electrolyte material *"... has the most significant near-term commercial potential for recovery of hydrogen from water on a large industrial scale."* 220p191 It is also more convenient to use on a smaller scale.

The two most common alkaline electrolytes used are sodium hydroxide (NaOH) and potassium hydroxide (KOH). NaOH is less conductive, but cheaper than, KOH. Since KOH combines with CO_2 in air to produce potassium carbonate, periodic replacement is needed in cells open to the atmosphere. However, air tight cells cut down on this loss.

High purity distilled water is needed because electrolytes produce chlorides and sulfates in the presence of tap water impurities. These chemicals slowly corrode the electrode material. Even under the best conditions, with distilled water, electrode materials need to be corrosion resistant. Among the readily available metals, iron cathodes and stainless steel anodes are recommended.

Electrolysis is a general phenomenon that may apply to other substances. Salt, a compound of sodium and chlorine, in the molten state may be electrically split by a suitably designed electrolyser to gather solid sodium at the cathode and chlorine gas at the anode. A zinc chloride solution under electrolysis yields solid zinc at the cathode and chlorine gas at the anode.

Separators

Electrolysers consist of four elements: a container, an electrolyte, an anode (positive electrode), a cathode (negative electrode), and a separator. The electrolyte consists of water and a chemical added to allow the conducting of current. The chemical may be a salt, an acid, or a base. The current passes between the electrodes. The separator is placed between the electrodes. It allows the current to pass through but prevents the hydrogen and oxygen generated by the electrolysis process to mix.

If both hydrogen and oxygen gasses are combined during the electrolysis process, there will be a substantial risk of explosion. Mixtures of between 4 and 75% hydrogen in air and 4 and 94% of hydrogen in pure oxygen are explosive. If the hydrogen content is less than 4% or greater than 75% in air the mixture will not explode but combustion will take place.

Electrolysers are designed with separators (also called membranes or diaphragms) between the anode and cathode to keep the hydrogen and oxygen from combining and also to allow ions to be transfered in the liquid electrolyte. For this reason, the space between electrodes should be minimized. The separator must be permeable to liquids but but not permit gasses to pass. Materials such as asbestos fiber work well as separator material because the capillary pressure is greater then the cell pressure. Artificial fiber cloth, rubber cloth, or metallic mesh may also be used. 630

In the simple low pressure electrolyser design that follows, a solid barrier is used to separate the gasses. A space is left at the bottom of each gas column for the ions to migrate from one electrode to another. The space is below where the gasses evolve so that the rising hydrogen and oxygen bubbles will be kept separate from each other.See **Exhibit 6.**

Measures of Efficiency

The *thermal efficiency* of electrolysis compares the energy of the combustion of hydrogen and oxygen with the energy needed to evolve the two gasses from water.

Thermal efficiency = H / (q + [w/e]) = H / Q = Energy input / Energy output.

Where:

H = energy input required to split water = 79.4 Wh/gram mole H_2 at 25°C (77°F) and 1 atm (0.1 MPa, 14.7 psi).

q = heat energy input.

e = efficiency of converting heat to electrical energy.

Q = total thermal energy required by the process.

Water electrolysis is typically 30 to 35% thermally efficient. **610**

The *voltage efficiency* of water electrolysis compares the theoretical minimum voltage needed to split water with the actual voltage needed in the cell.

Voltage efficiency = 1.24 V/cell voltage = Minimum V needed/Actual V needed.

This means that the voltage efficiency of a cell varies *inversly* with the cell voltage needed. At 1.9 V (for commercial electrolysers) cell efficiency is 65%. At 1.7 V some advanced cells with expensive platinum electrodes have a voltage efficiency of 73%.

The *cell voltage* of any particular electrolyser is the sum of several variables.

Cell voltage = E + iR + n.

Where:

E = required theoretical dissolution voltage of water = 1.24 V/electron.
iR = electrolyte resistance to current flow in the electrolyser (in ohms). This is minimized by reducing separator thickness and electrode spacing.
i = current passing through the cell.
R = area resistance (in ohms) determined by the conductivity of the electrolyte and the permeability of the membrane to fluid ions.

Energy Requirements

At 25°C (77°F) the voltage needed to split water is 1.24 V. It decreases with rising cell temperature by 0.82 millivolts (0.82 mV) per 1^{O}C (1.8^{O}F) and increases by 44.4 mV per 1^{O}C if the pressure is increased ten times.

Conventional electrolysers operate at 75 to 80°C (167 to 176°F) with current densities of around 2,000 amps per square meter (185.8 A/ft^2). Voltage requirements for electrolysers fall within a 1.9 to 2 volt range. The required energy input is 4.8 kWh per cubic meter (0.14 kWh/ft^3) of hydrogen produced. This includes the total energy requirements for pumps and other equipment.

Although the energy input to the electrolysis process may be varied over a wide range, the reaction always requires about 2 volts. **Exhibit 4** shows no upper limit for current input but voltage requirements taper off at 2 volt. The larger the current flow the lower the voltage becomes in relation to it. Electrolyser efficiency is thus increased. However, the current density on the electrodes also increases with increasing current. This increases the resistance in the electrodes. Electrode thickness must, therefore, be minimized at 0.00001 cm (0.000004 in) or less.

The smallest amount of energy needed to electrolyse one mole of water is 65.3 Wh at 25°C (77°F). When the hydrogen and oxygen are recombined into water during combustion 79.3 Wh of energy is released. 14 Wh more energy is released in burning hydrogen and oxygen than is required to split water. This excess must be absorbed from the surrounding media in the form of heat during electrolysis.**340p39**

Voltage vs Temperature

If all the energy to split water came from electric current and no heat flowed into the reaction, 1.481 volts would be needed. As temperature is increased, this voltage at 25°C (77°F) would just begin to produce waste heat. Over 1.481 volts, increasingly large amounts of heat is generated. This critical limit of 1.481 V is referred to as the *thermoneutral voltage.*

Exhibit 5 shows the relationship between electrolyte temperature and the required voltage. **630** At 25°C (77°F) for voltages of 1.23 to 1.47 V, the electrolysis reaction *absorbs* heat. At over 1.47 V at 25°C the reaction *gives off* heat. The horizontal scale shows the desired operating temperature of the cell. In general, for voltages between the

4. Electrolyser Polarization

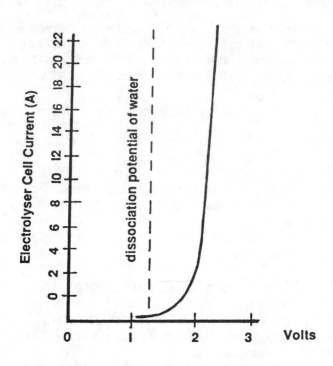

5. Temperature vs Voltage

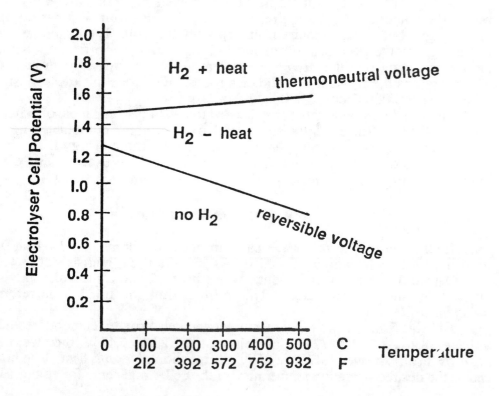

6. Cell Crossection

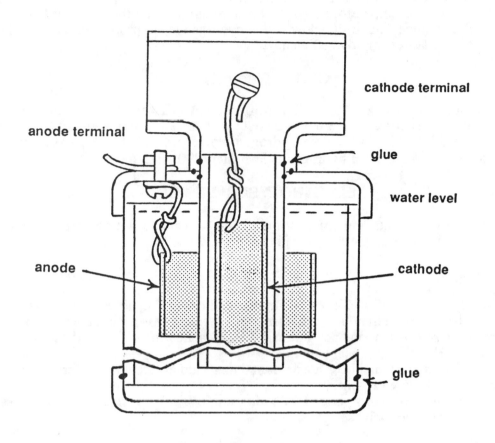

anode terminal

cathode terminal

glue

water level

anode

cathode

glue

7. System Schematic

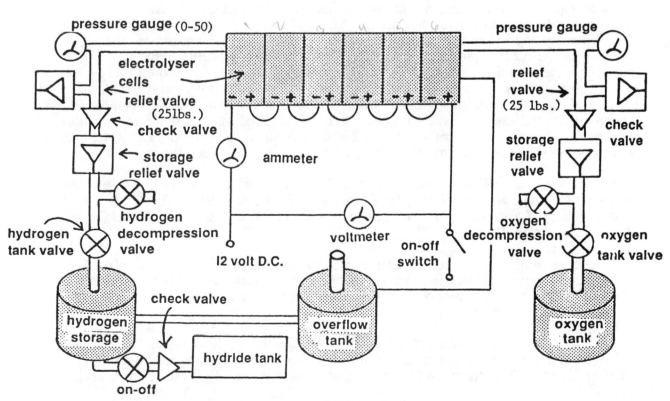

pressure gauge (0-50)

pressure gauge

electrolyser cells

relief valve (25 lbs.)

relief valve (25lbs.)

check valve

check valve

storage relief valve

storage relief valve

ammeter

hydrogen decompression valve

hydrogen tank valve

oxygen decompression valve

oxygen tank valve

12 volt D.C.

voltmeter

on-off switch

check valve

hydrogen storage

overflow tank

oxygen tank

hydride tank

on-off

24

thermoneutral (upper limit) voltage and the reversible (lower limit) voltage the electrolysis reaction absorbs heat. The electrolysis cell operates most efficiently in this range. No electrolysis occurs below the reversible voltage.

With increased temperature both the electrochemical and the electrolyte resistance diminish. This reduces the limit below which hydrogen is not produced. Lower voltages and higher temperatures improve efficiency.

Cost of Electrolysis

A homemade electrolyser is about 50 percent efficient. A certain number of watt-hours of electricity is converted into about half as many watt-hours of hydrogen. If electricity costs \$0.05/kWh then the hydrogen would cost \$0.10/kWh. At atmospheric pressure the energy content of hydrogen is 3wh/liter (290 BTU/ft^3).

ELECTROLYSER DESIGN

This section presents principles for building a homemade electrolyser. The various components should be obtainable at locally for around \$200.

- Use only distilled water. Chlorine in city water corrodes steel electrodes. Rainwater may be used.
- The electrolyte is 20 to 30% KOH in distilled or demineralized water. As a second choice baking soda may be used. It requires 4 volts but is a safer chemical to handle. Use 6 teaspoons per gallon. Water leached through wood ashes may also be used. Filter out the ashes first.
- Electrode material: nickle or nickle-containing stainless steel in the form of a sintered porous sheet, wire or gauze.
- Electric input: 3-4 volts per cell (allowing for 50% voltage efficency), 3 to 10 amps. Increased current increases gas output.

Exhibit 6 is a crossection of an electrolyser cell. It shows the basic components of the cell. Note that a nonconductive sleeve separates the cathode (shaded in center) from the anode (shaded outer electrode.) The two electrodes should have equal surface area. The sleeve prevents the hydrogen from combining with the oxygen. The two gasses must be kept apart to avoid an explosion hazard.

Virtually any nonmetallic container may be used so long as the gas is not allowed to build up in the electrolyser and generate a high pressure. **Exhibit 8** shows a senior engineer at the American Hydrogen Association running an electrolyser built into a glass jar. The hydrogen-generating electrode is seen in the top photo. Oxygen is generated in the central electrode, not shown. The current source is an auto battery. This is the safest current source to use for home experimenters. As the hydrogen collects in the short plexiglas container it displaces water into the larger container to the left. The water acts like a sink trap to prevent the hydrogen from backing up into the electrolyser.

WARNING: Leaking hydrogen could cause an explosion. Vent the oxygen at least 18 meters (60 ft) from the hydrogen. Keep all flames and sparks away from the electrolyser when it is in operation. Insulate all electrical connections.

A schematic for an entire hydrogen-generating system is presented in **Exhibit 7**. The various gauges monitor the amount of hydrogen generated and its pressure. The overflow tank and relief valves prevent excessive pressure build up.

Several cells can be connected in series for increased hydrogen production as shown in **Exhibit 9**.

The float-activated safety switch is shown in **Exhibit 9**. It works as follows. As hydrogen is generated and accumulates in the storage tank, pressure builds, forcing the water level down. The displaced fluid causes the level in the overflow tank to rise. As the

8. Cell in Operation

9. Six Cells Connected in Series

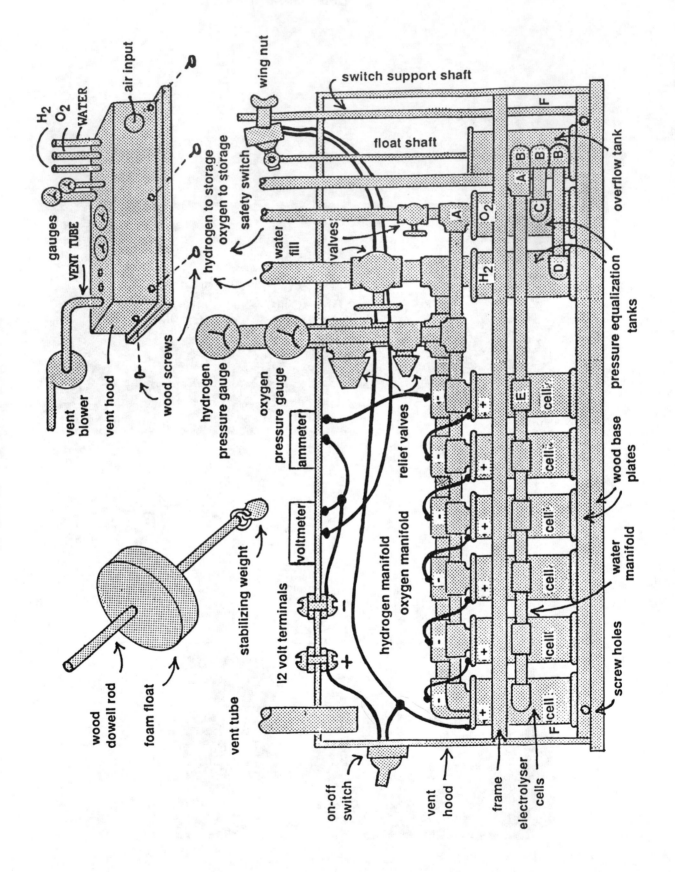

27

float rises, the shaft engages the safety switch turning the electrolyser off before the pressure reaches the danger point. A compressor, if used, may automatically turn off at this point. When the pressure drops, the fluid level also drops and the electrolyser is turned back on. The compressor should be automatically turned off. Wire as shown in **Exhibit 7** and **9**.

WARNING: Never reverse the terminals. This would cause hydrogen to be generated at the oxygen electrode, and oxygen to be generated at the hydrogen electrode. The gasses would mix causing an explosion hazard.

Adding the Electrolyte

Using an ohm meter to measure the electrical resistance of the electrolyte, add potassium hydroxide until the resistance equals 0.3 ohms, or a 30% solution, whichever comes first. Note that the higher the current of the cell, the less electrolyte needs to be used.

WARNING: When the electrolyser is first used, hydrogen and oxygen may be mixed. Discard the first hour's production.

Output

At 100% efficiency, 12 volts and 40 amps, 480 watts (0.6 horsepower) per hour of hydrogen fuel is produced. In practice, efficiency is usually about 50%. This means that output is one-half of what it would be if the unit were 100% efficient.

WARNING: Place the electrolyser at a safe distance from habitable buildings. Change the electrolyte every 1,000 hours of operation. Ground all circuits. Keep feet dry when touching the electrolyser.

The above design may be scaled up for higher output by increasing the height and width of the elecrolyte containers, the area of the electrodes, or increasing the number of cells. Larger designs with higher current may employ cooling fins around the cells so that the blower may dissipate heat more readily to avoid damage to the electrolyte materials.

If 115 volts of alternating utility current is used for electrolysis, a transformer and rectifier are neededto convert the current to 2 volts direct current with boosted amperage.

Using an independent source of electricity such as a windmill generator or photovoltaic cell the electrical output can be converted to hydrogen with about 50 percent efficiency. The following relations are useful in calculating how much hydrogen can be produced from a given electrical output.

- Hydrogen energy content = 3 wh/l (286 BTU/ft^3).
- 1 kwh = 3415 BTU.

If the electrolyser is 50 percent efficient one kilowatt hour of electrical energy will produce about 48,000 BTU of hydrogen. This about 167 l (5.9 ft^3) cubic feet of hydrogen.

HIGH PRESSURE CELL

The following is a general description of a relatively high pressure electrolyser. 340 It is designed to operate at 200°C (392°F) and 98.7 atm (10 MPa, 1,450 psi). The gap between the electrodes is 3 mm (0.12 in). These design features combine to give the device a 75% efficiency. Other features include:

- Sanded nickle electrodes to increase surface area.
- 30 to 50% KOH electrolyte.
- 1.6 volts and 1 amp/cm^2 (6.5 A/ in^2) at 200°C (392°F).

28

Since asbestos is corroded in caustic solutions at temperatures above 100°C (212°F) the diaphragms are made of metal screens covered with oxide ceramic. These are corrosion resistant and have a high hydraulic resistance with small pores. This feature eliminates the probability of passing significant amounts of gas bubbles. The separators also have a low electrical resistance of 0.05 to 0.10 ohm/cm^2 (0.3-0.65 ohm/in^2). Nickle electrodes will corrode in caustic solutions at high temperature. The anode in this design corrodes at the rate of 0.03 mm/year (0.001 in/year) at 0.01 amp/cm^2 (0.07 amp/in^2) and 0.10 mm/year (0.004 in/year) at 1.0 amp/cm^2 (7 amp/in^2). The cathode deterioration rate is 0.01mm/year (0.0004 in/year) at 0.01 amp/cm^2 (0.07 amp/in^2). The cathode corrosion rate increases to 0.0003 mm/year (0.00001 in/year) at 1.0 amp/cm^2 (7 amp/in^2).

In the high temperature region plastics cannot be used. In these areas all bodies and tubings are made of steel-lined with nickle because nickle does not absorb hydrogen as many other metals do. Steel is needed for its strength but must not come into contact with the hydrogen.

The electrodes are made of coarse screen: 0.6 mm (0.24 in) diameter wire layed out in a 0.52 mm (0.02 in) mesh. A 1 mm (0.04 in) perforated nickle plate may be substituted. The electrode may also be corrigated to increase surface area even further. Each corrigation has a 3 cm (1.2 in) radius.

High temperatures combined with caustic solutions destroy many high temperature plastic materials. Nafion (R) was found to be destroyed in days at 150°C (302°F) and in a 50% KOH solution.

An exploded view of the electrolyser cell "sandwich" is shown in **Exhibit 10.** Hydrogen is produced at slightly above the thermoneutral voltage shown in **Exhibit 5.** At this voltage, heat is produced in the electrolyser along with hydrogen. This cell can be connected to the meters, valves and storage tanks as shown in **Exhibit 7.**

Free electricity may be used to power the electrolyser. These can take the form of photovoltaic cells or windpower plants, such as the 32 volt, 40 amp Jacobs model. Connect the wind driven generator to batteries and then connect the batteries to the electrolyser to insure constant current supply.

SOLID POLYMER ELECTROLYTE

A basic problem in designing electrolysers is to allow *ions* to travel between the electrodes while at the same time excluding gas molecules. Liquid electrolytes transfer both the gas bubbles and the ions. Since the distance between electrodes must be small to minimize electrical resistance, the problem of keeping the evolved hydrogen and oxygen gasses separate becomes even more acute. Solid porus barriers known as *separators* are used with liquid electrolytes to keep the evolved gasses separate but to allow ion transfer.

With the advent of *solid electrolytes* the separator is no longer needed. The electrolyte alone performs this function. The electrodes are immersed in water but are separated by the solid electrolyte. See **Exhibit 11.**

Thinner solid electrolyte cells may be designed to accomplish the same task as a liquid electrolyte cell. This reduces internal resistance. Because the solid electrolyte typically has a high melting point, the cell may operate at elevated temperatures, thereby increasing efficiency.

General Electric has developed a solid electrolyte made of *perfluorinated sulfonic acid polymer* 0.1 mm (0.04 in) thick and capable of operating at temperatures between 120 to 150°C (248 to 302°F). Current densities of 20,000 amp/m^2 (1,859 A/ft^2) allow a 90% thermodynamic efficiency. Capital costs are $200 to 280/kWh. Hydrogen production costs range from $4.10 to 7.00/1,000 kWh assuming electric power costs of $0.06 to 0.23/kWh. **340**

By contrast, a current state of the art machine, the Teledyne alkaline liquid electrolyser, requires a capital investment of $260 to 320/kWh. A high temperature separator withstands a 150°C (302°F) operating temperature. Current density is 4,000 to 6,000 A/m^2 (372 to 558 A/ft^2). Hydrogen production costs are comparable to the GE electrolyser.

Exhibit 12 shows a Westinghouse solid polymer cell. It is configured as a tube.

10. High Temperature Electrolyser "Sandwich"

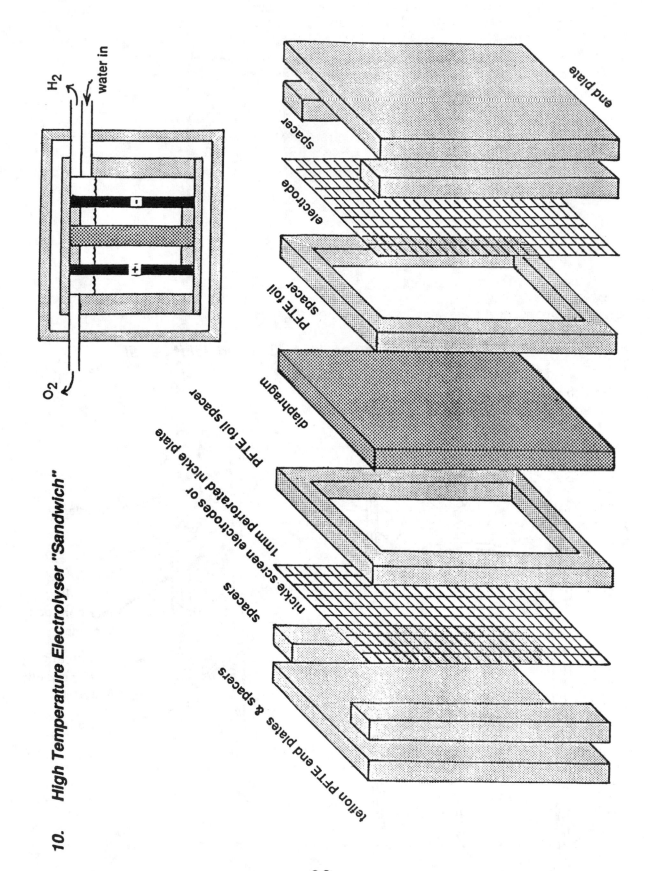

11. Solid Electrolyte Cell

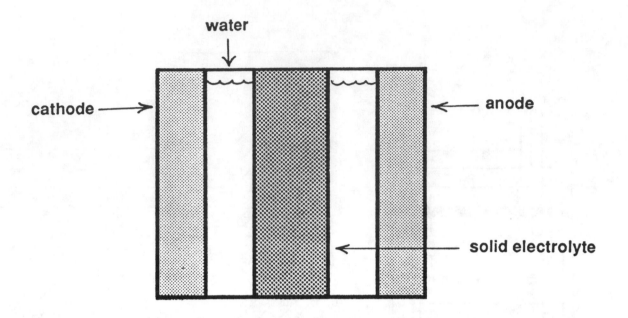

water

cathode

anode

solid electrolyte

12. Crossection of S.P.E. Cell and Joint Detail

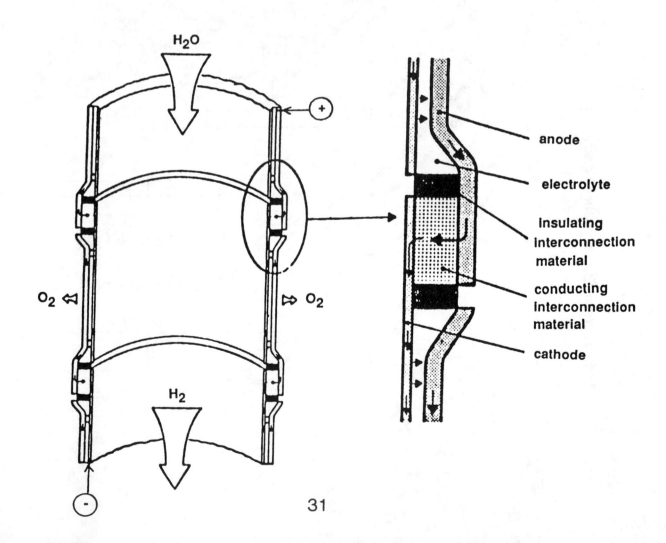

H_2O

+

O_2 ⬅   ➡ O_2

H_2

−

anode

electrolyte

Insulating
interconnection
material

conducting
interconnection
material

cathode

31

Water is injected as steam at one end of the tube and hydrogen gas comes out the other end. Oxygen emerges from the outside wall (anode) of the tube. The cathode forms the inner wall of the tube. The solid polymer separates the inner and outer walls of the tube. **Exhibit 12** shows that the cell tube is connected in sections and reveals the details of the joints.

CELL CONNECTIONS

A pair of electrodes and a container of electrolyte make up one elctrode *cell*. Several cells can be combined for greater output. Cells may be electrically connected in *parallel* or in *series*.

In the *parallel (or unipolar)* connection shown in **Exhibit 13**, each anode is connected separately to the positive terminal of the electric source. Each cathode is similarly connected to the negative terminal. Each cell can be switched off without effecting the neighboring cells. The electrolyte container for each cell is also kept separate from the other cells. This means that each cell can be removed and repaired individually without shutting down the whole unit. The voltage requirement for the entire unit is equal to that of one cell. However, the current requirements of this array are higher than for a single cell. The total current needed is figured as follows.

Current needed = current requirements of each X number of cells.

The *series (bipolar)* electrolyser is made up of cells each sharing an electrode with the next cell. Each electrode has a positive and a negative side. The positive side serves as the anode and the negative side serves as the cathode. The removal and repair of one cell means that the entire electrolyser must be shut down. Unlike the parallel electrolyser, the voltage needed for the entire electrolyser is:

Voltage needed = voltage requirements of each cell X number of cells.

The current consumed for the entire electrolyser is the same as the current consumption for any one cell.

Advantages of Parallel Compared to Series Electrolysers

- Individual cells may be isolated without effecting neighboring cells.
- Higher current density is possible, resulting in higher current efficiency approaching 100%. **Exhibit 14** Shows the performance for a four cell unit. Notice how the voltage requirements taper off when operating over 2,200 A/m^2 (200 A/ft^2).
- Longer service life is possible (25 years or more) with maintenance-free operation for the first 10 years.

Disadvantages of Parallel Compared to Series Electrolysers

- Low voltage and high current is needed resulting in the need for large conductors (bus bars) to keep electrical resistance low. Large current consumption also requires large transformers and rectifiers.
- Because each cell is separate and the components are not shared, as in the series type, more floor space is needed. Liquid electrolyte must be kept in motion in each cell to control heat and remove waste gasses. A manifold circulates the electrolyte in each cell separately. In **Exhibit 15** notice how the hydrogen manifold delivers gas to the overhead tank for collection "over water" as in small- scale lab experiments. This prevents reverse gas flow.

Advantages of Series Compared to Parallel Electrolysers

- High voltage and low current means more efficient AC-DC rectification.

32

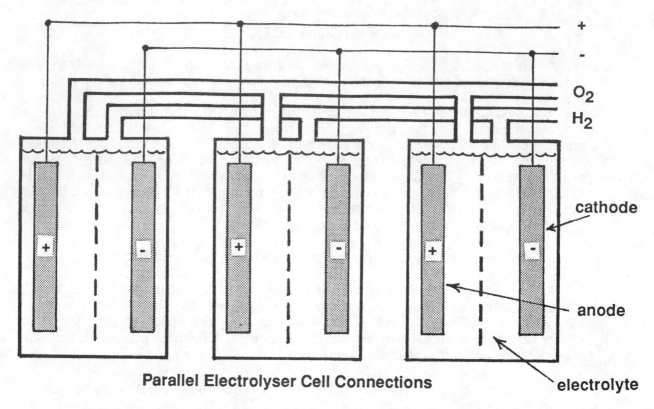

Parallel Electrolyser Cell Connections

Total current = number of cells X current for each cell.

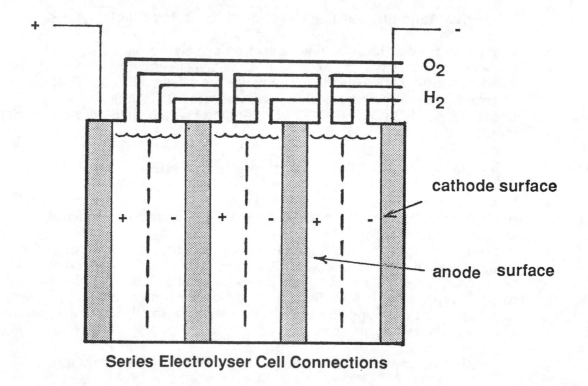

Series Electrolyser Cell Connections

Total voltage = number of cells X voltage for each cell.

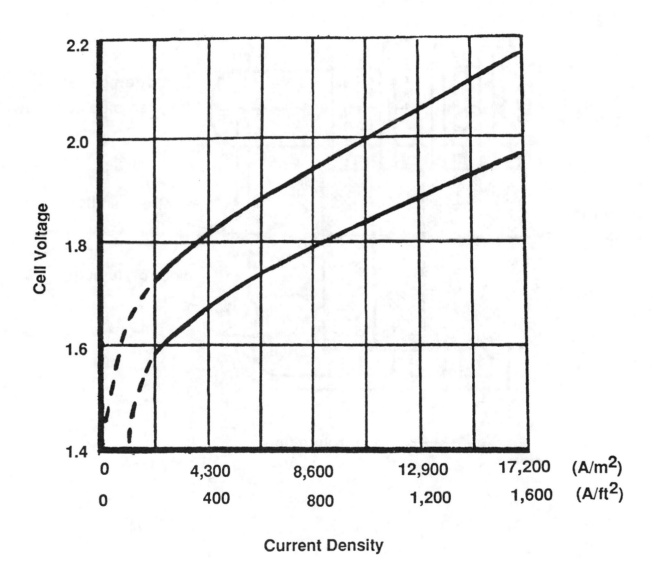

15.   *Electrolyte Circulation in a Four-Cell Parallel Unit*

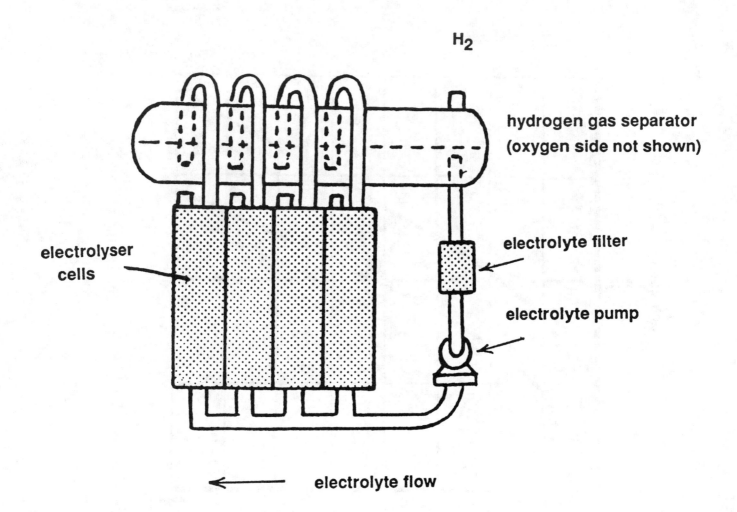

H_2

hydrogen gas separator
(oxygen side not shown)

electrolyte filter

electrolyte pump

electrolyser
cells

← electrolyte flow

- Less floor space is needed due to thinner cells.
- All cells share a common electrolyte bath allowing freer circulation of the electrolyte. Gas production also helps circulate the electrolyte.

Disadvantages of Series Compared to Parallel Electrolysers

- High voltage and low current input combine to give lower current efficiencies of 95% or less.
- Each cell must be engineered to be identical to all the other cells in the electrolyser to avoid overloads. Capital costs, therefore, are usually higher.

With a solid polymer electrolyte the need for electrolyte circulation may be avoided. **Exhibit 16** shows how the experimental solid polymer tubes, described earlier, may be connected in a single electrolyser module. The ends of the tubes are capped. Steam under high pressure enters one end of the tube and is converted to hydrogen. Oxygen is vented outside. The hydrogen gas at the capped end, still under pressure from the rising steam, is forced down a smaller diameter tube inside each electrolyser cell. Manifolds deliver steam to each tube and remove hydrogen as shown.

The material used for the gas ducts is a high temperature-resistant alloy while the base frame for the cells is made of aluminum. At high temperatures aluminum, the manifold, and the cell bodies all expand at different rates. Special joining techniques had to be devised to insure tight connections at prevent gas leaks. Their reliability has been proven in tests. **280p291-295** This and other problems illustrate the difficult of engineering high temperature electrolysers.

Commercial electrolyser may combine both series and parallel connections of cells to achieve the right combination of features and current-voltage characteristics. One such hybrid connection is shown in **Exhibit 16.** A typical electrolyser installation might have a row of cells connected in series. Auxilliary parallel connections allow each cell to be shut down without effecting the other cells.

COMMERCIAL ELECTROLYSERS

Electrolysers made for industry usually operate at high temperature and pressure to increase efficiency and reduce operating costs. The optimum voltage decreases about 0.83 millivolts per degree centigrade of temperature increase. For standard liquid electrolyte cells, as shown in **Exhibit 17** and **18**, at an operating pressure of 20 atm (2 MPa, 294 psi) and at 121°C (250°F) hydrogen is produced at about 0.04 m^3 per squre meter of electrode area per minute. Half as much oxygen is produced. Typical performance and components of commercial electrolysers can be illustrated by describing the Stuart Cell manufactured in Canada by the Electrolyser Corporation. **630**

- Hydrogen output: 818 m^3/hour (28,900 ft^3/hr). 99.9% pure.
- A.C. 4.7 kWh/m^3 (0.13 kWh/ft^3). D.C. 4.52 kWh/m^3 (0.13 kWh/ft^3).
- Current density: 1,350 A/m^2 (38 A/ft^2). State of the art for some electrolysers permits up to 5,000 A/m^2 (142 A/ft^2).
- Cell voltage: 2.04 volts.
- Current efficiency: 100%.
- Thermodynamic efficiency: 72%. State of the art ranges up to 85%.
- Electrolyte: 30% potassium hydroxide.
- Water feed rate: 25 liter/hour (6.6 gallon/hour).
- Cooling water feed rate: 1,098 liters/hour (290 gallon/hour).
- Electrode material: low carbon steel.
- Anode Material: low carbon steel, nickle-plated.
- Separator material: woven asbestos cloth.
- Operating temperature: 70°C (158°F).
- Operating pressure: 1 atm (0.1 MPa, 14.7 psi).
- Teflon gaskets, stainless steel cell frames and end plates.

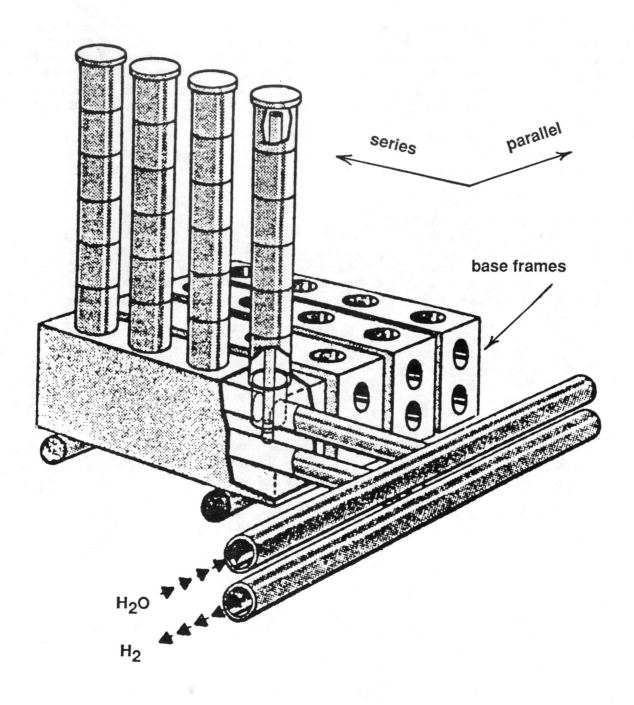

series   parallel

base frames

H_2O

H_2

17. Lurgi Parallel Electrolyser

The "Electrolytor" is capable of producing 740 m^3/hour (26 l00 ft^3/hour) of hydrogen gas. (Courtesy of Lurgi-Apparate-Technik GmbH.)

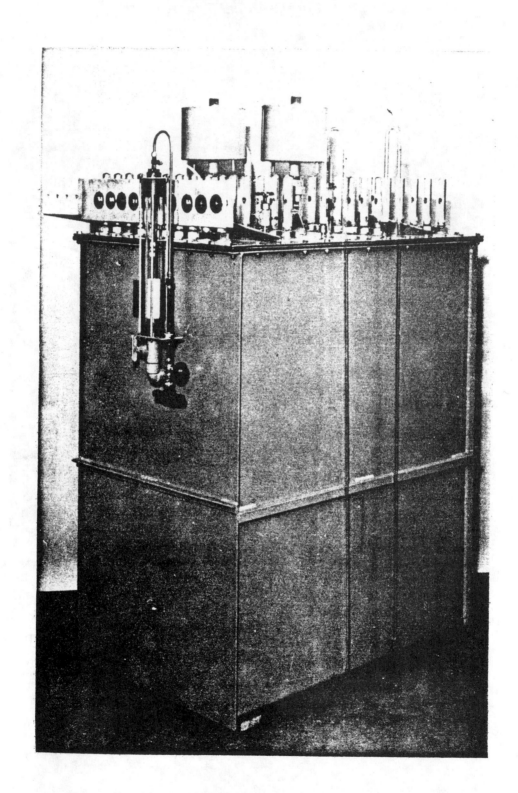

This electrolyser produces 818 m^3/hour (28 900 ft^3/hour) of hydrogen gas. (Courtesy of The Electrolyser Corporation, Ltd.)

For typical electrolyser installations hydrogen production costs range from $680 to 4,250/kW for small plants and from $350 to 680/kW for large plants. Capital costs are about 30% of total costs. The operating costs not directly related to power generation are 10% of the above figures. **220p191-201**

Few plants are larger than 5 megawatts (5 MW). A proposed plant in Canada would have an output of 3,000 kg (6,600 lb). This equivalent to 3,000 kW. This plant would need an input of 7 MW. Described as the "the largest of its kind" **221p297-303** the plant will provide gaseous hydrogen for a liquid hydrogen fuel production facility to service customers in Canada and the northeastern U.S. Cheap, readily available electricity from Hydro Quebec will be supplemented by surplus hydrogen from a nearby chloralkali plant. The $32 million cost is shared by the Canadian government ($4.1 million), the Quebec provincial government ($3.2 million) and private sources.

Electrical power fed to a commercial electrolyser plant from the utility must be converted from *alternating* to *direct* current (A.C. to D.C.). For the Candian plant described above 25,000 volt, 3 phase, 60 cycle A.C. power is converted to D.C. by two rectifiers into 100,000 A at 74.6 V.D.C.

HIGH PRESSURE ELECTROLYSIS

Some manufacturers specify operating pressures from 5 to 30 atm (0.5 MPa, 74 psi to 3 MPa, 441 psi). The advantages of operating at high pressures are given below.

- Reduced power consumption.
- Compressors used to prepare the product gasses for storage may operate at lower pressure if the electrolyser supplies some of the input pressure.
- Reduced cell size.
- Reduced voltage losses.

Disadvantages of high pressure operation also become apparent.

- Increased costs of pressure vessels.
- It becomes more critical to maintain a precarious balance between oxygen and hydrogen gas pressure to prevent separator failure.
- Increased dissolved gasses appear in the electrolyte. This may be overcome by using pressurized feed water.

Despite the engineering challenge the cost-benefit tradeoffs still weigh in favor of high pressure operation. The DeNora company of Italy produces units operating at 30 atm (3 MPa, 441 psi). **200**

HIGH TEMPERATURE ELECTROLYSERS

Increased Performance

As was seen in **Exhibit 5**, a large increase in the operating temperature of the electrolysis process requires only slight increases in voltage but provides a substantial increase in efficiency. Energy in the form of heat is partially substituted for the electrical energy needed to split water. According to K.H. Quandt, *"One has the possibliity of providing part of the splitting energy by thermal energy instead of electrical, thus achieving higher total efficiency"*. **740p309** This is particularly true if water is fed into the electrolyser as steam. Less energy is needed to split water in the vapor phase because of reduced demand for electricity at the electrode and the possibility of using increased current densities.

A high temperature electrolysis (HTE) development program called *Hot Elly* was begun in 1977 by the German Federal Ministry of Research and Technology. The technology, it is reported, *"has reached an advanced status"*. High temperature operation

40

allows a 30% reduction in energy input for each volume of hydrogen produced - from 4.5 to 3.2 kWh/m^3 (0.13 to 0.09 kWh/ft^3). For 1,000°C (1,800°F) experimental results are summarized below for two different energy inputs.

- 1.33 volts, 5,000 A/m^2 (465 A/ft^2).
- 1.07 volts, 3,000 A/m^2 (279 A/ft^2).

85% of the steam is converted to hydrogen.

For commercial applications, commercial requirements call for an steam conversion of 70% and current densities of at least 3,700 A/m^2 (344 A/ft^2) and voltages of no more than 1.33 volts. **Exhibit 19** compares the performance of three classes of electrolysers.

- Conventional commercial electrolysers using an alkaline electrolyte.
- Experimental advanced low temperature electrolysers including both liquid and solid electroltyes.
- Water vapor electrolysis with a temperature of around 1,000°C (1,800°F).

The second group has a clear advantage over conventional commercial electrolysers. The lower the voltage the higher is the efficiency. High temperature electrolysis (HTE) has an even greater advantage over experimental low temperature electrolysers.

Materials

At high temperatures other materials must be substituted for asbestos in the separator. Two materials, potassium titanite or perfluorinated sulfonic acid polymer, Nafion (R), may be used instead.

The General Electric solid polymer electrolyser, mentioned in a previous section, is designed to split 1,000°C (1,800°F) steam. The solid electrolyte serves a double function as a charge conductor and a gas separator. High temperature materials used were: **280p291**

- Base frame: alumina.
- Gas ducts inside tubes: high temperature-resistant alloy (Iconel 601).
- Electrodes: yttria-stabilized zirconia.

The main problem in working with such materials at high temperature is in joining materials with different expansion properties.

Modes of Operation

Electrolysers both consume and produce heat. For any electrolyser, operating at a specific temperature, there is a certain voltage (the *thermoneutral voltage*) at which as much heat is consumed as is produced. Above this voltage, the electrolysis reaction produces heat, and below the voltage, it consumes heat. **Exhibit 5** shows the electrolysis voltage-temperature relationship graphically.

In a presentation of a design for a high temperature electrolyser various modes of operation were analysed. **740**

A high temperature electrolyser operating exothermally (above the thermoneutral voltage) needs no external high temperature heat source. Only 200°C (390°F) steam is needed to insure a gas output temperature 70°C (160°F) greater than the input. This lowers both investment costs and thermal efficiency (39.3%).

In the thermoneutral mode the temperature of the output gasses equals the temperature of the input steam. At a 1.3 volt cell potential, 3.12 kWh/m^3 (0.09 kWh/ft^3) of energy was consumed. It was found that this balance of temperatures did not make the best use of the superheating equipment.

Operating below the thermoneutral voltage (endothermally), the electrolyser exhibited the highest efficiency. But the reduced voltage (below 1.3 volts) also reduced

19. Cell Voltage-Current Density in Conventional and Advanced Electrolysis

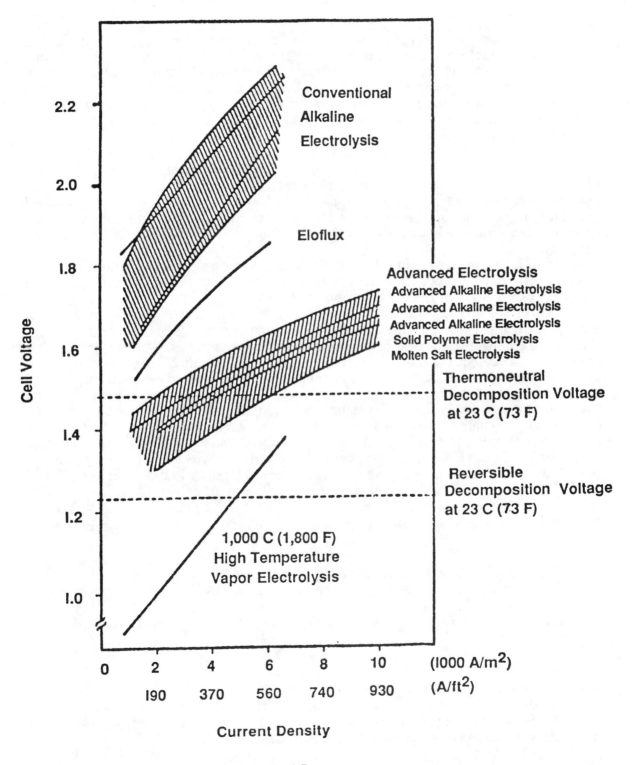

the allowable current density and the hydrogen output. At 1.07 volts and 3,000 A/m^2 (279 A/ft^2) the energy input needed is 2.6 Wh/m^3 (0.07 kWh/ft^3) for each volume of hydrogen produced. Increased capital costs were anticipated for coupling the electrolyser to a high temperature heat source. A heat input of 0.6 kWh provides a thermal efficiency of 44.7% at 19% less electrical power cost.

In all modes of operating pressures above 24.7 atm (2.5 MPa, 363 psi) incurred higher operating costs. Cell pressures at 3 to 5 atm (0.3 MPa, 44 psi to 0.5 MPa, 74psi) are more economical even when the output gas had to be compressed to a more useful 24.7 atm (2.5 MPa, 363 psi) storage pressure.

Costs

HTE can make use of waste heat from a veriety of sources including coal and nuclear power plants. Nuclear fusion is a form of nuclear energy, currently under research, that promises a nonpolluting and virtually endless supply of energy. Fusion derives its energy from fusing pairs of hydrogen atoms to form helium. Copious amounts of heat are also produced. *"The technical integration of fusion and high-temperature electrolysis appears to be feasible and that overall hydrogen production efficiencies of 50 to 55% seem possible."* **320p188**

With current technology, the waste heat from coal-fired plants can be used for HTE, but problems remain. *"Based on performance and cost figures available in 1983, high-temperature electrolysi s coupled with thermal electrical energy derived from coal is not yet competitive with processes which make hydrogen from hydrocarbons. If natural gas prices were to double (from $0.012/kWh to $0.027/kWh) catalytic steam reforming and high temperature electrolysis would have comparable hydrogen production costs."* **540p441**

An HTE plant converting 90% of the steam to hydrogen at a computed 38.2% thermal efficiency exceeds the 15% steam conversion and 30.6% efficiency of a comparable capacity coal gasification plant.

Exhibits 20, 21, and **22** show when the cost of hydrogen from HTE is economical compared to the cost of hydrogen from other methods of production. **740p314** **Exhibit 20** compares HTE with conventional forms of electrolysis. The higher the price of electricity becomes the more competitive HTE gets. **Exhibit 21** compares HTE with hydrogen from the steam reforming of natural gas. With the costs of electricity and natural gas shown on the two axes of the graph the "break even" line shows at what price of the two inputs the costs of HTE equals steam reforming of natural gas. At price combinations of electricity and natural gas above the line HTE is advantageous. Below the line natural gas steam reforming is more cost effective. **Exhibit 22** shows the cost relationship of coal gasification and HTE at various prices of coal and electricity. In the U.S., the current cost of electricity is too high (above $0.05/kWh) and the price of coal is too low ($0.007 to $0.008/kWh) for HTE to be economically competitive at the present time.

The initial costs of building conventional electrolysis plants is about $12/m^3/hr ($0.34/ft^3/hr) of hydrogen production capacity. With HTE this cost could be reduced by various means.

- Using circular vessels, thus eliminating the need for reinforcing ribs.
- Incorporating vertical stacks of modules into the design. This would reduce capital costs as much as 50%.
- Selling the pure oxygen produced at the current rate of $0.05/m^3 ($0.0014/ft^3) to reduce costs 15%.

M.A. Liepa has completed a study of HTE fed by electricity and heat derived from coal or natural gas. **540** He estimates hydrogen production costs of $0.07 to $0.22/m^3 ($0.002 to $0.006/ft^3). This is equivalent to $0.04 to $0.06/kWh for electricity. About 12% of this comes from thermal energy, the rest from electrical energy. These low estimates were based on the following assumptions.

43

20. Cost of Electrolytic Hydrogen

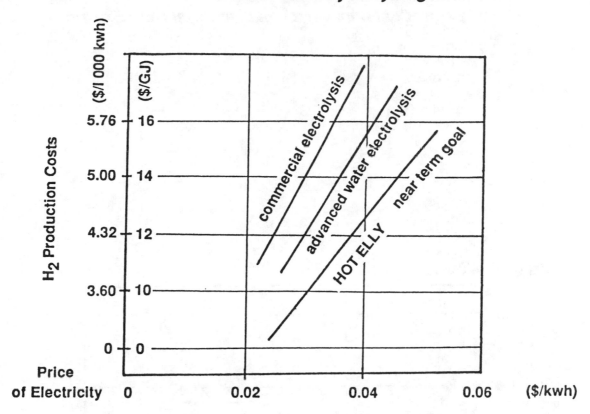

21. Cost Comparison of Electrolysis and Natural Gas

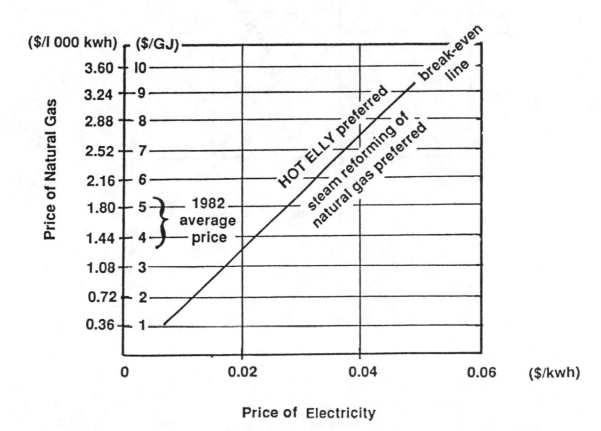

44

22. Cost Comparison of Electrolysis and Electricity

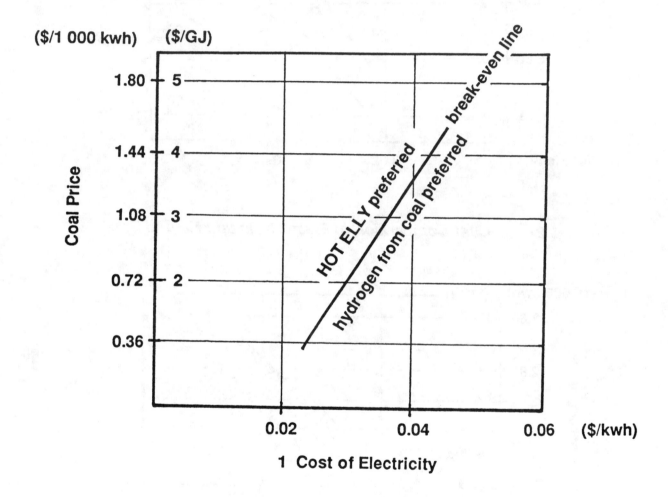

- Operating temperatures: 1,000°C (1,800°F) on average.
- Maximum temperature drop in HTE unit: 200°C (390°F).
- Cooling water temperature: 15°C (59°F).
- Hydrogen output temperature: 25°C (77°F).
- Cost of coal: $0.007/kWh.
- Cost of natural gas: $0.012/kWh.
- Cost of electricity: $0.050/kWh.
- Cost of fuel oil: $20/barrel.
- Annual capital cost recovery: 20%.
- Thermodynamic efficiency of electrical power generation: 35%.
- Gas-gas average heat transfer coefficient: 60 W/m^2/°C (3 W/ft^2/°F).
- Expansion gas-water heat transfer coefficient: 230 W/m^2/°C (12 W/ft^2/°F).
- Condensation gas-water heat transfer coefficient: 850 W/m^2/°C (44 W/ft^2/°F).

J.A. Fillo estimates even lower costs if waste heat from nuclear fusion reactors is used. According to his estimates the costs might be: $0.0017/kWh ($5.87/million BTU) at 1,300°C (2,370°F) and $0.002/kWh ($7.14/million BTU) at 1,150°C (2,100°F). *"Thus in the long term, the electrolytic process may well be able to compete with hydrogen production from fossil fuels, particularly in view of the expected raw material shortage after the year 2000, especially of natural gas."* [320]

PHOTOVOLTAIC-POWERED ELECTROLYSIS

Hydrogen as an Energy Carrier

Hydrogen is often erroneously regarded as a *source* of energy similar to petroleum or coal. This would be true if hydrogen were available naturally in large quantities. However, much of it is derived from the steam heating of hydrocarbons and water or by electrolysis. Hydrogen is similar to the energy storage characteristics of an electrical storage battery. Energy is needed to obtain hydrogen from either water or hydrocarbons. This is because hydrogen is rarely found in a pure state on earth. The energy used to obtain hydrogen from water is recovered when the gas is burned. Hydrogen is a carrier of the energy used to obtain just as an electrical battery carries the energy used to charge it.

Energy from sunlight can be converted to electricity by photovoltaic (PV) cells. This electrical energy can then be stored in batteries or as hydrogen from electrolysis. Hydrogen has much more energy per unit weight than electric batteries. In practical terms, *"A solar energy economy is not conceivable without hydrogen being used for storage and energy distribution."* [740p315]

At the earth's surface about 1 kWh/m^2 (317 BTU/ft^2) of solar energy is available. If it could all be harnessed it would supply 10,000 times the current annual world energy consumption. [630] Solar energy can be converted to useful energy by various technologies that harness the sun's radiation.

- *PV powered electrolysers.* PV cells convert sunlight to electricity. The electricity is then used by an electrolyser to produce hydrogen.
- *Photoelectrodes.* Electrodes immersed in water and an electrolyte combine PV cells and an electrolyser in one device. However, it is difficult to match the current and voltage output of the electrodes with the demand of the electrolysis process. At present, it is more efficient to carry out each of these processes separately.
- *Photochemical processes.* The energy of solar radiation is absorbed by various chemicals in solution and is used to drive hydrogen-producing reactions.
- *Biological sources.* Microorganisms in water absorb light to split water in the process of making their own "food" and in respiration. The use of similar processes to synthesize methane, methanol or ethanol is currently cheaper and more efficient than the process of producing hydrogen from microorganisms.

100p555-562

- *Direct thermal water splitting*. At 2,500°C (4,500°F) water decomposes into hydrogen and oxygen. A lens or reflector is employed to concentrate sunlight to supply heat. The problem here is to prevent the oxygen and hydrogen from recombining at the high temperatures used in the process.
- *Thermochemical cycles*. Relatively low temperature heat, 1,000°C (1,800°F), is used to drive reversible chemical reactions. These processes are promising but very experimental at the present time.

From Sunlight to Hydrogen

State of the art PV cells operate at about 10% efficiency. Nevertheless, one square kilometer can produce 26,000 kW. One square mile can produce 67,000 kW. A 120 by 120 km (75 X 75 mile) square array in sunny Arizona could produce 1,000,000 megawatts. This is equivalent to the projected electrical needs of the U.S. in the year 2000 AD. **580p6**

A PV cell converts light energy to electrical energy at a specific voltage and current level. The more light the cell receives the greater the energy output. However, the current and voltage do not increase equally. **Exhibit 23** shows that at various light levels the current doubles, from 10 to 23 milliamps, while the voltage remains around 0.5 volts. The temperature is constant.

To make the best use of single photocell or any array of cells, the load must operate at an optimal combination of current and voltage known as the *maximum power point* (M.M.P.). This point is shown on each of the curves in **Exhibit 23**. This point is where the tangent to the curve is 45°.

Changes in either the light intensity or cell temperature will shift the power curve and the M.M.P. **Exhibit 24** shows this shift in response to three different temperatures. In general, the power output of a PV cell increases with lower temperatures and higher light levels.

When PV cells are coupled to an electrolyser, light energy can be converted, indirectly, to hydrogen production. The current output of the PV cell is expressed in milliamps per square centimeter (mA/cm^2). The higher the current density, the higher the rate of hydrogen production and the lower the operating costs per unit of hydrogen produced.

The electrolyser electrode area determines the current requirements while the number of electrolyser cells (at 2 volts each) determines the voltage needed.

The amount of light striking the PV cell will vary with different times of day, weather conditions and season. The operating temperature of the cells will also vary when the cells are exposed to the weather. For these reasons, the electrolyser will not always be operating at the maximum power point for the cells.

Power conditioning equipment constantly adjusts the voltage and current characteristics of the cells so that the electrolyser always operates at the M.M.P. The efficiency of the power conditioning device is typically in excess of 90%. With power conditioning the rate of hydrogen production is higher than without such continual adjustments. However, the equipment needed is complex and costly. Direct coupling of the cells to the electrolyser (with a fixed voltage-current transformer) is cheaper and simpler even though hydrogen output is slightly lower. The simplest and cheapest power tracking method is a switching interface that changes the parallel and series connections of the cells to give relatively coarse changes in voltage and current from the cells. **370,497**

According to a recent study, in New Mexico, at a latitude of 35°C (95°F) and a hydrogen production rate of 4.4 kg/m² (0.9 lb/ft²) of cell area per year is possible. This is an average annual value. The summer peak rate is calculated to be 0.002 kg/m² (0.0004 lb/ft²) per hour. The average annual efficiency is about 7%. **350**

At a latitude of 48°, in central Europe, the hydrogen production rate is about half that for New Mexico.

A PV-powered electrolyser was constructed and studied at the Florida Solar Energy Center under a NASA grant. **410p153-160** The experimenters were interested in hydrogen as a means of storing solar energy. They noted the disadvantages of batteries.

23. Solar Cell Performance and Light Intensity

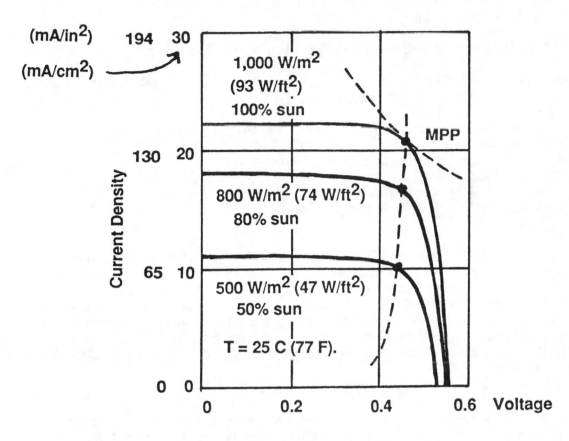

(mA/in²)
(mA/cm²)

1,000 W/m²
(93 W/ft²)
100% sun

MPP

800 W/m² (74 W/ft²)
80% sun

500 W/m² (47 W/ft²)
50% sun

T = 25 C (77 F).

Current Density

24. PV Cell Performance

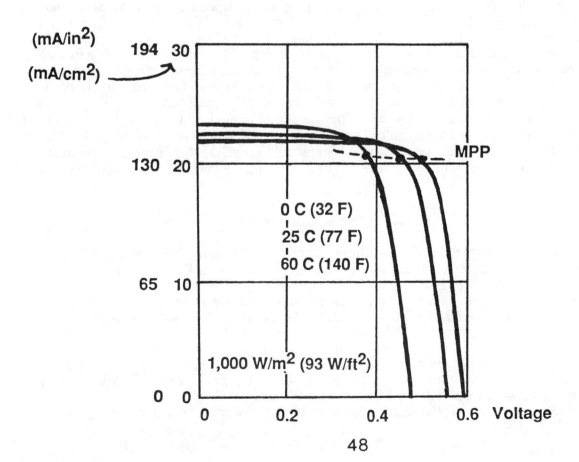

(mA/in²)
(mA/cm²)

MPP

0 C (32 F)
25 C (77 F)
60 C (140 F)

1,000 W/m² (93 W/ft²)

- Low energy stored compared with high weight.
- The use of scarce resources in their construction.
- Leaking of stored energy due to heating and long periods of nonuse.
- The need for standby charges.

The specifications for the experimental hydrogen plant were as follows.

- *Electrolyser cells:* 15 cells, each 5.19 cm (2 inches) in diameter and with an current output of 600 mA/cm^2 (3,870 mA/in^2).
- *Peak power output:* 1 kW.
- *Electrolyser power input:* 4 kWh, 500 kWh per month, in Florida.
- *Electrolyser pressure range:* 0 to 1.7 atm (0.17 MPa, 25 psi).
- *Electrolyser type:* Series (bipolar, or "filter press").
- *Separator:* asbestos fabric.
- *Electrolyte:* 25% by weight KOH.
- *Photovoltaic array:* 50 Solec Model 3135 modules.
- *PV efficiency:* 6.1%.

No power tracking was used. The peak power of the PV cell array was matched to the electrolyser demand. In 15 days the plant could generate 29.7 kWh of hydrogen (101,400 BTU) equivalent to 3 liters (0.75 gallon) of gasoline. A summary of the plant's performance is given in **Exhibit 25.** The result of a computer study concluded that the most power conditioning equipment could boost hydrogen output was 6% (assuming that the power conditioner was 100% efficient - a technical impossibility). The researchers concluded that, *"Maximum power trackers are probably not desirable in PV-electrolyser systems".* **520p93**

Solar Hydrogen Aircraft

PV cells have always been used in the space program because of their simple maintenance-free operation. The cost of the PV electrolysis is relatively high for a house, but is small compared to the total cost of a spacecraft.

For an application closer to earth, Lockheed has proposed a high altitude aircraft powered by photocells mounted on the skin of the craft. It is designed as a robot reconnaissance plane able to stay aloft for a year or more. The cells power an electric motor that turns a large diameter, low rpm propeller. The same cells also generate hydrogen by way of an on-board electrolyser. At night, the stored hydrogen is used to feed a fuel cell that supplies electricity to the motor. The oxygen from the electrolysis is also needed because of the thin atmosphere at 20 km (65,000 ft) altitude.

The *Solar High-Altitude Powered Platform,* as it is called, is designed to carry a 113 kg (250 lb) payload of communications relays or surveillance cameras. Although designed for continuous powered flight, it is expected to cost less than a communications satellite. The wingspan will be 91 m (300 ft) while the fragile craft will weigh only 907 kg (2,000 lb). **530p745-746**

Costs of Solar Electrolysis

The Solar Power Corporation in San Diego, California has built a 7 kW solar cell plant. Tracking solar concentrators focus sunlight on 76 m^2 (818 ft^2) of PV cells. The reflector also produces 45.8 kW of heat.

Relying on current data and future research and development activities, the company anticipates costs of $0.0285/kWh for a 1,000 Megawatt plant. This is comparable to current costs of electricity from hydropower or natural gas. This also compares favorably with $0.0775/kWh for nuclear power and $0.0993/kWh for coal-fired plants.

A study of the solar electric plant at the Florida Energy Center developed a program to estimate the costs of future solar hydrogen plants. The data in **Exhibit 26** summarizes the estimated cost of residential hydrogen from a PV array.

NASA has experimented with a 1 kilowatt commercial solar cell array. The experimenters used no power conditioning. They selected the number of electrolyser cells, and designed the electrolyser cells for the peak power output from the array. The electrolyser had 15 cells designed for a current density of 600 mA/cm^2 (3870 A/in^2). Each electrode was 5.19 cm (1 in) in diameter. Each cell had an asbestos separator. The energy value of the hydrogen produced had 50 to 75% of the solar cell energy input. The overall system efficiency from sunlight to hydrogen was about 4%. The experimenters calculated that for a 500 kWh/month plant located in Florida, the operating costs would be $0.73/kWh. The average residence in Florids consumes 1,000 kWh/month.

By 1995, with production of solar cells increased 100 times, the cost of solar electricity from a plant similar to the one studied, would be reduced to $0.17/kW. If present developments in solar cell technology become commercially feasible, further cost reductions can be expected. **920p1-2**

Stanford University is demonstrating a new silicone-based solar cell with a textured surface that has a efficiency of 27.5%. Combined with an electrolyser with 90% efficiency, the overall efficiency would be = 0.275 X 0.90 = 25%.

25. Electrolyser Peformance Summary

Day	Power Input (Ah)	Hydrogen Produced (l)	(ft^3)	Output Efficiency (real/ideal)	Energy Equivalent (Wh)	Energy of P.V.Array (Wh)	Energy Efficiency (%)	Gas Pressure (MPa)	(psi)	Electrolyte Temp. (^{o}C)	(^{o}F)	Day Light (hours)
1	121	733	26	97.0	2,511	3,426	73.3	0	0	55	131	8.25
2	139	759	27	87.3	2,601	4,093	63.5	0	0	70	158	11
3	123	726	27	94.4	2,488	3,382	73.5	0	0	70	158	8.25
4	131	744	26	90.6	2,549	3,796	67.1	0	0	60	140	11
5	123	616	22	80.2	2,110	4,022	52.5	28	40	70	158	8.25
6	98	607	21	98.4	2,080	2,798	74.3	28	40	35	95	8.25
7	126	661	23	83.7	2,265	3,600	62.9	28	40	70	158	8.25
8	101	462	16	72.9	1,583	2,903	54.5	28	40	70	158	8.25
9	121	592	21	78.0	2,029	3,421	59.3	28	40	70	158	11
10	122	607	21	79.0	2,080	3,454	60.2	21	30	70	158	11
11	109	582	21	84.4	1,994	3,009	66.3	14	20	70	158	8.25
12	124	608	22	77.9	2,084	3,653	57.0	14	20	75	167	11
13	101	486	17	77.0	1,665	2,871	58.0	14	20	60	140	11
14	80	397	14	79.6	1,360	2,391	56.9	14	20	60	140	8.25
15	29	108	4	59.3	370	1,493	24.7	0	0	40	104	8.25

26. Estimated Cost of Residential Hydrogen

Cost element	1983-1984$	1995$
PV array, 4 kWh	48,000	12,000
Electrolyser, 4kWh	15,000	05,000
Maintenance charges & electrolyte replacement	03,500	02,300
Replace module	03,200	01,500
Property tax	14,900	03,300
Insurance	07,300	00,500
Total present value	91,900	24,600

J.E. Nitsch, in a study of future solar electric costs, anticipates capital costs to decline to one-tenth the current levels over 20 years and by one-half to one- third over the next 10 years. Capital costs for electrolysis equipment are expected to decline one-third over next 40 years. **620p23-32**

Electrolytic hydrogen is expected to become cost competitive with fossil fuels in the 2005 to 2010 time period, assuming favorable conditions, which are:

- Interest rates on capital of no more than 6%
- Increasing plant life up to 30 years, due to technical improvements
- Increasing prices for fossil fuels by 4 to 5% per year.

Wind Power

The total windpower in the 48 contiguous states of the U.S. averages about 13 kW/hectare (5.2 kWh/acre) or 400 billion kW. This is about equal to the total U.S. residential electric consumption from 1970 to 1985. Residential electric consumption is about one-third of the total electric consumption. On average, each house in the contituous 48 states consumes 30,000 kWh/year and is 200 square meters (2,150 ft^2) in area. To be useful, the wind must be blowing at over 10 km/hr (16 miles/hour). In Oklahoma this occurs 80% of the time. To supply 30,000 kWh/year to a house on a continuous basis a wind energy plant must store 20% of 30,000 kWh or 6,000 kWh/year for use on relatively calm days. For two successive windless days, 165 kWh must be stored. This can be done in any of several ways. These alternatives can accomodate a peak home load of 15 kW. **1080p339-343**

- A water tower 10 m (33 ft) high storing 20 cubic meters (706 ft^3) of water.
- A volume of gaseous hydrogen stored at 1 atm (0.1 MPa, 14.7 psi) in a 1 cubic meter (35.3 ft^3) volume.
- One liter (1/4 gallon) of liquid hydrogen.

CHAPTER 3
CHEMICAL HYDROGEN PRODUCTION

ELECTROCHEMICAL REACTIONS PRODUCING HYDROGEN

S.B. Lalvani reports that the presence of sulfur in the anode during electrolysis reduces oxygen output and converts sulfur (S) to sulfate (SO_4^{-2}). The cell voltage needed to produce a volume of hydrogen is reduced by one-third, compared to conventional electrolysis. A minimum of 0.36 volts is required. At 1.2 volt the reaction proceeds as follows at the anode:

$$S + 4H_2O \longrightarrow 8H^+ + SO_4^{-2} + 6 \text{ electrons.}$$

At the cathode the reaction is:

$$6H^+ + 6 \text{ electrons} \longrightarrow 3H_2.$$

The overall reaction is:

$$S + 4H_2O \longrightarrow H_2SO_4 + 3H_2.$$

According to Lalvani, *"Preliminary investigations indicate that sulfur-assisted water electrolysis has the potential of becoming a viable economic process for co-generation of hydrogen and sulfuric acid"*. **500p639**

High material costs include an expensive platinum mesh electrode. The sulfur forms a layer and reacts with the electrolyte.

This process is similar to the *Westinghouse Cycle,* a process for producing hydrogen and sulfuric acid from sulfur dioxide and water.

$$SO_2 + 2H_2O \longrightarrow H_2SO_4 + H_2.$$

$$H_2SO_4 \longrightarrow H_2O + SO_2 + 1/2O_2.$$

The overall electrolysis reaction is:

$$H_2O \longrightarrow H_2 + 1/2O_2.$$

Ideally, the process has a 45% thermodynamic efficiency and requires less than 0.6 volts. For practical applications high concentrations of sulfuric acid are used, thereby increasing the voltage required. This process takes place at higher temperature than the pure sulfur process. In contrast, sulfur-assisted electrolysis requires a temperature of less than 75°C (167°F). Hydrogen production is also higher than with the Westinghouse process.

In comparison with conventional electrolysis, the hydrogen production rate for sulfur-assisted electrolysis is three times higher with electrical consumption one-half that required for ordinary electrolysis. Sulfuric acid is produced instead of oxygen, but the acid can be reacted with metals to produce still more hydrogen.

It is easy to see how it is possible to start with sulfur or sulfur dioxide and produce hydrogen, then add metal, like iron, and get still more hydrogen. Both sulfur dioxide and scrap iron are products of an industrial society that can be recycled into fuel production.

Either of the following two reactions produces hydrogen and sulfuric acid.

$$S + 4H_2O \longrightarrow H_2SO_4 + 3H_2.$$

$$SO_2 + 2H_2O \longrightarrow H_2SO_4 + H_2.$$

Sulfuric acid also reacts with iron to produce hydrogen.

$$Fe + H_2SO_4 \longrightarrow FeSO_4 + H_2.$$

For all three reactions no separator is needed because the reactions produce only one gas. Only liquids or solids form at the oxygen electrode.

PHOTOVOLTAIC PROCESSES

Solar Electric Hydrogen

Various research projects demonstrate how the functions of solar cells and electrolysers can be combined in one device. These experiments involve two main components.

- One or more photoelectrodes or photocatalysts.
- An electrolyte in solution with water.

Light striking the photoelectrode generates an electrical potential (voltage) at the surface of the semiconductor and the electrolyte. This potential then splits water into hydrogen and oxygen in an electrolysis process. The gasses are generated together. Some means of separating them is necessary.

Strong ultraviolet light can directly split water. As the water molecule absorbs this wavelength of light the energy is sufficient to overcome the molecular bonds holding the hydrogen and oxygen together. Since ultraviolet light makes up only 8% of solar radiation, this process is inherently inefficient.

Photoelectrodes

Certain chemicals can convert a wider spectrum of light to electrolytic energy. Each of these makes more efficient use of the solar spectrum. Candidate materials include some salts, organic dyes, semiconductors absorbing a wider spectrum of light (these need a bandgap over 2.3 electronvolts). Some species of algae also do this. 90p219-225

Photoelectrode materials generally share one or more of the following problems.

- *Photocorrosion* that causes the material to decompose under the influence of light reduces electrode life.

- *Temperature mismatch:* photovoltaic processes are more efficient at low temperature while maximum electrolytic production occurs at higher temperature.
- *Voltage mismatch:* the voltage output of the photoelectrode (1.5 volt) does not approximate the voltage input needed for the electrolytic reduction process (2.2 volts). **550p445-461**

These problems have led some researchers to conclude that a separate solar cell array is preferable. **980p225-232** Undaunted, other researchers continue the search, tempted by the elegance of a single process that converts light directly to hydrogen fuel. In the search, oxides of sulfur and phosphorous are specifically excluded from the role of photoelectrodes. **80,647-651**

Mixing ferric oxide and titanium dioxide with silicone produces a *photoanode* Ferric oxide and magnesium oxide comprise a *photocathode*. The two electrodes placed in a neutral electrolyte solution with water and in the presence of light yield electrolytic hydrogen and oxygen. The entire reaction normally takes place without the need for any input voltage. **810p137-145** However, a process which is *technically* possible is not necessarily *economical*. *"A cheap accessible industrial process for producing titanium dioxide is not now available."* **420p773-781**

Experiments compared relatively cheap zinc and cadmium sulfide precipitated onto Nafion (R) film then precipitated onto silicone dioxide with more expensive platinum mixed with cadmium sulfide. The conclusion was that:

- *"Relatively efficient photoassisted catalytic hydrogen generation can be realized without a noble metal catalyst."*
- The nature of the support for the surface coating of zinc and cadmium sulfide *"is not a crucial element"*.
- *"Intimate contact of zinc sulfide and cadmium is required for good activity.* **480p734**

In other experiments 1.0 grams (0.002 lb) of zinc sulfide in suspension in an electrolyte solution produced 16 liters (0.6 ft^3) of hydrogen in 35 hours with *"no observable deactivation of the photocatalyst"*. **750p5903-5913** There was no need for platinum to improve the charge transfer.

Electrolysis of Hydrogen Sulfide

Some hydrogen-containing compounds are easier to split than water. Hydrogen sulfide is an example. It is a derivative of natural gas, coal, and petroleum refining. It requires only 1/7 the amount of energy to electrolyse hydrogen sulfide as it does to electrolyse water. The energy required to split hydrogen sulfide is sufficiently low to allow the use of light as a source of energy to split the molecule.

$$H_2S + 2 \text{ photons of light} \longrightarrow 2H+ + S.$$

In one set of experiments light in a specific band of wavelengths stimulates cadmium sulfide to release an electron that splits hydrogen sulfide into hydrogen and sulfur. A small amount of rubidium dioxide (0.1% by weight) was mixed with the cadmium sulfide to form the catalyst. the catalysts were dissolved in a 0.1 mole solution of sodium sulfide illuminated with a 250 W halogen lamp shining through a 15 cm (6 in) water column to remove the infrared portion of the spectrum. This avoids heating the solution. The 25 ml (0.07 gal) solution produced 2.3 ml/hour (0.00008 ft^3/hr) of hydrogen. 90% of the hydrogen sulfide was converted to hydrogen. Doubling the rubidium dioxide increased the hydrogen output 50%. **150p118** The experimenters didn't need platinum as an electrocatalyst. Other experimenters, using the same chemical constitutents, discovered thermodynamic efficiencies of 2.85% . **470p23-26** The experimenters concluded:

"Apart from its importance for solar energy research, the process might be used in

industrial procedures where H_2S or sulfides are formed as a waste product whose rapid removal and conversion into a fuel, ie. hydrogen, are desired. Also, in intriguing fashion, these systems mimic the function of photosynthetic bacteria that frequently use sulfides as electron donors for the reduction of water to hydrogen." **150p119**

The Texas Instruments Solar Energy System

Texas Instruments has the *"only reported commercial photoelectrochemical program"*. **100** Hydrobromic acid is used as the photoelectrode while a sulfuric acid and water solution serves as the electrolyte. The photoelectrode coats microspheres 0.25 to 0.40 mm (0.010 to 0.020 in) in diameter. They use two types of microspheres: *photoanodes* and *photocathodes*. The photoanodes evolve bromine while hydrogen emerges at the photocathodes. The electrolyte-microsphere suspension is contained between two sheets of glass, one sheet has a conductive backing. Sunlight shines through the transparent side and produces hydrogen with 7% thermodynamic efficiency. Further developments are expected to increase this to 8 to 10% by before the year 2000.

In 1992 Texas Instruments Marketing Manager Eric Graf announced plans to produce the Spherical Silicone photovoltaic module by 1993. The main customer is Southern California Edison electric company. The panels could be put directly on the customer's roof. One kilowatt panels could generate one third of the homes electricity needs. As Graf says *"our goal is to help America lead in renewable technology for jobs, balance of trade, and the environment."* **442p7**

Summary

Photoelectrodes employ either semiconductor powder suspensions or photosensitizers that transform electrons to and from water molecules. Compared to solar cell powdered electrolysis, the current technology of photochemical processes for producing hydrogen have conspicuous disadvantages.

- The product gasses, hydrogen and oxygen, are mixed.
- Light energy corrodes the electrode material.
- The process has lower efficiency.

BIOLOGICAL SOURCES

Plants as a Carbon Source

All means of producing hydrogen from water are not man-made. Certain bacteria, in the absense of oxygen, will convert organic matter into methane. Municipal sewage can be used or algae can be grown and harvested specifically for this purpose.

In growing an algael "energy crop" heat is needed to boost the growth rate. The waste heat from the cooling towers of a 100 MW nuclear reactor will support a 4,047 hectare (10,000 acre) algae pond. The land around the nuclear plants is wasted, anyway, because it must be kept clear for safety reasons. This pond will yield 4.5 kilograms per square meter (20 tons/acre) of organic matter. Supplying extra carbon dioxide increases the rate 50 percent. 22,680 kilograms (25 tons) of algae can reasonably be converted to 10kWh (34,143 BTU) of methane. **50p331-338**

Biological Production of Hydrogen

Green plants and algae (microscopic one-celled plants) convert carbon dioxide, water, and sunlight to carbohydrates, water, and oxygen.

$$CO_2 + 2H_2O \longrightarrow CH_2 + H_2O + 3/2O_2.$$

Hydrogen can be produced by intercepting a plant's production of carbohydrates during photosynthesis. During photosynthesis the plant absorbs green light (a 500 nm wavelength). This is only about 16% of the visible solar spectrum. Hydrogen is briefly formed by water splitting and then used to construct carbohydrates that are used by the plant.

Researchers are trying to find a way to intercept the hydrogen before it is used to form carbohydrates. Work on this process is at an early stage. No working models have been developed and tested yet. In *Scientific American* (January 1986) two basic approaches are discussed.

- Using the active ingredient of photosynthesis in water (as a thylakoid membrane of ruptured chloroplasts).
- Preparing a solution of platinum and hexachloroplatinate in water.

When properly set up, light shining on either of these solutions will produce a brief electrical potential. The resulting electrolysis splits water molecules liberating hydrogen.

Some microorganisms produce hydrogen naturally. One species (*Rhodobacter sphaeroides* 8703) converts 7.9% of the light input energy at 50 W/m^2 (4.6 W/ft^2) to hydrogen gas. At 75 W/m^2 (7 W/ft^2) of light intensity the conversion efficiency drops to 6.2%. 600p147-149

In experiments using different growth media for hydrogen producing microorganisms a salt water blue-green algae (*Oscillatoria sp. Miami* BG7) was found to produce 30% more hydrogen when the cells were grown on a thick jelly and mobility was restricted. 720p83-89 Similar results were found with hydrogen-producing bacteria 950p623-626

Some researchers are trying to get around the problem of raising these fussy organisms by developing synthetic photosynthesis. 890p627 In one process under consideration, 70% of visible sunlight could be converted to electrical voltage and made available for electrolysis 250p825-828 During 1992 the University of Miami is selecting among 5,000 strains of cyanobacteria to find their hydrogen-producing enzymes so that they could be synthesized and used in artificial process that resemble photosynthesis.

Exhibit 27 shows the results of experiments with various hydrogen-producing microorganisms. Both algae and bacteria are represented.

Algae, as a green plant, produces hydrogen while making carbohydrates. Some bacteria, on the other hand, give off hydrogen as a by-product of digesting carbohydrates. The algae must be subject to artificial conditions to be "tricked" into producing hydrogen. This involves interrupting their photosynthetic activity. To the algae, making hydrogen is a "waste of time". Certain bacteria will produce hydrogen in oxygen-poor environments. For this reason, bacteria produce more hydrogen than algae. Under some conditions 25 percent of intestinal gas of mammals is comprised of hydrogen. Methane and carbon dioxode accounts for the rest. This process could be duplicated in man-made "digesters". The methane produced could be broken down under heat to yield hydrogen and carbon. The carbon could be used in a variety of products. The hydrogen could be used as a fuel. 441 and 792

Summary

The practical use of microorganisms remains a distant vision due to the current problem of low energy conversion rates, exacting biological requirements, and the periodic replacement of the microorganisms and their substrate.

56

Organism	Hydrogen Production		
	ml H_2/g of cells	(ft^3/lb)	ml/l culture
Photosynthesis (producing glucose)			
Oscillatoria sp. Miami BG7	15	0.24	10
Anabaena cylndrica	50	0.80	30
Rhodopseudomonas capsulata	202	3.2	131
Rhodosprillum rubrum	96	1.5	74
Fermentation (digesting glucose)			
Clostridium butyricum	270	4.3	---
Citrobacter intermedius	360	5.8	272
Enterobacter st. E. 82005	420	6.8	520

DIRECT THERMAL WATER-SPLITTING

Solar Thermal Energy

At 2,730°C (4, 946°F) water decomposes into hydrogen and oxygen. Solar energy focused by a parabolic reflector or a lens can achieve this temperature. According to Roy McAlister, President of the American Hydrogen Association, an area 110 miles on a side or 12,000 square miles (31,300 sq. km.) in a sunny climate is sufficient to gather enough sunlight to process water to supply all the current energy needs of the U.S. However, the amount of water needed each year would equal the volume of Lake Mead where Hoover Dam is located. Seawater could suffice. Once the hydrogen is burned pure water is results. One ton of hydrogen makes 9 tons of water. **568 and 235**

50% of solar energy is in the infrared spectrum - the heat producing part of solar energy. Based on this observation, direct thermal water splitting would seem to be the simplest method of producing hydrogen from water. However, there are two main problems.

● Keeping the hydrogen and oxygen separate.
● Finding high-temperature materials.

The latter problem is slowly being solved by materials engineers. Another general approach is to use a *fluid wall*. This is a boundary layer of gas injected into the container so as to keep the high temperature water vapor from the container wall.

"The work of these groups demonstrates that solar direct splitting of water can be accomplished in a reactor constructed of currently available materials." **960p91-100**

Various means of keeping hydrogen and oxygen separate have been proposed.

- *Centrifuging:* Oxygen is heavier than hydrogen. Spinning the gas mixture in a centrifuge will tend to fling the oxygen out farther toward the rim, in a shorter time than it would require for hydrogen.
- *Magnetic separation:* Some hydrogen molecules may be deflected in a magnetic field while others are not. This may be a partial solution.
- *A membrane:* Vanadium or paladium will transmit hydrogen selectively at temperatures above 730°C (1,350°F). The expense of this material and its intolerance of high temperatures makes this impractical.
- *Quenching:* Cooling the gas before it can recombine. The gasses then are carefully separated at lower temperature by other means. **630**

The most effective means used to quench the temperature of the hot product gasses before combustion takes place are the following.

- *Injection quenching:* injecting the hot gas as bubbles into water and collecting them at the top of the water container. **960** As the bubbles rise, the gasses can be separated by gravity. Hydrogen, being lighter and more bouyant, rises faster than oxygen.
- *Impingement quenching.* A jet of a high temperature gas mixture is forced under pressure against a flat plate. **510p3-11**

With impingement quenching, the jet strikes the "wall" at a flow rate of from $2 \times 10^{-5} m^3/s$ (7×10^{-4} ft/s) to $6.7 \times 10^{-5} m^3/s$ (2.4×10^{-3} ft^3/s). The portion closest to the wall is the coolest and gets hotter closer to the nozzel. The stream flares out as it hits the wall. There is a stagnation zone in the center of the stream as it impacts against the wall. This stagnation zone was thought to cause the gasses to recombine but an experimental device using this principal worked better than expected. *"Such a fast exchange* (heat transfer) *within the wall jet of the stagnation zone may be efficient enough to prevent back recombination by both rapid cooling and dilution of the cold medium."* **510p9**

Exhibit 28 shows the percent of water that is dissociated at various temperatures.

Inspite of current breakthroughs problems remain. Given the higher temperatures and materials problems involved we can conclude that *"this direct thermal decomposition of water is not feasible at an industrial level with the present technology."* **70p761-771**

28. Water Dissociation at Various Temperatures

Temperature		Amount Dissociated
(°C)	(°F)	(%)
1,730	3,146	0.69
2,030	3,686	2.64
2,430	4,406	10.35
2,730	4,946	22.40
3,230	5,846	57.43

Solar Thermal Collectors

The sun's rays can be focused by a lens or a parabolic dish concentrator. A lens would be impractical for large-scale operations. The parabolic dish can be easily and cheaply manufactured. Solar radiation is reflected off the surface of the dish and focused on a point near the center of the dish. The heat is focused on a target made of material that can withstand high temperatures. This is termed a "point-focus" solar concentrator. A circulating fluid is heated and, in turn, can turn a turbine to generate electrical power. Alternatively, a Stirling engine can be used. The Stirling engine employs heated gas to drive a piston. It is like a steam engine in that it uses a source of heat outside the engine to supply power.

This technology is not new. John Ericsson developed what he called "sun motors" in the 1880's. Thousands were sold to pump water until they were replaced by electric motors and utility power. **Exhibit 29** shows a sun motor that is being tested by Irving Jorgenson of the American Hydrogen Association. The mirrored dish focuses the sun on the black plug at the center of the dish. The finned tube below the plug is the cylinder of the Stirling engine. The air heated in the cylinder by the focused rays expands and drives the piston downward. A valve exhausts the air and returns the piston for a power stroke. The side view of the device shows the parabolic shape. This shape is necessary in order to focus all the incoming rays on a single point. Irving Jorgenson, a professional meterologist, is involved in constructing larger dishes for future use on an Arizona Indian reservation.
Generally, the larger the diamater of the dish the more power produced.

- A Sterling engine generator with 1/2 meter (18 inch) 310 stainless steel reflector would generate about 4 watts power in full sunlight.
- A 3 meter (10 ft.) dish gives 4 to 5 kilowatts.
- A 6.4 meter (21 ft.) dish produces 25 to 30 kilowatts.

Seasonal variations occur. In Arizona a dish and Stirling engine with stainless steel parabolic reflector will get about 1.2 kilowatt-hour per square meter (385 BTU/ sq.ft). in summer and 0.62 kWh per sq.meter (196 BTU/ sq.ft.) in winter. The operating cost is about $5.00 per kilowatt. This is equivalent to $0.19 per gallon of gas. (It costs $0.28 per gallon just to refine gasoline.) The typical efficiency of these devices is between 28 and 30 percent. According Paul Klimas of Sandia, *"Dish Stirling generators are a prooven, modular and efficient way of generating solar electricity. This program will be designed to let industry lead their own commercialization effort with technical and financial support from Sandia ..."* 442p7

The McDonnell Douglas Corporation has constructed a point-focus concentrator for the Southern California Edison Company in cooperation with the Electric Power Research Institute. The device uses a Stirling engine to generate 25 kW of electricity. In tests the generator converted 28 percent of the suns rays to electrical energy. Photovoltaic cells are typically no more than 12 percent efficient. **Exhibit 30** shows the McDonnel Douglas device. The Stirling engine is mounted on the end of the arm that extends from the dish.

In the background of **Exhibit 30** is the famous "Power Tower" near Barstow, California. It uses the point focus principal on a larger scale. The reflector is made up of individual mirrored panels mounted on the ground. Each panel can be moved independently. A computer controls the entire field so that the top of the central remains at the focal point of the suns rays all during the day. The top of the tower reaches 1,000 °C (1,800 °F) on a clear day to generate 10 megawatts of power. Molten salts carry the heat from the tower to thermal storage tanks. Inspite of this, if clouds block the sun for more than 30 minutes, the plant has to shut down until the sun reappears. Two new tanks were added in 1992 as part of a joint project between Scandia Labs and several utility

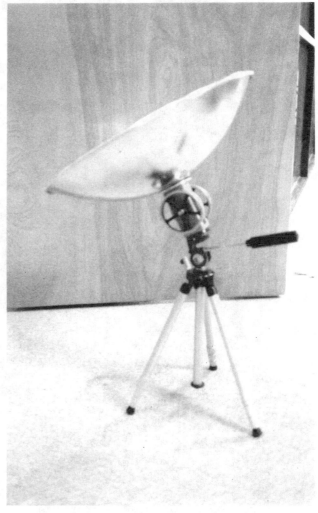

companies. The new tanks would allow generation even when clouds are overhead. In Southern California's climate, the plant can remain operating 60 percent of the time. The costs of power are within one to two cents of other ocal utility power. Daniel Alpert of Sandia predicts that with new improvements the plant will produce 100 megawatts by 1996-1999 and will be in full operation by 2001. By then the costs of power should drop below the costs of coal-fired power plants.

Germany plans to import solar energy from Saudia Arabia in the form of electrolysed hydrogen. According to Hartmut Steeb of the German-Saudi Hysolar Project, it is estimated that if five percent of Arabia's land were dedicated to solar hydrogen the hydrogen produced would equal Germany's total oil imports. Hysolar plans to build two 50 kW dish Stirling engine generators in the Saudi desert. Eventually this will be expanded to a 350 kW photovoltaic solar hydrogen production facility.

Since the earth rotates, solar collectors must track the sun to receive direct sunlight. The sun must be tracked up and down as it rises in the sky and from side to side as it travels from east to west across the sky. A parabolic circular dish-shaped collector needs to track the sun along both the vertical and east-west axis. A linear-focus system employs a trough that focuses sunlight along a line, not a point, as does the dish. If the trough is mounted horizontally the sun need only be tracked up and down, not side to side. Roy McAlister of the American Hydrogen Association has studied focusing solar collectors and concluded that the dish-type parabolic collector responds more rapidly to solar variations and focuses the suns rays more efficiently. [569]
There are several ways to produce hydrogen from this source of solar heat.

- Direct thermal water splitting, as mentioned above.
- The sun's rays can heat a fluid, such as water, producing steam. The steam can turn a turbine, generate electricity and produce hydrogen by electrolysis.
- Provide heat energy for thermochemical processes, discussed below.
- Heat water to provide steam for steam reforming of carbon. This is described in a following chapter.

Roy McAlister has described a way to store heat energy indefinitely without energy loss. Heat breaks down combines methane and carbon dioxide to form carbon monoxide and hydrogen. These two gasses can be recombined into their original form in the presense of a suitable catalyst to give off heat. Heat stored in this manner may be transported from sunny areas to distant locations that lack abundant solar energy. [569] The reactions are:

$$\text{Heat} + CH_4 + CO_2 \longrightarrow 2\,CO + 2\,H_2.$$

$$2\,CO + 2\,H_2 \longrightarrow \text{Heat} + CH_4 + CO_2.$$

THERMOCHEMICAL CYCLES

Isothermal Steps

Avoiding the high temperature requirements of direct thermal water splitting requires more complex chemical processes. "*According to the thermodynamic restraints, pure thermodynamical cycles operating at temperatures below 1,000°C (1,800 °F) consist of three steps or more.*" [300p291]
Unlike electrolysis, heat energy is used to directly decompose

hydrogen-containing compounds. These compounds are easier to thermally split than water and the thermochemical process is generally more efficient than electrolysis. **990p459-462** Some processes are designed to utilize both a thermal and an electrical input and are referred to as *electrothermochemical* processes or as *hybrid thermochemical* cycles. **70**

In general, higher temperatures increase the chemical reaction rate and help lower plant costs. Higher temperatures also reduce the number of steps needed for a chemical process. By taking bigger thermal steps, fewer steps are needed to arrive at the desired product. **270p67-72** The temperature required at each step must also match the heat input available.

Efficiency

Electrolysis is typically 25 to 30% efficient if a heat engine is used to generate energy. 40 percent of the engine's heat input is converted to electricity by turning a generator. If an electrolyser is 70% efficient then the overall proces efficiency is about 0.4 X 0.7 = 0.28 or 28%. A thermochemical may use the heat input in a more direct manner producing hydrogen at 40 to 50% efficiency, depending upon the temperature of the heat supplied.

Chemical processes for splitting water that require temperatures over $3000^{\circ}C$ (5400° F) are impractical because the temperatures are hard to achieve and production materials cannot withstand them. By breaking the water splitting process down into several steps lower temperatures may be used, around $800\text{-}900^{\circ}$ C ($1500\text{-}1650^{\circ}$ F). Thermochemical cycles operating at these temperatures may be used with high-temperature solar and nuclear fusion power plants. For example, future fusion reactors will produce $1,250^{\circ}C$ ($2,280^{\circ}F$) cooling water. This could support a sulfur-iodine thermochemical cycle at 45% efficiency because the thermochemical process can use the exact temperature ot the waste heat as it comes from the reactor. **590p178-183**

The efficiency of a thermochemical process is defined as:

$$79.42 / Q.$$

Where:

- 79.42 = combustion energy of 1 gram (0.0022 lb) of hydrogen in Watt-hours (Wh)
- Q = total energy required for decomposition at 100% efficiency.**70**

Costs

The chemicals used in a thermochemical process are reused over and over again with little or no loss. The main inputs are water and heat energy. In some processes electricity is used for electrolysis in one or more of the steps. The chemicals used include various catalysts, organic solvents, complexing agents and molten salts.

The range of projected costs of thermochemically produced hydrogen compared to gasoline and electricity are:

	COST / kWh	COST/million BTU
H_2 Thermochemical	$0.02 to 0.04	$7 to 11
H_2 Electrolysis	$0.05 to 0.06	$17 to 20
Gasoline ($1.10/gal.)	$0.03	$10
Electricity	$0.05	$15
Nat. Gas	$0.01	$3.50

In comparing alternative processes, economic costs, as well as the efficiency, of various choices must be considered. The costs of high temperature electrolysis with solid polymer electrolytes is comparable to the best thermochemical cycles. **90** *"The costs are close enough so that no clear choice can be made among the processes."* Coal gasification, however, remains a cheaper source of hydrogen. *"Hydrogen from water splitting will most probably be more expensive than hydrogen or other synfuels produced from coal gasification. Therefore, water splitting , either by electrolysis, or by thermochemical cycles is a long term energy conversion process."* **300**

A nation with sufficient deposits of coal doesnot have to be vitally dependent upon foreign sources of energy. The *Sasol* process developed in South Africa turns 5.4 billion kg (6 million tons) of coal per year into various oils, alcohols, and gasses at relatively low temperature and pressure making that nation 80% *independent of imported fuel.* **140**

Exhibit 31 shows the comparative costs of various commercial and experimental processes of generating hydrogen. **540**

31. Hydrogen Production Costs

Process	Cost per Unit Voltage	
	($/m^3)	($/ft^3)
Catalytic Steam Reforming	0.10-0.12	0.003
Partial Oxydation of Fuel Oil	0.12-0.16	0.003-0.005
Koppers-Totzek Coal Gasification	0.17-0.20	0.005-0.006
Conventional Electrolysis	0.34-0.41	0.01- 0.012
Advanced SPE Electrolysis	0.22-0.24	0.006-0.007
High Temperature Steam Electrolysis	0.22-0.24	0.006-0.007

Energy Input			
(Wh/m^3)	(Wh/ft^3)		
3,125-3,186	88.5-90.2	0.19-0.22	0.005-0.006
3,064-3,124	86.8-88.4	0.18-0.21	0.006-0.0062
2,711-3,064	76.8-86.7	0.17-0.18	0.005-0.0052

Process	Cost per Unit Voltage	
Sulfur-Assisted Conventional Electrolysis	125.7-170.9	3.56 - 4.48
Sulfur-Assisted SPE Electrolysis	43.8- 87.9	1.24 - 2.49
Formate-Bicarbonate Cycle	2.32+	0.008+

Demonstration Plants

In order to determine the practicality of alternative thermochemical cycles it is necessary to study the chemical features of the process.
- Thermodynamic requirements for each of the reaction steps.
- The chemical and energy outputs of each step.

64

- The effect of other chemical reactions that are not part of the main reaction.
- The effect of possible losses of chemical reactants, leakages, etc.
- Processes to separate the chemical reactants that are to be recycled from the hydrogen and other chemical outputs.
- Space requirements for the heat transfer machinery.
- High temperature and corrosion resistant materials.
- Availability of raw materials now and in the future. Are imports needed?

A study was conducted of over 1,000 possible thermochemical cycles which use materials that can be recycled. In hydrocarbon reforming processes the input materials are used up. The only inputs for each of these thermochemical cycles were water, heat, and electricity. Three promising cycles were selected and three small demonstration plants were built. The three cycles were:

- The Bismuth sulfate cycle, orginating at Los Alamos Scientific Laboratory.
- The Westinghouse sulfur cycle.
- The iodine-sulfur cycle devised by the General Atomic Company.
- The bromine-sulfur cycle, *Mark 13,* developed by the Joint Research Center in Ispra, Italy.

The first three require heat and electricity. The latter two processes need only heat as an energy input.

The bismuth sulfate cycle has estimated overall efficiencies of over 50% if the heat source is 1000°C (1800°F). The process can be operated at lower sulfuric acid concentrations than other processes. This reduces the voltage requirements at the electrolysis step (the first step shown below). Corrosion is also reduced. The process requires the use of solid chemicals.

$$2H_2O + SO_2 \longrightarrow H_2SO_4 + H_2 \qquad \text{Room Temp.}$$

$$H_2SO_4 + Bi_2O_3 + SO_3 \longrightarrow Bi_2O_3 \cdot 2SO_3 + H_2O \qquad \text{Room Temp.}$$

$$Bi_2O_3 + 2SO_3 \longrightarrow Bi_2O_3SO_3 + SO_3 \qquad 800^\circ C$$

$$SO_3 \longrightarrow SO_2 + 1/2\ O_2 \qquad 800+^\circ C$$

In the first step above water and sulfur dioxide are electrolysed to produce hydrogen and sulfuric acid. Next the sulfuric acid is transported to a tank that contains a bismuth oxysulfate compound ($Bi_2O_3 + SO_3$). This reacts with sulfuric acid to produce a bismuth oxysulfate compound ($Bi_2O_3.2SO_3$). This compound is dried and heated to about 800 °C (1500 °F). It then decomposes to the original bismuth oxysulfate compound along with sulfur trioxide gas. The sulfur trioxide is heated to 800°C to break it down to sulfur dioxide and oxygen. The sulfur dioxide is cooled, separated and returned to the electrolyser.

The oxygen in this process can be used for iron production and aeration of ponds. If processes like this were used on a large scale more oxygen would be produced than could be used, so it would be vented to the atmosphere.

As with other thermochemical cycles, each step in the above process is a separate chemical reaction. Each step must be modified so that the required amounts of products are produced for the next step - no more and no less.

The Westinghouse cycle is based on the following reaction at 300° to 375°C (570° to 700°F).

$$SO_2 + 2H_2O \longrightarrow H_2SO_4 + H_2. \qquad \text{Room Temp.}$$

$$H_2SO_4 \longrightarrow H_2O + SO_2 + 1/2O_2. \qquad 800^\circ C$$

As in the bismuth process, the first step involves electrolysing water to produce sulfuric acid and hydrogen.

The last reaction represents a simple splitting of the sulfuric acid molecule by heat at 1,200°C (2,190°F). Decomposition of 84% of the reactants can occur at 1,080°C (1,976°F).

The iodine-sulfur cycle involves thermally splitting surfuric acid and hydrogen iodide. The latter compound can be split at low temperatures and energy input.

$$2H_2O + I_2 + SO_2 \longrightarrow H_2SO_4 + 2HI \qquad \text{Room Temp.}$$

$$H_2SO_4 \longrightarrow H_2O + SO_2 + 1/2O_2 \qquad 300°C$$

$$2HI \longrightarrow H_2 + I_2 \qquad 800°C$$

The process gives low yields and presents difficulties in separating the sulfuric acid from the hydrogen iodide.

Here is another process investigated at Los Alamos. No electrolysis is used in the process. The main disadvantage is its high temperature requirements.

$$Cd + CO_2 + H_2O \longrightarrow CdCO_3 + H_2 \qquad \text{Room Temp.}$$

$$CdCO_3 \longrightarrow CdO + CO_2 \qquad 300°C$$

$$CdO \longrightarrow Cd + 1/2\ O_2 \qquad 1500+°C$$

The experimenters found that the most promising of the three processes to be the bromine-sulfur cycle. In May 1978 the demonstration of this process was the first complete thermochemical hydrogen production process by water decomposition.

$$2H_2O + Br_2 + SO_2 \longrightarrow H_2SO_4 + 2HBr$$

$$H_2SO_4 \longrightarrow H_2O + SO_2 + 1/2\ O_2$$

$$2HBr \longrightarrow H_2 + 2Br$$

The sulfuric acid in the first reaction is easily separated in a column still. It constitutes 75% of the total weight of the mixture. The acid is split at a temperature from 900 °C to 1,200 °C (1,650 °C to 2,230 °F) at a low pressure of 3 atm (0.3 MPa, 44 psi). Steel is used as a catalyst. No heat exchangers were required.

Hydrogen bromide is electrolysed in the third reaction at 0.80 volts. Hydrogen is produced at the rate of 0.1 m³ (3.5 ft3/hr). Because hydrogen is lighter than bromine, the two gasses are easily separated. No separator is needed. The following is a summary of the output and operating conditions of a plant that begun operation in 1984 and was run for 18 months.

- Hydrogen output: 1,000 m3/hr (35310 ft3/hr).
- Sulfuric acid processed: 43.7 kg/hr (96 lb/hr).
- Operating pressure: 24.7 atm (2.5 MPa, 362.6 psi).
- Maximum operating temperature: 950°C (1,740°F).
- Electrical input: 100 kW.

- Efficiency: 30 to 40%.
- Cost: $1.00/m3/hr. ($0.03/ft3/hr).

The efficiency compares with 28 to 32% for high temperature solid polymer electrolysis, but the overall costs are similar. According to G.E. Beghi, a researcher connected with the project:

"The operation of the plant showed no problems of major instabilities, and no formation of by-products or side reactions. The starting-up was also easy and rapid once the required levels were reached, the plant could be put on stream immediately at its normal hydrogen and oxygen production flow rate. Industrial pilot plants can already be built with the present knowledge, chemical engineering data and commercial materials are available, no critical breakthrough is necessary.... Thermochemical production of hydrogen is demonstrated and feasible." [70]

The Nitric Acid Process

Newell C. Cook has developed a process for recycling nitric oxide compounds and acid while splitting water to produce hydrogen. Nitric oxide is advantageous because of its low boiling point, low ionization potential, and its high thermal stabiltiy. A variety of acids may be used but phosphoric acid is shown in the following reaction.

$$2NO + 2HPO_3 \text{-----}> 2NO^+PO_3^- + H_2$$

The phosphoric acid decomposes, releasing hydrogen, and forming nitrosonium phosphate (a salt). When water is added to the salt, the acid and one-half of the nitric oxide is reconstituted. Heat is given off.

$$2NO^+PO_3^- + H_2O \text{-----}> 2HPO_3 + NO + NO_2$$

The NO_2 is reduced by heat and recycled to the first reaction.

$$NO_2 \text{-----}> NO + 1/2O_2$$

The overall objective is to "split" nitric oxide into a positive ion (NO^+) and a free electron (e^-). This reduction process is more efficient than electrolysis. The energy input required is 58.2 Wh at 20°C (68°F) and 1 atm (0.1 MPa, 14.7 psi). 60 to 80% of this can be fed back as heat from the later reactions.

Despite the low hydrogen yield the process is promising. It is simpler than other chemical cycles for making hydrogen, has fewer steps, and uses cheaper and more readily available chemicals.*"The reactions described above suggest that if yields can be improved, a cyclic process for making hydrogen from water and low-level energy may be possible through the use of the NO/NO+ redox system."* [70]

Summary

Regarding the costs of these and other thermochemical processes the observations of L.P. Bicelli are not so optimistic. *"Owing to the many problems involved, it is diffucult to predict whether one of these hydrogen production processes, which are extremely complex from a technical viewpoint, will ever reach a commercial stage."* [100p558]

Perhaps this, and similar observations, are correct only if we ignore the *environmental and health costs* of using fossil fuels and the *military costs* involved in defending our precariously overextended energy supply lines. Perhaps a crash program to develope all energy resources that can make us energy independent would be cheaper both now and in the long run.

Chapter 4:
FUEL FROM TRASH

STEAM REFORMING OF COAL

Hydrogen can be produced by steam reforming most carbon-containing materials. Some materials like coal are almost pure carbon. The general reaction for reacting carbon with steam to produce hydrogen and carbon monoxide is:

$$\text{Heat} + C + H_2O \dashrightarrow CO + H_2$$

It is an "exothermic reaction", meaning that a source of heat is necessary to make work.

The resulting mixture of carbon monoxide and hydrogen is called "town gas" because it was used in 1803 by William Murdock, a partner of James Watt, as a source of light in Watt's workshop. It was used for street lighting in London in 1810. By 1830 the use of town gas spread to Boston, New York and Paris. It was used for illumination because it was cleaner than burning coal or oil for lamps. It solved a growing problem of air pollution that was occuring before the use of town gas.

Town gas is also called water gas because of the reaction of water with carbon. Another name is synthesis gas because it is the first step in the synthesis of methanol.

The higher the temperature of the steam reforming reaction the more hydrogen is produced. At 550 °C (1,022 °F) 24 percent of the carbon reacts with the steam to produce hydrogen. At 600 °C (1,112 °F) 89 percent of the carbon reacts. A cobalt molybdate catalyst increases the hydrogen output at all temperatures.

Thermodynamic Cost

R.L. Wooley, an engineer working for the Billings Energy Corporation, compared the thermodynamic and economic costs of producing methane and hydrogen from coal. The essential results of that 1977 study are paraphrased and presented below.

The costs of investing in and operating a plant that produces synthetic fuel from coal depends upon many variables such as the following:

- How the plant is financed.
- Interest rates for invested capital.
- Land costs.
- The cost of mining and preparing the coal.
- The cost of other raw materials.
- The current and projected rate of inflation.
- Wages and salaries.
- Costs of protecting the environment.

68

- Engineering and design.
- The efficiency of the process.

The last two items in the above list depend the least upon the specific site choosen. Here we are concerned primarily with the thermodynamic efficiency of converting coal to three alternative synthetic fuels:
- Synthesis gas (carbon monoxide and hydrogen)
- Methane
- Hydrogen

First, let us consider the thermodynamic efficiency of a simplified and idealized process. In this way we can determine the maximum output for each of the synthetic fuels.

Thermodynamic Concepts

Here is a review of useful thermodynamic concepts.

The minimum amount of energy necessary to force together various elements to make a synthetic fuel is called the *heat of reaction,* or as the *enthalpy of reaction* . The amount of energy that a fuel give off when it is burned is the *combustion enthalpy.* Under ideal conditions of 100 percent efficiency, the synthetic fuel gives off the same amount of energy as it took to create it. Energy was consumed in creating the fuel. The same amount of energy was given off when the fuel was burned. This principal is known as the *First Law of Thermdynamics.* It applies to any use of energy to do work. It basically says that "there ain't no free lunch".

In reality the energy recovered is always less than what it took to create the fuel. This is the *Second Law of Thermodynamics.* According to it, "you can't even break even". Someone has to pay the energy price. In the case of coal, nature does. Millions of years ago solar energy was converted into carbohydrates in plants. The plants died and ended up at the bottom of a swamp. Sucessive layers of silt weighed down on the dead plant material so that through the ages mostly carbon was left - in the form of coal. The sunlight absorbed by the plants was not converted 100 percent to coal. There is always some energy loss, even in nature. When man arrives to mine the coal he only has to put energy into mining the coal which is less than the energy value of the coal itself. So mankind is getting an energy bargain. Synthetic fuels have to be made "from scratch" from their various constituent elements, and so, they never give the same amount of energy that it took to create them.

The maximum amount of energy from various fuels can be seen from a table of heats of formation. See **Exhibits 32** and **33.** When energy of combustion is harnessed to do work, the enthalpy of reaction leaves the system in one of three forms:

- Heat
- Work
- Exhaust enthalpy

This is in accordance with the *First Law of Thermodynamics.* Work is the most useful output but according to the *Second Law of Thermodynamics* the other two will never be zero. The Second Law of Thermodynamics states that it is impossible for a heat engine to convert all of the heat into useful work. Some heat must be rejected to the environment.

The maxiumu useful work that it it possible to obtain from a combustion process can be determined by assuming the fuel is used in a thermodynamically ideal heat eagine. This ideal engine performs better than any engine could in reality: there is no friction and heat flow takes place across any temperature difference, regardless of how small.

The amount of heat that must be given off by the engine to the environment depends upon the temperature of the environment. The maximum amount of useful work that may be obtained depends only on the process and the temperature of the heat being rejected to the environment. The maximum useful work produced by an ideal heat engine that rejects waste heat at a given temperature, T_o , is known as the *availability.*

The availability represents the maximum amount of work that can be obtained from

69

the fuel using thermodynamically ideal equipment. Real equipment produce less work because of friction and heat transfer losses.

The change in availability is the change in the maximum useful work that can be accomplished ideally for a process that begins and ends at the same temperature. This is the same as the change in the Gibbs function, g, at that temperature. The *Gibbs function*, is also called *free energy*, is related to enthalpy (h) and entropy (T_s).

$$g = h - T_s.$$

By selecting the initial and final temperature to be the temperature of the environment, approximately 25°C (77°F), the change in the Gibbs function at that temperature produces the change in energy availability. This is the maximum amount of useful work remaining to be extracted from the fuel.

Maximum Useful Work Available from a Synthetic Fuel

A comparison of the availability (Gibbs function at 25°C or 77°F) in the various fuels made from coal shows the thermodynamic cost to make the fuel.

The maximum useful work that may be obtained by burning carbon is given by the change in the Gibbs function for carbon combustion. See **Exhibit 33.** Some of this energy (94.2598 kcal/gram-mole) is wasted when the carbon is processed into other synthetic fuels. Some is consumed in making the fuel and the remainder is left in the final product. The thermodynamic cost of producing the synthetic fuel is the loss of availablity. This loss always takes place during fuel manufacture.

32. *Heats of Formation for Various Chemicals*

Substance	Heat of Formation of Formation (kcal/g-mole)	Free Energy (kcal/g-mole)
Carbon	0	0
Hydrogen	0	0
Oxygen	0	0
Carbon Monoxide	-26.4157	-32.8077
Carbon Dioxide	-94.0518	-94.2598
Water (steam)	-57.7979	-54.6351
Water (liquid)	-68.3174	-56.6899
Methane	-17.889	-12.140

70

Reaction	Heat of Formation (kcal/g-mole)	Free Energy (kcal/g-mole)
Carbon combustion (incomplete) $C + 1/2\ O_2 \longrightarrow CO$	-26.4157	-32.8077
CO combustion $CO + 1/2\ O_2 \longrightarrow CO_2$	-67.6361	-61.4521
Carbon combustion (complete) $C + O_2 \longrightarrow CO_2$	-94.0518	-94.2598
Carbon (coal) gasification $C + H_2O\ (l) \longrightarrow CO + H_2$	+41.9017	+23.8822
CO shift to hydrogen $CO + H_2O\ (l) \longrightarrow CO_2 + H_2$	+ 0.6813	- 4.7622
Methanation $CO + 3H_2 \longrightarrow CH_4 + H_2O\ (l)$	-59.7907	-36.0222
Hydrogen combustion $H_2 + 1/2\ O_2 \longrightarrow H_2O\ (l)$	-68.3174	-56.6899
Methane combustion $CH_4 + 2O_2 \longrightarrow CO_2 + 2H_2O\ (l)$	-213.7976	-195.4996

Thermodynamic Cost of Synthesis Gas Production

Synthesis gas ($CO + H_2$) is produced by reacting steam and carbon (coal). There is partial carbon combustion reaction when the carbon combines with oxygen from the steam. Complete combustion would produce CO_2. Combustion of 61% of the carbon is necessary to produce the energy (enthalpy of reaction) required by the gasification reaction. The partial oxydation reaction gives off heat energy (an *exothermic reaction*). The gasification reaction consumes energy (an *endothermoic reaction*) The exothermic reaction provides the energy needed by the endothermic reaction. **Exhibit 34** shows the proportions of materials used in these reactions needed to convert one atom of carbon into synthesis gas. The total energy (enthalpy) remains constant for this thermodynamically ideal process. All of the energy originally in the carbon is now in the synthesis gas. However, there has been a change in the Gibbs function. 11.6% of the availability originally in the carbon has been lost. When the synthesis gas is later burned, 100% of the energy may be extracted, but only a maximum of 88.5% of the energy may be converted into useful work. In spite of this synthetic fuels have other advantages such as the ease of gas cleanup and less pollution.

Producing methanol (CH_3OH) from the synthetic gas requires an extra endothermic step at high pressures.

34. Availability Loss for Carbon Conversion to Synthesis Gas in a Thermodynamically Ideal Process
$(T_O = 25^O C)$

Process	Enthalpy	Input Output	Free Energy	Input Output
Carbon (coal) gasification $C + H_2O\ (l) \longrightarrow CO + H_2$	+16.2018	-------	+9.2343	-------
Carbon combustion $C + 1/2\ O_2 \longrightarrow CO$	-16.2018	-------	-20.1222	-------
Total gasification reaction $3C + O_2 + H_2O \longrightarrow 3CO + H_2$	0	0	-10.8879	11.55%
Fuel combustion $CO + H_2 + O_2 \longrightarrow CO_2 + H_2O$	-94.0518	100%	-83.3719	88.45%
Total of all reactions $C + O_2 + H_2O \longrightarrow CO_2 + H_2O$	-94.0518	100%	-94.2598	100%

Thermodymanic Cost of Hydrogen Production

Hydrogen is produced from coal by first producing synhesis gas and then reacting the resulting carbon monoxide with steam. The energy loss in producing systhesis gas is the same as above. Since the hydrogen forming step (the *shift reaction*) is slightly endothermic, some combustion of the synthesis gas to CO_2 is necessary (10%) to provide the heat energy. In the ideal process considered here, the energy in the hydrogen is equal to that in the original carbon. However, the shift reaction has wasted an 5.7 percent of the input energy. 82.8% of the availability in the carbon is used when the hydrogen fuel is burned. The thermodynamic penalty to convert synthesis gas into hydrogen has been relatively small. There are several advantages to the extra steps.

- Hydrogen may be transported by pipeline over great distances.
- Hydrogen burns cleanly.
- Hydrogen fuel may be used in place of other fuels, often with only minor changes.

35. Availability Loss for Carbon Conversion to Hydrogen
for a Thermodynamically Ideal Process
($T_0 = 25°C$)

Process	Enthalpy	Input Output	Free Energy	Input Output
Carbon (coal) gasification $C + H_2O (l) ---> CO + H_2$	+16.2018	-------	+9.2343	-------
Carbon combustion $C + 1/2 O_2 ----> CO$	-16.2018	-------	-20.1222	-------
Total gasification reaction $2C + 1/2 O_2 + H_2O ---->2CO + H_2$	0	0	-10.8879	11.55%
CO shift to hydrogen $CO + H_2 + H_2O ----> CO_2 + 2H_2$	+.6745	-------	- 4.7147	-------
CO combustion $CO + H_2 + 1/2 O_2 ---> CO_2 + H_2$	-.6745	-------	- .6128	------
Total shift reaction $2CO + 2H_2 + 1/2 O_2 + H_2O ---->2CO_2 + 3H_2$	0	0	-5.3275	5.65%
Hydrogen fuel combustion $H_2 + 1/2 O_2 ----> H_2O$	-94.0518	100%	-78.0444	82.80%
Total of all reactions $C + O_2 + H_2O ----> CO_2 + H_2O$	-94.0518	100%	-94.2598	100%

Thermodynamic Cost of Methane Production

The steps for producing synthetic methane are shown in **Exhibit 36.** The gasification steps are repeated for clarity. After gasification, 65% of the gas stream must be converted to hydrogen in order to provide the ratio of 3 to 1 hydrogen to CO molecules necessary to produce methane. Since only two-thirds of the gas stream is shifted to hydrogen, the loss in availability is less than if it were shifted entirely to hydrogen. We are assuming there that all of the energy in the coal is transferred to the gas stream that is to be converted to methane.

73

The methanation step is very wasteful. The shift plus methanation reaction loses 16.8% of the energy originally available in the carbon. This was only 5.7% in the hydrogen shift. Only 72% of the original availability remains in the methane produced. The methanation step alone uses up more energy than the initial gasification.

Another loss occurs because the methane reaction is exothermic, heat must be removed during the process. The temperature for the methanation step is so low that it is not possible to place the heat back into the process. Even in ideal thermodynamic devices heat must still move from higher to lower temperatures. Even if some of this energy could be recovered by preheating water the change in the Gibbs function would be small. If none of the energy be recovered, only 78.8% of the original enthalpy remains in the carbon after methanation.

36. Availability Loss for Carbon Conversion to Methane for a Thermodynamically Ideal Process
$(T_0 = 25^oC)$

Process	Enthalpy	Input Output	Free Energy	Input Output
Carbon (coal) gasification $C + H_2O (l) \longrightarrow CO + H_2$	+16.2018	-------	+9.2343	-------
Carbon combustion $C + 1/2\ O_2 \longrightarrow CO$	-16.2018	-------	-20.1222	-------
Total gasification reaction $2C + 1/2O_2 + H_2 \longrightarrow 2CO + H_2$	0	0	-10.8879	11.55%
Partial CO shift to hydrogen $CO + H_2 + H_2O \longrightarrow CO_2 + 2H_2$	+.4418	-------	- 3.0880	-------
CO combustion $CO + H_2 + 1/2\ O_2 \longrightarrow CO_2 + H_2$	-.4418	-------	- .4014	-------
Not shifted $CO + H_2 \longrightarrow CO + H_2$	0	-------	0	-------
Partial shift reaction $3CO + 3H_2 + 1/2O_2 + H_2O$ $\longrightarrow CO + 2CO_2 + 4H_2$	0	0%	-3.4894	3.70%
Methanation $2CO + 6H_2 + CO_2$ $\longrightarrow 2CH_4 + 2H_2O + CO_2$	-20.6297	21.93%	-12.4288	13.19%
Methane fuel combustion $CH_4 + 2O_2 \longrightarrow 2H_2O + CO_2$	-73.4221	78.07%	-67.4537	71.56%
Total of all Reactions $C + O_2 + H_2O \longrightarrow CO_2 + H_2O$	-94.0518	100%	-94.2598	100%

37. Availability Loss for Manufacture of Synthetic Fuels from Coal in a Thermodynamically Ideal Process

	% Loss of Enthalpy for Synthetic Fuel Manufacture	% Loss of Availability for Synthetic Fuel Manufacture	Availability Remaining in Fuel
Carbon (C)	0%	0%	100%
Synthesis Gas (CO + H_2)	0%	11.6%	88.4%
Hydrogen (H_2)	0%	17.2%	82.8%
Methane (CH_4)	21.9%	28.4%	71.6%

Summary

It takes less energy to produce hydrogen from coal than it does to produce methane from coal. The maximum amount of useful work that can be extracted from synthetic fuel made from coal is shown in **Exhibit 37**. Coal gasification wastes much energy. Less energy is lost in reacting carbon monoxide with steam to produce hydrogen. Since methane and hydrogen have similar advantages as fuels, producing methane from coal makes less sense than producing hydrogen more efficiently from the same source. Hydrogen produces more heat energy per unit of air and can be sent through pipelines with only slightly more difficulty than methane.

Even though the analysis here was greatly simplified, the reactions taking place in the manufacture of synthetic fuels, whether separately or simultaneously, are the same. The thermodynamic conclusions reached here are, therefore, valid.

Real production facilities do not operate under ideal conditions. Various factors such as design differences in heat exchanger performance, catalyst performance, air blown or oxygen blown gasifieres, etc.; would reduce the amount of input energy that finds its way into the fuel, but would not change any of the conclusions reached herein. 1020

STEAM REFORMING OF BIOMASS

Part of the cost of producing hydrogen can be offset by converting organic waste material to hydrogen fuel. Those who create the waste usually have to pay to have it disposed of. Why not use this trash to produce a useful product? Income can be generated from two sources: disposing of waste material and selling a high grade fuel.

Most of rural and municipal garbage is made up materials that are a combination of hydrogen and carbon. Fuels like methane (CH_4) contain more hydrogen than any other hydrocarbon fuel in common use. By this process hydrogen is obtained from both the steam and the hydrocarbon inputs.

The general reaction for steam reforming any hydrocarbon is:

$$C_nH_m + n\ H_2O + Heat \longrightarrow n\ CO + (n+0.5M)\ H_2.$$

The carbon monoxide resulting from a steam reforming operation may be burned in air to recover some of the energy. The heat of combustion may be used to supply energy for the steam-reforming reaction. The temperature of combustion is low enough so that nitrogen is not converted to nitrous oxides. According to the above reaction, one volume of carbon monoxide yields three volumes of carbon dioxide and nitrogen.

$$CO + 0.5\ O_2 + 2N_2 \longrightarrow CO_2 + 2N_2.$$

The resulting gases could be injected into oil wells to sustain the pressure necessary to extract the fuels. Currently it is common to abandon a well if 50 percent of the oil is recovered. This is because of the drop in pressure that makes it uneconomical to recover the last 50 percent. By reinjecting a well more oil can be recovered. 565

OXYDATION OF HYDROCARBONS

The complete oxydation of hydrocarbons produces about three times as much carbon dioxide, by weight, as the original hydrocarbon. It is estimated that there are 500 million motor vehicles in the world. Assuming that the average weekly fuel consumption is four gallons per week 100 billion gallons of fuel are consumed per year worldwide. If each gallon of gasoline produces 20 pounds of carbon dioxode, about two trillion pounds (18 billion tons) of carbon dioxide are produced each year from motor vehicles. 566

$$C_n\ H_m + (1/4\ m + n)\ O_2 \longrightarrow nCO_2 + 1/2m\ H_2O.$$

$$(12n + 1m)\ kg\ hydrocarbons \longrightarrow 44n\ kilograms\ of\ CO_2.$$

As a means of reducing land fill space municipal garbage has been incinerated for years. The exhaust has only contributed to urban air pollution. Decaying refuse in landfills also puts an equivalent amount of carbon dioxide into the atomosphere.

PYROLYSIS OF HYDROCARBONS

As mentioned in the above section. Burning trash produces more carbon dioxide by weight than the unburned hydrocarbon. Roy E. McAlister, President of the American Hydrogen Association has suggested, in a paper entitled "Prosperity Without Pollution" that we stop "wasting waste". 568, This carbon resource is too valuable to be dumped into the atmosphere, where it may contribute to global warming. The pure carbon can be extracted from the hydrocarbons by heating them to several hundreds of degrees in the absence of oxygen. This process is called *pyrolysis*. The heat separates the carbon from the hydrogen. The general pyrolysis reaction is:

$$Cn\ Hm + Heat \longrightarrow nC + (1/2\ m)\ H2.$$

The pure carbon can be fashioned into a variety of carbon-containing materials.

- Activated carbon filter and hydrogen absorbing storage media.

- High strength fibers for various composite materials that can be used in car bodies, fishing rods and anywhere strong lightweight material is needed. They can be used in rust proof plastic building materials.
- Artificial diamond materials for cutting, electronic circuit plating (more heat resistant and having a lower resistance than silicone).
- Fullerenes, or "Buckeyballs" after Buckminster Fuller, the inventor of the geodesic dome. The molecular structure of the Fullerenes resembles a geodesic dome. (12 pentagons and 20 hexagons) The balls usually consist of 60, but may contain as many as 600, carbon atoms that form a hollow sphere. They can be fragmented to plate hard wear-resistant diamond films on electronic circuit boards, windshields, and engine parts. In combination with Fluorine the Fullerenes become $C_{60}F_{60}$. In this form they can be used as the lowest friction lubricants yet devised.
- Each C_{60} ball can absorb hydrogen atoms on its surface. This can become a method of hydrogen storage.

If an inexpensive source of heat is used, the process becomes economical. Refuse collectors pay to leave their garbage. Manufacturers pay for the carbon and hydrogen by-products. Land fill space is saved. Air pollution is reduced.

The source of heat may be solar. In areas of the world where there is little annual cloud cover the process is particularly attractive. Garbage from other areas may be shipped there. There should be little public protest because the garbage is not being stored but transformed into useful products and the operation would be a source of revenue for the local governments.

According to Roy McAlister a field of 2,000 mirrors, each the size of a billboard, could be angled to focus sunlight on the top of a central tower. The temperatures there could quickly reduce dry biomass to hydrogen and carbon-rich solids. The technology for processing the output is already available in the petrochemical industry.

Exhibit 38 shows the composition of annual U.S. garbage "production". 772
As can be seen in the exhibit almost one and a half times as much garbage is produced in the U.S. each year than is coal. The carbon content is similar. This means that more carbon is wasted than is mined. The cost of "mining" hydrogen and carbon from waste is estimated to be around $2.00 per million BTU depending on the efficiency of the process and how much can be charged for accepting the waste. This estimated cost is competitive with natural gas and less than for refined fuels such as gasoline and diesel fuel.

Sewage, garbage, and toxic hydrocarbons can produce 10 to 25 percent hydrogen by weight using the pyrolysis process. 568

38. *Annual U.S. Waste Production*

Type of Waste	Output (millions of dry tons)
Field Crop Residues	521
Animal Manure & Municipal Sewage	287
Forestry Wastes	283
Municipal Garbage	170
Miscellaneous	50
Industrial Organic Wastes	44
Total	1,355
Carbon Content of Total	40 - 60 %
Annual U.S. Coal Production	970
Carbon Content	50 - 85 %

Chapter 5:
STORING HYDROGEN

PERSPECTIVE

There are three main ways of storing hydrogen. Gaseous, liquid and solid (hydride) storage.

Hydrogen is stored as a gas under high pressure in containers made of light-weight but strong materials. Because it has small atoms, hydrogen can penetrate many materials. A hydrogen container must be able to contain the gas without leaking. High strength fibers (aramide, glass or carbon) are wound around this inner container to give it strength. Hydrogen emerges from the container under high pressure. Pressure regulators are necessary to reduce the pressure before the fuel is admitted to the engine.

Hydrogen liquifies at a temperature at about -253 $^{\circ}$C (-423 $^{\circ}$F). Storage containers must be highly insulated. Typical containers have double walls with a vacuum in between the walls. In spite of good insulation 1 to 2 percent of the liquified fuel is lost per day in evaporation. A specially designed pump is used to supply the engine with the fuel.

Gaseous hydrogen may be stored in solid metal. The metal absorbs the hydrogen gas at high pressure and low temperature. Heat and low pressure is applied to release the hydrogen from storage. A typical configuration has hydride -containing tubes surrounded by water. Heat is added or removed from the hydride in the tubes by heating or cooling the water.

The following list gives the energy content for equal weights of mechanical, chemical, and nuclear energy sources. **320**

Elastic bands, 2kg (1lb):	0.16 kWh / kg (248 BTU / lb)
Fossil fuel:	13 kWh / kg (20,000 BTU / lb)
Hydrogen:	35 kWh / kg (54,000 BTU / lb)
Uranium fission:	161,000 kWh / kg (2×10^8 BTU / lb)
Hydrogen to helium fusion:	1.68×10^{11} kWh / kg (2.6×10^{14})

Volume, as well as weight, must be used to compare fuels. One fuel may have more energy per *unit weight* but less energy per *unit volume*. This is particularly important to consider when comparing a very light gas, like hydrogen, to a relatively dense liquid fuel like gasoline.

A given weight of hydrogen has 2.8 times the energy of the same weight of gasoline, but on a volume basis liquid hydrogen has only 27% of the energy content of gasoline.

Exhibit 39 compares the energy content of some common fuels. **Exhibit 40** summarizes some of the information in the previous exhibit. A liter of gaseous hydrogen pressurized to 100 atm (10 MPa, 1,450 psi) has an energy content of only 300 Watt-hours compared to 8,890 Watt-hours for the same volume of gasoline. The weight of a container is usually 100 times the weight of the hydrogen gas stored in it.

The above figures indicate the impracticality of using pressurized gaseous fuels for use on long-range vehicles. Some gaseous fuels become liquid under pressure (such as propane). Vehicles powered by propane, with their conspicuous cylindrical tanks, are common in fleet vehicle applications.

Hydrogen can be stored in what is widely mistaken to be a "solid" form. Certain metals like magnesium, titanium, and iron absorb hydrogen when cooled, and release it when heated. Hydrogen remains a gas but is invisibly confined in the spaces between molecules in the metal. When the metal is charged with hydrogen gas it is called a *hydride* . Although only 1.5% of the weight of fully charged iron-titanium hydride contains hydrogen, the fuel density of the gas is comparable to liquid hydrogen.

Liquid hydrogen at -253°C (-423°F) is denser than hydrogen gas but requires costly and complex storage containers and elaborate refueling procedures. The energy required to liquefy hydrogen gas is approximately equal to one-third of the energy in the liquid produced.

Although hydrogen makes up only a few percent of the weight of hydrides the total volume and weight of the hydrogen gas stored is larger than for liquid hydrogen. Of the three methods of storing hydrogen (gas, hydride and liquid) pressurized gas comes in a poor third for both hydrogen content and energy per unit of volume. However, a hydride system may take up 50% more space than pressurized gas tanks. 76 cm^3 (4.6 in^3) of iron-titanium hydride weighs 680 kg (1,500 lb).

Hydride compares favorably to electric batteries used in vehicles. Even the advanced batteries predicted for the future (sodium-sulfur and lithium-sulfur) have less than half of the energy density (on a volume or weight basis) of magnesium-nickle hydride.

Hydride is the safest storage method. If a hydride tank is ruptured, the hydrogen gas remains in the hydride, posing little fire hazard. Pressurized gas vessels are subject to leaks and accidental punctures. With a properly designed system, liquid hydrogen has been found, after crash tests, to be no more dangerous than gasoline.

Exhibit 41 summarizes features and problems with using various fuels. This illustrates that factors other than energy content, like cost, availability, combustion characteristics and auxilliary equipment must be considered in comparing fuels and energy storage devices.

PRESSURIZED GAS

Low Pressure Stationary Storage

For stationary applications hydrogen can be stored at relatively low pressures. This is because the volume of the container is not as critical as when the fuel is stored on board a vehicle.

Atmospheric pressure is about 14.75 psi. Anything less is called a vacuum.

	Energy		Energy		Density	
	Wh/kg	1000 BTU/lb	Wh/l	1000 BTU/ft3	kg/l	lb/ft3
Gaseous Fuels						
Hydrogen, 1 atm	34 770	54	3	0.29	.00009	.006
Hydrogen, 100atm	34 770	54	300	29	.0063	.390
Natural Gas	14 900	23	10	0.97	.00008	.005
Methane	13 330	21	10	0.97	.008	.5
Propane	14 270	22	27	2.6	.0019	.119
Liquid Fuels						
Liquid Hydrogen	34 770	54	2 430	235	0.070	04.4
Liquid Methane	13 900	22	5 770	558	0.42	26.2
Methanol	5 560	9	4 430	428	0.8	49.9
Ethanol	8 260	13	6 540	632	0.8	49.9
Gasoline & Fuel Oil	12 360	19	8 890	860	0.72	45.0
Keroscene	12 630	20	10 360	1 001	0.8	49.9
Diesel Fuel	11 770	18	10 555	1 020	0.9	56.2
Ammonia	5 170	8	3 530	341	0.70	43.7
Hydrazine	4 660	7	4 710	455	1.0	62.4
Benzene	11 650	18	10 460	1 011	0.9	56.2
Methyl Ether	8 780	14	6 450	623	0.7	43.7
Solid Fuels						
Wood	4 710	7	2 600	251	.56	35
Coal	8 640	13	12 000	116	1.4	87.4
Hydrides						
$FeTiH_{1.95}$	630	0.9	2 070	200	3.3	206
$LaNi_5H_{6.7}$	570	0.8	1 280	124	2.2	137
Mg_2NiH_4	1 250	1.9	3 200	309	2.6	162
MgH_2	2 760	4.3	3 980	385	1.4	87
Electric Cells						
Lead Acid	32	.05	100	9.7	3.0	187
Nickle Cadmium	44	.07	--------	--------	--------	------
Silver Zinc	109	.2	--------	--------	--------	------
Sodium or Lithium	219	.3	--------	--------	--------	------

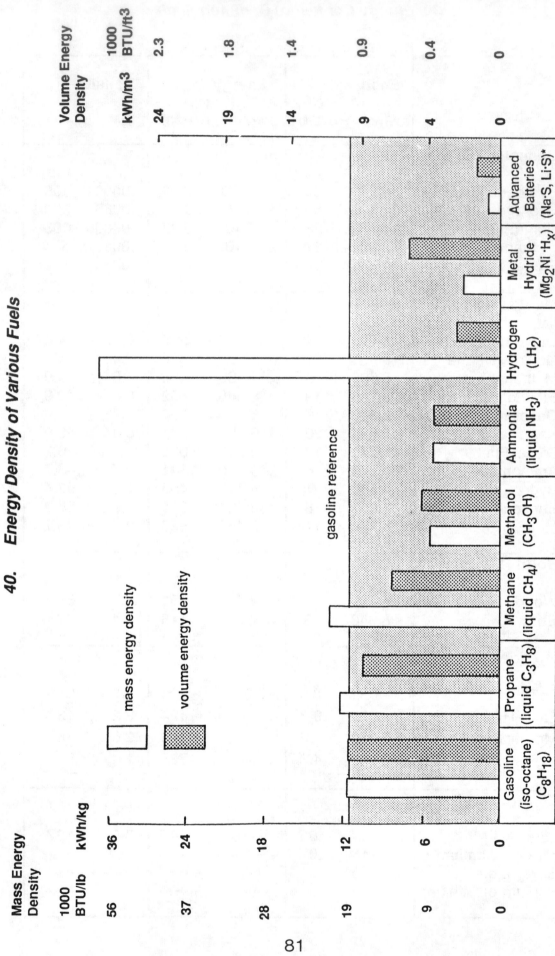

40. Energy Density of Various Fuels

*Includes adjustment for different energy conversion efficiency.

81

41. *Comparison of Fuel Storage Methods*

Fuel	Features	Problems
Gasoline	High energy to weight ratio. Already established as a fuel.	Short supply. CO, NO_x, HC_x pollutants.
Hydrogen gas	High energy to weight ratio.	Low energy to volume ratio. High pressure tanks needed. Highest overall weight.
Liquid hydrogen	High energy to weight ratio.	Low energy to volume ratio. Need expensive insulated tank. 30% liquefaction energy cost.
Hydrogen Hydride (FeTi)	Low dissociation temperature.	Heat loss when charging. Heaviest hydride.
Magnesium + 5% Nickle	Lighter weight.	Moderate dissociation temperature. Scarce materials.
100% Magnesium	Lightest weight.	Highest dissociation temperature.
Methanol	Liquid storage. Obtained from coal.	Moderate pollution. CO_2
Methanol + Water	Increased amount of hydrogen to engine.	Higher weight than pure methanol. Less pollution.
Electric Batteries	Non polluting. At-home charging.	Lowest energy to volume ratio. Short range.

Any more than atmospheric is "pressurized". Inflating a tire to 30 pounds per square inch includes the pressure of the atmosphere. The total pressure is 44.5 psi. The atmosphere presses on the outside of the tire so that the difference is measured as 30 psi.

Pressure and volume of a gas are inversely proportional. The higher the pressure the less the volume and vice versa. The same weight of gas at one pressure times its volume equals the product of another pressure and volume. This is the "Ideal Gas Law".

$$P_1V_1 = P_2V_2.$$

Assume that we have generated 50 cubic feet of hydrogen at atmospheric pressure. Storing hydrogen at 30 psi above atmospheric pressure would give a total pressure of 14.75 psi + 30 psi = 44.75 psi. What is the new volume?

$$V_2 = \frac{P_1V_1}{P_2} = \frac{14.75 \text{ psi} \times 50 \text{ ft}^3}{44.75 \text{ psi}} = 16.48 \text{ ft}^3$$

For storage at a stationary location (not on board a vehicle) hydrogen can be stored in propane tanks at 60 psi. If the tanks are stationary volume is not critical. The fuel can be stored at low pressure in 55 gallon drums. The drums can be open at one end. The open end is down and immersed in a pool of water. Water completely fills the drum. A tube that delivers hydrogen gas is inserted up inside the drum. As hydrogen collects, the gas fills the drum and forces the water out. The drum rises higher and higher above the surface of the water as more and more gas collects. The bottom of the drum should be tethered to the bottom of the pool to prevent the drum from tipping over and letting the gas escape. See **Exhibit 2.**

WARNING: Be sure that no air is in the drum prior to or during the storing of the hydrogen. Water and hydrogen must completely fill the space inside the drum. If air and hydrogen mix there is a danger of explosion.

High Pressure Storage on a Vehicle

Typically the weight of pressure containers is 100 times the weight of hydrogen contained in them. A 136 kg (300 lb) gas cylinder may store one percent of its weight at 408 atm (41.3 MPa, 6,000 psi) giving a range of 96 km (60 mi). 76 liters (20 gal) of gasoline weigh about 52 kg (115 lb). The same energy value of hydrogen weighs 18 kg (40 lb), yet requires a container 100 times heavier, if stored as a gas. The container mass required to store a certain mass of hydrogen is more or less independent of the pressure and container volume. 150 atmospheric storage tanks are commonly used. **190p1081** This means that lower pressure gas would require a larger container. A higher pressure would permit a smaller volume but require more container mass to withstand the higher pressure. The advantages and disadvanges of high and low pressure gas seem to cancel each other. An advantage of high pressure storage remains: the volume is less than with low pressure storage.

To convert a car with a 5.5 km/liter (13 mi/gal) fuel economy to a fuel system that uses hydrogen stored as a gas a 1,350 kg (3,000 lb) storage cylinder would be needed to give a reduced range of 418 km (260 mi) and a top speed of 96.5 m/s (60 mi/hr).

This weight penalty could be partly offset by taking advantage of the higher combustion efficiency of hydrogen compared to gasoline. New engines designed specifically for the use of hydrogen could weigh 50% less than their gasoline counterparts. **580p195**

Despite the problems, gaseous hydrogen is the simplest and cheapest form of hydrogen conversion. Its efficiency and range is sufficient for any local round trip under 96 km (60 mi).

Essentially, the conversion process involves mounting one or two gas cylinders traversly in either the trunk or behind the front seats. Stainless steel fuel lines are used to prevent *hydriding* or *embrittlement* of the fuel line metal by absorption of hydrogen gas. Hydrogen gas under pressure tends to permeate through regular steel or iron and many other metals.

Exhibit 42 shows the layout of a pressurized hydrogen storage system adapted for a vehicle used in a UCLA demonstration. Each tank weighs 135 kg (300 lb) and holds one percent of their weight in fuel. A sheet aluminum envelope around the tanks acts as backup to prevent any escaping hydrogen from getting into the trunk or passenger compartment. A small blower ventilates the envelope to the outside through the trunk lid or roof.

The range of this vehicle is 192 km (120 mi) with a postal Jeep straight six engine.

Two solenoid valves activated by ignition and by engine vacuum, respectively, control fuel flow to the engine. Fuel flow is diverted into two sets of pressure regulators. The first set reduces the tank pressure from 408.3 atm (41.4 MPa, 6,000 psi) to 1.1 atm (0.1 MPa, 16.0 psi). The second set reduces line pressure still further to a vacuum of 0.03 atm (0.003 MPa, 0.44 psi).

Inexpensive polyvinyl chloride (PVC) tubing may be used after the second set of regulators. The 100 mesh stainless steel screen breaks up any large droplets of water from the water injector system. Water injection is used to cool the combustion temperature to prevent preignition.

The Impco CA 300 gas mixer is usually mounted on top of the carburetor. If space is not available it may be attached to one side with an offset adaptor. Its functions being assumed by the gas mixer, the carburetor is now used to inject a water spray. The gasoline tank is converted to a water reservoir.

The estimated cost (in 1988) of this conversion is as follows:

Impco CA 300:	$80.00
Gas cylinder tube frame:	$40.00
Gas regulators:	$100.00
Direct adaptor:	$10.00
Gas cylinders:	$100.00
Stainless steel fuel lines:	$50.00
Valves:	$100.00
Miscellaneous:	$100.00
------------	-----------
Total:	$580.00

Parts suitable for natural gas are generally adaptable for hydrogen. These include tanks, pressure regulators, and delivery tubing. Check with the manufacturer to be sure that the equipment is rated for hydrogen. The tank should have the highest volume and the pressure gauge should be able to handle the highest pressures of those available. If the engine is tuned properly emissions for natural gas should be much lower than for gasoline. 10 percent hydrogen can be mixed without modification to the natural gas conversion. Emissions will be even lower with this mixture called *Hythane*.

Exhibit 43 shows the engine compartment of a Jeep converted to hydrogen. The hydrogen was stored and delivered to the engine in gaseous form.

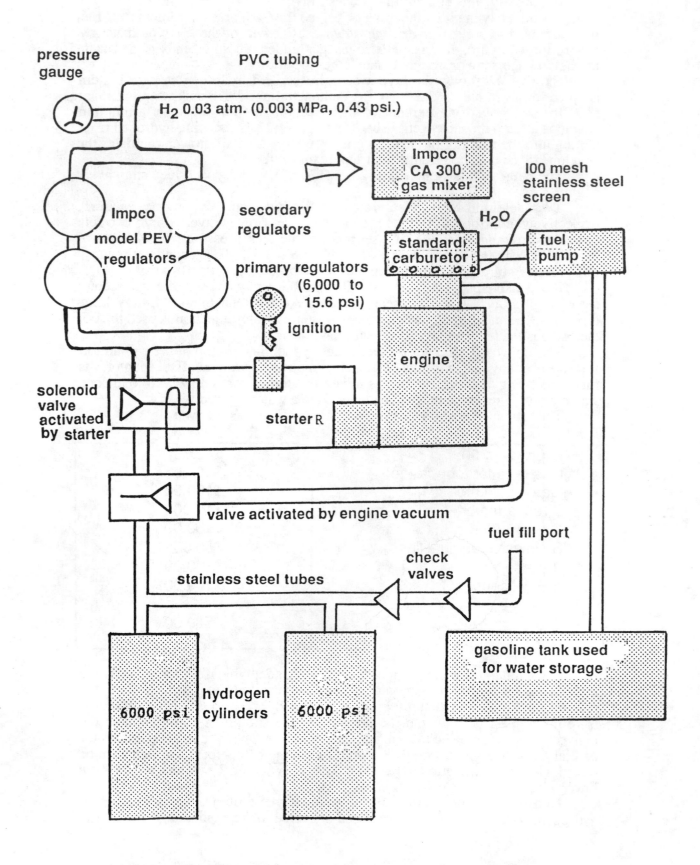

Modifications to UCLA Jeep with pressurized gas storage

LIQUID HYDROGEN

Comparisons

The 1991 Oldsmobile pictured in **Exhibit 44** was converted to liquid hydrogen as part ot the American Hydrogen Association's racing program under the direction of Demetri Wagner. The car has won awards for both horsepower and low exhaust emissions in competitions for alternate energy vehicles. The engine compartment is shown with its electronic ignition and fuel system controls. The liquid hydrogen tank is shown in the car's trunk. It has about a three gallon capacity and gives a range of about 100 miles.

As can be seen in **Exhibit 45**, a vehicle run on liquid hydrogen has the greatest range and highest energy density of the hydrides and liquid fuels listed. Compared to gasoline, liquid hydrogen has three times the energy and one-half the weight. The following table is a comparison of vehicle performance on gasoline and liquid hydrogen. The vehicle has the same range with both fuels. 1000p124

		Gasoline	Liquid Hydrogen
●	Range	650 km (400 miles)	650km (400 miles)
●	Tank size	80 liters (21 gal)	312.0 liters (82 gal)
●	Fuel weight	56 kg (123 lb)	21.8 kg (48 lb)
●	Fuel use	8.1 km / liter (19.1 mi / gal)	2.1 km /liter (4.9 mi)

If the liquid hydrogen vehicle carried around its own oxygen supply in the form of liquid oxygen the range would be reduced by 75%, as shown in **Exhibit 45**. Any other fuel would be similarly handicapped if it could not make use of atmospheric oxygen.

Liquid hydrogen and liquid oxygen in combination have long been the choice fuel for spacecraft.

Storage of liquid hydrogen requires new technology. Tanks with capacity of 3,400 m^3 (900,000 gal) have only 0.05 to 0.03% boil off per day, insuring a supply of liquefied gas lasting five years. 76 liter (20 gal) of liquid hydrogen weigh 54.4 kg (120 lb). 1870 m^3 (66,000 ft^3) of hydrogen weigh 900 kg (2,000 lb), including the cryogenic tank.

Exhibit 46 compares the properties of liquid hydrogen and liquid methane (or liquefied natural gas). Methane liquefies at a 38% higher temperature but requires about seven times as much energy to vaporize it (its heat of vaporization). The density of liquid methane is also about seven times that of liquid hydrogen. This accounts for the use of liquefied natural gas as a means of storing natural gas on supertankers. It stays liquid for the duration of the voyage and weighs less than gas pressure cylinders.

The energy required to liquefy hydrogen is equal to about one-third of the energy content of the hydrogen. For 0.5 kg (1 lb.) of hydrogen, 5 kWh of electrical energy is required. **200**

Liquefaction Plants

A proposed plant designed to liquefy and store electrolysed hydrogen is shown in **Exhibit 47**. The gasses from the electrolyser must have any residual

45. Characteristics of Fuel Systems

At Constant Range								
Fuel	**Total Wt.**		**Total Vol.**		**H2 Stored**		**Range**	
	kg	lb	liters	cu.ft.	kg	lb	km	mi.
TiFe	215	474	54	1.9	4.3	9.5	160	100
$LaNi_5$	290	639	72	2.5	4.3	9.5	160	100
Mg_2Ni	109	240	54	1.9	4.3	9.5	160	100
Mg	54	119	27	1.0	4.3	9.5	160	100
LH_2 + Air	7	15	65	2.3	7.0	15.4	160	100
LH_2 + LO_2	39	86	88	3.1	39.0	86.0	160	100
Propane	15	33	23	.8	----	----	160	100
Butane	11	24	20	0.7	----	----	160	100
Gasoline	11	24	11	0.4	----	----	160	100

At Constant Weight								
TiFe	98	216	54	1.9	4.3	9.5	160	100
$LaNi_5$	98	216	54	1.9	3.0	6.6	117	73
Mg_2Ni	98	216	108	3.8	4.3	9.5	320	199
Mg	98	216	108	3.8	8.6	19.0	640	398
LH_2 + Air	98	216	425	15.0	98.0	216	1051	653
LH_2 + LO_2	98	216	425	15.0	98.0	216	184	114
Propane	98	216	71	2.5	----	----	492	306
Butane	98	216	82	2.9	----	----	657	408
Gasoline	98	216	45	1.6	----	----	657	408

Property	Hydrogen	Methane
Boiling point of Liquid	-252.9°C -423.22°F	-156.0°C -248.8°F
Critical Temperature	-240.10°C -400.10°F	-82.7°C -116.9°F
Critical Pressure	12.98 atm 1.32 MPa 191.00 psi	45.80 atm 4.6 MPa 673.00 psi
Heat of Vaporization	2.226 kWh/kg 3447.6 BTU/lb 8.75 KWh/m^3 846 BTU/ft^3	0.26 kWh/kg 402.7 BTU/lb 60.0 kWh/m^3 5 802 BTU/ft^3
Density at at 1 atm and 20°C (68°F)	71.00 kg/m^3 4.43 lb/ft^3 0.59 lb/gal.	120.30 kg/m^3 7.51 lb/ft^3 1.0 lb/gal
Specific Gravity (water = 1.0)	0.07	0.47
Viscocity	1.82×10^{-6} poise 1.80×10^{-4} lb/ft.s	1400×10^{-6} poise 9.41×10^{-5} lb/ft.s

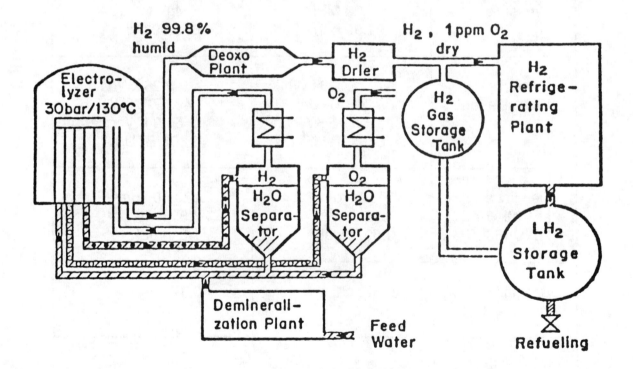

water vapor removed prior to storage. Some hydrogen is inevitably lost due to boil off from the liquid hydrogen. It is recycled and liquefied, as shown. **Exhibit 48** shows the capital and operating costs for the same plant. **30,576**

In typical commercial processes in the U.S., the liquefaction costs are about 20% of the price of the liquid hydrogen. The price of electricity ranges from 45 to 70% of the cost of liquefaction. **900p5-22**

Hydrogen was first liquefied in 1898. The first large scale plant in the U.S. was completed in 1952 at Boulder, Colorado for the National Bureau of Standards. Its capacity then was 450 kg/day (0.5 ton/day). Today it produces 55,000 kg/day (60 ton/day). The cryogenic storage tanks accomodate 3,400 m^3 (900,000 gal). **580**

If the process were 100% efficient, it would require only 7.7 kWh/kg (12,000 BTU/lb) for hydrogen liquefaction. Since the process is typically 33% efficient, three times the energy is needed, or about 28% of the energy content, 23.1 Wh/kg (36,000 BTU/lb), of liquid hydrogen. **140**

The current price of liquid hydrogen is about $1.20 to $2.60 / kWh ($350.00 to 760.00 / million BTU). **580**

Researchers are at work trying to improve the 30 to 33% efficiency of conventional refrigeration. One potential method makes use of the gas pressure generated during electrolysis. Oxygen coming from the electrolyser is under pressure. If allowed to rapidly expand, it can absorb heat from the hydrogen passing through a heat exchanger. This precooled hydrogen requires less energy to liquefy. **850**

Magnetocaloric Effect

Another experimental method exploits the effect that magnetic fields have on certain materials, such as gadalinium alloys. When placed into a magnetic field, the material heats up. It cools when removed. Through a series of stages, hydrogen gas is cooled by contact with these materials. Different materials are used at each cooling stage.

Rotating a wheel of the special material in a magnetic field alternately immerses and removes the material from the field. After the heating phase the material is cooled by a heat exchanger. During the cooling phase the temperature of the material is reduced below what it was originally. The *change* in magnetic flux is what produces the temperature change.

A strong magnetic field is needed (60,000 to 100,000 Gaus). Superconducting materials could be used in the magnets to reduce the current demanded to sustain such an intense magnetic field.

John A. Barclay of Los Alamos National Lab expects the efficiency of this process to exceed 60%. This is *double* the efficiency of conventional refrigeration. Liquefaction costs could also be cut in half.

In practice, the most economical method of liquefying hydrogen may be to combine gas compression with the magnetocaloric process. Four stages of compression and cooling would bring the gas temperature down sufficiently for a single magnetocaloric stage to efficiently cool it to the liquid stage. For gas compression the final stage is the most costly. Magnetocaloric technology would take only one eighth of the energy value of hydrogen to liquefy the hydrogen.

Cryogenic Tanks

In the early 1950's simple vacuum bottle type devices were used to store liquid hydrogen and other low temperature gasses. Later improvements put powder insulation (perlite) in the vacuum space and added a reflective heat shield on the inside of the tank to reduce radiant heat losses. The heat transfer through the wall is cut to one-tenth of the earlier "vacuum bottles".

The newest tanks use alternate layers of glass fibers and metallized plastic

48. Typical Liquid Hydrogen Plant Specifications

Gas Input ● Hydrogen Pressure ● Oxygen Concentration ● Dew Point	30 Atm (3.0 MPa, 441psi) 1 ppm 80°C (176°F)
Gas Purification o Temperature Range	27 to -193°C (81 to -315°F)
Liquefaction ● First Refrigeration Cycle Cooling with Liquid Nitrogen 2 Turbines ● Second Refrigeration Cycle 5 Turbines ● Third Refrigeration Cycle Joule Thompson with Ejector ● Ortho-Para Conversion 6 Steps	27 to -193°C (81 to -315°F) -193 to -247°C (-315 to -413°F) -247 to -254°C (-413 to -426°F) -193 to -253°C (-316 to -424°F)
Plant Capacity	9 m³/hour (318 ft³/hour) 14.9 ton/day
Electrical Power ● Per Unit of LH_2 Output o Total Power	12.5 kWh/kb (19360 BTU/lb) 9 MW
Evaporative Cooling Water	14.3 m³/hour (505 ft³/hour)
Area ● Refrigeration Equipment ● Maintenance	100m² (1 076 ft²) 300 m² (3228 ft²)

film in the vacuum space. This *quilted superinsulation* was pioneered by the Linde Corporation and reduces heat leakage by another one-tenth. The walls of the Linde tanks are about 5 cm (2 in) thick compared to the 91 cm (3 ft) thick walls of the previous technology. **580p51**

The largest tanks have a boil off rate of 0.06%/day. A 100 m³ (3, 500 ft³) tank has a boil off of 0.2%/day at 20ºC (68ºF). Demetri Wagner, manager of the American Hydrogen Association's Racing Program has drag raced a liquid hydrogen powered car. The boiloff loss for his 75 liter fuel system is 0.5 percent per day.

Approximate costs for liquid hydrogen fuel tanks are as follows. **900p7**

3,800 liters (1,000 gallons) 380,000 liters (100,000 gallons) 3,800,000 liters (1,000,000 gallons)	up to $100,000 up to $1,000,000 up to $10,000,000

Exhibit 49 shows the relative sizes of various containers storing 3,000 m³ (106 ,000 ft³) of hydrogen gas. **870p325** **Exhibit 50** presents summary data from experiements with liquid hydrogen storage tanks.

Ortho to Para Conversion

Hydrogen atoms tend to group into pairs to make up hydrogen molecules. In *orthohydrogen* the electrons in the atoms of each molecle spin in the same direction. In *parahydrogen* the electrons spin in opposite directions.

At 20ºC (68ºF) and atmoshperic pressure, hydrogen gas is 25% *para* and 75% *ortho*. When liquefied, all the orthohydrogen is gradually converted to parahydrogen.

Ortho to para conversion gives off heat: 196.8 Wh/kg (304.8 BTU/lb). This heat accelerates the evaporation of liquid hydrogen. In **Exhibit 51** the evaporation rates of liquid hydrogen for various beginning percentages of parahydrogen are given. **580p61**

A special catalyst increases the ortho-para conversion in hydrogen before the gas is liquefied. If all of the heat that would ordinarily go into the conversion is removed before liquefaction takes place energy is saved. Experts claim that this prodedure is cost effective only if the liquid hydrogen is to be stored for more than 36 hours. **580p55**

Using Liquid Hydrogen as a Coolant

Liquid hydrogen is evaporated back to the gaseous state just before it is burned as a fuel. The cooling properties of the liquid can be exploited to recover part of the production costs. Various possibilities for this thermal energy include food warehousing, liquid air production, and turbine blade cooling in jet engines.

Energy can also be recovered from liquefied natural gas. The energy is four times greater, on a weight basis, than that recovered from liquid hydrogen. This is due to the lower molecular weight of hydrogen. **900p5-22**

Liquid Hydrogen as an Aviation Fuel

The cooling properties of liquid hydrogen can be used in jet aircraft to cool engine parts and the skin of the craft flying at supersonic speeds. The cooling capacity of liquid hydrogen is 20 times higher than that for jet fuel. *"Moreover, it has been concluded by NASA and Lockheed that hydrogen is the only fuel*

94

Capacity = 3,000 m^3 (106,000 ft^3)

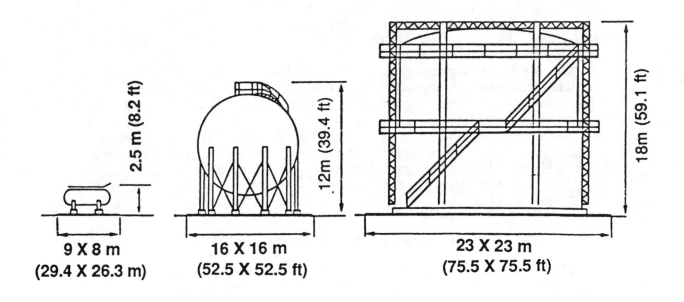

metal hydride

9 X 8 m
(29.4 X 26.3 m)

high pressure tank
10 kg/cm^2 (142 lb/in^2)

16 X 16 m
(52.5 X 52.5 ft)

low pressure
water-sealed reservoir

23 X 23 m
(75.5 X 75.5 ft)

50. Liquid Hydrogen Dewar Specifications

Dewar ($/Gal)	Capacity (liter) (Gal)	Energy Stored (10^3kWh) (10^6BTU)	Insulation Used	Boil-Off (%/day)	Cost
Linde-LSH 150	150.3 39.7	0.36 1.23	Linde SI-4 2.5 cm	2.5-3.0	13 50
Balloon Flight	450 120	1.08 3.69	Evacuated Santocel	-----	----- -----
Linde LSH 1000	1 000 264	2.37 8.09	Linde SI-4 3.2 cm	1.0	----- -----
Beech Transport Trailer	6 000 1 585	14.2 48.5	Powder	1.9	3 12
Semi-Trailer	30 000 7 900	69.8 238	Linde SI-4	0.5	----- -----
Conventional Trailer	49 000 13000	116 396	Evacuated Super Insul.	0.25	----- -----
Rectangular Trailer	61 000 16 000	143 488	-----	0.4	----- -----
Rail Tankcar	98 000 26 000	233 796	Evacuated Perlite	0.5	----- -----
Nevada	189 000 50 000	449 1 530	Evacuated Perlite	0.18	----- -----
	757 000 200 000	17 920 61 200	Evacuated	0.07	-----
	1 890 000 500 000	4 488 15 300	Evacuated Perlite	0.05	0.05 2
KSC	3 217 000 850 000	7 626 26 000	Evacuated Perlite	0.026- 0.03	0.3-.5 1-2

51. Liquid Hydrogen Storage Losses due to Ortho-Para Conversion

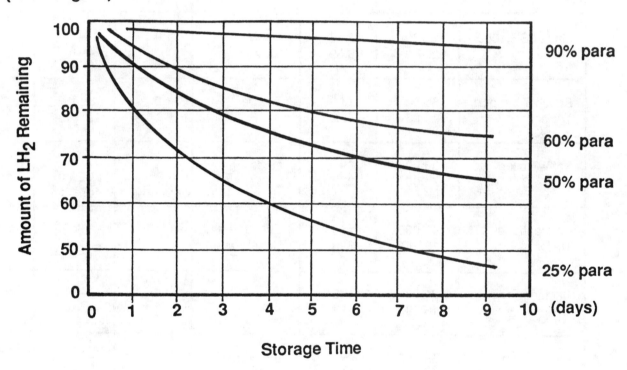

(% of Original)

Amount of LH₂ Remaining

90% para
60% para
50% para
25% para

Storage Time (days)

97

capable of powering hypersonic aerospace planes." **580p826**

Planes that fly 6,400 km/hr (4,000 mi/hr) may be in commercial operation early in the next century. See **Exhibit 52**. Only hydrogen burns fast enough to propel an air-breathing craft from London to Sydney in 67 minutes. This is possible with planes that fly part of their journey in orbital space at speeds usually associated with spacecraft.

This type of hybrid airplane/spacecraft is called a *transatmospheric vehicle*. It takes off from conventional runways to travel beyond the atmoshpere at 24, 000 km/hr (15,000 mi/hr). Once in space, high speeds are possible due to a lack of air resistance. After a brief flight the craft will plunge back into the atmosphere and land on a runway.

One such craft, under development, is the British *Horizontal Takeoff and Landing Launcher* (HOTOL). The plane is air-breathing at low altitudes and acts like a rocket with its own liquid oxygen supply in space. Using the atmospheric oxygen during part of its flight reduces the amount of liquid oxygen needed to be stored on board.

NASA's *Hypersonic Transport* (HST) design may serve a multitude of purposes: a transport, an orbital bomber, or a reconnaissance craft. Boeing, General Dynamics, and Rockwell are the major contractors. The ability of the HST to take off and land reduces operating costs compared to the space shuttle: to one-fifth for low earth orbits and one-half for geosynchronous orbits at 35, 200 km (22, 000 mi).

Aerojet General is developing a special engine, an *air turbo-ramjet*. The engine functions similar to a conventional turbojet, exploiting the unique properties of hydrogen fuel up to a speed of 4, 800 to 6,400 km/hr (3,000 to 4,000 mi/hr). This is the upper limit for turbojets on any fuel. After this, the supersonic ramjet takes over. In orbital space liquid oxygen is used for combustion. The U.S. Defense Department is spending $90 million on this technology in 1986 and plans to spend $90 billion over 10 to 15 years. **880p745-746**

At slower speeds, for more conventional aircraft, liquid methane, as well as liquid hydrogen has been proposed for an aviation fuel. **Exhibit 53** compares the relative placement and size of the fuel tanks on three converted Boeing 747's with the same range. **30p584** This subsonic plane flys at about 1,041 km/hr (650 mi/hr).

The petroleum based fuel widely used for aircraft ("jet A") has a synthetic counterpart: *synjet*. These fuels are generally stored in unused spaces in the wings. Liquefied gasses, on the other hand, must be stored in containers with a low surface to volume ratio - as close to a spherical shape as possible. Cryogenic fuel tanks are shown positioned in the fuselage, one behind and one in front, of the wings, for balance.

The diagram shows that liquid hydrogen takes the most space but since it is lighter it imposes no weight penalty. **Exhibit 54** shows that a liquid hydrogen craft when fully loaded weighs less than a similar craft with liquid methane. For shorter distances of 3,250 km (2,020 mi) liquid hydrogen imposes a 20% weight penalty when the tanks are empty and the plane is unloaded. See **Exhibit 55**. For the shorter range, the volume of the tanks is less than for the longer range, but the weight of the tank is proportionately more than for a larger volume tank on the longer distance craft in **Exhibit 54**. In other words, liquid hydrogen has the greatest advantage at longer distances and higher speeds.

Cryogenic Auto Fuel

Liquid hydrogen offers some of the same advantages and disadvantages for automobile fuel as it does in aviation. This is seen in examining several conversion projects.

Researchers converted a 1973 Chevrolet V8, 5.6 liter (350 in^3) to liquid

52. Hypersonic Aircraft

53. Aircraft With Alternative Fuels

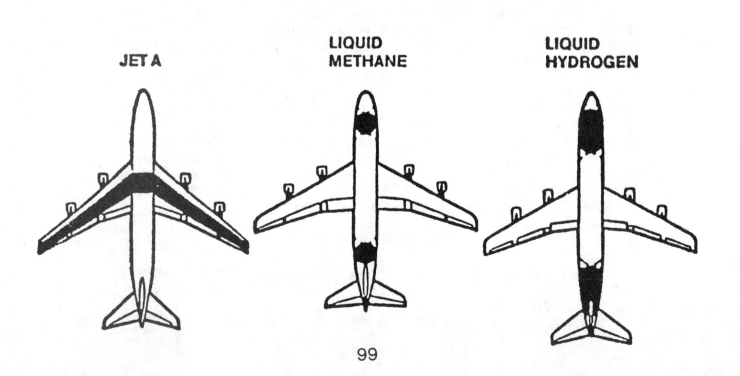

JET A

LIQUID
METHANE

LIQUID
HYDROGEN

54. Alternative Fuels
In Long-Range, High-Payload Aircraft

Range: 10,200 km. (6,340 mi).
Speed: 0.85 Mach.
Payload: 36,000 kg (79,400 lb) or 400 passengers.

Parameter	Jet A or Synjet	Liquid Methane	Liquid Hydrogen
Relative Empty Weight	1.0	1.0	1.0
Relative Gross Weight	1.0	0.9	0.7
Relative Mission Energy	1.0	0.9	0.7

55. Alternative Fuels
In Short-Range, Low-Payload Aircraft

Range: 3,250 km (2,020 mi).
Speed: 0.85 Mach.
Payload: 18,000 kg (39,700 lb) or 200 passengers.

Parameter	Jet A or Synjet	Liquid Methane	Liquid Hydrogen
Relative Empty Weight	1.0	1.1	1.2
Relative Gross Weight	1.0	1.1	1.0
Relative Mission Energy	1.0	1.2	1.2

100

hydrogen. It had a range of 483 km (300 mi) and an energy use equivalent to 11 km/liter (25 mi/gal) of gasoline.

A 1975 Datsun B210 with 1.4 liter (84 in^3) displacement with 2,784 km (1,730 mi) on 231 liters (61 gallons) of liquid hydrogen. Two tanks, each 20.3 cm (8 in) in diameter and 109.2 cm (43 in) long stored 32 kg (70 lb) of liquid hydrogen. 586 kwh (2,000,000 BTU) of energy was effectively stored. The gasoline fuel use equivalent was 12 km/liter (28 mi/gal). The total cost of the stored hydrogen was $263.

In another experiment a postal Jeep was converted to liquid hydrogen. It takes 15 minutes to refill. The researchers used 1.3 cm (0.5 in) bayonet fittings. To refuel, the manual fill vent was opened before opening the fill valve and transferring the liquid gas under high pressure. The fuel lines were vacuum insulated to prevent thermal losses during transfer.

The engine produced only 0.04 grams per mile of nitrous oxide compared with the 1977 federal standard of 0.49 grams per mile.

The six cylinder Jeep postal truck used a Minnesota Valley Engineering ULH-50G spherical tank. Two concentric shells separated by a vacuum space kept the liquid hydrogen at -253°C (-423°F) and prevented water condensation. The diameter of the outer sphere was 86.4 cm (34 in), and the inner sphere was 71.1 cm (28 in). The material was spun aluminum with 1.2 % manganese. The total weight of the tanks was 42.6 kg (94 lb) empty and 56.3 kg (124 lb) when full. The 189 liter (50 gal) of liquid hydrogen had a boil off rate of 3.3% per day.

A heater in the tank, see **Exhibit 56** and **57**, maintains gas pressure for fuel flow when the engine is running. It uses 25 to 30% of the heating value of the fuel to vaporize the gas. Its composition was 22 gauge nichrome wire in a conical-shaped spiral wrapped around four phenolic supports epoxied to the bottom of the fuel withdrawl tube.

An automatic feedback shuts off the heater when the tank is empty to avoid heat damage to the tank. A Motorola 320M7348 diode wired in parallel with the heater is short circuited when the temperature goes over 21°C (70°F). A fuse blows and the heater goes off.

A 0.15 cm (0.06 in) thick stainless steel splash shield separates the passenger compartment from the liquid hydrogen tank which is also vented through the rear roof.

In crash tests, the mail truck did not catch on fire, nor did it spill any fuel. The researchers report that liquid hydrogen fuel is as safe as gasoline. **380**

Billings Energy Corp. converted a 1979 Buick Century to liquid hydrogen for use at the Los Alamos National Laboratory in New Mexico. See **Exhibit 59**. Notice the large liquid hydrogen storage tank in the background.

Fuel consumption is 2.4 km/l (5.6 mi/gal). Energy consumption is 2,557 kWh/km (5.4 million BTU/mi). Acceleration to 80 km/hr (50 mi/hr) took 13 seconds. Range was 354 km (220 mi). The tank is 66 cm (26 in) high and 86 cm (34 in) in diameter and holds 151 liters (40 gal) of liquid hydrogen. Liquid hydrogen costs the experimenters $0.97/l ($3.66/gal). The tank has an insulated space between double shells.

When refueling, a hydrogen detector checks for leaks. Then, air is removed from the fuel lines after the refueling hose is hooked up. The tank is filled, the fuel line is purged of hydrogen, and the hose is disconnected. If the empty tank is at atmospheric temperature, chilling is necessary before fuel is introduced. Under these conditions, the refill operation may take 15 to 30 minutes.

In a later development, a 150 liter (39.6 gal) tank delivered liquid hydrogen to the engine by a single cylinder receiprocating pump. The pump is located *inside* the liquid hydrogen tank. With the piston held stationary, the barrel receiprocates up for the delivery stroke and down for the suction strike. In this arrangement, the piston rod is under tension, not compression. This permits a thinner piston rod with less mass and with less heat inflow. Clearance between the plunger and barrel is minimized to around 1.5 micrometers (0.00006 in). See **Exhibit 60.**

56. Liquid Hydrogen Fuel System

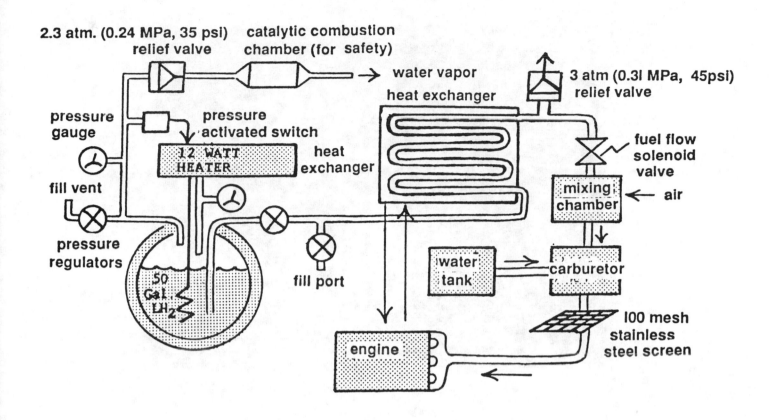

57. Flow Control Wiring Diagram

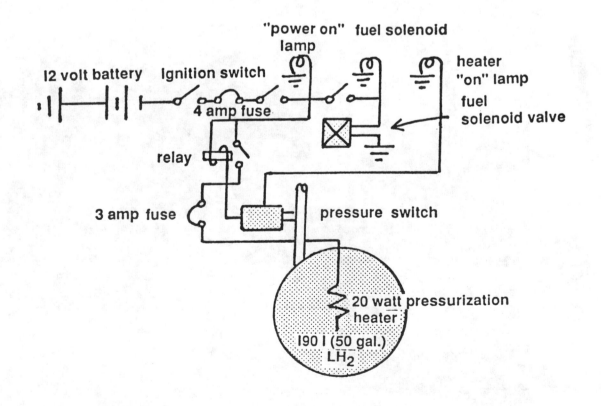

102

58. Liquid Hydrogen-Powered Buick

59. Liquid Hydrogen Storage and Filling Apparatus

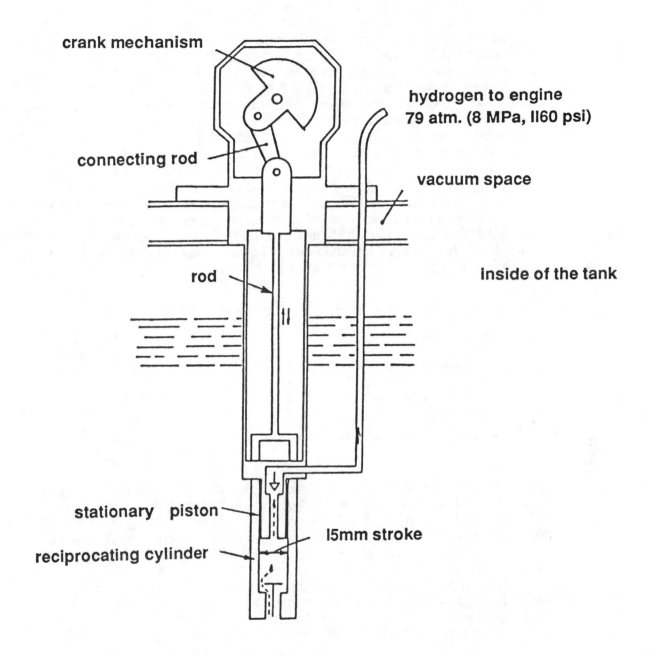

crank mechanism

hydrogen to engine
79 atm. (8 MPa, II60 psi)

connecting rod

vacuum space

rod

inside of the tank

stationary piston

I5mm stroke

reciprocating cylinder

A heat exchanger evaporates the liquid hydrogen in the fuel line. A small tank between the pump and the engine stores the gaseous hydrogen. As can be seen in **Exhibit 61**, a computer-controlled electric motor drives the pump at the right rate to maintain a constant pressure in the gaseous hydrogen tank.

A fuel vaporizer is needed te evaporate the liquid hydrogen fast enough. A fuel consumption of 5.5 km/liter (13 mi/gal) on gasoline is thermodynamically equivalent to 3.2 km/liter (5.2 mi/gal) on liquid hydrogen. If only boil off gas is used to fuel the engine, a speed of only 0.04 m/s (0.1 ft/sec) is possible. Therefore, more heat is needed to evaporate the liquid hydrogen. 650 W of power input are needed to sustain a speed of 44.7 m/s (147 ft/sec.).

Fuel is injected into the liquid hydrogen tank at the rate of 56.8 liters/min. (15 gal/min) through a 1.3 cm (0.5 in) inside diameter fill line and a 5.1 cm (2 in) inside diameter vent line. Refills take 3 min. without *"excessive fill losses "*. 319 The tanks are cleaned annually to remove dirt to and discover leaks.

The experiments measured a 1% boil off per day but no loss of hydrogen through venting of the safety valve. Y. Rotenberg has discovered that the boil off rate of a liquid hydrogen tank being vibrated, as while driving, increases up to 12 times when compared to the resting rate. **790p729-735**

The vehicle using the above system, a small diesel truck, has a range of 230 km (143 mi) on one tank of liquid hydrogen. There was no change in power compared to its former diesel operation. See **Exhibit 62**. **780p427**

Shoichi Furuhama, a longtime experimenter with liquid hydrogen-fueled vehicles, entered the converted diesel truck in the Vehicle Design Competition as part of the Vancouver, British Columbia *Expo 86* . The project was sponsored by the Musashi Institute of Technology of Japan as the culmination of a 16 year development. Vehicle specifications are as follows.

● Manufacturer:	Hino Motor Co.
● Weight:	2,550 kg (5,622 lb).
● Engine:	diesel, 4 cylinder.
● Compression ratio:	17:9.
● Fuel mixing:	injection, turbo.

This was judged to be the optimum combination for *"best engine performance, low noise, vibration and nitrous oxide emissions "*. **780p429**

The fuel is ignited by a hot ceramic surface at 950°C (1,740°F). The temperature is electronically controlled for ignition at all operating temperatures.

The vehicle won second place in the 150 km (94 mi) 3 hour race. Only 30% of the experimental vehicles that started in the race finished.

The German DFVLR (Institute for Energy Conversion) in Stuttgart experimented with a liquid hydrogen tank. Like the Musashi truck, they minimized boil off during operation by removing both liquid and vapor from the tank in response to engine demand. The cylindrical aluminum tank is 40 kg (88 lb) in weight and holds 120 liters (32 gal). The maximum design pressure is 7.9 atm (0.8MPa, 116 psi) but usually operates at about 40 to 45% of this. A boil off of 5.2 liters (1.4 gal) per day implies a heat leak of 2 W for this storage system. See **Exhibit 63**.

During the Ninth World Hydrogen Energy Conference in 1992 at Paris, France BMW reported developing a hybrid gasoline-liquid hydrogen vehicle. With their new tank design practically no hyrogen is lost during filling. The tank can be filled in 15 minutes.

61. *Crossection of Liquid Hydrogen Tank Showing Fuel Pump*

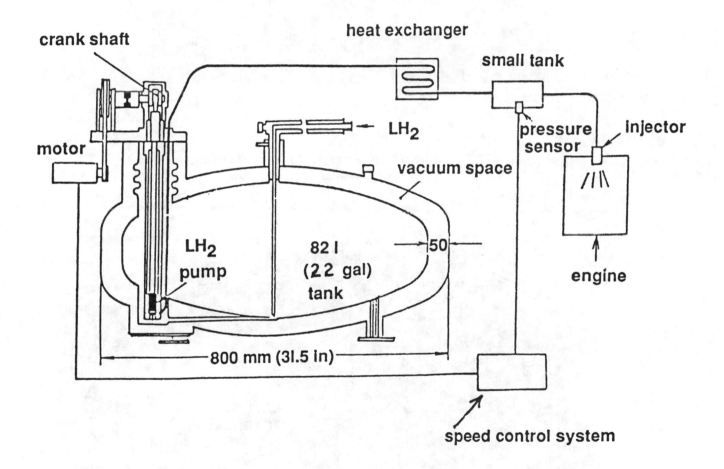

150 l LH₂ tank

**63.   Liquid Hydrogen Tank and Pump
for BMW Experimental Car**

Liquid hydrogen can be used in race cars. With 50 million car race fans in the U.S., putting hydrogen on the track is a good way to publicize hydrogen fuel.Demetri Wagner, manager of the American Hydrogen Association's Racing Program has drag raced an Oldsmobile at 439 km/hr (273 mph) on 2.3 liters of liquid hydrogen at 7500 rpm. See **Exhibit 44**. The Olds is a "Quad-4", 2.3 liter engine with a forged steel crank and pistons. It also has a double overhead cam and 4 valves per cylinder. He races in the "Unlimited Fuel" class. The cars can use any fuel: gasoline, alcohol, nitromethane, hydrogen, etc. The 75 liter tank is refueled from a larger 500 liter tank at the pit stop. Prior to refueling liquid hydrogen is circulated to cool the tank to reduce boiloff. For safety, there is a breakoff valve with instant seal when the fill nozzle is removed.

Exhibit 64 summarizes the major liquid hydrogen vehicle experiments. 710p721 See the title page illustration of a Tennessee State race car.

Recovering Refrigeration Energy

It is possible to use the cryogenic properties of liquid hydrogen to boost the efficiency of the vehicle. The boil off can be used to cool the engine when the ignition is off or to supply hydrogen to a fuel cell to charge batteries.

Air is a mixture of gasses. It is approximately 70% nitrogen and 20% oxygen. Each of the atmoshperic gasses liquefies at different temperatures. Nitrogen liquefies at a higher temperature than oxygen. The boiling point of liquid hydrogen is below most atmoshperic gasses. For example, air coming into contact with uninsulated liquid hydrogen fuel lines will liquefy nitrogen before the oxygen. Oxygen can thus be separated out from the air and used in pure form in engine combustion. Suitable devices that accomplish this have yet to be designed and tested in vehicles.

In stationary applications, evaporating liquid hydrogen can drive a Stirling engine which, in turn, can turn a generator. The engine is too heavy to use on board a vehicle. The Sterling engine was invented over 100 years ago. It runs on *temperature differences*, - not combustion. 580 The engine has high efficiency but a low power to weight ratio, but is relatively quiet and vibration free.

A new alloy was developed by the Lewis Research Center in Cleveland, Ohio. It is low in chromium and cobalt, low cost, resists oxydation and corrosion, does not become excessively brittle at cryogenic temperatures or promote hydrogen permeation, and is capable of being welded and fabricated.

Railroads

In a 1976 U.S. Department of Transporation study, liquid hydrogen was found to be preferable to hydride storage in railroad locomotives. Iron-titanium hydride would increase the weight of locomotives 12 times and cost by 10 times. Both cases assumed high pressure injection at 238 atm (24.1 MPa, 3,500 psi).

Diesel locomotives have from 8 to 20 cylinders, are naturally aspirated and turbocharged, with 750 to 2240 kW (1,000 to 3,000 hp) power output.

With liquid hydrogen, a separate car would be towed behind the engine. The 106,000 liter (28,000 gal) storage car would weigh 35,800 kg (79,000 lb).

Liquid hydrogen would increase power output by 15 to 20% while decreasing thermal efficiency 1 to 2%. However, there would be a 5% increase in efficiency with exhaust heat recovery. Turbocharging would boost power by another 32 to 44%. Longer life and lower hydrocarbon emissions can also be expected.Liquid hydrogen is more expensive, at present, than diesel fuel but future increases in imported fuel prices can make hydrogen competitive. *"With regard to technological and operating feasibility, the DOE study concluded that locomotive diesels can be converted successfully to hydrogen"*. 201p60

Date	Producer	Model
1971	Perris Smogless Automobile Assn.	Ford F250 Truck
1973	Billings Energy Corp.	Ford Monte Carlo
1973-74	Los Alamos National Laboratory	1.5 Ton Pick-Up Truck
1973-74	University of California at Los Angeles	AMC Jeep
1975	Musashi Institute of Technology	Datsun E210 Musashi III
1978-79	DFVLR and University of Stuttgart	BMW 520
1979	Los Alamos and DFVLR	Buick Century
1980	Musashi Instutute	Musashi IV
1981	DFVLR	BMW 520
1982	Musashi Institute	Musashi V
1984	BMW and DFVLR	BMW 735i
1984	Musashi Institute	Musashi VI
1986	Musahsi Institute	Musashi VII

HYDRIDE ENERGY STORAGE

Using Heat to Store Hydrogen

P. Solvani describes a hydride energy storage system as *"...the only system where energy and environment are not adversaries "*. **830p169** Hydrides use special metals that absorb hydrogen when cooled and release the gas when heated. The hydrogen atoms dissolve into the metal and "hide" until released by heat.

The hydrogen content of a *volume* of fully charged hydride exceeds an equal volume of liquid hydrogen. However, the energy content for an equal weight of hydride is less than for an equal weight for liquid hydrogen. Liquid hydrogen contains from 10 to 100 times as much hydrogen as hydride, on a *weight basis* . **770p22** Nevertheless, the power requirement of refrigerating and the problems of storing liquid hydrogen make hydride preferable in some cases.

When being charged with hydrogen, the hydride material is cooled. Absorption proceeds up to a certain equilibrium pressure called the *dissociation pressure* . The exact value of the dissociation pressure depends upon the hydride material used and the temperature. When this pressure is reached, the pressure of hydrogen being forced into the hydride must be increased in order to get the hydride to absorb more hydrogen.

Exhibit 65 shows the amount of hydrogen that can be absorbed at different pressures. Several curves are shown. **460** Each curve shows hydrogen absorption taking place at a constant temperature. The top curve shows results for the highest temperature. The bottom curve assumes the lowest constant temperature. The higher the temperature, the higher the pressure needed force hydride to accept the hydrogen.

For each curve, increasing pressure is needed to get the hydride to absorb more hydrogen. The broad flat *plateau area* of each curve means that at a certain pressure (the dissociation pressure) hydrogen can be absorbed without increased pressure. When the hydride becomes saturated, more pressure must again be applied to absorb more hydrogen.

When discharged, heat is applied to the hydride and hydrogen is driven out of the metal. Unless the hydrogen gas in the hydride container is removed, pressure will build up and the discharge will stop. The gas must be continually removed to relieve pressure so that the process can continue.

Sievert's Law gives the approximate concentration of hydrogen in hydride.

$$H_2 \text{ concentration} = kP^{1/2}.$$

Where:

k = equilibrium constant of the hydride material.
P = equilibrium pressure (as shown on the curve).

The efficient use of heat is crucial to getting maximum storage volume for the charge and discharge process. The amount of heat added to the hydride must be able to fully discharge the hydride without increasing the hydride temperature and losing heat to the environment. The amount of heat (not the temperature)withdrawn when charging and the amount of heat added when discharging must be as close to equal as possible to minimize energy losses.Thermal storage absorbs the amount of heat needed force all the hydrogen into the all the hydride without waste of either. The thermal capacities of selected materials are given in **Exhibit 66**.

65. Composition-Pressure Isotherms

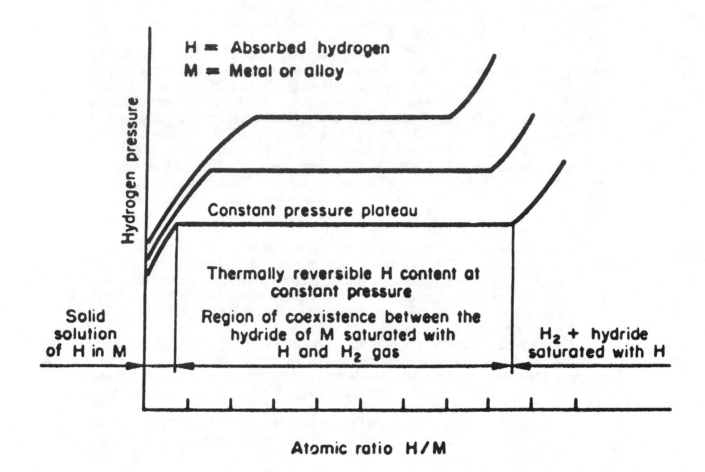

66. Thermal Capacities of Selected Materials

Material	Density (kg/m^3) (lb/ft^3)		Energy per Unit Weight (Wh/kg) (BTU/lb)		Energy per Unit Volume (Wh/m^3) (BTU/ft^3)	
Aluminum	2,707	169	0.139	0.215	372.3	36
Water	1,000	62.4	0.646	1.00	641.3	62
Concrete	1,906	119	0.136	0.21	289.6	28

111

Heat Exchange Fluid

The temperature of water from the local water company is sufficient to cool iron-titanium hydride during charging. The heat absorbed by the water can be stored in the thermal materials mentioned above. If this water is kept out of contact with the hydride it may also be used in a domestic hot water system.

Assuming the use of an aluminum hydride container and iron-titanium hydride, the amount of water needed for heating and cooling a given mass of hydride can be calculated as follows. **201**

$$M_{H2O}/M_{mH} = (M_H/M_{mH} \times hsg/dT) - C_{mH} - (M_{al}/M_{mH}) \times (C_{al}/C_{H2O}).$$

Where:

M_{H2O} = mass of cooling water.

M_{mH} = mass of hydride.

M_H = maximum weight of hydrogen that can be stored.

$M_H/M_{mH} = 0.016$

C_{mH} = heat capacity of metal hydride = 0.026 Wh/kg°C (0.04 BTU/lb°F).

M_{al} = mass of aluminum container = 27% weight of hydride (typically).

C_{al} = heat capacity of aluminum container = 0.139 Wh/kg (0.215 BTU/lb).

C_{H2O} = heat capacity of water coolant = 0.646 Wh/kg (1.0 BTU/lb).

hsg/dT = 6,500°C/ temperature change.

Typically, iron-titanium dT = 88.0 - 4.4°C (190 - 40°F) = 83°C (166°F). Solving for the typical values given above we get 48.3%. Therefore, in this case, the cooling and heating water makes up about 50% of the weight of the iron-titanium in an aluminum container.

Types of Hydride

A wide variety of metals can be used to absorb hydrogen according to the general reaction:

$$M + xH_2 -----> MH_{2x} + heat.$$

The metal (M) releases (desorbs) hydrogen in a similar manner. **940p990-129**

$$MH_{2x} + heat -----> M + xH_2.$$

The curves in **Exhibit 65** apply to most hydride materials. Any particluar hydride curve will have its own unique characteristics, but the general shape, including the plateau, is the same for all.

Absorption/desorption curves for specific hydrides are shown in **Exhibit 67**. **190p214** The plateaus for some hydrides are steeper than for others. The steeper the platcau, the less *stable* the hydride is. All the curves are held constant for 25°C (77°F). Hydrogen is realeased from iron-titanium (FeTi) at pressures above 1 atm (0.1 MPa, 14.7 psi) and temperatures above -20°C (-4°F) when fully charged. A different curve is shown for FeTi at each of four different temperatures in **Exhibit 68**. The temperature of auto exhaust is sufficient to guarantee a supply of hydrogen fuel from a FeTi hydride-powered car. For comparison, **Exhibit 69** shows curves for a different hydride - lanthanum nickle. Most of the hydrides in **Exhibit 67** also contain nickle.

At atmospheric pressure, magnesium hydride holds more hydrogen per unit weight than FeTi but must be heated to higher temperatures, 204°C (400°F), as opposed to 20°C (68°F), to release its stored hydrogen. In both LaNi and FeTi

57, 68 & 69. Pressure-Hydrogen Content Isotherms

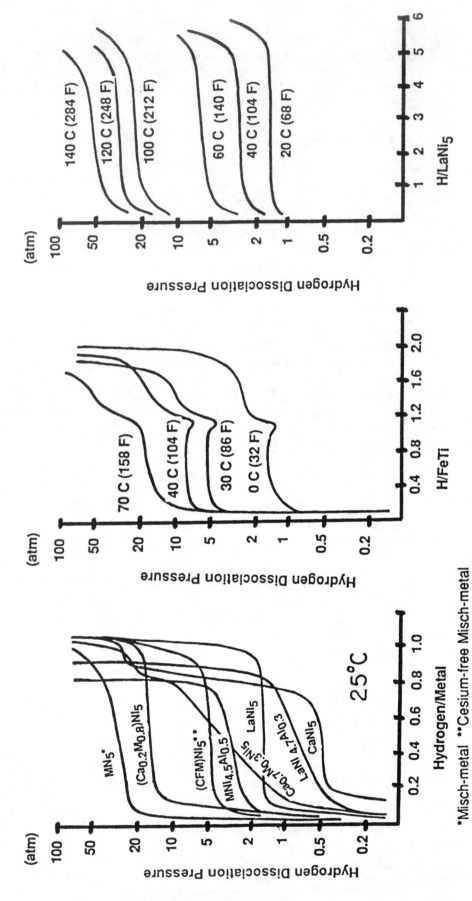

*Misch-metal **Cesium-free Misch-metal

Source: R.L.Cohen, "Intermetallics for Hydrogen Storage", *Science*. Dec. 1981, p.1082.

113

hydrides the equivalent of 10 % of the energy of the stored hydrogen is needed to absorb and release hydrogen from the metals, or 8.3 Wh/mole of hydrogen stored.

FeTi weighs two times magnesium hydride and holds only one-fourth as much hydrogen on a weight basis.

Each hydride has a different combination of properties as shown in **Exhibit 70**. However, for automotive applications only certain properties are needed. 870p325

- *Rapid* absorption and desorption of hydrogen.
- *Reversibility* of the hydriding/dehydriding reaction.
- *Sensitivity* to changes in pressure and temperature.
- *Rejection* of all gasses except hydrogen.
- *Holding a high percentage* by weight of hydrogen fuel.
- *Durability*: hydride must hold up under 300,000 or more cycles.

In some hydride alloys expensive metals may be replaced with cheaper ones to give similar performance. Lanthanum is sometimes replaced with *mischmetal* : a mixture of rare earth metals as found in nature . It is possible to substitute aluminum for nickle in MnNi hydride. This reduces the hydrogen capacity but increases thermal stability. 460

Exhibit 71 shows the "bottom line" comparison between FeTi, magnesium nickle (MgNi), and pure magnesium (Mg) hydrides. For the same volume of hydrogen stored, a vehicle using Mg can go twice as far as either MgNi or FeTi. FeTi has twice the weight of either MgNi or Mg. When the weight of the hydride material is held constant magnesium holds four times, and MgNi holds twice, the amount of hydrogen as FeTi. For a constant distance traveled, a vehicle using FeTi has a substantial weight penalty.

Magnesium has the highest storage capacity: 6 to 7% by weight. One-fifth m^3 (7.1 ft^3) of magnesium is equivalent to 216 liters (57 gal) of gasoline. 201 221 kg (488 lb) of magnesium hydride store 16.8 kg (37.0 lb) of hydrogen or the energy equivalent of 45 kg (100 lb) of gasoline.

Magnesium hydride loosely packe in a container has empty spaces between grains of hydride. These void spaces typically take up 40 percent of the total volume. The void space is not wasted, however. This space allows for gas to enter and leave the hydride. The above amount of magnesium hydride takes up 253 liters (8.9 ft^3). This is equivalent to 237 liters (8.37 ft^3) of liquid hydrogen. 580p207

Magnesium is also the cheapest hydride material at less than $5.00/kg ($2.27/lb).

Disadvantages include a high working temperature, over 280°C (536°F) at 1 atm (0.1 MPa, 14.7 psi) and a large amounts of energy needed for dissociation: 10,331 Wh/kg (16,000 BTU/lb) of hydrogen. Engine heat is not enough to flush out this much hydrogen at a fast enough rate. The energy to dissociate magnesium hydride requires 15% more than the hydrogen energy supplied. 201

Magnesium and magnesium nickle hydrides have a tendency to fracture with repeated charge/discharge cycles. The pea-sized hydride particles are reduced to a fine powder that packs down and impedes gas flow. This reduces the storage capacity.

Contaminants are also a problem with magnesium hydride. The dehydrided metal, when contaminated with oxygen, forms oxides such as magnesium oxide and magnesium hydroxide. These compounds form a film around the metal particles and reduce hydrogen absorption. 830

With half the weight of FeTi, Magnesium nickle hydride has the same advantages as pure magnesium: 870p325 high hydrogen content (over 7% by weight) and low storage costs $5.00/kg ($2.27/lb) and low mass density. 650p1821

70. Properties of Metal Hydrides

Name	Symbol	% Weight Hydrogen	Heat of Formation (Wh/mol)(BTU/mol)	
Lithium Hydride	LiH	12.7	-25.3	-86.4
Aluminum Hydride	AlH	----	-3.14	-10.7
Calcium Hydride	CaH_2	5.1	-48.5	-165.6
Magnesium Hydride	MgH_2	6.6	-21.00	-71.7
Sodium Hydride	NaH	5.1	-15.8	-53.9
Titanium Hydride	TiH	9.1	-34.9	-119.2
Zirconium Hydride	ZrH_2	7.3	-46.2	-157.7
Lanthanum Hydride	LaH_2	6.8	-57.9	-197.7
Iron-Titanium Hydride	$FeTiH_{1.95}$	1.95	-8.7	-29.7
Uranium Hydride	UH_3	8.4	-35.9	-122.6

71. Comparison of Hydrides

Volume Held Constant									
Hydride	**Volume**		**Weight**		**H_2**		**Range**		
	(cm3)	(in3)	(kg)	(lb)	(kg)	(lb)	(km)	(mi)	
Iron Titanium	39 329	2 400	76.5	169	1.5	3.3	306	190	
Magnesium Ni.	39 329	2 400	38.4	85	1.5	3.3	306	190	
Magnesium	39 329	2 400	38.4	85	3.0	6.6	612	380	
Weight Held Constant									
Iron Titanium	39 329	2 400	76.5	169	1.5	3.3	306	190	
Magnesium Ni.	78 658	4 800	76.5	169	3.0	6.6	612	380	
Magnesium	78 658	4 800	76.5	169	6.1	13.5	1223	760	
Range of Operation Held Constant									
Iron Titanium	39 329	2 400	76.5	169	1.5	3.3	306	190	
Magnesium Ni.	39 329	2 400	38.4	85	1.5	3.3	306	190	
Magnesium	19 665	1 200	19.2	42	1.5	3.3	306	190	

Working temperatures are similar to pure magnesium, but magnesium nickle requires less energy for storing and releasing hydrogen: 8,846 Wh/kg (13,700 BTU/lb).

FeTi has the lowest hydrogen capacity of the three hydrides mentioned here (1 to 1.9% by weight). 134 kg (295 lb) of FeTi is equivalent to 75.7 liters (20 gal) of gasoline. Because hydrogen burns more completely than gasoline, it could increase engine efficiency over the 23% typical with fossil fuels. Only 103 kg (227 lb) of hydride would be needed.

The density of FeTi exceeds that of the other two hydrides. Energy densities are high compared to lead acid or nickle cadmium batteries: 143 Wh/kg (222 BTU/lb). **580**

The main advantage of FeTi is in its low heat of dissociation 25°C (77°F) at 5 atm (0.5 MPa, 73.5 psi) The energy involved in storing hydrogen is 4,681 W/kg (7,250 BTU/lb) at 1 to 10 atm. (0.1 to 1.0 MPa, 14.7 to 147 psi). **201**

FeTi also does't decompose as readily with repeated hydriding cycles as do the other two hydrides.

For the above reasons, FeTi is the most commonly used hydride in automotive applications. The metal is ground into pea-sized particles as seen in **Exhibit 72**. The coal-like texture of each particle is seen in the closeup view in **Exhibit 73**.

Hydride Packing

The process of hydriding and dehydriding expands and contracts the hydride material. This tends to split the granules into finer and finer particles with each charge/discharge cycle. This is a problem with magnesium, magnesium nickle, and lanthanum nickle hydrides. After several thousand cycles, the particles may assume the consistency of flour. A filter may have to be installed to keep this powder out of the fuel flow system. As the particles and void spaces get smaller, the hydride may tend to pack down in the container so that the expansion and contraction of the material puts greater stress on the container - perhaps bursting it.

Even if the container remains intact, increasingly less of the hydride's surface area is exposed to the incoming hydrogen during charging. Storage capacity is thereby diminished. Solutions include:

- Increasing the absorption and desorption times to allow the particles to adjust more gradually to the thermally induced stresses.
- Using hydride material ground into a powder form and squeezed into pellets. An inert metal is used as a "glue" and serves as a thermal ballast to reduce the rate of thermal change in the hydride.
- Suspending hydride powder in a liquid and bubbling hydrogen through it. This improves the access of hydrogen to the particles and eliminates packing stresses on the vessel. However, the added mass of the liquid reduces the system's overall energy content per unit weight. Experimenters used 2,2,4 trimethylpentone (isooctane) as the liquid and lanthanum nickle aluminum as the hydride. **650p1821**
- Using FeTi essentially eliminates these problems.

Contamination

Hydrides are also susceptible to contamination by reactive chemicals such as carbon dioxide and oxygen. 300 parts per million (300 ppm) of carbon dioxide reduce the capacity of hydride 50% over five cycles. Oxygen, similarly, impairs the storage efficiency of hydride materials. Hydrogen must avoid contact with the air to operate most efficiently. The air in the tank and fuel lines should be vented prior to charging to prevent contamination of the hydride and to avoid explosions. Nitrogen could be used to purge the tank of gaseous contaminants.

116

72 & 73. Iron-Titanium Hydride

117

Heat Exchange Systems with Magnesium Hydride

For 100 g (0.2 lb) of hydride, or less, no heat exchanger may be needed. This is particularly true if the tank is aluminum or any other metal with an equal or better rate of heat transfer. Magnesium hydride fuel systems adapted for use in an automobile need heat to start discharging. Heat from the engine exhaust or coolant is used for this purpose. Lanthanum nickle starter hydride can be used to start the engine and get it warmed up to the point where it has enough heat ot release hydrogen from the magnesium hydride. Lanthanum nickle requires over 30ºC (86ºF) to discharge. Magnesium hydride requires more heat than lanthanum nickle to discharge hydrogen. The system also has a booster heater powered by hydrogen from the lanthanum nickle tank to add even more heat. This dual hydride system is used where the hydride tank is very large in relation to the size of the motor.

An auxillary heater is needed to start discharging lanthanum nickle. A separate high pressure small gaseous hydrogen tank could accomplish this.

A thermostatically controlled blower could circulate part of the hydrogen through an exhaust or engine coolant heat exchanger. The heated hydrogen is used to liberate more hydrogen from the tank. The engine must be already running and warmed up for this to work.

Heat Exchange Systems with Iron-Titanium Hydride

FeTi, with a relatively low dissociation temperature compared to magnesium or magnesium nickle, needs some auxillary source of heat other than from the engine. The required heat may come from the *engine exhaust or from the coolant*.

Engine exhaust can pass through metal tubes running through the hydride tank. An intermediate heat exchanger may also be used. An intermediate heat exchanger, like the one employed in the system shown in **Exhibit 74** absorbs heat from the exhaust and pases it on to a circulating fluid that runs through tubes in the hydride tank or circulates in a jacket around the hydride tank. The fluid used can be a water and antifreeze mixture. This liquid can transfer heat to the hydride more efficiently than can the exhaust.

The exhibit shows that the exhaust system has a valve that can be set to divert all of the exhaust to the heat exhanger. The valve may also allow only half of the exhaust to bypass the heat exchanger and be vented directly outside. To start the hydride tank discharging hydrogen, all the exhause heat is needed. When a sufficient rate of dehydriding is reached, half of the exhaust is diverted to avoid boiling the circulating fluid. During brief periods when the hydride may be overheated, all the exhaust passes by the heat exchanger. There are, however, two main drawbacks to this system.

- Reduced dependability of parts immersed in the highly corrosive exhaust stream.
- The heat exchanger impedes the flow of the exhaust thereby creating backpressures against which the engine must work, and thereby, reducing engine power.

Under most conditions only 13% of the engine coolant heat energy is needed to discharge hydrogen from FeTi hydride. 35% of the heating value of the engine fuel (whether gasoline or hydrogen) ends up in the engine coolant. **201 Exhibit 75** shows a system than exploits this property. The engine block serves as the heat exchanger between exhaust and liquid coolant. The coolant that goes to the hydride tank can be diverted from the radiator. The hydride tank serves as a kind of second radiator. Varying amounts of the coolant can be diverted depending upon the heating needs of the hydride.

A combined approach would allow both the exhaust and engine coolant to be used to heat the hydride.

118

74. Hydride Heating Using Engine Exhaust

1975 Pontiac

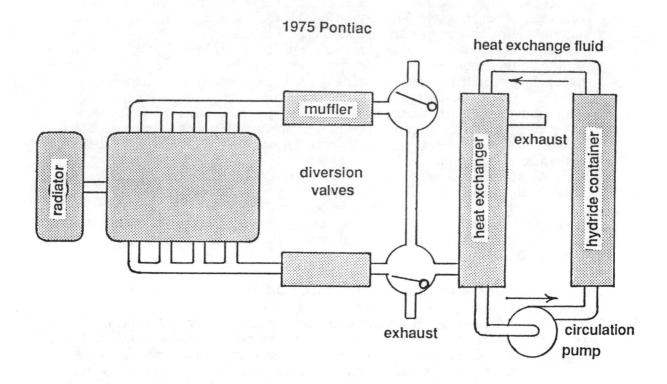

75. Hydride Heating Using Engine Coolant

1977 Cadillac

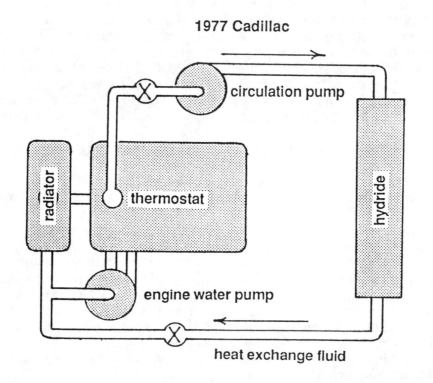

A Hydride Tank Design

Exhibit 76 shows an effective home-made hydride tank design. It is essentially a bundle of hydride-containing tubes surrounded by an aluminum sheet. Fewer welds are needed than with one large tank. A variety of bundle configurations are possible. One manifold attaches to the ends to deliver the heat exchange fluid and another manifold directs the released hydrogen to the point of use.

The circulating heated fluid may flow around and between the tubes inside the sheet metal covering. As an alternative, coolant can be directed through small tubes inside of the larger hydride tubes. **570**

Researchers tested a small hydride tank made from two stainless steel tubes: 5 cm (2 in) diameter and 39 cm (15.4 in) long. The container held 3 kg (6.6 lb) of FeTi hydride. Canon Muskegon Corp., of Muskegon, Michigan supplied the hydride. The experimenters placed a metal screen particle filter in the outlet manifold. The device delivered hydrogen at 4 liter/min. (244 in^3/min.) at 20°C (68°F) at atmospheric pressure.

76.   Tube Bundle Hydride Tank

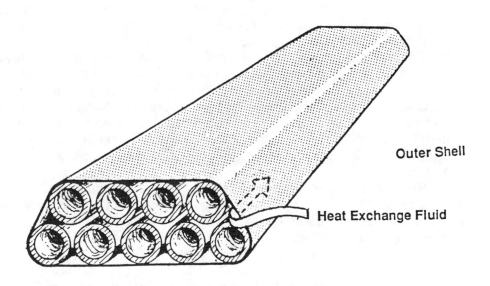

Outer Shell

Heat Exchange Fluid

Hydride Tubes

1975 Pontiac

Billings Energy Corporation converted a 1975 Pontiac to hydrogen hydride operation. It uses 198 kg (437 lb) of hydride in a tank weighing 136 kg (300 lb). The dimensions of the tank are: 25.4 cm (10 in) in diameter by 119.4 cm (47 in) long. This car has a range of about 241 km (150 mi) consuming 2.4 kg (5.25 lb) of hydrogen.

The hydride vessel assumes 40% of full charge in the first minute at 17°C (63°F). 80% charge is attained within 15 minutes and 100% in 60 minutes. A water-jacketed aluminum tank holds the FeTi hydride. Pressure is regulated by an Impco model PEV-2 regulator connected to an Impco model CA50 gas mixer. The hydrogen supply to the engine is turned on and off by way of a solenoid valve.

The ignition system was modified by decreasing the spark plug gap and eliminating the centrifugal spark advance. The standard compression ratio for the air-cooled Kohler engine was left unchanged.

Nitrous oxide emissions are lowered by using water injection to cool the combustion temperature. This is accomplished by two spray nozzels mounted above the intake valves. The induction pump and solenoid valve are controlled manually. The engine is air-cooled.

The conversion to hydrogen in this vehicle was accomplished without any sacrifice in power and performance. The researchers were able to cold start the vehicle many times even when the hydride was nearly discharged.

1977 Cadillac Seville

This vehicle, along with the garden tractor mentioned later, was converted to hydrogen as part of the Billings Hydrogen Homestead. A car of this size usually gets poor mileage. The weight of the hydride tank imposes even more severe penalties. To partly overcome these limitations, the car was modified to use *two fuels* : *hydrogen and gasoline.* hydrogen is used for short commuter trips. These trips made the largest proportion of the vehicle's use. Gasoline is used for longer trips on the highway. It is possible to switch from one fuel to another while the car is in motion. A home-based electrolyser charges the hydride overnight. The fuel system is shown in **Exhibit 77.**

This car was driven in President Carter's inaugural parade in January 1977. It was also displayed at various energy fairs and symposia nationwide.

The engine displacement is 5.7 liters (350 in^3). The car's standard electronic ignition and fuel-injection systems are very compatible with hydrogen conversion. Propane regulators and a propane mixer accomodate the hydrogen fuel. The existing carburetion system was left intact for use with gasoline. Engine coolant is circulated through the hydride tank to release hydrogen at low pressure.

Researcher J.J. Reilly suggests that *"since this vehicle will use primarily hydrogen as a fuel (using gasoline only when necessary, ie in nonurban areas) pollution abatement equipment could be largely discarded and an increase in fuel economy realized ".* 760

Dodge Omni

Billings also converted a Dodge Omni to dual hydrogen and gasoline fuel. The standard engine has 4 cylinders, in line, with an overhead cam. The compression ratio is 8.2 : 1. The 1.7 liter (104 in^3) block is cast iron, with an aluminum head and forged steel crankshaft. The aluminum head provides better heat transfer and less weight. The intake manifold and water pump are also aluminum.

A microprocessor controls the ignition system and timing with three

77. Water Heated and Cooled Hydride

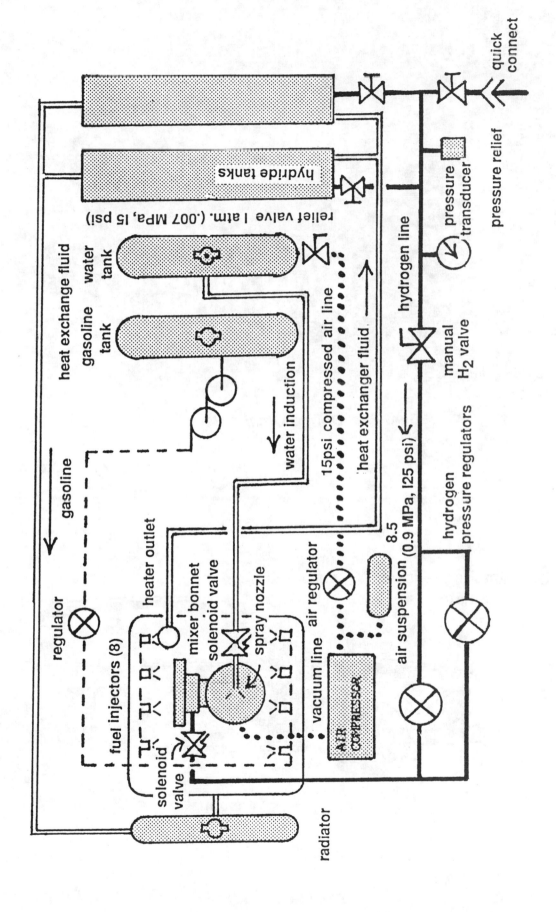

78. *Dual Fuel Dodge Omni*

79. *Crossection of Dodge Omni*

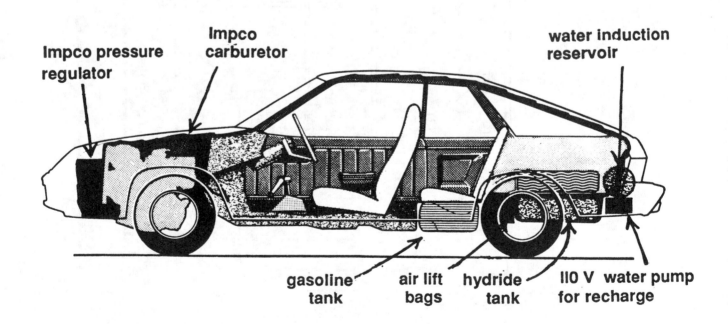

Impco pressure regulator

Impco carburetor

water induction reservoir

gasoline tank

air lift bags

hydride tank

110 V water pump for recharge

Photo courtesy of Billings Energy Corp.

integrated circuits. A Hall-effect speed and angular relationship pickup electric ignition coil replaces the standard induction coil for optimum performance with both hydrogen and gasoline.

Radiator coolant is circulated to the hydride tank to release hydrogen. If excess heat is applied, a thermostatically controlled fan turns on to cool down the hydride. This onboard fan is used along with an electric pump when the hydride is being recharged. At this time outside electricity is needed to run the fan.

The position of the hydride tank and other components of the system can be seen in the cross section of the vehicle in **Exhibit 79**.

The hydride tank is approximately the same size of the spare tire and fits inside the spare tire pocket in the trunk. The hydride tank is unique in that it has an *internal heat exchanger* . This design replaces earlier models that had surrounding water jackets. The new design provides better heat exchange and takes up less space. The exchanger is made of copper tubing coiled up inside the hydride tank. See **Exhibit 80**. The tank adds 180 kg (400 lb) to the rear of the vehicle but holds only 2.5 kg (5.5 lb) of hydrogen. The range when operating on hydrogen alone is 169 km (105 mi). To compensate for the increased weight in the rear, lift air bags were installed.

A Billings BE-5A electrolyser produces 2.3 kg (5 lb) of hydrogen per day. It takes 35 kWh at 220 V.A.C. to evolve 0.5 kg (1 lb) of hydrogen. The device operates at 65% efficiency to make 10,874 to 26,054 liters (383 to 920 ft^3) of hydrogen per day.

The fuel economy with gasoline is 13 km/liter (30 mi/gal) and 19 km/liter(44 mi/gal) with hydrogen. Top speed is 129 km/hr (80 mi/hr).

Hydride on the Racetrack

In May 1984 Kenji Watanabe demonstrated a hydride powered 1973 Mazda RX-4 on the Fuji race course in Gutemba, Japan. He averaged 130 km/hr (80 mi/hr). The top speed was 210 km/hr (130 mi/hr) over a range of 200 km (124 mi).

The exhaust temperature of the 1.2 liter (73 in^3) rotary engine was half that for a comparable engine running on gasoline. At 128 km/hr (80 mi/hr) the temperature was 565°C (1050°F). At 59 km/hr (37 mi/hr) it was 460°C (860°F). This is expected to double the engine life. The car has large diameter exhaust pipes, 3.81 cm (1.5 in) to increase the cooling effect. Nitrous oxides were measured at 15 ppm at 6,500 rpm. The Japanese standard is 240 ppm. There were no detectable levels of carbon monoxide or hydrocarbons.

Mitsui and Co. designed and built the $20,000 stainless steel hydride tank. Japan Metals and Chemical Co. supplied the FeTi hydride. In production, using aluminum, the tank cost could be reduced to $8,000.

The 480 kg (1,060 lb) of hydride holds 70 m^3 (2,472 ft^3) of hydrogen. The energy content of one m^3 (35 ft^3) of hydrogen is equivalent to 0.5 liters (1/8 gal) of gasoline. It takes from 10 to 15 minutes to refill the tank. Water injection is used to increase engine power. Inside the cylinder, at 374°C (705°F) water expands 1,700 times applying a force of 225 kg/cm^2 (3,200 lb/in^2). Fuel combustion contributes 175 kg/cm^2 (2,500 lb/in^2) to give a total force of 400 kg/cm^2 (5,700 lb/in^2).

According to a passenger, "*on balance, the ride was very smooth. Pickup was very good* ". **970p52**

Watanabe has experimented with hydrogen power for 25 years without government help. He has been the president and owner of Hydrogen Energy Laboratory Project (H.E.L.P.) since 1982. He estimates that future conversion costs for similar cars will be $ 1,000 per car on a mass production basis.

Hydrogen Tractors

As part of the Billings *Hydrogen Homestead* , a Jacobsen lawn and garden tractor was converted to operate solely on hydrogen. If a source of hydrogen is nearby, this vehicle can prove that hydrogen is practical for work vehicles.

The vehicle specifications are shown in **Exhibit 81**. A schematic diagram of the hydrogen system is given in **Exhibit 83**. A 29.8 kW (40 hp) gasoline-powered Massey Ferguson Model 65 tractor was converted to hydride and tested at Rockhaven Farm, near Clarksburg, Ontario, Canada. A propane carburetor and gas mixer (Impco CA50) was slightly modified for hydrogen fuel for the 2.9 liter (177 in^3) engine.

Dynamometer tests showed a 30% loss in power compared to gasoline. Exhaust gas recirculation and a Holly low compression water injector system prevented even more power loss.

The extra weight of the hydride tank is not seen as a liability because farm tractors often use ballast to improve traction and prevent upsets. Tractors are generally used close to home; this simplifies the problem of finding a recharging station. A 20 kW electrolyser with a potassium hydroxide electrolyte supplies hydrogen at 6.8 atm (0.70 MPa, 100 psi).

The hydride selected is a misch-metal alloy ($MNi_{4.5}Al_{0.5}$) with hydriding characteristics similar to FeTi. See **Exhibit 67**. The Hystor 208 hydride was supplied by Ergenics, Corp. of New Jersey. The minimum absorption pressure is less than the electrolyser output pressure. This makes the tractor easy to start in cold weather.

The hydride is also relatively resistant to atmosphperic impurities such as water, carbon monoxide and oxygen. In the event of contamination, reactivation of the hydride is easily accomplished by using a mechanical vacuum pump for 24 hours to "suck" the impurities out of the hydride.

A tubular structure stores the hydride with input and output manifold on either end of the tube bundle. See **Exhibit 82**. The 11 stainless steel tubes are each 6.35 cm (2.5 in) in diameter and 83.8 cm (33 in) in length giving a total hydride capacity of 80 kg (176 lb) , enough for four hours of operation. The overall gross weight is 154 kg (340 lb). The tank stores up to 1 kg (2.2 lb) of hydrogen to supply 14.2 kW/hr (19 hp/hr) of hydrogen during operation.

The tractor could also be run on gasoline from the standard fuel system. Either fuel is selected by a switch. The ignition timing has to be manually adjusted for peak performance on either fuel.

Located under the front cowling on top of the engine, the hydride container is heated by engine exhaust through a single pass heat exchanger. A thermocouple is installed in the manifold to measure the hydride temperature. During charging, the hydride temperature increases less than 50°C (122°F), as shown in **Exhibit 84**. An initial discharge at 15°C (59°F) is sufficient to supply hydrogen for ignition. The temperature while driving is 25°C (77°F) with a hydrogen pressure of 4.1 atm (0.413 MPa, 60 psi). *"Measurement of the bed conditions during charging and for a typical running cycle indicate the system as designed can meet farm tractor requirements "*. **260p39**

Hydride fragmentation during repeated cycles makes a filter necessary to catch particles 1 micrometer (0.00003 in) in size. The filter is installed outside the bed. Particle accumulations of 3 g/m^3 (1.9 X 10^{-4} lb/ft^3) were reported during the test.

The researchers conclude: *"regular operation of a tractor by non-technical personnel makes the choice of an easily regenerable hydride alloy a necessity. As well, simplicity of operation and operator safety are paramount requirements and these reqirements can be met."* **260p42**

80. *Hydride Tank with Internal Heat Exchanger*

Heat exchanger in hydride tank for a converted Dodge Omni. Coiled copper tubing replaces earlier water-jacketed tank design. New design transfers heat more efficiently, weighs less and is more compact. Photo courtesy of Billings Energy Corp.

81. *Hydrogen Tractor Specifications*

Vehicle Specifications	**Hydride Vessel**
Manufacturer: Jacobsen Drive Train: 2 speed rear axel	Manufacturer: Luxfer U.S.A. Construction: Aluminum Outer Diameter: 20.3 cm (8 in) Tank Length: 83.8 cm (33 in) Mass of Hydride: 47 kg (104 lb) Mass of Tank + Hydride: 64.8 kg (143 lb) Mass of Usable Hydrogen Stored: 0.77 kg (1.7 lb)
Engine Specifications	
Manufacturer: Kohler Power: 14.9 kW (20 hp) Bore: 8.6 cm (3.38 in) Stroke: 7.6 cm (3 in) Displacement: 0.9 l (54.9 in^3) Cooling system: air cooled Mass of engine: 84.2 kg (186 lb) Cycles: 4 cycle engine Cylinder head: L-head Cylinder configuration: 2 opposed Construction: cast iron with Aluminum heads	**Hydrogen Engine Hardware**
	Hydrogen regulator: Impco Hydrogen mixer: Impco
	Performance
Hydride Storage System	Range of Vehicle: 75 minutes Recharge Temperature: 15.6C (60F) Recharge Pressure Range: 25.2 - 40.8 atm 2.56 - 4.12 MPa 370 - 600 psi
Metal Hydride Material: iron-titanium Metal Hydride Capacity:1.6 % by weight	

Notice the manifold connecting the outputs of the hydride tanks in series.

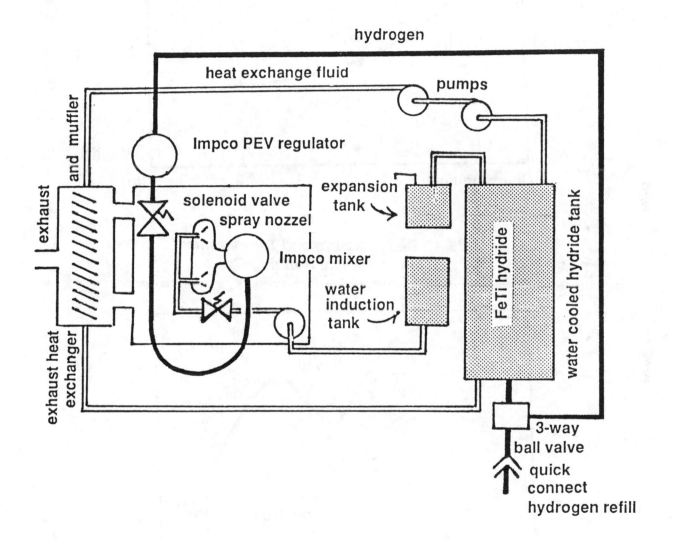

This system shows a water-cooled and water-heated hydride
fuel system.

84. Hydrogen and Bed Temperature for Air-Cooled Cell Refueling

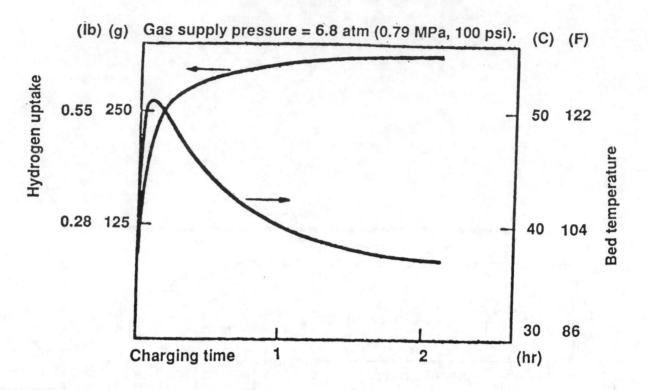

Gas supply pressure = 6.8 atm (0.79 MPa, 100 psi).

85. Bed Pressure and Temperature During Typical Running Cycle

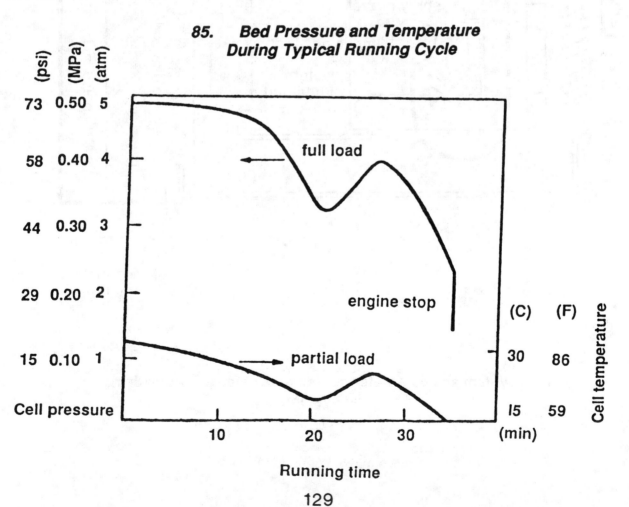

129

The Riverside Bus

The city of Riverside, California, with funding from the Department of Energy, and $125,000 from the California Transportation Department has converted one of the six minibusses to hydrogen fuel. Billings Energy Corporation provided the design and engineering. The firm owns the bus and leases it to the city for testing on a two year renewable lease option. The bus is the first hydrogen vehicle opeated in regular service by a transit authority.

The vehicle is a 21 passenger 7.3 m (24 ft) Argosy. See **Exhibit 86**. Some seats were removed to accomodate the water induction reservoir, thereby limiting the bus to 19 passengers as seen in **Exhibit 87**.

Hydrogen is the prinicpal fuel for the vehicle, but propane is used as a backup source of power if needed. Enough hydrogen is stored in the aluminum hydride tanks for a range of 129 to 145 km (80 to 90 mi). The hydride is $Fe_{4.4}Ti_{5.1}Mn_5$ developed by Brookhaven National Lab.

Ten hydride-containing tubes are linked together by a manifold and mounted under the floor. Data for each tube is as follows.

Diameter:	20.3 cm (8 in)
Wall thickness:	0.92 cm (0.36 in).
Length:	122.2 cm (48.1 in).
Volume:	29.45 liter (1.04 ft^3)
Weight:	22.6 kg (49.8 lb).
Service pressure:	137.2 atm (13.9 MPa, 2,015 psi).

Each tube is surrounded by a large diameter tube that contains a circulating water jacket used to control the tempeature of the tubes for charging and discharging. End plates support the concentric tube arrangement. Manifolds that collect the gas are separate from those that circulate the coolant. Coolant flows from one tube to another in series, as shown in **Exhibit 88**. The hydrogen manifolds are in parallel. The flow of the hydrogen from any tank may be turned off without effecting the others

A 83.3 liter (22 gal) propane tank boosts the range another 241 km (150 mi). The changeover from one fuel to another is accomplished by simplly turning a switch on the dashboard. It takes an hour to recharge the iron-titanium hydride tanks. The twice daily refueling stops are scheduled for the driver's lunch breaks or at night when the bus is out of service. The bus cannot travel beyond the availability of hydrogen fuel.

Hydrogen is considered for fleet vehicle use because:

- It helps reduce pollution in urban areas.
- Route travel simplifies fuel distribution problems.
- The percentage of the weight of larger vehicles devoted to hydride is less than for smaller vehicles.

95% of auto trips occur within 48 km (30 mi). This is equivalent to 60% of all vehicle miles. **201** It takes 3 hours to recharge the hydride completely, but a short recharge can supply much of the capacity the hydride is designed to take.

- 40% recharge takes place in the first 5 minutes.
- 55% recharge takes place in the first 10 minutes.
- 78% recharge takes place in the first 30 minutes.
- 86% recharge takes place in the first 60 minutes.

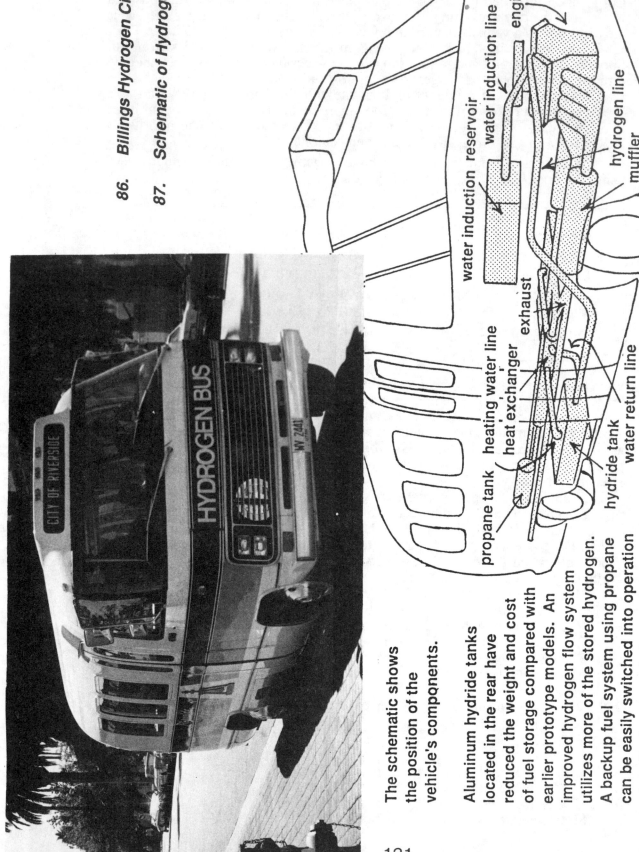

86. *Billings Hydrogen City Bus*

87. *Schematic of Hydrogen Bus*

water induction reservoir

water induction line

engine

hydrogen line

muffler

water return line

hydride tank

exhaust

heat exchanger

heating water line

propane tank

The schematic shows the position of the vehicle's components.

Aluminum hydride tanks located in the rear have reduced the weight and cost of fuel storage compared with earlier prototype models. An improved hydrogen flow system utilizes more of the stored hydrogen. A backup fuel system using propane can be easily switched into operation when the bus travels beyond its hydrogen range.

131

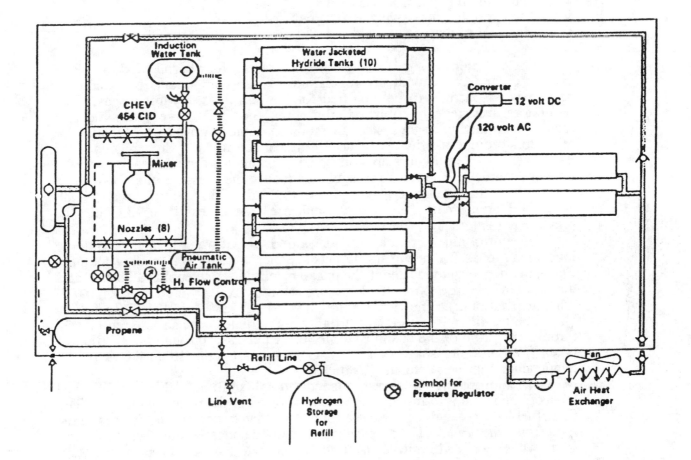

When charging with hydrogen the heat exchange circuit is tapped at two points. Cooling water is circulated through the hydride tanks from the outside. A thermostatically controlled water pump varys the flow rate in response to the hydride temperature. The 907 kg (2,000 lb) of FeTi stores up to 58.6 kWh (200,000 BTU) of energy.

The nearby Linde Division of Union Carbide in Fontana, California makes delivery of hydrogen from steam-reformed natural gas, economical.

Engine coolant provides the heat necessary to release stored hydrogen from the hydride. The coolant is circulated by a water pump turned by the engine as shown in **Exhibit 88**. (An extra 120 V.A.C. pump is installed and runs on converted 12 V.D.C. durrent from the battery.)

A schematic diagram of the Riverside Bus is shown in the exhibit. Six flow circuits make up the fuel system.

- Hydrogen delivery.
- Heat exchaging.
- Water induction.

- Pneumatic air for controls.
- Fuel and air mixing.
- Propane fuel delivery.

The main hydrogen ball valves are activated by air pressure from a small pressurized (pneumatic) air tank only when all of the following conditions are met.

- The ignition key is ON, and
- The hydrogen flow switch is ON, and
- Manifold vacuum is sensed.

The 7.4 liter (452 in^3) Chevrolet engine has a four barrel Mudd CA 425 carburetor and two model EV regulators. These components are made for propane fuel but had to be modified for the less dense hydrogen gas. The regulators are made by Impco Carburetion, Inc. To save space the two regulators in the hydrogen system are mounted in the left front wheel well. The regulators provide the final pressrue adjustment before the hydrogen goes to the gas mixer. Two regulators are connected in parallel to "check" each other for greater accuracy. The pressure regulators reduce the pressure of the hydrogen gas delivered to the engine from 51.0 atm (5.2 MPa, 750 psi) to 13.6 atm (1.38 MPa, 200 psi). When the hydride tank pressure is less than 13.6 atm the pressure regulators are bypassed.

To control nitrous oxide emissions a fine mist of water is injected into the intake manifold. The pneumatic air tank supplies pressure to a small water tank. The spray nozzels are located in the intake manifold. A solenoid valve activates the spray in response to manifold vacuum. Nitrous oxides were 1.27 g/kWh (0.9 g/horsepower hour). The 1977 California standard was 9.4 g/kWh (7.0 g/hp·hr).

The air filter is mounted in front of the radiator. It can be seen clearly through the grille of the bus in **Exhibit 86**. Air coming through the air filter is taken from a cooler space than the engine compartment. Reduced air intake temperature improves combustion efficiency.

When propane fuel is used, it is fed through an Impco VFF fuel filter and lock-off and a single model EV combination vaporizer and regulator. The filter/fuel lock-off and the regulator for the propane system are positioned in the right front wheel well. The propane tank is nestled under the floor behind the left front wheel well. Manifold vacuum activates a separate propane pressure regulator. The driver can switch between hydrogen and propane while driving. This fuel is best used for light loads only unless the ignition timing is changed to accomodate the different combustion characteristics of propane.

Specifications and performance data **201** for the bus are given below:

Number of Passengers:	19
Manufacturer:	Winnebago
Weight without hydride:	3,690 kg (8,135 lb)
Weight of FeTi hydride:	1,002 kg (2,209 lb)
Weight of stored hydrogen:	12.6 kg (28 lb)
Weight of FeTi tanks :	400 kg (882 lb)
Weight of structural reinforcement:	54 kg (119 lb)
Weight of payload:	1,612 kg (3,554 lb)
Total H$_2$ available at 80 km/hr (50 mi/hr):	7.7 kg (17 lb)
Fuel economy at 80 km/hr (50 mi/hr):	16km/kg (4.5 mi./lb)
Range at 80 km/hr:	121 km (75 miles).

The experiment in Riverside met with numerous technical failures and was discontinued 1979 due to lack of funding.

Application of hydrogen is not limited to transit systems. Industry is finding hydrogen attractive for powering forklifts, underground mining vehicles, tractors, and other kinds of people and equipment movers without danger of contaminating closed-in air space.

Mercedes Benz Van

Daimler Benz, of Germany, has developed a van that uses *two hydrides*. The vehicle is designed to exploit the advantages of both FeTi and magnesium nickle hydride. TiFe makes up two-thirds of the weight of the total amount of hydride. Magnesium nickle (Mg_2Ni) comprises the remaining third.

TiFe holds only 1.6 to 1.95% of its weight in hydrogen but dissociates at a relatively low temperature. Mg_2Ni has the opposite feature: dissociating at 200° to 400^oC (390° to 750^oF) and requires twice the energy for dissociation as TiFe. The hydrogen stored in the Mg_2Ni can be recovered only when the engine coolant is hot enough.

The engine uses water injection to control backfiring and preignition.

Hydrogen is withdrawn from the hydride in discrete cycles, unlike most hydride-powered vehicles. First, the hydride is heated enough to increase pressure in the tank. Then, the heat is cut off as the hydrogen build-up is drawn off. As this happens, the temperature of the hydride drops and the cycle repeats. The temperature is allowed to vary between -20° and 20^oC (-4° and -68^oF). The pressure varies between 0.99 atm (0.1 MPa, 14.5 psi) and 1.97 atm (0.2 MPa, 30 psi).

Vehicle specifications are as follows **700p481-499**:

Number of cylinders:	4
Displacement:	2.3 liters (140 in^3)
Power output:	44 kW (59 hp) at 4,800 rpm.
Compression ratio:	9:1.
Exhaust gas recirculation:	25%.
Hydride:	67% FeTi, 33% Mg2Ni.
Range on highway:	152 to 200 km(95 to 124 mi).
Range in city traffic:	120 km (75 mi).
Heat exchange fluid:	standard engine coolant.
Recharge by cooling water.	75% recharge in 10 minutes.

The Mercedes van also incorporates hydride air conditioning. Heat from the passenger compartment can be used to heat the hydride and cool the passengers, as well.

Exhibit 89 and 90 reveal the mechanical details of the van. **Exhibit 91** shows a cross section of the hydride vessel. The performance of the vessel is given in **Exhibit 92**. **201**

A Mercedes Benz passenger car was converted to run on both gasoline and hydrogen. **Exhibit 93** shows an inside view of the major components of the car. This scheme allows flexible use of available fuel. Gasoline is to be used for long distance journeys, while hydrogen provides the power for shorter trips. **Exhibit 94** presents the test data for the car running on hydrogen at various distances.

Daimler-Benz hydrogen powered bus

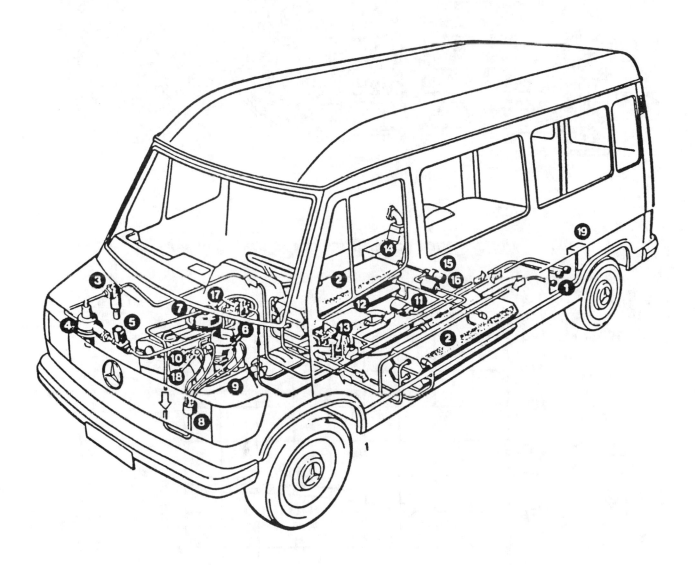

I. refill connections 2. hydride storage 3. filter 4. pressure
regulator 5 solenoid valve 6. hydrogen flow regulator 7.
differential pressure regulator 8. flow distributor 9. intake
manifold 10. hydrogen nozzles 11. pump for water circulation
12. exhaust gas/water heat exchanger, exhaust flaps 14. water
tank 15. water pressurization pump 16. filter 17. water flow
distributor 18. water nozzles 19. electronics system
(Photo courtesy of Daimler-Benz A.G.)

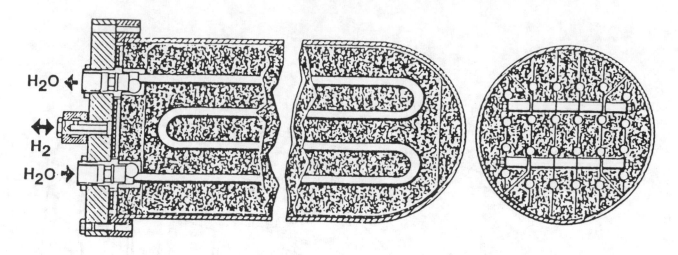

92.   *Performance of Iron Titanium Hydride Vessel*

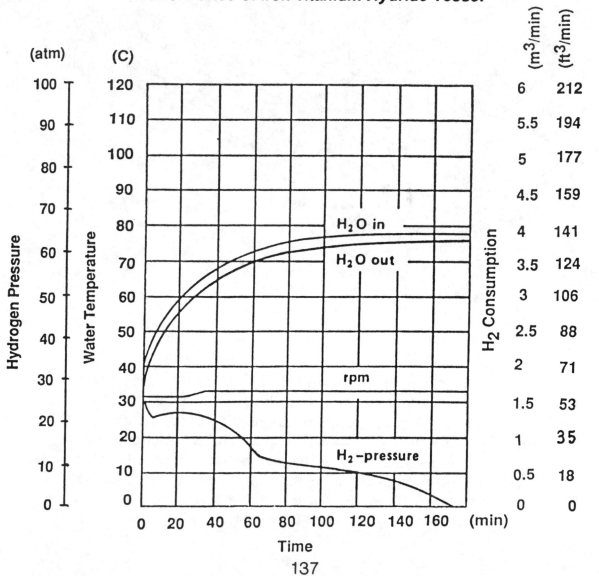

93. Details of the Mercedes-Benz with Gasoline and Hydrogen Operation

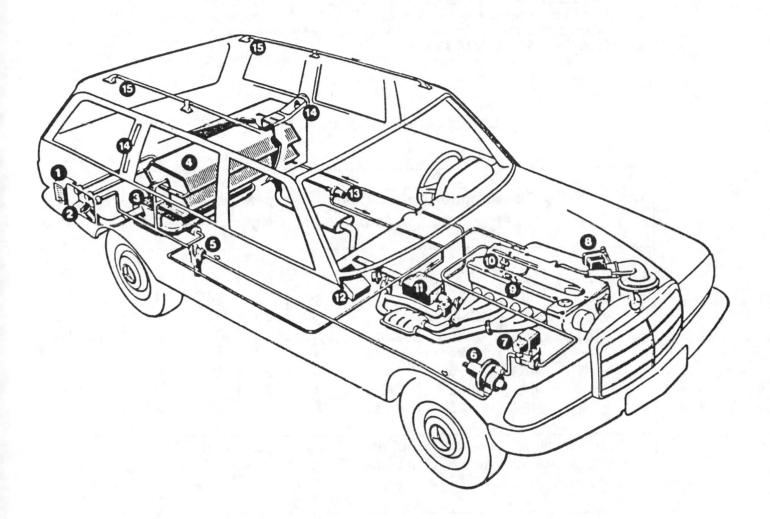

1. electronics system 2. refill connections 3. gasoline tank (50% regular size) 4. hydride storage 5. filter 6. pressure regulator 7. shutoff valve 8. throttle flap driver motor 9. hydrogen injectors 10. gasoline injectors, exhaust gas heat exchanger and controlling flaps 12. electronic engine management 13. heat exchanger recirculation pump 14. hydride storage vent line 15. passenger compartment vent line
(Photo courtesy of Daimler-Benz A.G.)

STORING HYDROGEN IN CARBON

The disadvantages of gaseous, liquid, and hydride storage can be summarized as follows for a car with a 500 km (310 mile) range.

- Pressurized gas range: **4,500 kg (10,000 lb.)** a pressure of 3,000 psi requires 100 lbs of tank for each pound of hydrogen stored. For practical applications range is limited to 60 to 80 miles.
- Lead acid batteries for an electric motor: **3,000 kg (6,600 lb.)**
- Titanium hydride: **2,600 kg (5,700 lb.)** Hydride systems are about 18 times heavier than a liquid hydrogen system. For a 500 km (310 mile) range the hydride system would weigh 2,600 kg (5,700 lb.)
- Liquid hydrogen: **136 kg (300 lb.)** Equal to to gasoline in weight and range. Twice the weight and four times the storage volume
- Gasoline: **63 kg (138 lb.)**

94. Test Data for Hydride Vehicle

Test	H$_2$ Consumption (m^3)	(ft^3)	Distance (km)	(mi)	Speed (km/h)	(mi/h)	Gear
1	32	1,130	88	55	60	37	4
2	40	1,413	86	53	70	44	4
3	45	1,589	81	50	80	50	4
4	48	1,695	76	47	60	37	3
5	48	1,695	79	49	30	19	3
6	48	1,695	66	41	30	19	2
7	48	1,695	69	43	70	44	4
8	48	1,695	130	81	60	37	4

Source: Buchner, H. and Staufferer, H., NATO/CCMS, 4th Int. Conference for Automotive Propulsion Systems, Vol. 2, Session 6, Arlington, VA, Apr. 1977.

The prospect of hydrogen power for bus fleets has resurfaced in 1992. The City of Tempe, Arizona is planning to spend $3 million to convert 25 fleet vehicles to operate on hydrogen within two years. The project will incorporate technological modifications that over come the difficulties encountered in the Riverside experiment. With the assistance of Arizona Senator John McCain, federal government through the EPA, and the Departments of Energy and Transportation may fund the project. This will be largest fleet of hydrogen-fueled vehicles in the world. It will also involve research by Arizona State University on the most cost effective method to extract hydrogen from sewage and city garbage. Also, a solar thermal powered dish built by McDonnel Douglas and a Sterling engine developed by Cummins will provide electrical power for electrolysers. The local utility will provide power by night during off peak hours. If the cost of the utility electricity can be held to 3 to 4 cents per kilowatt hour the cost of the hydrogen will be equivalent to gasoline costing $1.00 to $1.40 per gallon. Considering the environmental, health and military costs of gasoline use, this would be a bargain.

The hydrogen fuel for the Tempe bus project is stored on-board the bus in carbon. Carbon has a high surface area that readily absorbs a variety of gasses including hydrogen. The surface area is about 2,000 square meters (21,500 sq. ft.). per gram of storage material. Researchers at Syracuse Univerity in New York are developing lightweight carbon composites to store hydrogen. The hydrogen must be chilled to -123 °C (-190 °F) at a pressure of 1,500 psi. As with hydrides, the captive hydrogen is released by increasing the temperature and reducing the pressure. The weight and volume of the storage device is similar to fully loaded gasoline tanks. The carbon granules resemble in size and weight what Harry Braun describe as "kitty litter". [165]

Roy McAlister President of the The American Hydrogen Association is in the process of developing a activated carbon fabric that is capable of storing hydrogen for use on board vehicles at about one third the energy density of gasoline.

95. Volumetric and Mass Densities Storage Alternatives

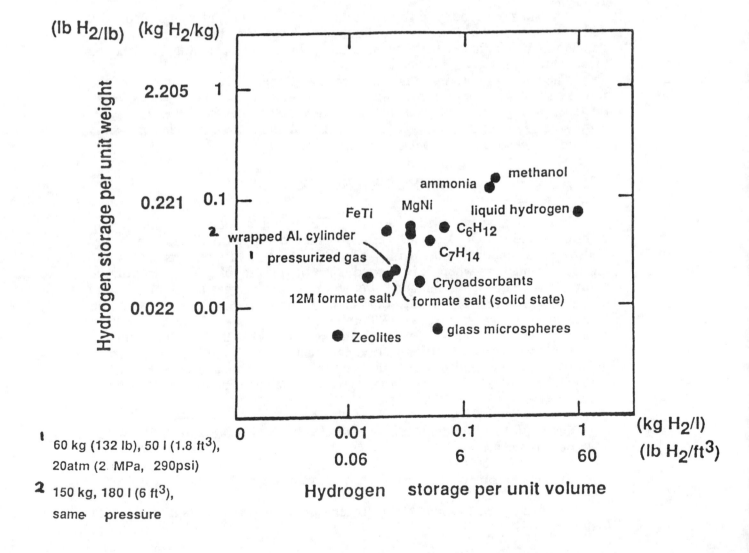

FORMATE SALTS AS STORAGE MEDIA

The major problem in finding a suitable media for storing hydrogen is in meeting three criteria.

- Low temperature and pressure reaction.
- Reversibility.
- High storage capacity.

The various hydrides meet all three criteria to some degree. One may excell in one area better than the others. A new experimental process that uses formate salts to store and release hydrogen seems to meet all three criteria.

A formate salt (sodium formate in this case) is mixed with water to yield sodium bicarbonate and hydrogen. This takes place at 20°C (68°F) and 1 atm (0.1 MPa, 14.7 psi). The process uses a charcoal catalyst coated with palladium. The reaction works in reverse by adding hydrogen to the bicarbonate to reconstitute the formate.

In practical applications, the hydrogen gas being stored may be include carbon monoxide without effecting the absorption of the hydrogen. Synthesis gas, a combination of CO and H_2, is a common by-product in petroleum refining and other chemical manufacturing processes. *"In this way, low value solid fuels (eg. inferior coals or waste) can be discretely transformed into a gaseous fuel of high quality (thermic and environmental) in a form easy to store and transport "*. **1060p344**

The storage capacity of formate salts exceeds zeolites, glass microspheres, and some metal hydrides. The conditions for charging and discharging are too demanding and cumbersome to be used for on-board vehicle storage but may be practical for stationary applications.

The hydrogen produced is estimated to be about 30% of the weight of the formate salts. *"Based on the data presented, one can conclude that the storage and transport of hydrogen by the intermediate of the formate-bicarbonate cycle is promising. The transformation of low value solid fuel in high caloric gas by this method can proove itself especially attractive "*. **1060p346**

MICROSPHERE STORAGE

In a process developed by Robert J. Teitel, and associates of San Diego, California under a Department of Energy grant, hydrogen is diffused into tiny hollow glass spherical containers. At 350°C (662°F) hydrogen gas passes into the glass containers where it is trapped when the glass cools. To get it out, the hydrogen is heated again but at a lower temperature. The gas is stored at 272 to 409 atm (27.5 to 41.3 MPa, 4000 to 6000 psi) in tiny spheres with the consistency of powdered sugar. A thimble full contains 4 million. They store hydrogen with less container weight than pressurized gas tanks. The diameters are 25 to 150 microns (millionths of a centimeter) with walls .25 to 5 microns thick. The amount needed store a given volume of hydrogen takes up more space than pressurized gas. The 3-M compay gives tit he trade name *Fillite* . It is made in two grades.

- Grade 300/7 : high temperature is needed but higher pressures and storage density are achieved.
- Grade 32D/4500 : lower temperatures are used along with lower pressures. This grade is more practical for automotive use.

The energy used to store the hydrogen cannot be recovered as it can be with hydrides.

EVALUATING HYDROGEN STORAGE SYSTEMS

The estimation of storage capacity is the first step for evaluating the efficiency of a hydrogen carrier. This property has two components.

- *Volumetric density*, measured in kg of hydrogen per liter (or lb per cubic foot).
- *Mass density*, measured in kg of hydrogen per kg of carrier (or lb per lb of carrier).

The storage efficiency of any system combines both of the above measures. **Exhibit 95** compares the storage capacity of some selected hydrogen storage alternatives. **1060p342** The upper right area of the graph shows high volumetric density and high mass density. For the lower left, the reverse is true. Formate salts hold an intermediate position in the graph.

There are about about 9.2×10^{22} atoms per mole of fully charged iron titanium hydride. Solid hydrogen holds about 5.3×10^{22} atoms per mole. Liquid hydrogen has about 4.2×10^{22} atoms per mole.

According to the latest research presented at the ninth World Hydrogen Energy Conference in 1992 at Paris, France liquid hydrogen was compared with hydride. Liquid hydrogen is generally more efficient but more expensive. BMW presented plans for a car with a liquid hydrogen tank that weighs 43 kg (95 lbs). full, giving a range of 306 km (190 miles). Hydride is cheaper but heavier. To give the same range, a hydride tank would weigh 295 kg (650 lbs).

ON - BOARD HYDROGEN GENERATION

Hydrogen From Gasoline

Gasoline may be *reformed* to hydrogen and simple gasses by incomplete combustion using small amounts of oxygen at a high temperature.

The university of Arizona modified a 29.8 kW (40 hp) Volkswagen engine to run on 100% hydrogen from reformed gasoline. The fuel reformer had a *catalytic reactor*. In this reactor, water and liquid hydrocarbon reacted to produce hydrogen. **1040p67** Nickle pellets were used as a catalyst in the $816^{\circ}C$ ($1,500^{\circ}F$) reactor. 18.9 liters (5 gal) of water and 75.7 liters (20 gal) of gasoline were stored in separate tanks. Water was recycled from the exhaust. **1070p56-57**

Pollutants were reduced to within one-fourth to one-half of federal standards. The engine produced no soot. Mileage increased by 50% at a slightly lower horsepower. The researchers reported smooth running over the entire range of rpm's

The design recycled exhaust heat to the reformer. About one-third of the energy in gasoline is waste heat.

The researchers used only a fuel atomizer for the engine. No carburetor was needed. **Exhibit 96** shows the process used. Steam plus gasoline goes to a *superheater* (a vaporizer) then to a *reactor* where the mixture is partially burned in a small amount of oxygen. The hot hydrogen is used to thermally decompose the steam, thereby producing more hydrogen gas. The *condenser* dries the hydrogen gas before storing the fuel. The water precipitated from the condenser is recycled. **Exhibit 97** shows another process that uses no water. Air and liquid hydrocarbon fuel are introduced separately into the reactor. Spiral tubes in the start up burner impart a swirling motion to the gasses to mix them thoroughly. Parial oxydation produces hydrogen and other flammable gasses for the engine. As the hollow jacket imparts heat to the incoming air up to a specified temperature, a thermocouple activates a two-way control valve that diverts fuel to

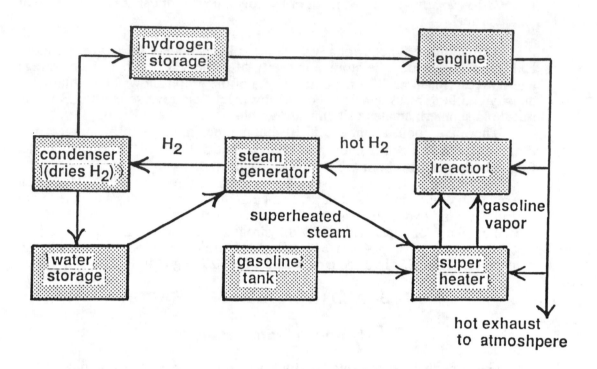

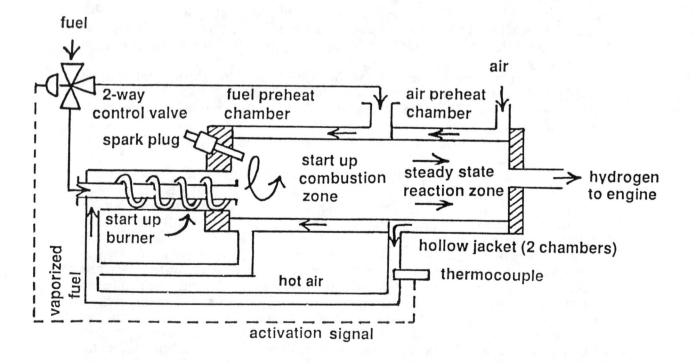

143

the hollow jacket surrounding the reactor (the preheat fuel chamber). Then fuel and air are now mixed before going to the burner.

In an alternative design a catalyst bed may occupy about two-thirds of the start-up combustion zone. Gasses react at the surface of the catalyst at 527°C (980°F).

Simultaneous hydrogen and gasoline operation is possible. The best mixture of hydrogen and gasoline is about 30% by volume of hydrogen. **1050**

Hydrogen From Methanol

Methanol can be split into hydrogen and flammable hydrocarbons by engine waste heat according to the following reaction.

$$Heat + CH_3OH \text{ -----> } 2H_2 + CO.$$

$$Heat + CH_3OH + H_2O \text{ -----> } 3H_2 + CO_2.$$

The first reaction uses heat to decompose methanol, the second reaction uses both heat and steam. The advantage of the first process is that when carbon monoxide and hydrogen are burned together the combustion helps to reduce overall engine temperatures. A zinc oxide or copper oxide catalyst is used. In either case, 26.7 Wh/mole of methanol is needed to "split" methanol. **325p 485**

Using engine waste heat hydrogen can be forced from methanol at the rate of 7,363 to 13,027 liters/hr (260 to 460 ft³/hr). A typical catalyst for automotive applications is copper chromite (70% CuO + 20% Cr_2O_3 + 3% graphite). Temperatures around 316°C (600°F) are needed. Higher temperatures damage the catalyst.

1.8 kg (4 lb) of catalyst is used in a typical automotive application. It would take the form of 9 tubes, each 2.5 X 17.8 cm (1 X 7 in).

The overall size of the reactor for the above amount of catalyst is determined to be 7.5 X 7.6 X 17.8 cm (3 X 3 X 7 in). For a larger volume of hydrogen, a larger reactor would be needed. See **Exhibit 98**. **40p107**

The mixture of methanol and water in this process contains from 1.12 to 1.13% hydrogen. Because of this solution's greater density, methanol and water contains from 1.4 to 1.5 times the amount of hydrogen as liquid hydrogen. **160**

Hydrogen From Iron

Iron reacts with water to form iron oxide and hydrogen at 700 to 900 °C (1,300 to 1,700 °F). The iron oxide can be reduced to iron and water at 800 to 1,100 °C (1,470 to 2,000 °F). Sponge iron, a porus form of cast iron with a large surface area, is usually employed. The two reactions are:

$$3Fe + 4H_2O \text{ -----> } Fe_3O_4 + 4H_2.$$

$$Fe_3O_4 + 4H_2 \text{ -----> } 3Fe + 4H_2O.$$

The temperatures needed may obtained by burning some of the hyrogen produced. H-Power Corp. has developed a process for lowering the temperatures required for oxidation to 90 to 100 °C (200 to 212 °F) with the aid of special catalysts. This lower temperature is within the range of exhaust temperatures from an internal combustion engine or fuel cell. This makes possible on-board production of hydrogen from iron and water.

With conventional process employing this reaction conversion to hydrogen is about 55 percent. The H-Power approach may improve this to 75 to 80 percent.

144

A car would carry around iron and water in a special tank. It would be twice as heavy as a conventional gasoline tank. The range would be 6 kilometers (3.75 miles) per kilogram (2.2 lb.) of iron. A car with a 500 km (310 mile) range would need 82.6 kg (182 lb.) of iron. The amount of iron oxide left over when all the fuel has been used up weighs about 1.4 times as much as the original iron. This is because oxygen has been added in the process of generating hydrogen. About 10 percent of the water has been used up. A lightweight tank could be made of plastic. The total fuel storage system could hold 4.5 to 5 percent hydrogen by weight.

H-Power figures that the hydrogen would cost the equivalent of $0.48/liter ($1.80/gallon) of gasoline. The cost would be even less if the iron oxide could be recycled. The user would be given cash credit for turning in his used iron oxide.

The advantage over methanol as an on-board source of hydrogen is that iron is renewable and nontoxic. **434**

98. Volume of Hydrogen from Methanol

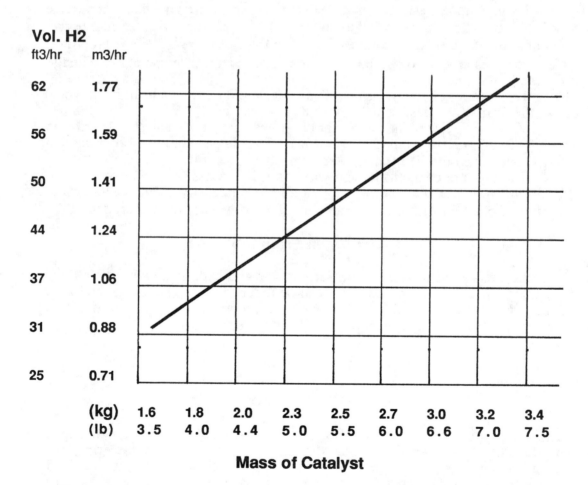

Chapter 6:
ENGINE MODIFICATIONS

BENEFITS AND PROBLEMS OF USING HYDROGEN FUEL

General Considerations

125 MILLION cars and trucks use 16% of current U.S. energy consumption and one-third of its liquid fuel production. Obviously, an acceptable substitute for gasoline which would be less costly and in more plentiful supply will help alleviate this dependency upon imported petroleum.

Hydrogen has 2.7 times the energy of gasoline on a weight basis but only one-third on a volume basis. Engines convered to hydrogen get only 80% of the power normally achieved with gasoline. Hydrogen, however, burns 50% more efficiently.

Hydrogen has a higher flame speed than gasoline, wider flammability limits, and higher detonation temperature. Hydrogen can produce more nitrous oxide emissions than gasoline, but water injection during the combustion process lowers nitrous oxide output of hydrogen below that of gasoline. Water vapor is the only other significant emission from hydrogen combustion.

Hydrogen burns hotter , but takes less energy to ignite, than gasoline. This means that hydrogen burns faster, but carries the danger of preignition and flashback.

With only one-tenth of the density of gasoline, hydrogen nevertheless takes up 4 times the volume. Hydrides are used like a "sponge" to store hydrogen gas. Iron-titanium hydride stores 1.5% of its weight as hydrogen. This material usually takes an hour to recharge, at atmospheric pressure. About 40% is recovered in the first minute and 80% is recharged after 15 minutes.

Hydrogen is a gaseous fuel. It shares many features in common with other gaseous fuels. The following are characteristics of using gasses, rather than liquids, as automotive fuel. These advantages of gaseous fuels apply equally to hydrogen, propane, butane, or liquefied petroleum gas (LPG).

- *Better fuel and air mixing.* No incomplete vaporization or vapor lock. No flooding.
- *No cold wall quenching.* Gaseous fuel does not precipitate on the cold walls of an engine that has just been started.
- *Cooler operating temperatures.*
- *Better engine lubrication:* Gasoline dissolves oil on cylinder walls, thereby increasing engine wear.
- *Less (or no) carbon deposits.* Gaseous fuels burn more efficiently. The oil stays clean. It may be possible to get 300,000 miles on an engine before it needs replacement.

146

- *Insignificant air pollution,* especially with water injection.

Disadvantages of gaseous fuels include the following:

- *The faster burning properties of gaseous fuels may overheat valves,* particularly on cars designed for unleaded gasoline. The valves may need more frequent replacement. To avoid this, valves and seats designed for high temperature operation may be installed.
- *Misfirings may occur,* particularly if the original ignition system is in poor condition.
- *Lower fuel economy:* Propane gives 75% of the range as an equal volume of gasoline.
- *Danger of leaks:* The fuel system must have an excess flow valve to shut off the fuel flow in case of a leak.
- *Danger of overpressurization:* Just as in the case of a water heater in a home, a relief valve is needed on a pressurized tank to avoid overpressure that may, among other causes, be a result of excess heat. Fuel lines should be made of high pressure neoprene reinforced with stainless steel, similar to high pressure aircraft hoses.

Hydrogen's low energy per unit volume means less energy in the cylinder compared to gasoline. An engine run on hydrogen produces less power than with gasoline. **Exhibit 99** shows that this difference is more noticeable in spark-ignited two-stroke engines than with four-stroke engines or two-stroke diesels. Supercharging may help remedy this. Compressing the incoming fuel before it gets to the cylinder increases the amount of energy per volume of fuel.

Preignition and Flashback

Hydrogen burns fast and has a low ignition temperature. This may cause the fuel to be ignited by hot spots in the cylinder before the intake valve closes. The same properties may cause *flashback, preignition, or knock.* [201]
These problems are particularly acute with high fuel/air mixtures. Uncontrolled preignition resists the upward compression stroke of the piston thereby reducing power. Remedies for backfire include:

- *Timed port injection* (late injection) to make sure the fuel detonates only after the intake valve is closed.
- *Water injection* . Raising the temperature of liquid hydrogen from -253° to 27°C (-423° to 81°F) requires 1,100 Wh/kg (1 703.66 BTU/lb). The heat of vaporization of water is 631Wh/kg (977.28 BTU/lb). The optimum ratio by weight of water to hydrogen is 1.75. [690p653-659]

Efficiency of Combustion

Hydrogen burns more *completely* than gasoline. The thermal efficiency of an engine running on hydrogen is 25 to 100% higher than with gasoline. This is measured in lower exhaust temperature, indicating less waste heat. The efficiency tends to be higher at reduced load. [319]

Emissions

Carbon monoxide and other hydrocarbon emissions result from *incomplete combustion* of gasoline. The list of pollutants also includes nitrous oxides, sulfur oxides and lead oxides. [580] The economics of using hydrogen must take into account the health costs for humans of breathing poisoned air.
With hydrogen, nitrous oxides are the only pollutant. These can be brought

Engine speed = 2 000 rpm.

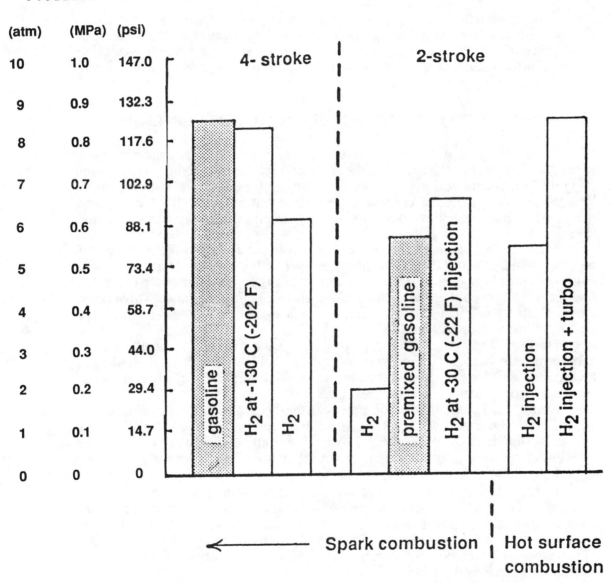

well below government standards with proper combustion techniques. Nitrous oxide emisions are lower than for gasoline even when the gasoline engine is using emission controls. With hydrogen, increasing engine load reduces nitrous oxide emissions to 10% of those at low loads. **319**

Wider Range of Combustion

Internal combustion engines can burn hydrogen in a wider range of fuel/air mixtures than with gasoline. This makes hydrogen more efficient in stop and start driving.**940p99-129**

Summary

"The combustion and emission characteristics of hydrogen appear so favorable that reseach into hydrogen engine technology has expanded at a rapid rate, expecially in the last few years. Results have been so favorable that all of the previously defined engine types have been operated on hydrogen with relative success." **580**

HISTORY OF HYDROGEN CONVERSION EXPERIMENTS

In the early years of the development of internal combustion engines hydrogen was not considered to be the "exotic" fuel that it is today. Otto, in the early 1870's, considered a variety of fuels for his internal combustion engine, including hydrogen. He considered gasoline but rejected it as being too dangerous. Only later developments in combustion technology made gasoline safe to use.

Most early engine experiments were designed for burning a variety of gasses, including natural gas and propane. When hydrogen was used in these engines it would backfire. Since hydrogen burns faster than other fuels, the fuel-air mixture would ignite in the intake manifold before the intake valve could close. Water was injected to control the backfiring. Hydrogen gave less power than gasoline with or without the water.

During World War I hydrogen and pure oxygen were considered for submarine use because the crew could get drinkable water from the exhaust. Hydrogen was also considered for use in powering airships. The gas used for bouyancy could also be used for fuel.

Rudolf A. Erren, first made practical the hydrogen-fueled engine in the 1920's. He converted over 1,000 engines. His projects included modifications to trucks and buses. After World War II the allies discovered submarine converted by Erren to hydrogen power that also had hydrogen powered torpedoes. **430**

In 1924 Ricardo conducted the first systematic engine performance tests on hydrogen. He used a one cylinder engine and tried various compression ratios. At a c.r. of 7 the engine achieved a peak efficiency of 43%. At c.r. of 9.95, Burnstall obtained an efficiency of 41.3% with an e.r. range of 0.587 - 0.80. The next year R. Erren, in Germany, studied direct injection of hydrogen to reduce preignition and flashback.

After World War II, King found the cause of preignition to be *hot spots* in the combustion chamber resulting from the high temperature ash from oil and dust. Flashback was traced to high flame velocity at high equivalency ratios. **200**

M.R. Swain and R.R. Adt at the University of Miami developed modified injection techniques with a 1,600 cm^3 (98 in^3) Toyota engine with a 9:1 c.r. The Illinois Institute of Technology converted a 1972 Vega using a propane carburetor.

Roger Billings, in collaboration with Brigham Young University, entered a hydrogen-converted Volkswagen in the 1972 *Urban Vehicle Competition* . The vehicle won first place in the emissions category over 60 other vehicles even though peak emissions were greater than for other hydrogen researchers. The nitrous oxides exceeded previous levels obtained by other experimenters using direct injection. **580p139**

Robert Zweig converted a pickup truck to hydrogen power in 1975. It has been running ever since. He solved the backfiring problem by using an extra intake valve to admit hydrogen separately from air. It is a simple elegant vehicle that uses compressed hydrogen. The Zweig Hydrogen Pickup is now a display vehicle used by the American Hydrogen Association in public exhibits.

The Brookhaven National Laboratory converted a Wankel (rotary) engine to hydrogen. The experimenters concluded that all types of engines are adaptable to hydrogen fuel, *"particularly , the Wankel engine seems to be predetermined for pure hydrogen rather than for conventional fuel because its combustion chamber enhances the emission of hydrocarbon pollutants "*. **70p725**

Mazda has converted one of their rotary engine cars to run on hydrogen. The unique design of the rotary engine keeps the hydrogen and air separate until they are combined in the combustion chamber.

MODERN CONVERSION PROJECTS

Diesel Conversion in China

An experiment in China demonstrates the higher efficiency of hydrogen compared to gasoline. Tests were performed on a stationary mounted, single cylinder, four stroke, air-cooled diesel engine. Specifications are given below.

Bore:	75 mm (3 in)
Stroke:	75 mm (3 in)
Compression ratio:	20:1
Injection advance:	21^0

Exhibit 100 shows thermal efficiencies using hydrogen and gasoline at different load conditions but at a constant 3,000 rpm. Hydrogen is seen to be more efficient through the entire load range. The thermal efficiency of hydrogen is 16% greater than gasoline at 20% load. **545p661-668**

Billings Postal Jeep

The Billings Energy Corporation in Independence, Missouri converted a U.S. postal Jeep to hydrogen hydride. Previously it got 3.9 km/liter (9.2 mi/gal) on gasoline. The hydrogen fuel consumption is 4.9 km/liter (11.5 mi/gal) per gasoline energy equivalent. This was in improvement of 24%. A special gaseous carburetor was used.

High flame speed and low ignition energy necessitated reducing the spark gap. Problems of rusting and pitting on the spark plug tip developed. The plugs were replaced with Champion stainless steel plugs to eliminate the problem. Rusted plug tips can cause preignition through the valves (backflash).

The ignition timing also had to be changed to compensate for faster firing.

The researchers added a water injection system to lower the combustion temperature and nitrous oxide production. A 4:1 ratio by weight, of water to hydrogen, is used. Typically, 1.4 kg (3 lb) of hydrogen and 5.4 kg (12 lb) of water were used daily. The water was injected as a fine mist directly into the

100. Thermal Efficiencies of Gasoline and Hydrogen

Engine speed = 3 000 rpm.
Compression ratio = 6.2.

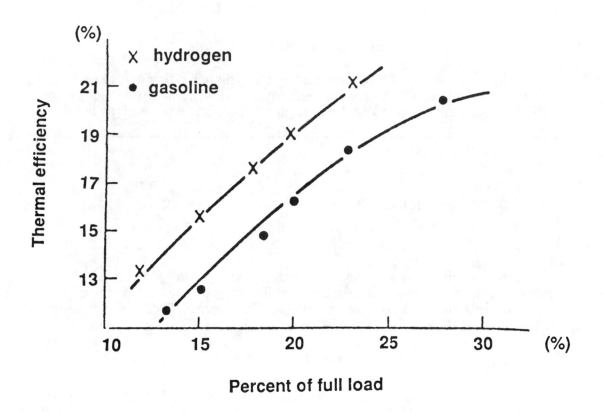

manifold of the straight six engine. This reduced backflashing into the manifold of the straight six engine. This reduced backflashing and boosted power.

The Fe-Ti hydride tank had an internal heat exchanger. This took the form of copper tubing coiled up inside the hydride tank, similar to the arrangement for the Dodge Omni tank shown in **Exhibit 101**.

Diesel Conversion in India

The Indian Institute of Technology has tested spark ignition engines converted to hydrogen and has come to the following conclusions:

- Hydrogen permits a wide range of fuel/air mixtures.
- Very little throttling, if any, is needed. The fuel/air ratio and the amount of fuel is varied, instead.
- Conversion requires higher compression ratios: up to 11:1.
- Hydrogen is 30 to 50% more efficient than gasoline. *"Significantly above the range of gasoline-fueled spark ignition engines."*

The Indian researchers also reached some conclusions regarding the use of hydrogen in addition to diesel fuel in diesel engines.

- Reduced compression ratios are used: 16.5:1 to 14.5:1.
- Because of hydrogen's high, and potentially explosive, rate of combustion only a small smount should be used when mixed with diesel fuel.
- A high ignition temperature is necessary: 585°C (1,085°F).
- The more hydrogen is added to the fuel mix the lower is the level of toxic emissions. **810p137-145**

Hydrogen Mining Vehicle

In experiments with a diesel converted to run on 100% hydrogen, the U.S. Bureau of Mines, in collaboration with EIMCO Mining Machinery, found that the nitrous oxide emissions for hydrogen is *one-tenth* of the amount for the same vehicle on diesel. With hydrogen, the only other emission was water vapor. This is important for vehicles operating in confined spaces, such as a mine.

The 63.4 kW (85 hp) engine was mounted on a 4,500 kg (10,000 lb) utility truck in 1980.

The Diesel required the addition of spark ignition. Compression alone would not ignite the hydrogen at the reduced compression ratio. A turbocharger was also added to increase the density of incoming fuel.

The fuel induction system provides two intake paths: one for hydrogen and the other for air. The fuel and air are kept separate until entering the cylinder to prevent backfiring.

FUEL MIXING

Keeping the air and fuel separate until burned in the cylinder is an important strategy for controlling a host of combustion difficulties arising from the fast-burning properties of hydrogen.

The low flammability limits and low energy required for ignition, of hydrogen cause preignition and flashback when using hydrogen fuel. Preignition occurs when a fuel/air mixture ignites in the combustion chamber before the intake valve closes. Preignition can cause flashback when the ignited fuel/air mixture explodes back into the intake system. These phenomena are most prevalent at higher power demands and at higher fuel/air mixtures near open throttle.

Hydrogen researcher F.E. Lynch does not see preignition as a problem under normal circumstances. *"Preignition is not a necessary precursor to*

**Iron-Titanium tank mounted in sparetire well of postal Jeep. Jeep was modified for selective dual fuel hydrogen or gasoline.
Photo courtesy of Billings Energy Corp.**

backfiring and probably does not occur under normal circumstances at moderate compression and equivalence ratios."

Because of the low volumetric energy content of hydrogen, higher compression ratios or higher fuel delivery pressures are needed to avoid reduced power.

- Supercharging spark ignition engines compresses the fuel/air mixture before being inducted into the cylinder.
- Direct fuel injection involves mixing the fuel with air inside the combustion chamber. The fuel and air are kept separate until then.

If fuel and air are mixed before entering the combustion chamber, the arrangement is called *external mixing* . A carburetor is generally used to accomplish this. *Internal mixing* describes any system where fuel and air are introduced separately into the combustion chamber.

External Fuel Mixing

Exhibit 102 shows an external mixing system inside an engine compartment. When air and fuel are mixed outside the combustion chamber the light hydrogen fuel displaces air in the mixture, thereby reducing power 20 to 30% compared to gasoline.

Hydrogen fuel passes through a pressure regulator where it is reduced in pressure for delivery to the fuel mixer.

The German Institute for Energy Conversion (DFVLR) in Stuttgart converted a BMW with a 3.5 liter (214 in^3) engine to liquid hydrogen. It uses an external mixing system with timed port injection, exhaust turbocharging and variable rate water injection. Fuel injection is controlled by digital engine controls. The car runs on either hydrogen or gasoline.

The power output at 5,000 rpm on gasoline is 170 kW (228 hp) on hydrogen compared with 120 kW (161 hp) on gasoline. **560p725** Another BMW with a 4 cylinder engine was converted to selective hydrogen or gasoline fuel. Power output on hydrogen was 67 kW (90 hp) at 5,000 rpm compared to 75 kW (101 hp) for gasoline. **710p721**

Supercharging has been found ineffective with external hydrogen fuel mixing over a lower power range. **560**

Internal Fuel Mixing

Air and fuel are mixed internally, inside the combustion chamber, when an internal fuel mixing system is used. This is generally done in the following sequence.

- Air is injected. This cools any hot spots in the cylinder.
- The air intake valve closes.
- Fuel is injected.
- The fuel intake valve closes.
- The fuel/air mixtue is ignited.

The air intake ports of an internally mixed fuel system can be seen in **Exhibit 103. 690,654**

When hydrogen is inducted into the cylinder under pressure no air is displaced in the combustion chamber. This prevents the power loss from externally mixed fuel/air systems. Theoretically, 20% more power is possible with directly injected hydrogen fuel than with the same engine using externally mixed gasoline. **201p16** All types of engines can be modified in this way: four stroke, two stroke, diesel, and rotary. With internal mixing, high pressure is

**Notice two hydrogen regulators (foreground) and the Billings
fuel mixer above the valve covers.**

103. Hydrogen Intake Ports

View of the intake ports and the cold hydrogen fuel rail during operation (continuous port injection). Fuel formation is due to the cold hydrogen gas flow. For clarity, the air intake manifold has been removed from the inake ports.

needed: up to 99 atm. (10 MPa, 1,450 psi). 710 A fuel pump is needed to supply fuel to the cylinder under pressure.

W.D. Van Vorst and associates conducted an experiment testing direct fuel injection. They found that high pressures up to 66 atm (6.7 MPa, 970 psi) were necessary to overcome compression in the cylinders. Hydrogen is injected immediately after the intake valve closes and before the combustion chamber pressure reaches maximum. 201

The induction of air separately, rather than in a fuel/air mixture *"allows the air flow rate of a low density hydrogen engine to be essentially that of a carbureted engine operated on a higher density fuel such as gasoline"*. 580p160

Since liquid hydrogen is 10 to 20 times denser than gaseous hydrogen direct injection of liquid hydrogen allows reduced valve size and mass. The relatively high density of liquid hydrogen, compared to gaseous hydrogen causes it to generate pressure when evaporating. Because of this, internal fuel mixing when combined with liquid hydrogen *"has the potential to surpass external mixing for gasoline or hydrocarbons "*. 710p653

In a hydrogen converted engine at Oklahoma University direct injection eliminated preignition and provided smooth operation throughout a wide range of fuel/air mixtures. 580

There are two main types of internal mixture formation: *early injection* and *late injection*. With early injection fuel is introduced at the start of the compression stroke and continues until 90° before top dead center (b.t.d.c.). With late injection fuel is introduced at 5° b.t.d.c. High pressure is needed to get enough fuel into the chamber in a short period of time. With liquid hydrogen fuel, the fuel pump can supply some of this pressure, and fuel expansion supplys the rest of the 99 atm (10 MPa, 1,450 psi) pressure needed. Fuel injection in general, and late injection in particular, make fuel/air mixing difficult because of the short periods of time involved. Uneven mixtures cause:

- Increased nitrous oxide formation.
- Erratic ignition.
- Ignition delay.
- Incomplete combustion.
- Delayed combustion.

These problems can be overcome by increasing the turbulance in the combustion chamber. This is accomplished in one of two ways.

- Changing the combustion chamber geometry.
- Modifying the fuel injector arrangements. 700p481-499

Both early and late induction require further research to overcome problems.

"However, both approaches need a lot of technical effort and do not exhibit the flexibility provided by electromagnetically activated injector arrangements. With the increasing trend towards digital engine electronics the way to go will be purely electromagnetic or electrohydraulic activation of the injector."

If the problems of internal mixture formation are overcome hydrogen fuel becomes competitive to gasoline. *"Because of controlled combustion it allows an operational performance comparable to hydrocarbon type fuels accompanied with a significantly reduced emission of pollutants "*. 700p491-492

Hydrogen injectors must be able to handle compressible fluids and changes in engine power. They must be able to accept varying pressures to the injector and changes in pulse duration.

Equivalency Ratio

The equivalency ratio compares the fuel/air mixture in the engine with the mixture needed for the maximum energy output. This ideal mixture is called the *stoichiometric ratio*. The stoichiometric ratio is the mixture of fuel and air at which all the air and fuel is combined during combustion with no leftover unburned fuel or unreacted air.

Equivalency ratio = e.r. = Actual fuel mixture / Ideal mixture.

Generally, the higher the engine load the higher will be the equivalency ratio needed. For hydrogen fuel, normal operation requires an e.r. of 0.5 to 0.65. High loads need e.r. of 0.8 to 1.00. **201** The range of e.r. for gasoline is 0.72 to 2.40 **700p7**

The higher the e.r. the higher will be the combustion temperature. At low e.r. the fuel is burned completely but some oxygen is left over. This unreacted air cools the combustion.

If the e.r. is lowered the flame velocity of any fuel is reduced.

The lower flammability limit for gasoline (1.3%) is close to its stoichiometric mixture (1.7%). The stoichiometric ratio of hydrogen is in the middle of a wide flammability range (4 to 75%). This means that lower temperature operation is possible. **201**

Engine Governing

There are three methods of delivering fuel to an engine.

- Constant equivalency ratio where the *volume* of fuel, not e.r., is changed.
- Varying the proportion of air while keeping the volume of fuel constant. This is accomplished by installing a third valve to inject the fuel. **See Exhibit 104. 840**
- Varying the proportion of fuel by direct injection of fuel into the cylinder. To accomplish this, the carburetor and intake manifolds are removed. Reseachers at Cornell, Miami, and Oklahoma Universities used this method.

An engine governed by changing the e.r. in response to changes in load runs the risk of preignition with increased e.r. To avoid this, tight tolerances and quick response by the fuel injection control system is necessary. Only a digital electronic engine control system can make the quick responses necessary - *in less than 10 milliseconds.*

Methods of Reducing Preignition

Based on the foregoing discussion and material presented previously in this book it has been concluded that preignition can be minimized by taking the following precautions.
- Excluding excessive oil from the combustion chamber. Less oil is needed with gaseous fuel.
- Using low temperature spark plugs.
- Using sodium-filled exhaust valves to avoid heat buildup in the valve. **201**

The autoignition temperature of hydrogen is approximately one-tenth that of other fuels. Carbon deposits and manifold temperatures that are too low to ignite gasoline may be high enough to lead to preignition in hydrogen. Hot surfaces that can initiate preignition include:
- Spark plug electrodes.
- Exhaust valves.
- Carbon deposits from unburnt lubricants. **545p662**

Liquid hydrogen can be injected near the end of the piston stroke to cool any potential hot spots. In one conversion experiment the injection valves were mounted on top of the cylinder head and opened 40° after top dead center. **710**

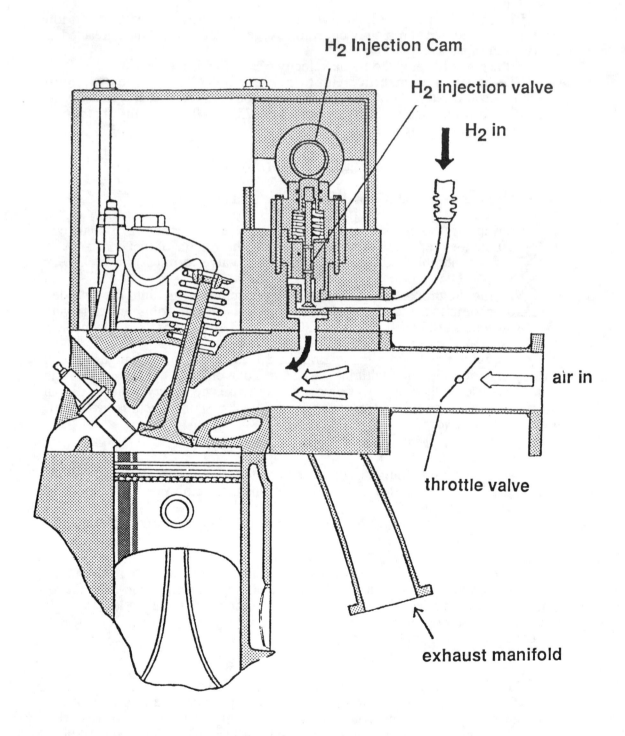

H₂ Injection Cam

H₂ injection valve

H₂ in

air in

throttle valve

exhaust manifold

105. Crossection of Combustion Chamber
Showing Internal Hydrogen-Air Mixing

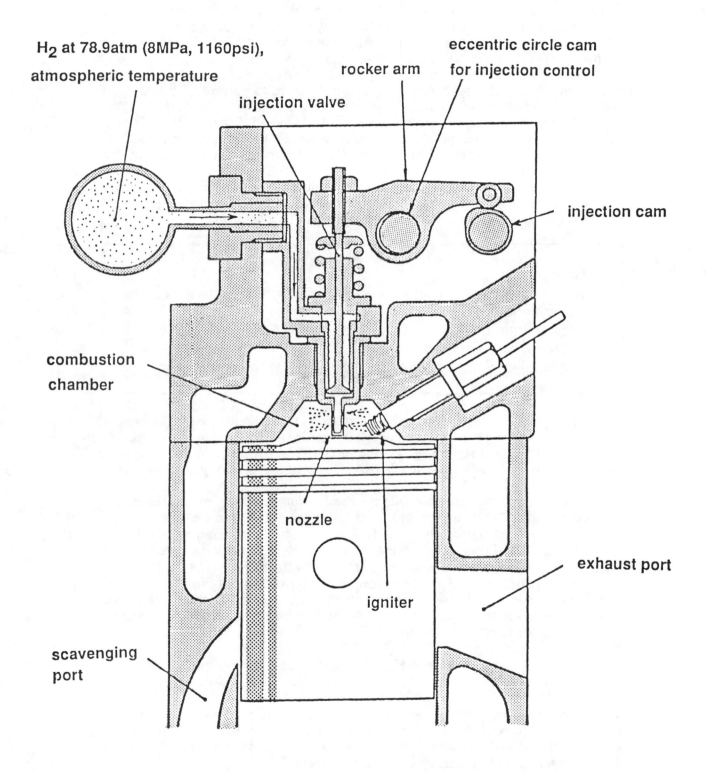

H_2 at 78.9atm (8MPa, 1160psi), atmospheric temperature

rocker arm

injection valve

eccentric circle cam for injection control

injection cam

combustion chamber

nozzle

igniter

exhaust port

scavenging port

160

The Musashi Liquid Hydrogen Diesel

In 1973, a University of California researcher, (Feingold) converted a vehicle to liquid hydrogen with external mixture formation. This was followed by W.F. Stewart at the Los Alamos Laboratory in 1983. In 1984, A.N. Podgorny in the U.S.S.R. and H.C. Watson in Australia conducted similar experiments.

The Musashi Institute of Technology in Japan introduced an operational liquid hydrogen car in 1975. The company later experimented successfully with internal mixture formation in 1982-84 with a 2 stroke spark ignition engine and a 2 and 4 stroke diesel. **700** Their first liquid hydrogen powered car for road use was tested in a 1975 road rally for experimental vehicles. Low temperature hydrogen at -120°C (-184°F) entered the engine's cylinders.

More recently, Musashi has converted a 2 stroke Suzuki diesel to liquid hydrogen. A turbocharger uses exhaust gas pressure to pump liquid hydrogen for direct injection into the combustion chamber at a pressure of 9.9 atm (1 MPa, 145 psi) and at a temperature of from 0° to -50°C (32° to -58°F). Direct injection and low fuel temperature combined to prevent preignition and reduce the nitrous oxide emissions. The fuel is injected during the first half of the compression stroke.

The combination of features employed in this vehicle increased power output 50% beyond a comparable gasoline or diesel without a turbocharger.

Engine specifications in the experiment are as follows:

Bore:	76 mm (3in)
Stroke:	80mm (3.2in)
No. cylinders:	3
Displacement:	1,100 cm^3 (67 in^3)
2 stroke, water cooled.	
Direct injection during 30° of crank angle at maximum point.	

The hydrogen injection device is installed in the cylinder head. The poppet valve is opened by a cam shaft and rocker arm driven by the engine. Injection pressure without the turbocharger is 59.2 atm (6 MPa, 870 psi). With the device, the pressure is 80 atm (8 MPa, 1,176 psi). The stainless steel injection nozzle is seen in **Exhibit 105**.

The injection pipe *projects into the combustion chamber* so that the fuel is sprayed into the cylinder away from the cylinder head. Holes in the pipe distribute hydrogen uniformly. The fuel jet is mounted in a depression in the cylinder head, as shown. This arrangement was compared with several other alternative designs and was found to be the most effective. **390p399-405**

The experimenters replaced the original manifold with a *blow down* type. See **Exhibit 106**. This modification puts the turbocharger within roughly an *equal distance* of each exhaust port. The new manifold insures higher exhaust velocities and increased air flow rate.

The A.H.A. "Smart Plug"

Roy McAlister of the American Hydrogen Association is developing a means of converting almost any spark ignition engine to hydrogen power. Hydrogen fuel injectors deliver fuel to the cylinders exactly when needed. This is similar to the "stratified charge" of a diesel. The experimenters expect to exceed the performance and efficiency of gasoline. **442p12**

106. Exhaust Manifold Variations

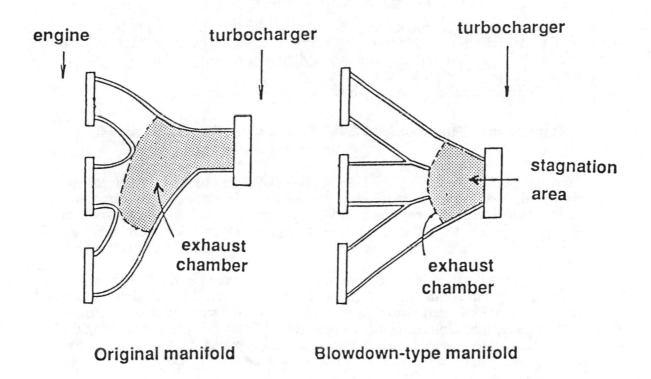

Original manifold   Blowdown-type manifold

107. Thermal Efficiency of Hydrogen

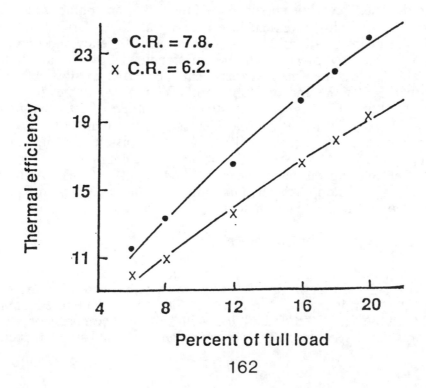

COMPRESSION RATIO

Spark Ignition Engines

In addition to compressing the fuel outside the cylinder with a turbocharger or liquid hydrogen fuel pump, the piston can be adjusted to increase the compression of fuel and air inside the cylinder prior to ignition. This means increasing the *compression ratio*.

The compression ratio is defined by the following. **390p188**

$$\text{Compression Ratio} = \frac{\text{Volume of cylinder with piston at lowest point}}{\text{Volume at highest point.}}$$

Increasing the c.r. decreases the ratio of piston head area to the cylinder volume containing the fuel. A decrease of c.r. from 6.2 to 7.8 increases the area/volume ratio at maximum compression. More area per unit volume increases heat dissipation from the cylinder walls. **545** Higher compression also increases combustion and exhaust gas temperature along with elevated nitrous oxide levels. **810**

Compressing the fuel/air mixture to greater degree permits lower fuel/air mixtures to get the same output as higher fuel/air mixtures. Leaner mixtures help reduce the risk of preignition. Since the combustion properties of hydrogen permit leaner mixtures at any c.r., compared to hydrocarbon fuels, increasing the c.r. is almost always indicated in hydrogen fuel conversions. Increasing the c.r. improves engine efficiency according to the relationship below.

$$n_e = 1 - (1e^{k-1})$$

Where:

n_e = engine thermal efficiency.
e = compression ratio.
k = specific heat ratio = heat increase due to compression.

In specific tests, experimenters increased the c.r. of an engine from 6.2 to 7.8 and noticed a 19% improvement in efficiency at 20% of full load. **545** **Exhibit 107** shows the relationship between thermal efficiency and two c.r.'s for the engine. Improvement in engine efficiency is obvious at all load conditions. This is the same Chinese experiment depicted in **Exhibit 100**.

Experimenters at the Indian Institute of Technology achieved engine efficiencies of 30 to 50% "*significantly above the range of gasoline-fueled spark-ignition engines* ". **810** The c.r. was increased to less than 11.0.

Changing the c.r. may require modifications of the piston. Billings Energy Corp. adapted a 6.6 liter (400 in^3) 1975 Pontiac V8 by changing the c.r. from 7.7 to 12.7 after shaving the piston heads 0.254 cm (0.010 in). At higher pressure in the combustion chamber, lubricating oil may leak past the piston rings. The remedy for this is to install double piston rings.

Diesel Engines

Diesel engines do not have spark plugs. Fuel is ignited by compression. This is based on the principle that any gas, when compressed, increases in temperature. If the c.r. is increased from 14 to 25 the gas temperature increases from 700°C (1,290°F) to 900°C (1,650°F). With sufficient compression, diesel fuel/air mixtures ignite spontaneously by *autoignition* . Fuel and air are inducted separately. The air is inducted during the piston downstroke, and the fuel is inducted at the point of maximum compression.

Hydrogen requires a c.r. of over 28 for autoignition. **201p19** Since this is impractical, hydrogen converted diesels require an ignition source. This can take the from of:

- Mixing hydrocarbon fuel with the hydrogen.
- Using a glow plug.

The latter solution involves a kind of "non-spark" plug. It remains hot continuously but provides just enough heat to ignite the mixture. *"The hot surface ignition is conducted in such a way that combustion takes place while hydrogen is injected which is similar to the conventional diesel engine. "*

The glow plug used in the Musashi experiments in Japan is shown in **Exhibit 108. 380p405** It is essentially a porcelain pipe 6 mm (0.24 in) in diameter. A 0.5 mm (0.02 in) diameter platinum wire is wrapped around the pipe. Each pipe requires 24 W. The 3 cylinder diesel engine in the test required 23 X 3 = 70 Watts. The plug requires current at startup, idling, and low loads; otherwise it maintains its $1,000^{\circ}C$ ($1,800^{\circ}F$) temperature by absorbing and retaining combustion heat without current input.

FUEL DILUTION

Sources of Pollution

There are two main sources of emissions problems from the use of hydrogen. They are not unique to hydrogen. Gasoline and diesel fuel combustion also produces these, and other pollutants, in greater quantity.

- Hydrocarbons from burning lubricating oil.
- Nitrous oxides from high temperature combustion of nitrogen in the atmosphere.

The combustion of hydrogen in pure oxygen results in only water vapor.

$$2H_2 + O_2 \text{-----> } 2H_2O \text{ at } 3,353^{\circ}C \text{ } (6068^{\circ}F).$$

Nitrogen makes up about 70% of the atmosphere. Under some conditions, nitrogen absorbs some of the heat during combustion.

$$2H_2 + O_2 + 3.76 N_2 \text{-----> } 2H_2O + 3.76N_2 \text{ at } 2,673^{\circ}C \text{ } (4,844^{\circ}F).$$

With an excess of air, combustion of hydrogen forms nitrous oxide.

$$2H_2 + O_2 + N_{2x} + O_{2x} \text{-----> } 2H_2O + 2NO_x.$$

The combustion temperature is reduced further to less than $2,673^{\circ}C$ ($4,844^{\circ}F$). **580**

In 1984, researchers in Germany tested a 3.5 liter (214 in³) engine converted to run on either gasoline or hyrogen. Engine nitrous oxide emissions on hydrogen were found to be only 7% of those for gasoline. **700** R.G. Murray and R.J. Schaeppel at Oklahoma State University tested a hyrogen-injected single cylinder engine. The nitrous oxide emissions were only *one-fifth* the minimum for fossil fueled spark ignition engines of the same size.

The combustion temperature and nitrous oxide emissions increase with the

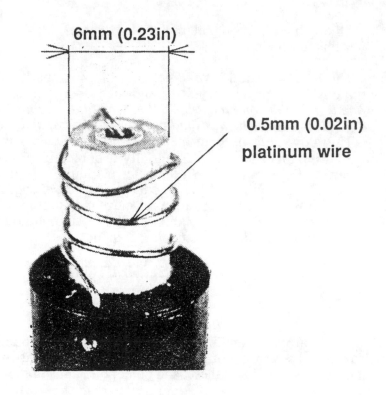

6mm (0.23in)

0.5mm (0.02in)
platinum wire

109. Impco Gas Mixer

Original gasoline carburetor used for water induction.

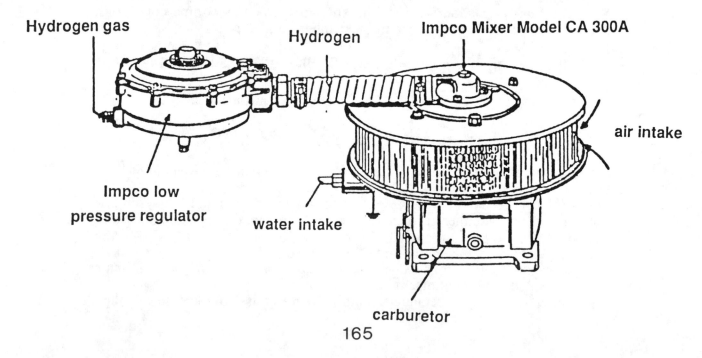

Hydrogen gas

Hydrogen

Impco Mixer Model CA 300A

air intake

Impco low
pressure regulator

water intake

carburetor

165

fuel/air mix (and the equivalency ratio). This relationship is exponential. In other words, slight increases in temperature bring much greater increases in nitrous oxide formation.

Water Induction

Internal combustion engines waste about two thirds of combustion energy as heat. Adding water to hydrocarbon fuels allows the heat of combustion to combine the oxygen in the water to unburned carbon in the exhaust. This produces a combination of hydrogen and carbon monoxide. The hydrogen then burns creating additional power and reduced pollution.

The induction of water vapor into the cylinder reduces the combustion temperature nitrous oxide formation. Nitrous oxides are reduced in increasingly large amounts for each small decrease in combustion temperature. Similarly, small increases in combustion temperature cause large increases in nitrous oxide formation. *"Water induction is an effective means of controlling nitrous oxide without loss of power, efficiency, or exhaust temperature. The effectiveness of water induction increases with rpm. "* **580p138**

It has been found that some cylinders of the same engine produce more nitrous oxide than others. With direct injection the equivalency ratio can be varied to each cylinder in response to individual emission characteristics. This is not possible with external mixing in carburetors where a uniform mixture is delivered to all cylinders. The nonuniformity of nitrous oxide formation from cylinder to cylinder requires a similar nonuniformity in water induction to compensate for this. With direct induction water vapor is mixed with the hydrogen before the introduction of air.

When the equivalency ratio exceeds 1.0 to 1.6 for maximum power output, the possibility of preignition is greatly increased due to hot residual gas or solid combustion residues such as oil ash. This can be remedied by the cooling effect of liquid hydrogen mixture formation or by water injection.

As water induction reduces combustion temperature it also reduces the probability of preignition and flashback. By reducing the reaction rate of hydrogen and air in the cylinder and increasing the energy needed for ignition, a larger range of mixtures may be used. Reducing the time, as well as the temperature, of combustion greatly reduces nitrous oxide emissions. This also serves to prolong engine life. Experimenters in India used a modified Bosch L-Jetronic water injector along with a Bosch-Motronic computerized engine injection control. **690p653-659**

More water is needed with higher engine rpm. To accomodate this fact experimenters in Germany varied the water induction rate with engine rpm. No water is inducted at engine speeds up to 2,000 rpm and 140 Nm (1,033 ft.lb.). Up to 4,000 rpm and 220 Nm (1,623 ft.lb.) the water induction rate was varied from 1 gram/second to 8 gram/second (0.0023 lb/s to 0.018 lb/s). **710p725**

The standard gas tank, carburetor, and fuel pump may be adapted for water. **Exhibit 109** shows an externally mixed hydrogen-converted engine with water injection. The hydrogen fuel and water enter the gas mixer through different ports. Two spray nozzles are installed on each side of the intake manifold just below the plenum chamber throttle plate. The water flow rate must be adjusted to avoid excess water leaking past the piston rings.

Exhaust Temperature and Combustion Efficiency

The higher the temperature of a heat engine compared to the exhaust temperature the higher the efficiency will be.

$$\text{Thermal Efficiency} = \frac{\text{High temp. - Low temp.}}{\text{High temp. - Abs. Zero}}$$

Where:

High Temp.   = maximum combustion temperature.
Abs. zero   = -273°C (-459°F).
Low Temp.   = exhaust temperature.

The lower the exhaust temperature the greater the proportion of combustion energy that is converted to mechanical work. An operating temperature of 2,670°C (4,838°F) with an exhaust temperature of 500°C (932°F) implies an efficiency of 74%. Reducing the exhaust temperature to 300°C (572°F) raises the efficiency to 81%.

Exhibit 110 shows the effects of compression ratio and engine load on exhaust temperature in one engine experiment. Exhaust temperature is used as a measure of engine efficiency. The engine was run on gasoline as well as on hydrogen. The results for the two fuels are shown. Increasing the compression ratio improves engine efficiency. More energy is converted to turning the drive shaft and less is sent out the exhaust pipe. **545**

Cryogenic Cooling

Liquid hydrogen avoids the need for water induction for both internal and external mixing. This was prooven in tests for speeds up to 5,000 rpm. The cooling effect of liquid hydrogen was found equivalent to water induction in reducing nitrous oxides. The liquid hydrogen tank was under a pressure of 247 atm (25MPa, 3,630 psi). A pressure regulator in the fuel line reduced this pressure to 19.7 atm (2 MPa, 290 psi). A second pressure regulator reduced this pressure still further to 3 atm (0.3 MPa, 44 psi).

Exhaust Gas Recirculation

Another method to reduce engine hot spots and nitrous oxide emissions is to recirculate the engine exhaust back to the combustion chamber. In experiments by Finegold, 35% of the exhaust was recycled. Combustion temperature and nitrous exode emissions fell, but so did engine power.

In conjunction with the development of a hydrogen fueled farm tractor the relative effectiveness of different methods of fuel dilution were measured. The engine was tested in three modes.

- No fuel dilution.
- Exhaust gas recirculation with the rate adjusted to maximize power.
- Water injection adjusted for maximum power.

The brake thermal efficiency was indicated by measuring the fuel consumption. This data was collected from a gas Rotometer corrected for temperature and pressure. Power was measured at the drive shaft by a water-cooled friction type dynamometer. The fuel consumption was 7.9 kWh/kg (4.8 hp·hr/lb). The maximum power without backfire was 19.4 kW (26 hp) at 1,800 rpm. This was 67% of gasoline power.

Exhibits 111 and **112** summarize the test results. Water induction increased power more than exhaust gas recirculation at both full and partial loads. The thermal efficiency of the engine was lower with either water injection or with exhaust gas recirculation. The highest efficiencies were achieved with no fuel dilution.

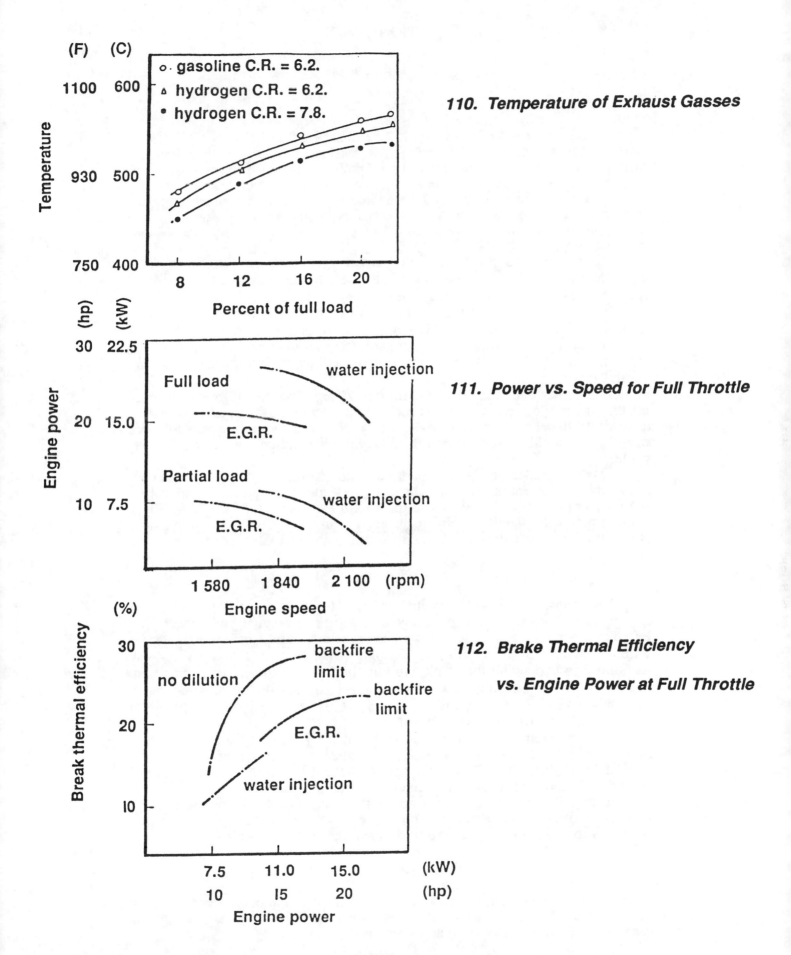

110. Temperature of Exhaust Gasses

111. Power vs. Speed for Full Throttle

112. Brake Thermal Efficiency

vs. Engine Power at Full Throttle

168

IGNITION TIMING

Spark Advance

The flame speed of hydrogen is 2.87 m/s. (9.4 ft/s). This is 10 times the flame speed for gasoline. Because it burns faster, hydrogen may backfire through the intake valve unless the ignition timing is modified for hydrogen fuel. The spark advance is moved close to the top dead center of the cranking angle.

Increased timing exponentially increases combustion temperature, and thereby, nitrous oxide formation. Decreasing the ignition advance reduces power. However, a tradeoff between reduced power and nitrous oxide emissions can be made.

Spark advance must be varied *inversely* with any changes in the equivalency ratio. If a fixed e.r. is used, the spark timing may also be fixed at all rpm and manifold vacuum settings. 330

The *lean best torque setting* for various e.r. values is shown in **Exhibit 113**. 1030 These figures should be regarded only as approximations. **Exhibit 114** summarizes experimental results indicating an *inverse relation* between spark advance and e.r. The tests were conducted under three different c.r. and engine speeds, as shown. 560

If the spark advance is too high, *backfiring* through the manifold may occur. If the spark advance is set too low, it may cause *delayed combustion* instead. With delayed combustion the fuel is still burning when the exhaust valve opens. This could cause overheating of the valve and preignition during the next cycle.

Once found, the optimum spark advance can remain constant from 0 to 5,000 rpm. The optimum spark advance does not seem to depend upon fuel temperature. The advance used for mixtures over 373 $^{\circ}$C (703 $^{\circ}$F) is approximately the same as for hydrogen at ambient temperature. Similarly, there is no significant difference for liquid hydrogen or for internal or externally mixed fuel.

Spark Gap

Less energy is needed to ignite hydrogen, therefore,less voltage is needed for the spark plugs. Reduced voltage also serves to prevent preignition. W. Peschka reports on a hydrogen conversion experiment using a spark plug gap of 1 mm (0.04 in). Bosch W300 T2 spark plugs were used. 690 W.C. VanVorst recommends narrowing the spark gap one-third to one-fourth the normal gap distance, thereby reducing the spark energy needed. 200 Billings, with his 6.6 liter (400 in^3) Pontiac V8, reduced the gap to 0.015 mm (0.0006 in). Finegold used a width of 0.012 mm (0.0005 in).

The researchers also recommended that the plug electrodes must have *square and clean edges* , otherwise excess voltage is required for them to work.

If an engine, normally used at heavy loads, is being place in a light load condition, it may be necessary to increase the spark gap slightly.

It may also be necessary to increase the spark gap when driving for long period of times at higher altitudes in order to compensate for the increased voltage necessary to overcome the higher electrical resistance of thinner air.

Avoiding Cross Induction

When a spark plug is being fired the voltage in the cable may induce a voltage in another spark plug cable. This is most likely if the spark cables touch each other. Several precautions are necessary.

113. Lean Best Torque Setting

	Equivalence Ratio (fuel/air mix)	Spark Advance (degrees before top dead center)
	0.45	24
	0.60	14
	0.85	7
	1.00	2

114. Spark Advance at Various Fuel Mixtures

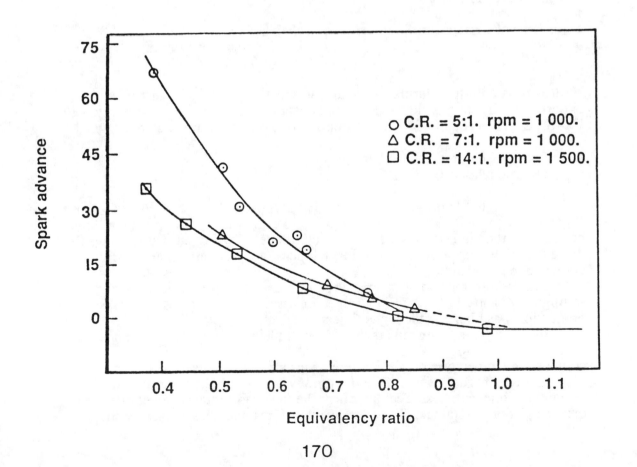

170

- Shield the ignition cables. Billings used a high temperature silicone radio suppression type. Tygon tubing slip covers is another alternative. **1030**
- Alter the ignition system to ground all plugs not being fired.
- Make sure the ignition cables do not run parallel to one another.
- Use heavily insulated cables. **201**

The Ignition Sequence

The manual vacuum switch or ignition switch is used to activate the fuel supply solenoid switches mounted on the fuel lines. This insures a fuel supply while the engine is cranking.

In one experiment, a relief valve is mounted between the solenoid shut off valve and the manual shut off valve. The relief valve used was a Nupro SS-4CA-3. The valve is activated at 2.2 atm (0.22 MPa, 32 psi). **1030**

HYDROGEN AS A SUPPLEMENTAL FUEL

Diesel and Hydrogen

The mixture of hydrogen with diesel fuel has been found to reduce smoke, hydrocarbons and nitrous oxides in the exhaust. The higher the proportion of hydrogen in the fuel mix the lower the level of pollutants. The following are specifications for an engine tested with simultaneous diesel and hydrogen fuel.

- Single cylinder.
- 4-stroke.
- Air-cooled.
- Bore: 75mm (3 in).
- Stroke: 75 mm (3 in).
- Compression ratio: 20:1
- Injection advance: 21°.
- Type of combustion chamber: pre chamber.
- Rated power: 4.5 kW (6 hp) at 3,000 rpm.
                                              4.1 kW (5.5 hp) at 2,600 rpm.

Hydrogen is admitted during the intake stroke along with air. During any one experiment, hydrogen flow was kept constant. The results, summarized in **Exhibits 115, 116**, and **117**, are given for two different flows of hydrogen:

- 35 grams/hour (0.08 lb/hour).
- 60 grams/hour (0.13 lb/hour).

The effect of hydrogen is greater at lower rpm and high load. At 2,600 rpm (high load) the exhaust contains more smoke than at 3,000 rpm (low load) because of the high flame speed and reaction rate of hydrogen that shortens the diesel combustion period, increasing temperature dissipation, and increasing combustion turbulance.

Smoke production was measured for two different injection advance settings: 20° and 21.5^o. A 5% hydrogen mix was used for both settings. Smoke production was higher at the higher injection advance setting.

Increasing the hydrogen content in diesel fuel was found to cause knock and reduced power output. Water induction remedied the knock problem by reducing combustion temperature but further reductions were experienced.

Hydrogen fuel was injected along with air, then compressed. The researchers injected diesel fuel later near the top dead center using conventional diesel injection equipment. The experimenters found that diesel conversions

171

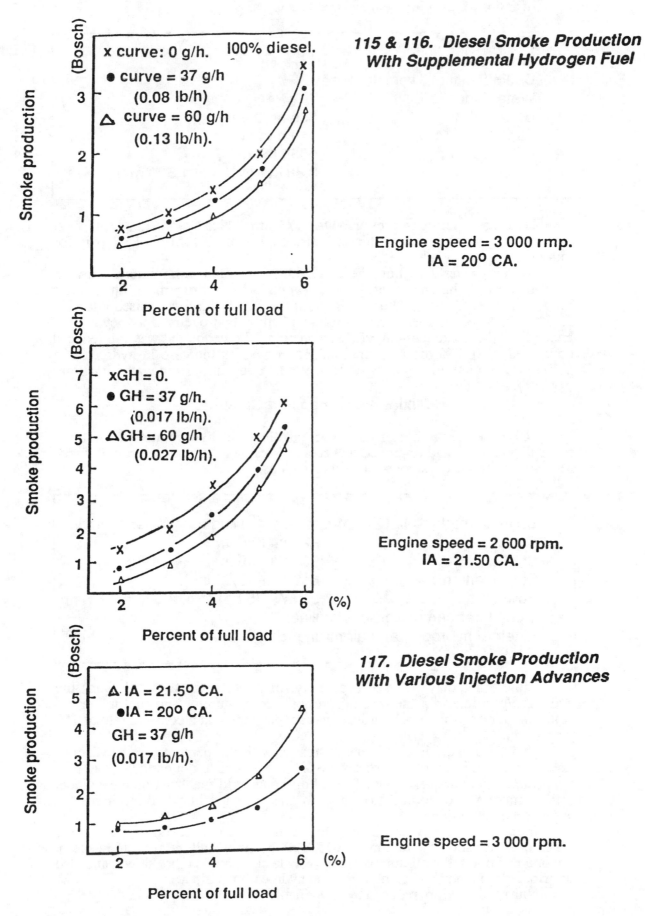

115 & 116. Diesel Smoke Production With Supplemental Hydrogen Fuel

Engine speed = 3 000 rmp.
IA = 20° CA.

Engine speed = 2 600 rpm.
IA = 21.50 CA.

117. Diesel Smoke Production With Various Injection Advances

Engine speed = 3 000 rpm.

172

allowed easier uninterrupted fuel selection than spark ignition engines. Specifications for the diesel engine used in this test were:

One cylinder.
Water cooled.
Direct injection, verticle diesel.
Water induction.
Bore: 80mm (3.2 in).
Stroke: 110 mm (4.3 in).
Displacement: 553 cm^3 (33.7 in^3).
Power: 3.68 kW (5 hp) at 1,500 rpm.

Hydrogen delivery pressure was 173 atm (17.5 MPa, 2,538 psi). A pressure regulator reduced this pressure to 1 atm (0.1 MPa, 14.7 psi) for introduction into the manifold.

With no water induction, the knock limit was found with mixtures between 50 and 84% of the fuel energy being supplied by hydrogen. With a water induction rate of 7 liters / hour (1.8 gal/h) the knock limit was raised allowing 53.5 to 87.5% of the fuel energy to be supplied by hydrogen. Only beyond the knock limit did brake thermal efficiency increase. Power output was still reduced compared to 100 % diesel operation. There was an increase in hydrocarbon pollution from unburnt fuel due to temperature quenching from water injection.
730p177-186

Mixing Hydrogen and Gasoline

Chinese researchers found that gasoline and hydrogen fuel mixtures reduced pollutants and improved fuel economy using lean mixtures of both fuels. The engine used had the following specifications.

Chinese made "492 Q".   4-stroke.   4 cylinder.   Water cooled.
Bore: 92 mm (3.6 in).
Stroke: 92 mm (3.6 in)
Displacement: 612 cm^3 (37.3 in^3).
Power: 56 kW (75 hp) at 4,000 rpm.
2 chamber carburetor for gasoline.
External hydrogen and air mixing for hydrogen fuel.

Either fuel may be used separately, or simultaneously. To vary the hydrogen/gasoline mix the throttles in both the carburetor and fuel mixer are adjusted. During the tests hydrogen was supplemented at a constant rate of 750 grams/hour (1.7 lb/hour).

Carbon monoxide emissions decreased with the percentage of hydrogen used. The amount of hydrocarbons in the exhaust depended upon fuel temperature and the quenching effects of the condensed fuel layer on the cylinder wall. Incomplete combustion due to these and other factors increases hydrocarbon emissions.

Increasing the fuel/air mixture reduces hydrocarbons up to the stoichiometric ratio (the mixture at which all the air and all the fuel are reacted). Beyond this point, the mixture is excessively lean. It burns more slowly and also contributes to incomplete combustion and hydrocarbon output.

Nitrous oxides are reduced by lowering the amount of oxygen in the fuel mix and reducing the temperature and duration of combustion.

Reducing oxygen tends to increase hydrocarbon emissions. Obviously, an optimum balance between the two pollutants must be found. Rapid burning reduces all pollutants.

"Experiments showed that adding a small amount of hydrogen to a gasoline-air mixture can make rapid buring and improvement of emission characteristics possible. "   Also,*"When hydrogen - gasoline mixed fuel is used in a multi-fuel engine, the emission characteristics are improved. "* Pure gasoline was found to have a consistently lower volume efficiency than hydrogen at all engine speeds than did gasoline and hydrogen mixtures. The experimenters found that engine efficiency *"Increased under all operating conditions, particularly under partial load conditions. This will be a very effective means of improvement of the fuel economy of automobiles. "* 545

Information gathered by the American Hydrogen Association, under the direction of Roy McAlister, shows that hydrogen can reduce polluting emissions when used in combination with standard hydrocarbon fuels. This is because hydrogen breaks down larger hydrocarbon molecules creating a larger surface-to-volume ratio allowing oxygen to more completely burn the components.   567

Selective Use of Hydrogen or Gasoline

In Germany, Mercedes Benz converted a car to dual fuel hydrogen and gasoline operation. **See Exhibit 118.** BMW also converted a sedan to dual fuel hydrogen and gasoline. The fuel tank can be seen in **Exhibit 63. Exhibits 119, 120,** and **121** show the engine compartment, and the intake manifold and injectors. 710p727-728 Specifications for the vehicle are given below.

Storage system : LH$_2$ tank 130 liter (34 gal), Empty
weight 70 kg (154 lb), boil-off rate 1.7%
per day. Gasoline tank 22 liter (5.8 gal).

Engine: 3.5liter(214in^3).External mixing, lean
mixure, exhaust gas turbocharger,
computer controlled ignition timing, fuel
mixing and water injection, dual fuel

Power output on hydrogen : 115 kW (154 hp) at 5,000 rpm.
Power on gasoline : 180 kW (241 hp) at 5,000 rpm.
Top speed on hydrogen : 160 km/hour (100 mi/hour).
Top speed on gasoline : 230 km/hour (143 mi/hour).
Nitrous oxide with hydrogen : 0.27 gram per ECE (6 X 10^{-4} lb).
Nitrous oxide with gasoline : 2.5 gram per ECE (6 X 10^{-3} lb).
Range with hydrogen : 400 km (250 mi).
Range with gasoline : 160 km (100 mi).

The liquid hydrogen tank was fabricated from an aluminum-magnesium alloy (Al$_{3.5}$Mn) by Messer Griesheim GmbH. A safety valve vents the tank if the pressure exceeds 2.5 atm (0.3 MPa, 36.7 psi). The fuel is fed through vacuum insulated lines and activated by a solenoid valve. A heat exchanger vaporizes the fuel.

A turbocharger boosts the fuel pressure to 0.5 atm (0.05 MPa, 7.3 psi) at 2,000 rpm. Fuel flow rate, fuel pressure , and equivalency ratios are varied according to engine demand by an engine load management system controlled by

118. BMW 745i Experimental Vehicle

119. *Engine Compartment of Hydrogen BMW 745i*

(Photo courtesy of DFVLR.)

120. Intake Manifold of BMW 745i

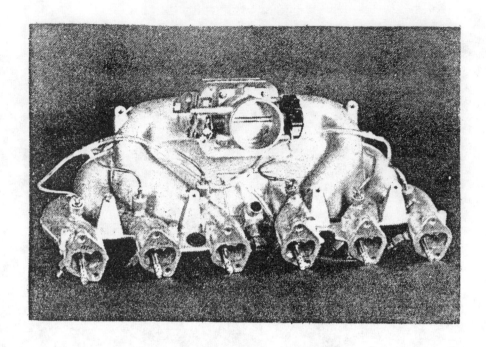

121. Computerized Engine Control System for BMW 745i

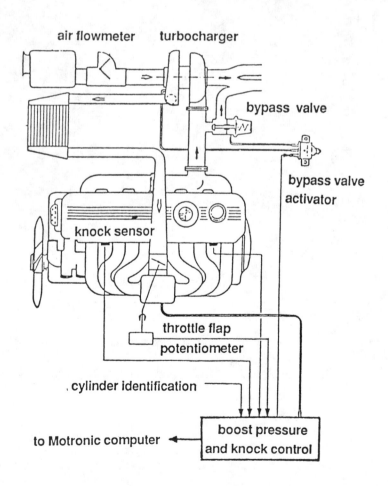

a Motronic microcomputer. Sensors located at different points on the vehicle feed information the the computer on:

- Intake air flow (an indicator of engine load).
- Engine speed.
- When the crank angle reaches top dead center.
- Cylinder identification.
- Intake air temperature.
- Cooling water temperature.
- When engine knock begins to occur.
- Turbocharger boost pressure.

Ignition timing and the fuel injection rate are easily programmed for either gasoline or hydrogen. Either fuel, or a mixture of both, can be selected.

A standard Motronic engine control computer was supplied with an additional memory storing the hydrogen fuel ignition sequence. See **Exhibits 122** and **123**. It is activated only when hydrogen is used. The electronic engine control facilitates easy switching from one fuel to another.

During hydrogen operation the *fuel/air ratio* is varied but not the *volume* of fuel. The engine is unthrottled. The throttling flap in the intake manifold is bypassed during hydrogen operation. The air input no longer automatically depends upon the fuel flow rate. With hydrogen fuel, the air flow is *manually governed*. The air flow meter signal which is an indicator of changing load conditions with gasoline fuel. With hydrogen it is ignored. A sensor activated by the accelerator pedal tells the control system about load conditions. Another control circuit that operates only with hydrogen fuel regulates the *water injection rate* .

At the Ninth World Hydrogen Energy Conference in 1992 at Paris, France, BMW propose a gasoline-hydrogen hybrid vehicle as the best near term compromise between the availability of gasoline and the environmental benefits of hydrogen. Hydrogen and gasoline would be used for stop and go driving in town while hydrogen alone would be used for long distance driving with few stops. According to the company they have the technology ready now.

Precision Spark Ignition

Roy E. McAlister, President of Trans Energy Corporations is developing a "kit" that will convert almost any car to run on either gasoline or hydrogen selectively. It is called the "Precision Spark Ignition" system. There is no power penalty for converting to hydrogen. It converts the car to stratified-charge, direct-injection with specially designed "smart plugs". The system permits improvements in fuel economy and engine efficiency of about 20 percent on gasoline. Hydrogen fuel can be added by installing a new fuel storage tank, safety valves, a pressure regulator, the PSI system "smart plugs" in place of the standard plugs, safety sensors, and the integration of the mechanical and electronic controls of the car. Trans Energy Corporation of Tempe, Arizona provides the PSI System, engine controllers, and "smart plugs". Manufacturers of components for storing and regulating natural gas supply the rest of the parts. Currently Trans Energy lends its expertise to a Hydrogen Racing Program under the direction of Demetri Wagner. According to McAlister, PSI technology allows engines to produce more power than with hydrocarbon fuels. [566]

PSI creates a stratified-charge combustion following the firing of the spark plugs. The air is admitted unthrottled into the combustion chamber to receive the largest amount possible. Fuel is injected into the air and at the same time is ignited by an electronically timed spark plug. Some parts of the cylinder have too much air for ideal combustion, other parts are fuel rich and have have too little air. The spark plugs ignite the fuel air mixture. When the burning fuel reaches the

178

excess air region of the cylinder flame speeds are increased. The flame speed is increased over what would occur if the fuel air mixture were uniform prior to spark ignition. Because of the unthrottled intake, "higher compression and power cycle pressures are developed". 565

Fuel and air are injected separately. Fuel is injected through the center of the PSI spark injector. As the fuel enters the cylinder it passes through the spark "flame" (a plasma) and the fuel is ignited. Combustion takes place after the intake valve is closed. Air in the fuel poor region of the cylinder surrounds the burning fuel. This serves to insulate the combustion region from the cooler cylinder and piston surfaces. A few milliseconds later the burning fuel expands into the fuel-poor, excess air region. The extra oxygen insures complete combustion. In other combustion in stratified-charge engines occurs at one part of the cylinder before it occurs at another. The flame front progresses from a fuel-rich region to a fuel-poor region. This staged form of combustion is different from regular engines where the fuel-air mixture detonates uniformly throughout the piston because the fuel-air mixture is uniform before ignition. PSI avoids the backfiring when using hydrogen that is common with homogenous mixture engines.

Stratified charge promotes more complete combustion, more power, and reduced emissions of unburned fuel components such as carbon monoxide, hydrocarbons and oxides of nitrogen. "Diesel and spark-ignition engines that have been modified to utilize PSI technology are able to burn efficiently fuel alcohols, diesel fuel, gasoline and L-P gases, or hydrogen interchangeably." 565 This is due to:

● Fuel is injected directly into the cylinder through the spark gas.
● The fuel flow is electronically controlled.
● A computer automatically adjusts the injection and ignition timing according to engine speed and load and the fuel used.

Herb Hayden of Trans Energy designed the electronic controls for PSI. PSI increases efficiency up to 10 percent for diesels and 20 to 50 percent for carbureted engines. "Fuel savings help amortize the cost of the system within months in many applications". 565 The unthrottled air of PSI reduces upper-cylinder vacuums, and thereby, increases engine power.

Cold weather startup is assured with the system. Engine power is limited under extreme starting conditions with throttled carburetors, not so with PSI. The burning fuel is insulated from the cylinder walls at the beginning of combustion. Heat energy is conserved at the beginning of combustion. The excess air allows fuel to burn more completely. Auxiliary air pumps, catalytic mufflers, and particulate filters may be eliminated.

The PSI system combines the functions of a fuel injector and spark plug. In Diesel engines this is an advantage. Diesels ordinarily don't have spark plugs . Compression is used to ignite the fuel-air mixture. In cold weather this can lead to delayed combustion due to heat loss through the cold cylinder wall.
In summary, PSI has the following advantages:

● The cylinders no longer have produce vacuum to "suck" in the fuel. Power is saved.
● Increased air intake promotes complete combustion.
● Heat loss during early combustion is reduced.
● Ignition occurs later but combustion is faster. This prevents early detonation from working against the rising piston during the power stroke.

According to Roy McAlister of Trans Energy Corp., combining water injection with the hydrocarbon fuel to produce carbon monoxide and hydrogen to boost power and the use of PSI can lead to 50 percent improvement in fuel economy compared to homogeneous-charge engines. 565

122. Diagram of the Engine Control System Microprocessor

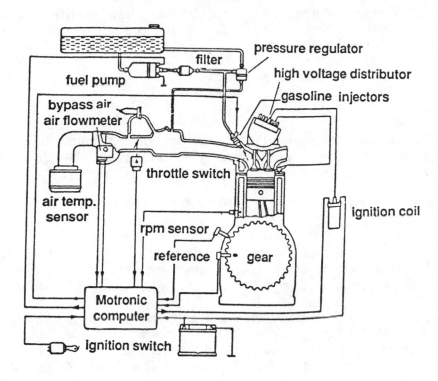

123. Operation Principal of the Motronic Computer

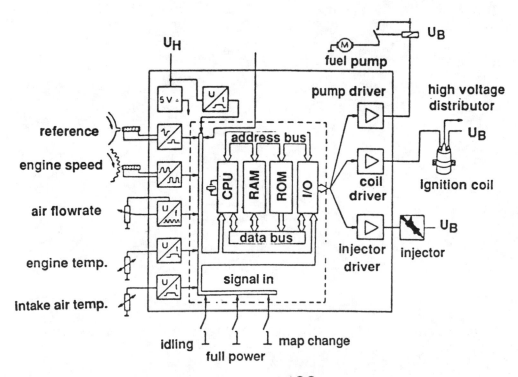

CONTINUOUS FLOW ENGINES

A Pratt and Whitney J-57 gas turnine was converted to liquid hydrogen. The researcher concluded that "*the stable operation of the J-57 confirmed that conventional gas turbines could be readily adapted to hydrogen fuel*". **580p140** Continuous flow engines like turbojets require only slight modification to be converted to hydrogen fuel. Compared to piston engines, continuous flow engines have the following advantages.

- Relatively low pressurization is needed.
- A simple continuous injection process is used.
- There are no intake and exhaust valves.

A significant disadvantage is the accumulation of high temperature heat in the engine materials due to continuous unrelieved combustion. **200** However, if liquid hydrogen is used as the fuel, the cryogenic properties can be used to cool the engine.

In another experiment, a Pratt and Whitney 304 jet engine was converted to hydrogen. The expanding liquid hydrogen helps turn the compressor while combustion energy provided thrust. *All performance predictions for this engine were confirmed within the first 25 hours when the project was terminated in 1958*

The Saturn Rocket Booster uses liquid hydrogen under 58 atm (6895 MPa, 1,000 psi). The low-temperature properties of the liquid hydrogen is used in the thrust chamber cooling jacket.

"*Hydrogen fueled engine research and development is far from complete; however the preliminary efforts performed to date indicate that all existing engine types can be operated with hydrogen. All of these engines appear to be capable of excellent performance characteristics at very low levels of pollution.*" **580p140-140**

Exhibit 124 gives a summary of major experiments in running internal combustion engines on hydrogen fuel. **580p154-164**

Investigator	Number Cy'der	Displacement	C.R.	Speed (rpm)	Power (kW)	Power Pis.area	E.R.	Eff. (%)	MEP (MPa)	NO$_x$ (ppm)
Tizard	1	2.1	-----	-----	-----	-----	-----	-----	-----	-----
Ricardo	1	2.1	5.45	1,500	26.9	0.26	0.9	33	0.51	-----*
							0.9	40	-----	-----**
Burstall	1	2.1	7.0	1,000	14.0	0.14	0.85	37	0.81	-----
							0.50	38	0.53	-----
Erren	-----	-----	8.0	-----	-----	-----	-----	45	-----	0
							-----	45	-----	0
Omichen	----	-----	12.0	1,500	-----	-----	-----	-----	-----	----
								52		
King	1	0.6	20.0	1,800	9	0.17	1.0	38	0.99	-----
							0.39	52	0.41	-----
Downs	1	0.5	20.0	1,500	-----	-----	-----	-----	-----	-----
Anzilloti	1	0.6	12.0	900	-----	-----	-----	-----	-----	-----
Holvenstot	8	63.1	8.0	550	162	0.06	1.0	29	0.57	-----
Karim	1	0.6	20.0	900	-----	-----	-----	-----	-----	-----
Swain	4	1.6	9.0	2,600	11.9	-----	-----	-----	0.35	1,900
Billings	1	0.1	5.5	2,900	1.2	0.04	0.9	33	0.46	7,000
							0.5	34	0.37	2.5
Adt	4	3.2	10	1,400	5.1	0.02	0.28	17	0.13	2.2
Finegold	8	5.8	8.9	-----	-----	-----	-----	-----	-----	-----
Adt	8	3.2	10	1,450	12.5	0.04	0.47	25	0.32	-----
							0.37	28	0.26	-----
Breshears	8	-----	-----	2,000	-----	-----	-----	-----	-----	-----
							0.35	39	-----	-----
Finegold	8	5.7	8.5	1,500	32.1	0.05	0.6	31	0.45	12
Stobar	1	0.6	8	1,200	1.0	0.02	0.2	40	23	13
Thomas	4	2.3	8	2,500	9	0.04	-----	23	0.19	-----
Erren	-----	-----	8	-----	-----	-----	-----	45	-----	-----
								45	-----	0
Murray	1	0.1	6.5	4,000	2.1	0.07	1.89	12	0.52	340
							0.78	17	0.43	752
Morgan	1	0.05	12.7	4,000	3.8	0.35	6	32	1.31	-----

* Top row of figures for E.R., Efficiency, MEP, and Exhaust NO$_x$ are measured at the maximum reported power.
** Bottom row of figures are for the maximum reported efficiency.

Chapter 7:
ELECTRICITY FROM HYDROGEN

ALMOST 100 years ago electric cars were introduced to a public skeptical about any means of transportation that didn't draw flies. For a time electric cars competed for public favor with internal combustion engines. By 1920 the gasoline-powered engine prevailed over all other transportation technologies. The electric car's demise was not due to the electric motor. The efficiency of electric motors is between two and three times that of internal combustion engines. The weak link in electric vehicle technology is the battery. There is not, as yet, any means of storing electrical energy that can come close to the energy density of combustible fuels.

HYDROGEN VS ELECTRIC POWER

Exhibit 125 presents the results of a study comparing hydrogen fuel with electric batteries. Present and future improvements were anticipated in both hydrogen and battery technology in the years 1990 and 2000. The researchers also considered capital costs, service life, efficiency, power output, recharge time and energy storage density.

Taking into consideration the use of the cryogenic properties of liquid hydrogen to cool an internal combustion engine and to provide air conditioning, the researchers concluded that this fuel provided the lightest weight, cheapest operating costs, best range and lowest energy consumption (including its manufacture) of all the non petroleum fuels studied.

FeTi hydride was found to be competitive with liquid hydrogen in 1990 but not in 2000.

Current lead acid batteries were worst in all categories. Future nickle-zinc and zinc-chloride batteries were best in overall efficiency in using the electric energy generated from nuclear fuel. This takes into account an electric vehicle's use of *regenerative breaking* . This feature uses the deacceleration force during breaking to feed current back into the batteries. This strategy can increase an electric vehicle's range by 8 to 13%. However, the use of on-board battery-powered accessories can reduce the range from 14 to 25%. In the year 2000 lithium-aluminum and iron sulfide batteries were predicted to be comparable in cost of maintenance to liquid hydrogen. This assumes a 20% improvement over the efficiency of zinc-chloride batteries in 1990. **201p70** Even with the most up-to-date technology the figures are not encouraging.

Propulsion System	Range		Weight		Cost		Energy	
	(km)	(mI)	(kg)	(lb)	($/km)	(mi)	(kWh/km)	(mi)
1985 MODEL YEAR								
LH2 I.C. Engine	137	85	1007	2220	20.9	13.0	1.24	0.77
FeTi I.C. Engine	137	85	1334	2940	26.4	16.4	1.40	0.87
Lead Acid Battery	103	64	2140	4718	29.1	18.1	1.11	0.69
Nickle-Zinc Battery	130	81	1587	3499	28.6	17.8	0.90	0.557
1990 MODEL YEAR								
LH2 I.C. Engine	137	85	953	2100	19.6	12.2	0.85	0.53
FeTi I.C. Engine	137	85	1243	2740	23.7	14.7	1.18	0.74
Advanced Hydride	137	85	1200	2640	24.6	15.3	1.47	0.91
Zinc-Cl. Battery	179	111	1476	3254	25.7	16.0	0.84	0.52
2000 MODEL YEAR								
LH2 I.C. Engine	137	85	860	1896	18.8	11.7	0.71	0.44
Advanced Hydride	137	85	1061	2340	23.2	14.4	1.24	0.77
LiAl/FeS2 Battery	150	93	975	2149	18.7	11.6	0.41	0.26

For an electric car with a range of 500 km (310 mi.) lead-acid batteries would weigh about 3,000 kg (6,600 lb). General Motors plans to market an electric car called the "Impact" before the turn of the century. The advanced lead-acid batteries in the car would weigh just 40 percent of that. More advanced zinc-air batteries would reduce the weight of electric vehicles powered with today's lead-acid batteries by one-sixth.

Utilities produce electricity at about 30 to 40 percent efficiency. They also produce about 35 percent of the CO_2 emissions, transportation produces 30 percent. Only about 20 percent of the U.S. electricity production comes from nuclear and a much smaller percent from hydroelectric plants. These produce virutally no air prollution. With coal-fired plants cars indirectly produce pollution and operate at a much lower overall efficiency. This is inspite of the electric motors's 80 percent efficiency compared to 30 to 40 percent for the internal combustion engine. efficiency.

The only way to take full advantage of the electric motor's efficiency and low environmental impact is to use renewable sources of energy such as hydroelectric plants, wind-driven generators, and various forms of solar power.

Although coal-fired utilities are inefficient and polluting at lease they have the virtue of using energy sources that we control. We don't have to fight wars to keep our lights burning.

THE HYDRIDE BATTERY

Perhaps the best way to store electricity is to use hydrogen. The U.S. Department of Energy, the auto industry, and several public utilities have joined together to form the Advanced Battery Consortium. They have given their first.

development grant to the Ovionic Battery Co. of Troy, Michigan. The company won the $18 million contract award in competition with 60 other designs. The winning design is a nickle hydride battery. The design has been tested at 80 wH per kilogram. An earlier Japanese design was rated at 70 wH/kg. This compares with 30 to 35 wH/kg for lead acid batteries. The new technology is half the volume and half the weight of nickel cadmium batteries. This gives a range of double or triple that with conventional batteries.

Gasoline has 200 wH/kg, apparently an insurmountable obstacle for battery technology. But electric motors are about 2.5 times as efficient as internal combustion engines. This gives the new Ovionic technology an effective energydensity of 2.5 X 80 wH/kg or approximately the same as gasoline.

In 1987 Ovionics produced the world's first nickle hydride battery. It was subsequently used in electronic devices. The company has finished testing an experimental cell. They plan to install and test a larger battery in a car. The new technology achieves its remarkable performance from an amorphous mix of hydride materials: vanadium, titanium, zirconium, and nickel.

The battery is charged by electrolysing water into hydrogen and hydroxyl ions (OH^-). The hydrogen is absorbed into the crystalline structure of the hydride. The hydroxyl ions migrate to the nickel hydroxide electrode. The electrode is then oxydized to nickel-oxy-hydroxide.

During discharge the reverse occurs. Hydrogen is oxydized into water. Electrons are released in the process and are conducted between the terminals to power a load. At the positive terminal nickel-oxy-hydroxide is converted back into nickel hydroxide.

An earlier Japanese design used Magnesium Nickel hydride ($MnNi_5$).

Ovionics has seven Japanese and eight worldwide patents on its system.

FUEL CELLS

Reactions

Electrolysis generates hydrogen from electricity, fuel cells create an electricity from the combustion of hydrogen. A fuel cell is a reverse electrolyser.

Exhibit 126 shows the operation of a hydrogen-oxygen fuel cell. Comparing this diagram with **Exhibit 3** (*Schematic of a Hydrogen-Oxygen Electrolyser*) we see that hydrogen enters on the anode side and oxygen enters on the cathode side. Water, hydrogen and oxygen leave the cell. Instead of current flowing *into* the electrolyser, current flows *from* the fuel cell.

Both electrical storage batteries and fuel cells convert chemical energy to electrical energy - directly. Batteries run down but fuel cells may operate as long as a supply of fuel and oxygen is available.

The chemical reactions that govern a hydrogen-oxygen fuel cell are given below. The reaction at the anode is:

$$2H_2 + 4OH^- \longrightarrow 4H_2O + 4 \text{ electrons.}$$

At the cathode the reaction is:

$$O_2 + 4 \text{ electrons} + 2H_2O \longrightarrow 4OH^-.$$

The overall reaction is:

$$2H_2 + O_2 \longrightarrow 2H_2O.$$

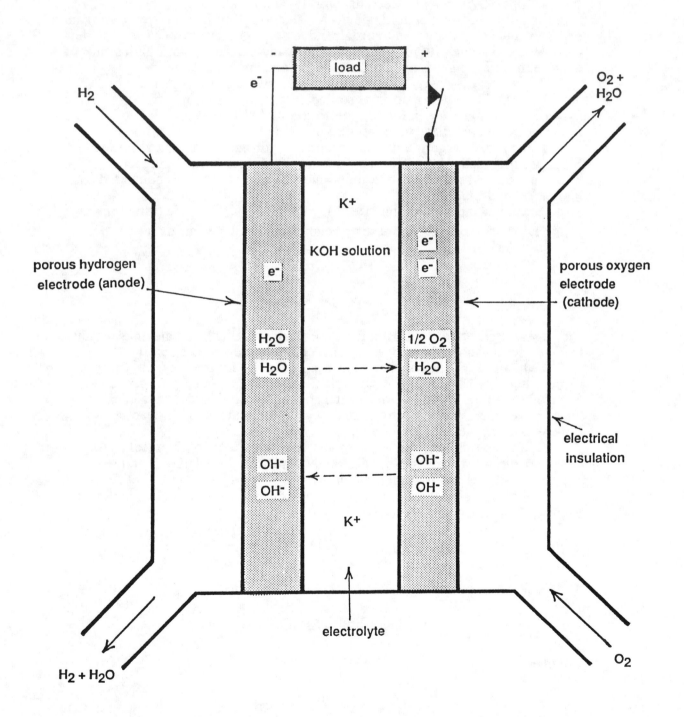

Hydroxyl ions (OH⁻) flow from cathode to anode through the electrolyte. Electrons flow from anode to cathode through the *external circuit* . When the external circuit is broken, the cell stops.

If the cell is 100% efficient, the energy from one mole of water produced in a fuel cell is 66 Wh. One kWh of energy is produced from every 421 grams (0.9 lb) of water in the exhaust. Output voltage is 1.23 volt (similar to the input voltage for 100% efficiency electrolysis).

In practice, fuels cells are currently 73 to 90% efficient. Compare this with a maximum of 55% for steam power. Output voltages range from 0.7 to 1.12 volt. Typical cell voltage varies with the current density of the electrical output .

Current Density (Amps/square meter)	Voltage (Volts)
11	1.01
108	0.95
538	0.70

For fuel cells up to 15kW the current output is typically 50 to 100 mA/cm^3 (819 to 1,639 mA/ in^3) of water produced.

As with electrolysers, fuel cells may be connected in *series* to boost voltage or *parallel* to boost current.

Fuel cells were developed in 1939 by Sir William Grove, in England. It wasn't until NASA space program in the 1960's that fuel cells were used for a practical purpose. The Gemini and Apollo spacecraft used hydrogen-oxygen fuel cells to generate electrical power and a pure water supply used on board.

Materials

Electrolytes may be acids, bases, or salts. For hydrogen-oxygen fuel cells potassium hydroxide (KOH) is less corrosive and gives higher cathode voltages. Phosphoric acid electrolyte is used with hydrocarbon fuels.

Air may be used as a source of oxygen but nitrogen and other gasses dilute the effect of oxygen at the cathode. Oxygen makes up only 20% of the air. Contaminants in the air poison catalysts, thereby increasing maintenance costs. In spite of this, the ready availability of air eliminates the cost of separating pure oxygen from the atmoshpere.

Fuel cell catalysts assist the ionizaion of fuel and oxygen. Many catalyst materials are precious metals such as platinum, palladium, or rhodium. Nickle, however, may be used with hydrogen-oxygen fuel cells. Catalysts with low *ion exchange current densities* minimize the *activation potential* . In other words, these catalysts minimize the build up of charges at the electrode-electrolyte interface. **170p151-157**

Electrodes are typically made of plastic bonded composites of teflon, platinum and carbon compressed and heated into thin durable sheets. This process prevents water saturation of porous electrode materials yet allows them to remain porous to gas. In general, electrode materials should combine the properties of *thickness*, *low electrical resistance* and *porosity*. Minimizing thickness and electrical resistance also reduces *ohmic polarization* . This is a potential that builds up across the electrode due to the electrode resistance to current flow. Reducing the thickness of electrodes to 0 . 0001 cm (0.000004 in) helps minimize *concentration polarization* . This is the build up concentrated charges in the electrolyte on either side of the electrode. **580**

Solid Electrolyte

The Argonne National Laboratory in Illinois is developing a solid electrolyte fuel cell. The new light weight cell would be ideal for automotive applications. It is designed to burn hydrocarbon fuels, particularly methanol, in air at 800° to 1,000°C (1,470° to 1,800°F).

At elevated temperatures, hydrocarbon fuels breakdown into hydrogen and carbon oxides in a process called *reforming*. The hydrocarbon fuel is a carrier for hydrogen, the actual fuel used in the cell.

The solid electrolyte greatly reduces weight. The researchers used *yttria stabilized zirconium oxide* in a ceramic-type material.

A cross section of the cell is shown in **Exhibit 127**. The cells are stacked in layers like corrugated cardboard. The entire array is a "sandwich" of individual cells connected in series. Each layer adds to the voltage of the next. This voltage is tapped on both sides of the fuel cell. The negative pole is on one side and the positive pole is on the other.

Electrons released from the anode travel accross the interconnection material to the cathode of the next cell above. The cathode releases oxygen ions through the electrolyte to the anode to repeat the process. Current flows in this zig-zag path until it reaches the surface of the cell stack.

This arrangement is an improvement on an earlier Westinghouse prototype. The new cell has shorter current pathways to reduce resistance. The main problem the researchers face is in keeping the different components, which have different rates of thermal expansion, together at high temperatures. With recent tests, this does not appear to be an insurmountable problem.

Garrett Ceramics Corp. intends to develope mass production of fuel cells utilizing this technology.

A cube 38 cm (15 in) on each side can deliver 50 kW (67 hp).

Automotive Applications

The fuel cell cannot produce torque. It cannot be used directly in vehicles to turn the drive wheels. Like storage batteries, a fuel cell can provide current to an *electric motor*. Unlike batteries, a fuel cell delivers far more power at a substantially less weight penalty. Fuel cells in cars may be 60 percent efficient. Combined with an electric motor's 80 percent efficiency, the overall efficiency of a fuel cell vehicle would be 48% - almost twice that of an internal combustion engine.

Electric motors have a higher power-to-weight ratio than internal combustion engines, and also have twice the efficiency. Fuel cells are 50 to 70% efficient compared to 35 to 38% for fossil fuel internal combustion engines. 80 to 90% efficiencies are expected with advanced technology. A fuel cell in combination with an electric motor has *twice* the efficiency of an engine powered by gasoline or diesel fuel. **940p105**

The cost of hydrogen from advanced electrolysis is about one-third more costly than natural gas. Adding delivery charges and other costs of making the fuel available to the consumer, the costs of hydrogen become twice as much as diesel fuel or natural gas. However, if hydrogen fuel is used in an electric vehicle to power a *fuel cell,* hydrogen is equivalent in cost to premium gasoline and half the cost of using hydrogen with an internal combustion engine. **180**

In 1964 General Motors experimented with a fuel cell-powered *Electrobus*. The vehicle used potassium hydroxide electroltye and liquid oxygen to avoid electrolyte contamination with carbon dioxide.

Dr. Karl Kordesch in 1970 converted a 1961 Austin A-40 four passenger sedan. He combined a fuel cell with lead acid batteries for acceleration. The fuel cell was used for low speed and cruising. A device to remove carbon dioxide enabled the cell to use atmospheric oxygen. The electrical system is shown in

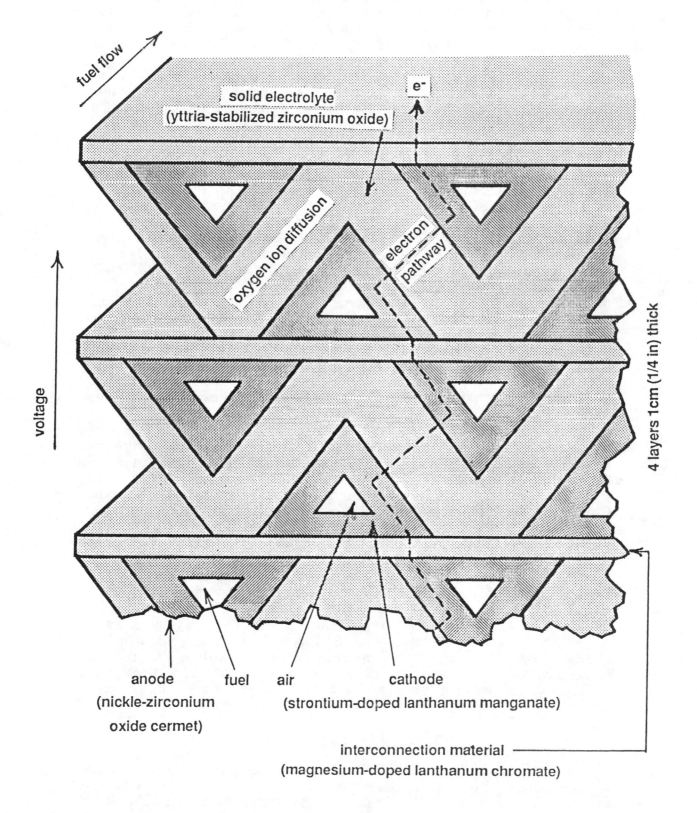

fuel flow

solid electrolyte
(yttria-stabilized zirconium oxide)

e⁻

oxygen ion diffusion

electron pathway

voltage

4 layers 1cm (1/4 in) thick

anode
(nickle-zirconium
oxide cermet)

fuel

air

cathode
(strontium-doped lanthanum manganate)

interconnection material
(magnesium-doped lanthanum chromate)

189

Exhibit 128. Exhibit 129 presents data showing how the batteries were charged and discharged at different speeds. The fuel cell is used for speeds up to 51.3 km/hour (32 mi/hour). At these speeds, the batteries are being charged. At higher speeds the batteries contribute a larger and larger proportion of the current used by the motor. A schematic drawing of the air-breathing Kordesch vehicle is shown in **Exhibit 130**.

Despite the inability of these experiments to reach commercialization, one researcher concludes that "*A hybrid fuel cell - battery vehicle could meet the performance standards of a conventional internal combustion engine while providing far more efficiency and less pollution*". **201,41** That assessment was made in 1977.

A Belgian - Dutch company, Elenco NV, in 1976 converted a VW van to hydrogen-powered fuel cells. They use a 30% solution of potassium hydroxide for the electrolyte. The electrolyte was circulated to promote cooling. It operated at 65°C (149°F) at atmospheric pressure. The electrodes were comprised of three layers. The first layer was a metal current collector. The second was a catalyst made up of platinum-coated carbon granules, and other constituents. The amount of platinum used was 0.7 mg/cm^2 (9 X 10^{-6} lb/in^2). A porous support structure formed the last layer.

Three stacks of fuel cell modules were used. Eight modules were used in each stack as shown in **Exhibit 131**. Each module had a plastic frame that contained 24 cells with two electrodes each. See **Exhibit 132** and **133**. Each electrode is 17 X 17 cm (6.7 X 6.7 in). Each module weighed 5 kg (11 lb), including the electrolyte. The dimensions were 26 X 25 X 16 cm (10 X 9.8 X 6.3 in). The total output of the fuel cells was 12 kW.

During the 8-year development program, the company improved the fuel cell's performance. **Exhibits 134** and **135** show the voltage-current output and voltage-time relationship of a 24 cell module at 65°C (149°F). At 0.67 volt the specific power of the modules is about 10 kg/kW (22 lb/kW) when using air. Higher performance could be expected using pure oxygen. The electrolyte was not changed during the period when the data was collected. Soda lime was used to remove carbon dioxide from the air. The vehicle's range was 200 km (124 mi) compared to 60 km (37 mi) with batteries, alone. **910p471-474**

In 1992, Dr. Paul Cherry of the American Academy of Science in Independence, Missouri has modified a compact car powered by a hydrogen fuel-cell. LaserCel 1 is a converted postal delivery vehicle. It took part in the first annual Canyonball Run, a rally for alternative powered vehicles, from Flagstaff, Arizona to Las Vegas, Nevada. The car had to be refueled every 75 km (120 miles). It cruised at 89 km/hr. (55 mph). A grant from the Pennsylvania Department of Energy paid for the research. The car was sponsored in the rally by a special contribution from Demetri Wagner, head of the American Hydrogen Association's racing program. It won Special Vehicle Award. Further developments for LaserCel 1 include a "reversible" fuel cell. When charging, the fuel cell can electrolyse the stored exhaust water to generate more fuel. **815**

During the Ninth World Hydrogen Energy Conference in 1992 at Paris, France many fuel cell projects were discussed. Despite many incremental advances there were no reports of a practical working fuel system for vehicles. Problems abound. Experts at the conference predict that it will be 5 to 10 years before a practical fuel cell vehicle can be available for electric cars. BMW and Mercedes predict that dual-fueled gasoline and hydrogen engines will be the norm well into the 21st century.

Stationary Power Generation

The Energy Research Corp. of Danbury, Connecticut has developed fuel cells for utility power. They operate on 58% methanol and 42% water. They tested two 3 kW units. The units were 26% efficient with direct current output and 23% with

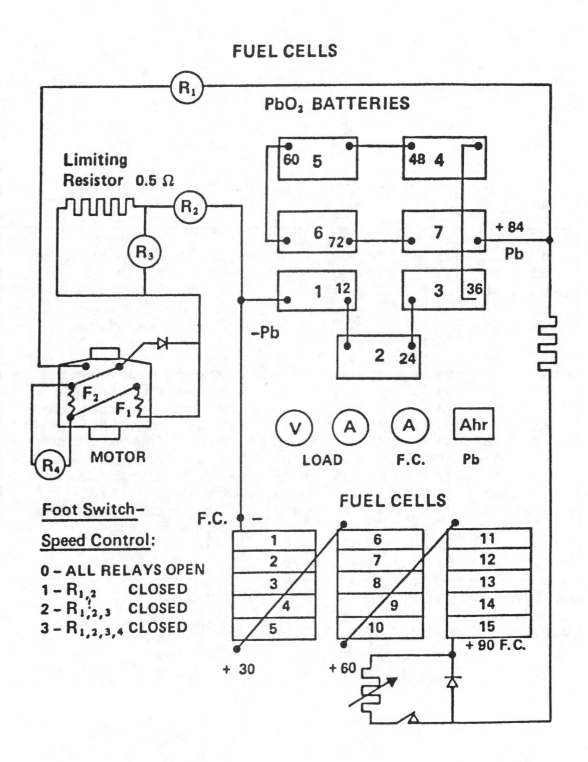

FUEL CELLS

PbO₂ BATTERIES

Limiting Resistor 0.5 Ω

Foot Switch–

Speed Control:

0 – ALL RELAYS OPEN
1 – R₁,₂ CLOSED
2 – R₁,₂,₃ CLOSED
3 – R₁,₂,₃,₄ CLOSED

MOTOR

V LOAD   A F.C.   A   Ahr Pb

FUEL CELLS

191

129. Load Sharing of Combined Fuel Cell and Battery System

Output (kW)	(V)	(A)	Battery Charge	(A)	Fuel Cell (A)	Operating Conditions
11.0	85	125	1/1	-80	45	88 km/h (55 mi/h) fourth gear
9.5	80	115	3/4	-60	55	83 km/h (52 mi/h) reduced field
8.0	75	105	1/2	-40	65	77 km/h (48 mi/h) battery temp.
6.5	70	95	1/4	-25	70	67 km/h (42 mi/h), 65 C (149 F)
20.0	75	260	1/1	-200	60	Steep hill, second gear
14.0	65	210	3/4	-140	70	
12.0	60	195	1/2	-120	75	Battery temp. 45 C (113 F)
8.0	90	90	1/1	-60	30	72 km/h (45 mi/h) fourth gear
7.0	85	80	3/4	-40	40	67 km/h (42 mi/h) full field
5.6	80	70	1/2	-20	50	61 km/h (38 mi/h) battery temp.
4.5	72	60	1/4	0	60	56 km/h (35 mi/h) 65 C (149 F)
4.0	70	58	1/4	+7	65	90 km/h (56 mi/h) fourth gear
3.0	84	35	1/2	+8	48	32 km/h (20 mi/h) third gear
2.0	88	22	1/2	+13	35	16 km /h (10 mi/h) second gear
0.5	110	5	1/1	+5	5	Car stopped
2.0	100	20	3/4	+20	20	Charging depends on state of charge and temperature.
2.8	95	30	1/2	+30	30	
4.2	85	50	1/4	+50	50	

Note : 60 A current equals 100 mA/cm^2 (645 mA/in^2) current density.

Source : from Crowe, B.J., NASA SP-5115, NASA, Washington, D.C., 1973.

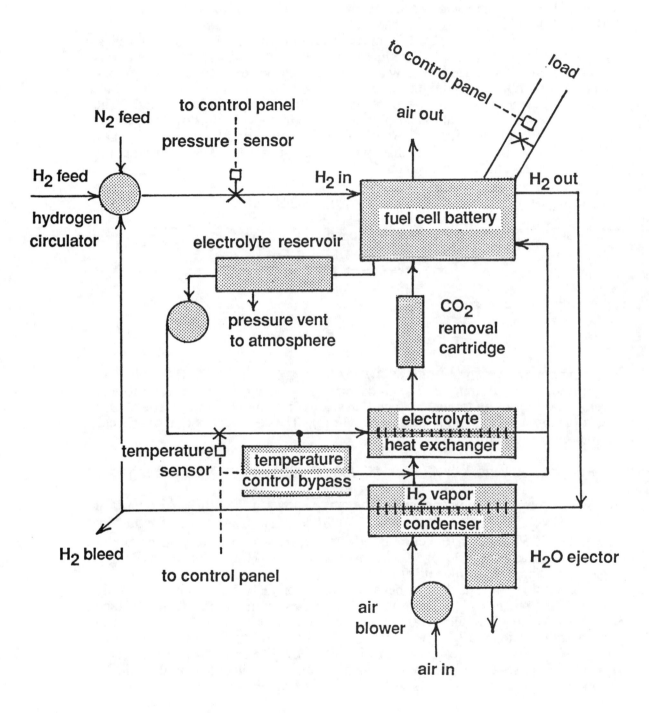

130. Schematic Diagram of Hydrogen-Air Fuel Cell Automobile

alternating current. The water-fuel mix is heated to 300ºC (572ºF) in a steam reformer and converted to a flammable gas rich in hydrogen. The fuel cell operates at 190ºC (374ºF). 60 to 65% of the hydrogen is used to produce electricity, the rest is burned separately to supply heat for the reforming process. The fuel cell uses phosphoric acid as an electrolyte. A microcomputer controls the fuel cell operation. **10**

Fuel cells may be in household use by the year 2000. Small decentralized units providing 7 to 70 kWh/day would operate off of utility gas lines thereby saving electric transmission costs. With mass production, the units would cost about $300/kW in 1987 dollars. **940**

B. Dandapani and J. O'M. Bockris, researchers at the University of Texas, have described a fuel cell that produces both electricity and hydrogen in various combinations. The current density and voltage may be adjusted to give different outputs of current and hydrogen.

The device consists of two electrodes immersed in a sulfuric acid bath. The anode is iron while the cathode is platinum. The iron electrode slowly dissolves during a series of chemical reactions to produce both current and hydrogen gas. The platinum cathode does not dissolve. See **Exhibit 136**. The reaction at the anode generates an electrical potential.

$$Fe \longrightarrow Fe^{2+} + 2e^-. \quad .041 \text{ volt}$$

The reaction at the cathode evolves hydrogen.

$$2H^+ + 2e^- \longrightarrow H_2. \quad 0 \text{ volt}$$

The overall reaction is:

$$Fe + 2H^+ \longrightarrow Fe^{2+} + H_2$$

At operating conditions of 10 mA/cm^2 (9300 mA/ft^2), 0.2 volt, and maximum power output, 10.7 kWh of current are generated for every mole (1 gram, 0.002 lb) of hydrogen produced. An equal amount of iron is needed. One mole of iron is equivalent to 0.055 kg (0.12 lb). The electrical output of this cell in Wh/mole of hydrogen is:

Fuel cell voltage X 2 X9.65 X 10,000 / 3,600 = 53.61 X cell voltage.

The maximum power point in the curve shown in **Exhibit 137** occurs at about 0.2 volt. 0.2 volt X 53.61 = 10.72 Wh/mole H_2. If the price of industrial electricity is $0.05/kWh, the current may be sold back to the utility at the rate of $0.000536/mole of hydrogen produced or about $0.536/kg of hydrogen produced. The hydrogen could also be sold, or otherwise used.

The fuel cell costs are low because no membrane material is needed - only one gas is produced. In 1985 operating cost estimates range from $120 to $1,400/kW. At low temperature the researchers assume $440/kW. At an amortization rate of 12 % per year over 10 years and assuming it runs 8,000 hours/year, the costs are assumed to be $0.0127/kWh of hydrogen produced. Electrolysis costs about 3.5 times as much. Steam reforming of natural gas is 2.3 times higher. The researchers conclude that "*taking into account the credits for the electrical energy generated, hydrogen gas can be produced at a cost significantly less than the cost of hydrogen from natural gas and by electrolysis of water*". **130p101-105**

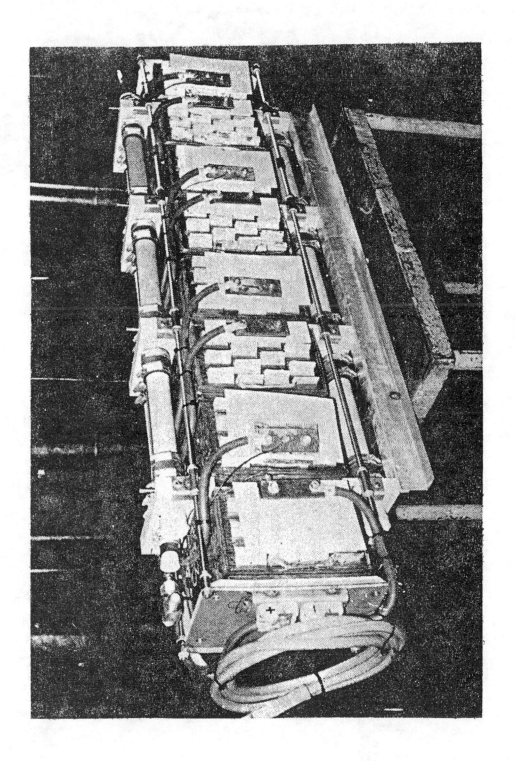

131. Fuel Cell Stack with Eight Modules

195

132. Fuel Cell Module with 48 Electrodes

133. Elenco Fuel Cell Electrode

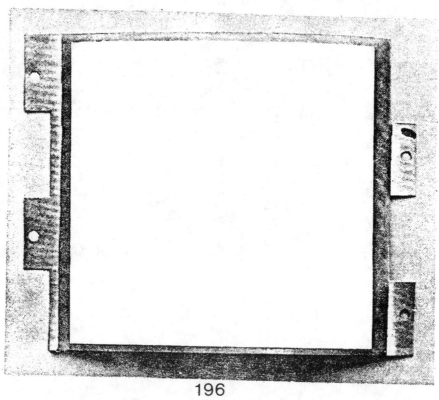

134. Voltage vs. Current of a 24-Cell Module at 65°C (149°F)

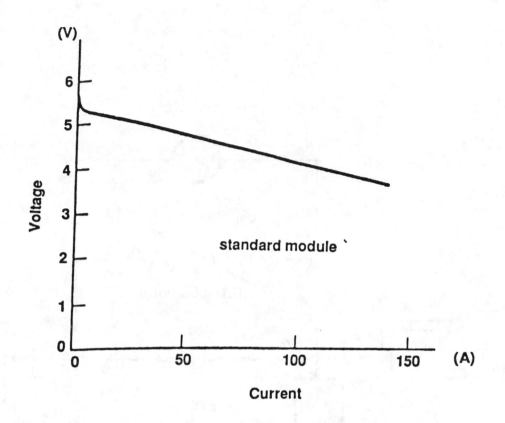

standard module `

135. Voltage vs. Time of a 24-Cell Module at 65°C (149°F)

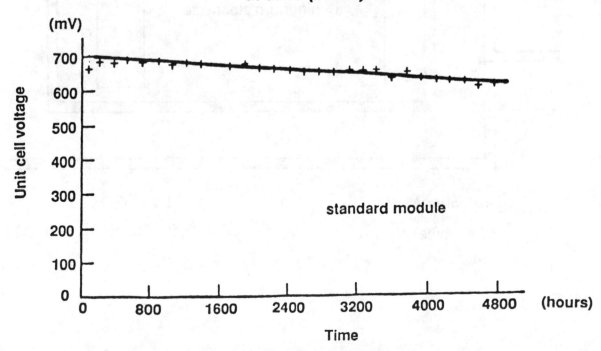

standard module

197

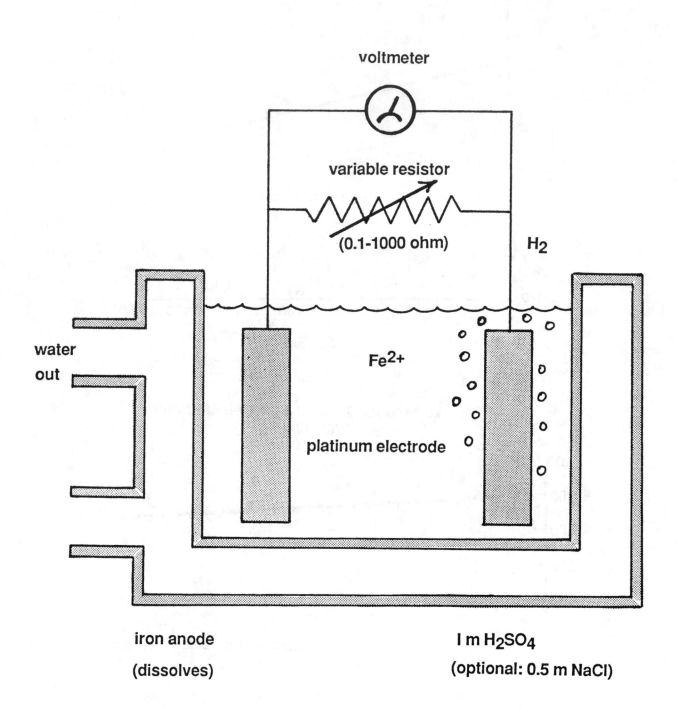

voltmeter

variable resistor

(0.1-1000 ohm)

H_2

water
out

Fe^{2+}

platinum electrode

iron anode

(dissolves)

I m H_2SO_4

(optional: 0.5 m NaCl)

137. Voltage and Current
of Experimental Electrolyser and Fuel Cell

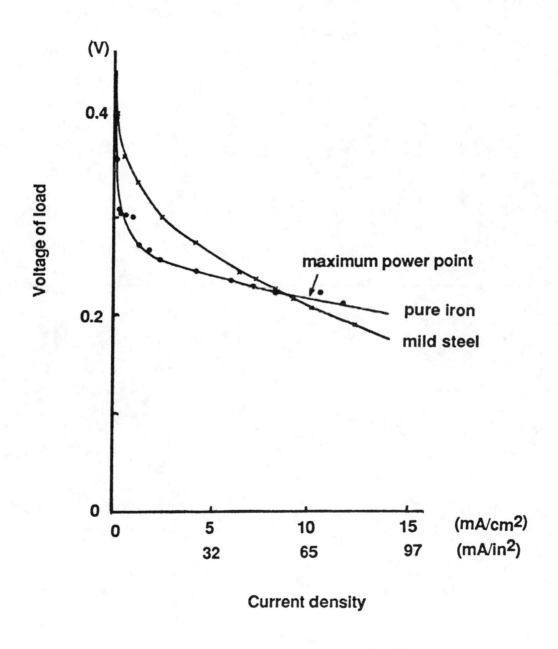

Chapter 8:
STATIONARY APPLICATIONS

ON - SITE POWER GENERATION

The Energy Carrier

HYDROGEN fuel has been studied and applied in virtually every way in which conventional fuels are used, in domestic non-commercial use.

- Cooking.
- Water and space heating.
- Cooling and refrigeration.
- Lighting.
- Farm Implements.
- Transport.
- Generating electricity.

"In all these applications, it is superior to conventional fuels and other synthetic alternatives". **201**

With the demand for energy increasing worldwide four times faster than the population new energy sources have to be found. The problem with wind, solar, water, and nuclear power is in *transporting* the energy from where it is generated to where it is needed. Hydrogen can serve as this link between the new sources of energy and the end uses. With engine-driven generators or fuel cells the energy consumed in generating hydrogen can be converted to electrical power for use, on-site, in homes, businesses and factories.

Hydrogen vs Natural Gas

Some advantages of hydrogen as compared to natural gas (methane) are:

- A minimum of 4% hydrogen in air is needed for combustion. For natural gas it is 5%. An explosion of 4% hydrogen has only *one-fourth* the energy of a 5% natural gas and air mixture. This means that if an explosion with leaking hydrogen gas occurs, it would be less damaging than a similar explosion with natural gas.
- Leaking hydrogen rises faster and dissipates more readily. The high density of propane makes it a particularly hazardous gas, in this respect.

Some disadvantages of hydrogen, as compared to natural gas are as follows.

- Because of the small size and high kinetic energy of the hydrogen molecule it is more likely to leak out of containers, and leak more rapidly, than natural gas. Hydrogen can reach its explosive limit four times faster.
- The flame is invisible and radiates less heat than a natural gas flame. This makes it easier to accidentally contact a hydrogen flame.
- Because all other gasses except helium and neon liquefy upon contact with liquid hydrogen only these two gasses may be used as a purge gas when liquid hydrogen is used as a fuel. A purge gas is used to flush air out of storage tanks and fuel lines before fuel is put in the tanks.
  140p224-226

HARNESSING HYDRIDE

Heating and Cooling

In the *Brayton cycle* a gas is compressed to increase temperature. The gas is then heated by combustion, or some other means, and allowed to expand. It is the expanding gas that does work, either by pushing a piston or turning a turbine.

During refrigeration, the Brayton cycle is reversed. First, a gas is compressed to increase its temperature. Because of the increased temperature, heat can flow out of the gas more easily. The gas is now expanded. The expanding gas cools to a temperature lower than what it originally was. A series of such steps are used to liquefy gasses, including hydrogen.

Heat pumps operate to either remove or add heat to a living space. In the cooling mode it compresses a heat exchange fluid in contact with outside air. The fluid now has a temperature higher than the outside air. Heat flows out of the fluid. The fluid is then expanded and brought into contact with the inside air. The inside air transfers heat to the lower temperature fluid. This heat is again transferred to the outside, and the cycle repeats. In the heating mode the process is reversed. Heat is taken from the outside air during expansion of the fluid and is released inside during compression.

Hydrides can be used in a heat pump. Hydrides absorb heat when releasing hydrogen and give off heat when absorbing hydrogen.

Pairs of hydrides can be selected for various desired heat transfer characteristics. Hydrogen gas is shuttled back and forth between these hydrides, absorbing and emitting heat in the process. *"For energy storage applications, the hydrides offer the possibility of performing work over a much wider temperature range than the classical absorption engines"*. 250p797 **Exhibit 138** compares FeTi hydride with other heat storage systems. 630

The efficiency of a heat engine is a measure of the work done by the engine compared to the heat energy input.

$$\text{Efficiency} = \text{work output} / \text{heat input} = 1 - (T_{out} / T_{in}).$$

Where:

T_{out} = exhaust temperature.

T_{in} = temperature of the heat applied to the engine or the temperature of combustion inside the engine.

In refrigeration, work is done to *remove* heat. The efficiency of a cooling process is:

$$\text{Efficiency} = \text{work input} / \text{heat removed} = (T_{in} / T_{out}) - 1.$$

The absorption - desorption characteristics of hydrogen hydride materials can be used in a chemical heat pump. This is a method developed at the Argonne National Laboratory. It uses two tanks of two different hydrides: $LaNi_5$ and $CaNi_5$. During the loading cycle the $CaNi_5$ is heated to 100° to $150^\circ C$ (212° to $302^\circ F$). Solar energy could be used for this purpose. Hydrogen is released from the $CaNi_5$ and is absorbed by the $LaNi_5$. Heat is then released by the $LaNi_5$. The input - output temperature difference is about $30^\circ C$ ($86^\circ F$). At pressures of less than 0.5 atm (0.05 MPa, 7.35 psi) cooling is provided at $0^\circ C$ ($32^\circ F$).

When the $LaNi_5$ has been fully charged, heat from room temperature can cause hydrogen release. The hydrogen is released and is absorbed by the $CaNi_5$ which then gives off heat that can be vented outside. In this way, heat is taken from the room. Researchers claim that this is cost competitive with conventional refrigeration technology. **190p1082**

This principle can also be employed in a hydride - driven compressor if high differences in pressure and low differences in temperature are used.

Iron - titanium is not used for either of these approaches because it has a break in its absorption cycle which decreases its efficiency for heat transfer applications.

Complex Hydride Energy System (CHES) Project

A hydride heating and cooling system has been designed to supplement a solar - assisted heat pump and water heater for use in a university building. At night a fuel cell provides electricity for the heat pump. The thermal energy storage unit was completed in 1986. It supplies 385 kWh of heat to the building. A second stage of the project, completed in 1987, uses heat from a 150 kW fuel cell to drive a hydride heat pump with an output of 60 kW.

In another experiment, Daimler - Benz, in Germany, converted a van to hydrogen. Heat from the passenger compartment is used to discharge a hydride tank, the cooled air is returned to the passenger compartment.

Power From Hydride

The pressure generated by hydride discharge of hydrogen can be used to perform work. In one possible application, solar or waste heat is used to dischage hydrogen. The pressurized gas then turns a turbine, gives up its heat, and is reabsorbed in another hydride tank. Heat can then be applied to the second tank and the flow reverses. If a reversible turbine is used continuous power is possible.

In practical applications the hydride beds can transmit heat at the rate of 0.2 to 1.0 W/m (0.06 to 0.3 W/ft.).

APHOID BURNERS

Hydrogen burned in pure oxygen produces steam at $3,300^\circ C$ ($6,000^\circ F$). Additional water can be added to reduce the temperature. This process produces no flue gasses, thereby avoiding the 25 to 35% heat loss from burning hydrocarbon fuel. **870**

No "boiler" is needed because steam is produced directly from combustion. This allows for smaller sized units. The total volume of an aphoid heating plant can be *ten percent* of the size of fossil-fueled boilers. A six story building could be heated by a furnace that can fit into a small living room.

Fossil fuels are typically burned at $1,600^\circ C$ ($2,900^\circ F$) to produce steam at

138. Comparison of Heat Storage Systems

Medium	Heat Stored	
	(Wh/l)	(BTU/ft^3)
Pebble Bed 1/3 Voids, 20°C (36°F) Temperature rise	8.9	860
Water 20°C (36°F) Temperature rise	23.2	2 240
NaSO$_4$.10H$_2$ Dehydration equilibrium	99	9 570
Iron Titanium Hydride	155	14 990

139. Principal Parts of a Typical Atmospheric Burner

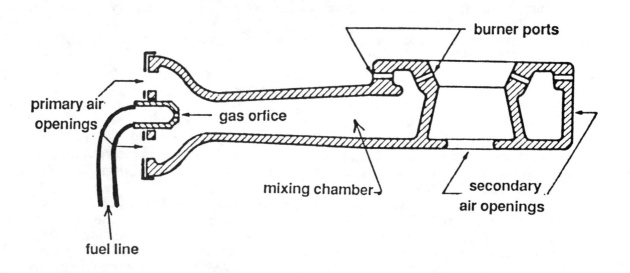

burner ports

primary air openings

gas orfice

mixing chamber

secondary air openings

fuel line

490°C (914 °F) with a 44% efficiency. Pollutants include: soot, sulfur dioxide, carbon monoxide, and carbon dioxide. The aphoid burner avoids this and has an efficiency of around 90%.

The main disadvantage of the aphoid burner is the high combustion temperature. It is difficult to design economical materials to withstand these temperatures. As a partial solution, water can be sprayed into the flame to reduce the temperature and produce a larger volume of steam at around 2,200°C (4,000°F) and 88% efficiency. Other losses may reduce this to 70%.

"This burner is still in the experimental stage but there appears to be no serious obstacle to either its development or the development of its associated turbine equipment. " 580p137

OPEN AIR BURNERS

How a Burner Works

The purpose of a burner is to mix air with gaseous fuel and impart a velocity to the fuel to keep it from burning back into the fuel line. The principal parts of an open air burner are shown in **Exhibit 139**.

Fuel flows from the fuel line through the gas orifice. As the gas flows through the mixing chamber it draws air in through the primary air openings. The fuel-air mix emerges under pressure from the burner through the burner ports. As the velocity of the fuel increases through the burner ports more air is drawn up through the secondary air opening.

It takes 9.56 m^3 (338 ft^3) of air to burn 1 m^3 (35 ft^3) of natural gas. 55 to 60% of this is primary air for most range-top burners. For a water heater or range oven, 35 to 40% is primary air and for a space heater it is 65%. 670

The velocity of the fuel must be carefully adjusted. If the fuel velocity exceeds the rate at which the fuel burns (the flame speed) the flame will blow itself out or combustion will take place too far from the burner. If the fuel velocity is less than flame velocity the combustion will *flash back* into the mixing chamber.

Because hydrogen burns faster than other fuels, the flame has a greater tendency to burn back into the mixing chamber. This may cause a loud (but generally harmless) "pop". For this reason, hydrogen burners should be designed to minimize the space between the gas orifice and the burner ports. The primary air fed is generally eliminated in hydrogen burners. 200

Hydrogen vs Natural Gas

Natural gas (methane) is the most commonly used gaseous fuel. Hydrogen is adaptable to almost every application where natural gas is now used. Some modifications are necessary to switch from one to the other. These modifications are based on the differences between the two fuels.

The minimum amount of hydrogen necessary to burn in air is 4%, the maximum is 75% by volume. The flammability limits for natural gas are 5% and 15% in air.

A hydrogen flame gives off almost no visible light. Natural gas burns with a blue flame. Hydrogen is hotter during complete combustion: 2,130°C (3,870°F) than is natural gas : 1,900°C (3,480°F).

The *combustion energy* for hydrogen is 1,000 Wh/m^3 (93 BTU/ft^3). For methane it is 3,000 Wh/m^3 (290 BTU/ft^3). Three times as much hydrogen as methane is needed to deliver equivalent amounts of energy. However, the flow rate for hydrogen is about three times that for methane (through the same size port). This means that about the same size gas orifice is needed for hydrogen as for natural gas. In practice, the energy value of the hydrogen flow is about 10%

less than with natural gas. A slightly larger fuel *orifice* is needed for hydrogen to compensate for this. (Note: the orifice is not the same thing as the burner port.)

The flame speed for hydrogen is ten times faster than for natural gas. This poses a greater danger of flashback with hydrogen. Hydrogen, therefore, requires smaller *burner ports* to prevent the fuel from burning back into the body of the burner. In other words, the burner port size for any fuel must be smaller than a certain maximum size in order to have a *quenching effect* to prevent the flame from burning back beyond it. If the burner port opening is below a certain diameter the flame will not pass through it. This maximum diameter is the *quenching distance* .

- For hydrogen the quenching distance is 0.06 cm (0.024 in).
- For methane the quenching distance is 0.23 cm (0.091 in).

Burner Port Sizing

The diameter needed for the burner port for any gaseous fuel is determined using the *Bernoulli Theorem* to solve for the area of the burner port opening.

$$A = Yc(h_L / P)^{1/2} / q.$$

$$\text{The diameter} = 2(A / 3.14159)^{1/2}.$$

Where:

A = area of orifice.
Y = expansion factor determined by the *specific heat ratio*, the port diameter/orifice diameter, and gas pressure leaving the orifice / gas pressure entering the orifice.
c = coefficient of discharge.
h_L = pressure inside burner - pressure outside burner (in cm or inches of water column, typically it is 1.52 cm [0.598 in] of water column).
P = specific gravity of the gas in air. Air = 1.0, hydrogen = 0.0696.

Appliance Regulators

Fuel line pressure may vary, thereby giving an unstable supply of fuel to the burner. Laws require that gas appliances have *pressure regulators* installed on the fuel line to even out the pressure of gas to the burner and to vent periodic excess pressure.

A natural gas regulator may be adapted to hydrogen. Hydrogen requires a smaller size vent because of the lower specific gravity of hydrogen. The maximum vent rate should be 0.06 m^3 / hour (2 ft^3 / hour). For natural gas the maximum rate is 0.07 m^3 / hour (2.5 ft^3 / hour) according to ANSI standard # Z 21.18 - 1969. This standard "*would apply to a regulator handling hydrogen fuel*". "*Informed opinion is that residential gas appliance regulators designed to regulate natural , manufactured, and mixed gasses would accomodate hydrogen without deterioration of the diaphragm or other working components.*"
670p183-184

CATALYTIC BURNERS

Flame Assisted

When hydrogen burns in the presence of iron or steel, combustion takes place very close to the surface of the metal at 1,500°C (2,730°F) or less. The combustion is controlled and the metal absorbs the heat of combustion. As a consequence, nitrous oxide emissions are reduced.

Billings Energy Research has developed a hydrogen flame stove top for a Winnebago recreational vehicle. The project was sponsored by Mountain Fuel Supply.

The Institute of Gas Technology, with the sponsorship of the Southern California Gas Company, has researched catalytic combustion for use in water and space heaters.

Hydrogen catalytic burners usually employ a stainless steel wire mesh over the burner ports and are designed so that the inflammable zone is within the diameter of the mesh surface. The larger the surface area of the mesh the smaller will be the diameter of the flammability zone. See **Exhibit 140** and **141**. 201

The catalyst requires a high temperature to function. Therefore, a primary ignition source is needed (such as a pilot light or glow plug) to start combustion and allow the temperature of the catalyst to increase. Such burners are about 70% efficient. Conventional natural gas burners are 60%.

Flameless Combustion

Hydrogen combustion in the presence of certain catalysts (such as platinum or palladium) occurs *without a flame* . Water vapor and heat are the only byproducts. Flameless catalytic combustion reduces nitrous oxide formation to a negligible amount. This form of combustion is found to be from 85 to 98% efficient. 670 No venting is required but is desirable to avoid excess humidity in the air. Other forms of flameless combustion occur naturally (the body's oxidation of carbohydrates, the yellowing of old newspapers, and rust).

Low temperature combustion reduces nitrous oxide emissions to 0.1 parts per million, compared to conventional burners at 200 to 300 ppm. 610 The combustion temperature for catalytic combustion must be kept at less than the autoignition temperature for hydrogen: 580° C (1,085° F). No pilot light or glow plug is needed to initiate combustion. This helps prevent the accidental buildup of unburnt gas.

The temperature of the catalysts start out at room temperature but, over time, the temperature increases due to accumulated heat. The rate of fuel flow, fuel velocity, and the surface area in contact with the fuel combine to influence the temperature of the catalyst.

Temperature resistant ceramic substrates are used for the burner material.

Water heaters equipped with catalytic burners were tested to be 80% efficient.

The cost of catalyst material is minimized by using a thin coating of platinum over a less costly metal, like stainless steel. The estimated cost of the catalyst is estimated to be $0.34 /kWh. If a 110 m^2 (1,200 ft^2) house uses 439 kWh/day (1.5 million BTU/day) of natural gas, only $12.00 is required as a one time extra cost to supply the catalyst material for hydrogen conversion. For low cost do-it-yourself projects stainless steel wool (3% to 22% nickle) works well enough and is easy to come by even though nitrous oxides are not as low as with more expensive catalysts. Using these low cost catalysts it is fairly simple to convert appliances that use propane.

Exhibit 142 shows test results on nitrous oxides comparing natural gas and hydogen for use in range burners. Open flame and catalytic combustion are also compared for both fuels. 670   In open air combustion hydrogen produces considerably higher levels of nitrous oxides than natural gas. With catalytic combustion the nitrous oxide emissions are lower for both fuels. The nitrous oxides for low temperature hydrogen catalytic combustion are lower than those for natural gas with the same form of combustion.

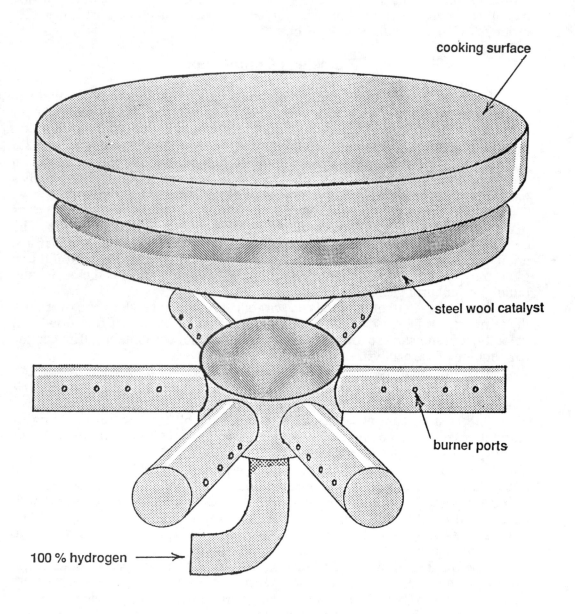

cooking surface

steel wool catalyst

burner ports

100 % hydrogen

141. Hydrogen Flame Stove Top

Lighting

The hydrogen flame is almost invisible, but it can be made useful for lighting. Peter Hoffman, in his book *The Forever Fuel* , describes a process of using a phosphorous - coated metal screen to react with a hydrogen flame to produce visible light. This is similar to gas camping stoves. A copper flame spreader will give a green flame. **430**

Water Production

Hydrogen combustion yields either water or steam. At 25°C (77°F) 0.21 Wh/m^3 (0.02 BTU/ft^3) of energy must be removed from the steam from hydrogen and oxygen combustion to produce water. If less energy than this is removed, the product gas remains as steam. **330** 7 kWh/day at 70% efficiency produces 2.5 liter/day (0.6 gal/day) of water. **670** Hydrogen makes twice as much water, per unit energy, as natural gas. See **Exhibit 143.**

THE HYDROGEN HOMESTEAD

Billings Energy Corporation recently constructed a large home and fueled it with hydrogen, electricity and solar energy. The *Hydrogen Homestead* includes a three-level 557 square meter (6,000 ft^2) home and a hydrogen powered tractor and Cadillac. The project was developed in cooperation with several companies and government agencies. The Hydrogen Homestead provides a glimpse of a hydrogen economy on a small scale, and is a showcase for the various applications being used in this setting.

The appliances in the home have been converted to hydrogen fuel. These include a Tappan range and oven, barbeque, fireplace, boiler, and water heater. Two hydrogen powered vehicles are also associated with the homestead: a Jacobsen tractor and a dual fuel Cadillac Seville. Hydrogen for these vehicles is stored in a metal hydride.

During the first phase of this project, hydrogen is being produced using an electrolyser that produces 1.4 kg (3 lb) per day of hydrogen. The electrolyser was designed and manufactured by Billings. The electricity to generate hydrogen now comes from a commercial hydroelectric plant.

During the second phase of the project, all electric power will be produced on-site using wind turbines, solar collectors, and a small hydroelectric plant. In phase three, hydrogen will be produced for the homestead, the residential subdivision, and an industrial park using a nearby *coal gasification* plant.

In a project funded by the U.S. Department of Energy through Brookhaven National Laboratory, Billings designed a metal hydride storage system and filled it with 1,800 kg(4,000 lb) of iron-titanium hydride. A computer monitored the tests for one year collecting storage and operational data.

Solar collectors are mounted on the south-facing roof and side wall. There are ten roof-mounted collectors to heat a water and antifreeze mixture for use with the metal hydride vessel. Two 1,000 liter (264 gallon) insulated holding tanks are provided for hot water storage, one for each solar collector array. Experimental equipment currently in use include: a metal hydride vessel, an electrolyser, hot water storage tanks, and the computer monitoring system. The hydrogen system shown schematically in **Exhibit 144** has been installed in the Hydrogen Homestead. Initial funding for planning the system was provided by the Four Corners Regional Commission and the Mountainland Association of Governments.

142. Nitrous Oxides from Hydrogen and Natural Gas at Maximum Combustion

Combustion Method	Hydrogen (ppm)	Natural Gas (ppm)
Open Flame		
Air Valve Fully Open	257.00	221-319
Air Valve Fully Closed	335.00	159-235
Catalytic		
Low Temperature Chimney	0.08	0.10
Vertical Fin	0.03	0.30
Flame Assisted Catalytic		
Regular Alum. Range Top	5.2	5 - 7
Stainless Steel	1.8	2
Aluminum Oven	4.5	4 - 6
Cast Iron	4.0	3 - 5

143. Water Production form Combustion of Various Fuels

Fuel	Water Production (kg/Wh)	(lb/BTU)
Gasoline (C_8H_{18})	0.00012	0.000077
Methane (CH_4)	0.00016	0.00010
Hydrogen (H_2)	0.00027	0.00017

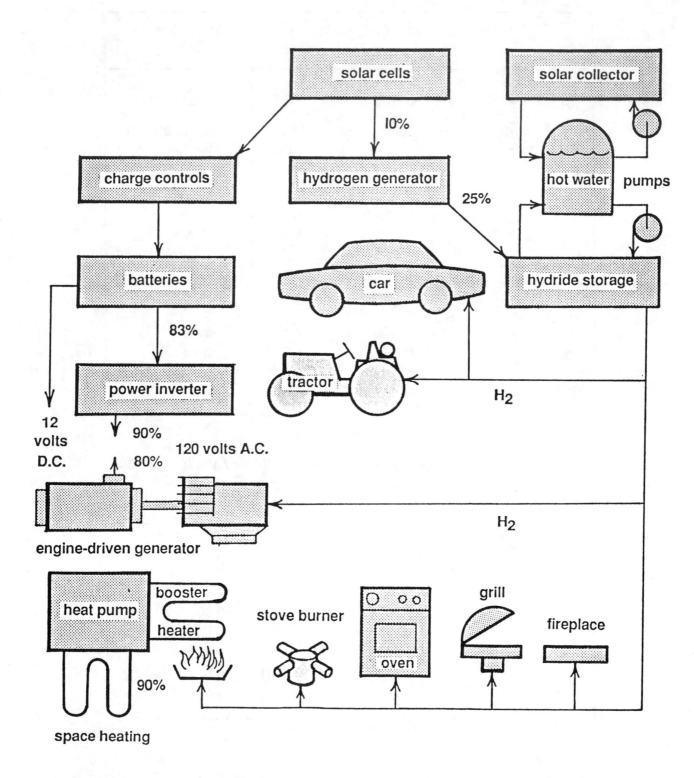

The Hydrogen Delivery System

Hydrogen is produced by electrolysis of water using a Billings Solid Polymer electrolyser. After passing through a water trap in the electrolyser unit, hydrogen flows either to the Homestead or to the metal hydride storage vessel, according to demand. The gas passes through a molecular sieve dryer. Hydrogen pressure for the flow is 34 atm (3.4 MPa, 500 psi). The pressure for recharge equilibrium with the hydride and the design output pressure of the electrolyser are identical.

Hydrogen equilibrium for the design recharge pressure is approximately 55°C (131°F). The entire hydride bed and vessel is maintained at this temperature under equilibium conditions by heat liberated from the hydriding reaction as hydrogen enters and by heat exchange with solar heated water. When homestead demand exceeds the electrolyser output, the hydrogen flows from the hydride vessel and the pressure drops. The temperature of the hydride also drops as heat is used to release the hydrogen. Hydrogen flows back through the purifier at reduced pressure because of the use of large lines and few restrictions.

In the homestead, hydrogen is used for the gas appliances, to boost the heat input to the heat pump used for space heating, and to fuel the two vehicles. The operation of each of these experiments is described below.

Hydrogen Production

In the first phase of operation, hydrogen is generated by electrolysis using power from a commercial hydroelectric source. Later, the electrolyser will be interfaced with a wind machine and with several types of solar-electric generators. An industrial park south of the Homestead is available for future installation and test of a prototype coal gasifier for hydrogen production to supply the proposed *Hydrogen Village*.

The electrolyser installed in the energy storage shed at the Homestead is designed to deliver 1.36 kg (3 lb) of hydrogen per day at pressure of 34 atm (3.4 MPa, 500 psi). Hydrogen from the electrolyser recharges the hydride vessel for the Homestead and the vehicle hydride tanks.

The Billings electrolyser uses a DuPont membrane material known as Nafion (R) for its electrolyte. This plastic absorbs water and conducts hydrogen ions between electrodes. The membrane, which replaces acid or caustic electrolytes, allows use of deionized tap water in the cell. The Nafion (R) membrane also acts as a separator to prevent mixing of hydrogen and oxygen within the cell.

Disc-shaped electrodes 8.9 cm (3.5 in) in diameter, are pressed against the membrane to obtain good electrical contact. 20 cells are fitted within the housing to make up a 0.5 kg/day (1 lb/day) module.

Hydrogen evolves at a pressure sufficient to charge the hydride vessels *without the use of a compressor*. Oxygen is generated at atmospheric pressure. The pressure difference across the membrane forces the Nafion (R) against the anode for better electrical contact.

Water consumption is 12 liters (3.2 gallons) per day and electrical consumption is 6 kW. The electrolyser operates at a high current density of 4,000 A/m^2 (372 A/ft^2) in order to minimize capital cost and size. Lower current density units may be constructed for higher electrical efficiency, if desired.

All of the transducers, flow controllers, water circulation pumps and switches are interfaced with a Billings computer monitor system. The computer records pertinent data periodically on magnetic discs. It also controls water flow in the heat exchanger and solar collectors and performs hydrogen mass flow integrations and other data analysis. See **Exhibit 146.**

As a consequence of the swelling of the hydride as it absorbs hydrogen, it is possible for the hydride to become *locked up*. This reduces the effective surface

145. Hydride Vessel Specifications

Parameter	Dimensions	
Height	123.2 cm	48.5 in
Diameter	97.3	38.3
Wall Thickness	2.38	0.937
Internal Volume	0.5969 m^3	21.08 ft^3
Service Pressure	3.447 MPa	500 psi
Test Pressure	6.895 MPa	1,000 psi
Hydride	$Ti_{0.51}Fe_{0.44}Mn_{0.05}$	
Hydride Mass	1 791 kg	3 950 lb
Service Temp.	55 C	131 F
Pressure Excursion	0.007 - 3.4 MPa	1 - 500 psi
Useable Weight	1.72%	
Stored Hydrogen	30.81 kg	67.94 lb
Stored Energy	1 213 kWh	4.14 million BTU

146. Computer Data System

Components	Technical Specifications
Microprocessor Computer	Billings BC-102
Word Length	8 Bits
Instructional Lengh	1 - 3 Bytes
Internal Storage	48 K
Access Time	450 ns
Dual Floppy Disc	B2FD
Capacity	480 K
A/D - D/A Channels	16

area available to hydrogen. Tests by the Brookhaven National Lab on small containment vessels have revealed vessel strain beyond the elastic limit. It is believed that the hemispherical shape of the Homestead vessel will be less conducive to lockup than other shapes. To insure against lockup, a loosening jet was installed in the bottom of the tank for the purpose of lifting and loosening the hydride bed with blasts of hydrogen. The same port will also be used to evaluate methods of hydride heat transfer with hydrogen recirculation.

Cooking and Nitrous Oxide Formation

Nitrous oxide is formed when nitrogen and oxygen, the two main constituents of air, are heated above a threshold temperature of about 1,315°C (2,400°F). The higher concentrations for hydrogen are a result of the fact that the laminar flame speed of a stoichiometric mixture of hydrogen and air is 3.24 m/s (10.7 ft/s) compared to 0.46 m/s (1.5 ft/s) for natural gas and air mixtures. This higher hydrogen flame speed results in a large fraction of hydrogen being burned in a smaller area and, consequently, a higher peak temperature with resulting increase in nitrous oxide formation. Although the compbustion temperatures vary only modestly, the natural gas combustion takes place right on the bottom edge of the nitrous oxide formation threshold, so that only a modest increase in temperature makes a significant contribution to the concentration of nitrous oxide formation. Appliance conversions were accomplished using a technique developed under a contract from the Mountain Fuel Supply Company of Salt Lake City, Utah. In this technique, nitrous oxide formation is controlled by the appication of two interacting phenomena.

- Hydrogen-air mixing is inhibited by blocking all primary air.
- A stainless steel wire mesh is placed around the burner ports.

The placement of the wire mesh in a proper configuration will allow the gradual mixing of hydrogen and air througout the operating flow rates of the burner design. A hydrogen rich condition exists in close proximity with the burner, with the oxygen concentration increases when moving away from the burner head. If the stainless steel material is properly placed, there will exist a region immediately surrounding the burner openings, consisting of a flammable hydrogen concentration. This region is the *flammable zone*. The flammable zone will move in and out from the burner head depending on the hydrogen flow rate. A proper burner design will incorporate sufficient stainless steel material so as to insure that the flammable limit zone is always located within the outside perimeter of the stainless steel material. See **Exhibit 140**.

The stainless steel also provides a very important secondary function in addition to the mixture inhibiting function just described. At high temperatures, stainless steel is an excellent catalyst for hydrogen combustion. Shortly after ignition, the temperature of the stainless steel is raised by hydrogen combustion to the region where the catalyst starts to work. At this point, the hydrogen in the previously described flammable zone begins to react with the dilute quantities of oxygen present through the action and on the surface of the stainless steel catalyst. In this manner, a controlled reaction occurs in the flammable zone where mixture limitations will not permit the rapid combustion of hydrogen which would occur under normal conditions. Therefore, peak combustion temperatures are maintained below the threshold level for nitrous oxide formation.

The Hydrogen Homestead uses a Tappan Convectionaire range. The oven has the same hydrogen modifications in the burner design as does the stove. The furnace, barbecue, and fireplace are similarly modified. The catalyst screen is placed directly above the burner. The metal grid glows when hot, indicating that the otherwise invisible hydrogen flame is present. The hydrogen burner heats eight times faster than with natural gas, while using 24% less energy.

The Lorenzen Homestead

John Lorenzen of Woodward, Iowa has, over the past 50 years, gradually converted most of his farming operations to hydrogen. Powered by windmills his homemade electrolysers supply most of his energy needs. Even is his truck runs on compressed hydrogen. It has sufficient range for his farm errands.

Determining the Needed Hydrogen Production Capacity

In order to convert some or all of a homes appliances to hydrogen it is first necessary to calculate how much fuel will be necessary. The energy content of propane is 24 kWh (82,000 BTU). Natural gas has about 10.3 kWh/m^3 (1,000 BTU/ft^3). 1 BTU = 0.00029287 kWh. Lets assume a house uses 20 cubic feet of natural gas every day for cooking and we want to replace it with hydrogen. We can calculate how much hydrogen we need assuming a 50 percent efficiency for the electrolyser. Since electricity is about five times the cost of natural gas per unit of energy this is not economical unless a source of alternative electrical energy is used.

Hydrogen can be stored at 4.1 atm (.4 MPa, 60 psi) in propane continers. It can be used in combination with propane up to 20 percent without modifications to appliances. Hydrogen gas can also be stored "over water" in 55 gallon drums as mentioned in Chapter 4.

Conclusions

The Hydrogen Homestead demonstrates the possibility of near-term application of combined hydrogen, electricity and solar energy for residential use. The key elements are: production, storage, and utilization of hydrogen in ways that complement the solar and electrical system.

In this example, production is by electrolysis of water using hydroelectric energy. Electricity could also be generated from other renewable energy sources such as solar and wind. Future plans call for hydrogen supply by pipeline from direct conversion of coal. Hydrogen is stored in a vessel containing iron-titanium hydride. Operational characteristics of the vessel and hydride are being studied. Hydrogen fuel is used to replace natural gas and gasoline in the Homestead.

The Billings Hydrogen Homestead has served as a test facility for evaluation of hydrogen systems and the interface with electrical and solar systems. **120** Since 1980 it has ceased operations because of technical and funding problems. The Lorenzen Homestead still continues in operation.

Chapter 9:
SAFETY

VENTING

PRESSURE builds up inside storage vessels containing hydride or liquid hydrogen. The accumulated pressure must be vented before the tank ruptures. This is the purpose of a *safety valve*.

Once outside the tank, this vented gas must not be allowed to accumulate in explosive mixtures. It must be safely burned during the venting process. **Exhibit 147** shows a cross section of a catalytic device that is mounted on the outlet of a safety valve. 110 When the maximum tank pressure is reached, at 9.2 atm (0.93 MPa, 135 psi), the built up gas is vented until the pressure is reduced. The blow off gas enters the jet nozzle, where it is mixed with air and passed through a catalyst of platinum coated aluminum pellets. Combustion takes place at low temperatures close to the surface of the pellets. In this way, the flammable vented gas is converted to water vapor.

Government regulations require that an outlet for vented gas be at least five feet above any nearby building opening.

SAFETY-RELATED PROPERTIES OF HYDROGEN

The various properties of hydrogen that make it safer or more hazardous than other fuels are listed in **Exhibit 148.** 580,594 They will be discussed in the order presented in the table.

Density and Specific Gravity

Hydrogen has a lower density than air. Because of this, the fuel rises and accumulates at high points in a building. These areas must be vented when hydrogen is used indoors in order to avoid fire hazards. Its low molecular weight also makes hydrogen more prone to leaks than other gases.

Diffusivity

Hydrogen has a high rate of *diffusion* in air. It dissipates more rapidly than other gases or liquid vapors.

The safety of liquid hydrogen was tested in an experiment. 1,890 liters (500 gallons) were spilled on the ground simulating an accidental rupture of a cryogenic tank. In 60 seconds the concentration in the air was less than the 18% of the explosive limit. 580

In another test, the Billings Energy Research Corp. shot a hole in a

147. Catalytic Safety Burner for Escaping Gas

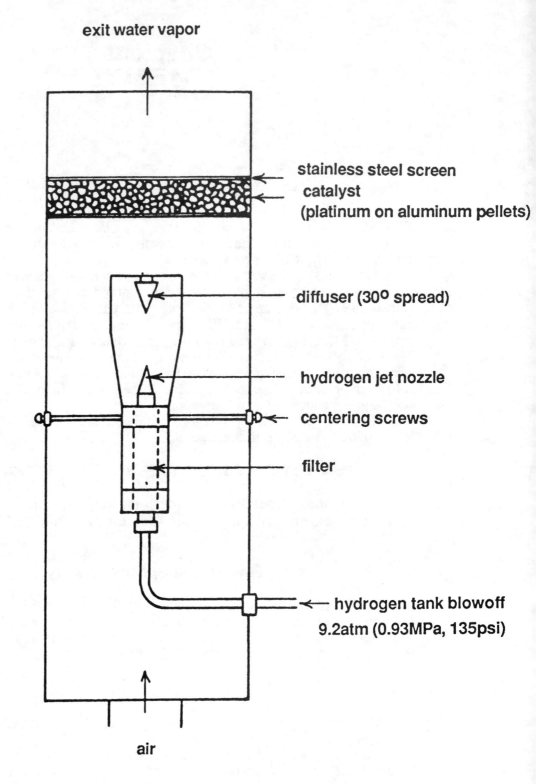

exit water vapor

stainless steel screen

catalyst
(platinum on aluminum pellets)

diffuser (30° spread)

hydrogen jet nozzle

centering screws

filter

hydrogen tank blowoff
9.2atm (0.93MPa, 135psi)

air

148. Safety Related Properties of Hydrogen

Property	Hydrogen	Methane	Propane	Gasoline
Density at 20°C (68 F), 1 atm				
kg/l	0.000083	0.00078	0.00187	0.72
lb/ft3	0.00518	0.0485	0.1168	44.95
Specific Gravity (Air - 1.0)	0.0696	0.641	1.56	3.90
Diffusion Coefficient				
m/s	0.0061	0.0016	0.0012	0.008
ft/s	0.0200	0.0052	0.0039	0.026
Heat Energy Weight Basis				
Wh/kg	34770	13330	14270	12360
BTU/lb	53776	20650	22000	19145
Volume Basis				
Wh/l	2.89	10.36	27	8889
BTU/ft^3	290	970	2600	860
Explosion Energy				
kg TNT/kg fuel	24	11	10	10
Flammability Limits				
% volume in air	4 - 75	5 - 16	2 - 12	1.4 - 7.6
Optimum Air/Fuel Mix				
% volume in air	29.3	9.48	4.03	1.76
Autoignition Temp.				
°C	580	540	487	295
°F	1076	1004	908	563
Ignition Energy, Air				
Wh	6×10^{-9}	8×10^{-8}	7×10^{-8}	7×10^{-8}
BTU	2×10^{-8}	3×10^{-7}	3×10^{-7}	2×10^{-7}
Flame Temp. in Air				
°C	2045	1875	2100	2197
°F	3713	3407	3812	3987
Flame Speed				
m/s	2.7	0.3	0.3	0.3
ft/s	8.9	1.0	1.0	1.0

iron-titanium hydride tank charged to full capacity. The armor-piercing incendiary bullet ripped through the casing of the tank but there was no explosion. Only burning gas escaped from the bullet hole. If a hydride tank is pierced, pressure is released and an *endothermic* (heat absorbing) reaction occurs as hydrogen is given off. This absorbs some of the heat required for combustion. For comparison, a gasoline tank was shot with the same ammunition. The explosion threw flaming fuel over a wide area. This is an advantage of all gaseous fuels: they dissipate more rapidly. **120**

There is a special hazard associated with *magnesium* hydride, however. The combustion of magnesium takes place at high temperatures and is difficult to extinguish. This is why magnesium is used in signal flares. Some finely divided powders of magnesium, aluminum, or iron will burn spontaneously when exposed to air. Special precautions need to be taken to keep oxygen away from those substances.

In 1937 a giant rigid frame passenger-carrying baloon, the *Hindenburg,* caught fire near Lakehurst, New Jersey. The hydrogen cells in the baloon exploded and 36 people were killed. This disaster is generally cited as an example of the special dangers of hydrogen fuel. However, it must be remembered that :

- The hydrogen was not used as a fuel for the aircraft but was stored in large bag-like containers to provide lift.
- The Hindenburg had completed 18 round trips between Europe, the U.S. and Brazil.
- Two-thirds of the passengers survived. The passenger gondola was below the gas cells. The burning hydrogen rose as it burned. Many of the 35 passengers who died *jumped* to their deaths.
- A 747 airliner crashed in the Canary Islands during the 1970's killing 400 people.

In general, hydrogen is not particularly hazardous compared to other flammable substances. It does have some unique properties that require special safety considerations. Its high rate of diffusivity enables it to penetrate some materials, such as cast iron.

Heat Energy

On a weight basis hydrogen has three times the energy content of hydrocarbon fuels. On a volume basis it has about one-third less. This means that a given volume of hydrogen will not give off as much energy as other gases, such as methane.

Explosion Energy

A concentration of hydrogen of 18% or more in air can cause *detonation* (an explosion). Only 6% is needed for methane and propane. **290p117-124** The amount of pressure that exploding hydrogen will exert on an enclosed container depends upon the detonation velocity and the density of the unburnt mixture. Since hydrogen burns quickly, it has the *highest* explosion potential of any gas, *on a mass basis*. On a volume basis, it has the *lowest* explosion hazard. For an equivalent storage of energy, hydrogen has a similar explosion potential as methane or propane.

Flammability Limits and Optimum Mix

The limits of flammability of hydrogen in air are from 4% to 75%. This means that a minimum of 4% and no more than 75% hydrogen mixed (by volume) in air are necessary to support combustion. The range of flammability for hydrogen is wider than methane, propane, or other hydrocarbon fuels. *"In most accidental situations, the lower flammability limit is of particular importance. This is due to the fact that in realistic accident sequences, ignition sources with sufficient energy are nearly always present, once leaking fuels and combustibles have reached flammability concentrations in air."* 360p595

The minimum limit of flammability for hydrogen is *higher* than for either propane or gasoline (2%).

Related to the above safety considerations, is the fact that hydrogen requires three times higher concentration in air (29.3%) for maximum combustion energy than methane (9.48%).

Ignition Temperature

The temperature needed to start the combustion of hydrogen in air is slightly greater than for methane and *double* that for gasoline. This means that hydrogen is usually not ignited, at atmospheric pressure, by ignition sources such as a lit cigarette, but only by an open flame.

Exhibit 149 gives a more detailed comparison of ignition temperature ranges for various levels.

Ignition Energy

The minimum amount of *energy* (not temperature) necessary to start the combustion of hydrogen is about *one-tenth* the minimum for any hydrocarbon fuel. Most ignition sources, such as electrostatic sparks, exceed this energy level. Electrostatic sparks from the human body ("carpet shock") have about three times the amount of energy needed to set off a hydrogen explosion.

Flame Luminosity and Temperature

Hydrogen gas is colorless, odorless and nontoxic. It produces a barely visible blue flame with very little radiant energy compared to hydrocarbon fuels. It is possible to come into contact with a hydrogen flame, accidentally, because of its near invisibility.

Flame Speed

The flame speed of any combustible gas is the sum of its burning velocity and the speed with which the flame displaces the unburnt gas mixture. The flame speed for hydrogen is *ten times* that for hydrocarbon fuels. Therefore, automatic check valves designed for methane must be able to respond quickly enough to prevent hydrogen fuel-air mixtures from burning back into a fuel line.

EMBRITTLEMENT

This phenomena could best be described as *unwanted hydriding*. Steel and other iron-containing metals become brittle and crack when absorbing hydrogen. Metal containers and pipelines designed for natural gas may not be suitable for hydrogen. Steels with a high proportion of nickle (stainless steels) are relatively resistant to hydriding. If the right materials are used, hydrogen presents no unique storage problems.

Since 1940 a German pipeline has carried hydrogen with no significant embrittlement problems. The pipeline extends 220 kilometers (137 miles) and connects 18 industrial centers. Fuel flow is 250 million cubic meters per year (8.83 billion ft^3/year). The pipe diameter varies from 15 to 30 cm (6 to 12 inch). Pressure varies from 10.9 atm (1.1 MPa, 160 psi) to 24.7 atm (2.5 MPa, 363 psi). *"With this network very high operational reliability and safety have been*

220

149. Ignition Temperature of Various Fuels

Fuel	In Air		In Pure Oxygen	
	(C)	(F)	(C)	(F)
Hydrogen	580 - 590	1,076 - 1,094	580 - 590	1,076 - 1,094
CO	644 - 658	1,191 - 1,216	637 - 658	1,179 - 1,216
Methane	540 - 750	1,004 - 1,382	556 - 700	1,033 - 1,292
Propane	487	909	490 - 570	914 - 1,058
Acetylene	406 - 440	763 - 824	416 - 440	781 - 824
Methanol	728	1,340	555	1,031
Ethanol	558	1,036	425	797
Keroscene	295	563	270	518
Gasoline	295	563	270	518

150. American Regulations for Distributing Hydrogen

Distribution Method	Equipment Specifications	Shipping Regulations	Installation Standards
Liquid Cylinder	TCG Title 49 CFR 178.57	TCG Title 49 CFR 173.316	NFPA 50B (22)
Liquid Trailer	ASME (Ref. CGA 341)	Special Permit	------------------
Liquid Tank Car	TCG 1.73.316 Title 49 CFR 179.400	TCG 173.316 Title 49 CFR 173.316	------------------
Liquid Customer Station	ASME (23)	------------------	NFPA 50 B
Gas Cylinder	ASME/TCG Title 49 CFR 178.36 - 37	TCG Title 49 CFR 173.301	NFPA 567 50A (24)
Gas Pipeline	ANSI B 31.8/25	------------------	DOT Title 9, part 192

221

established."

The pipeline was originally designed for natural gas but at the pressure under which it operates, the pipe material should experience negligible levels of embrittlement. Embrittlement does not become a significant problem in pipeline steels until a pressure of around 100 atm (10 MPa, 1,470 psi), or more, is encountered. Comparing hydrogen with natural gas is the pipeline, *"replacement of parts in the hydrogen pipeline network has shown that, in contrast to gas pipelines, only negligible deposition or corrosion damage exists."* 360p593

At temperatures over 220°C (430°F) the two-atom hydrogen molecule (H_2) splits into two atoms of hydrogen. Steel is more likely to be permeated with single atoms than with molecular hydrogen. Corrosion or electrolysis reactions can also produce atomic hydrogen. Pressures over 680 atm (68.7 MPa, 10,000 psi) promote hydriding.

Titanium tubing specifications require hydrogen concentrations to be below 150 ppm, otherwise the titanium becomes *titanium hydride*. An titanium oxide film accumulates on the metal with exposure to air, but this film protects the metal from hydriding.

General precautions against hydriding include:

- Use alloy linings and vented inner liners for large hydrogen gas containers.
- Minimize the presence of nonmetallic inclusions in metal.
- Use quenched and tempered, rather than rolled steels. Embrittlement is lowest in 300 series stainless steels, beryllium-copper alloys, and aluminum and copper alloys. All alloys should have minimal manganese content.
- Avoid the use of water when welding to prevent the hydrogen in the water from getting into the metal. Use low hydrogen electrodes and any other method to reduce the presence of hydrogen in the weld.
- Preheat the metal before welding and allow the weld to cool slowly.

REGULATIONS

U.S. hydrogen consumption exceeds 65 billion cubic meters per year (2,300 billion ft^3/year). Use increases about 7% per year. Hydrogen has been used for years in the petroleum and chemical industries. It has an excellent safety record and can be handled without significant risk. Government regulations have evolved regarding gaseous fuels, and in particular, hydrogen. The main regulations are shown in **Exhibit 150.** 580p196

Containers with over 85 cubic meters (3,000 ft^3) must be located outdoors. The regulations applying to containers over 425 cubic meters (15,000 ft^3) are the most stringent. For hydrogen fuel in cylinders, as much as possible of the supply should be outdoors.

Researchers testing hydrogen in a stationary engine located indoors used a delivery pressure from the cylinders of 1.4 atm (0.14 MPa, 21 psi). They voluntarily conformed to *National Fire Prevention Association* standards 54(14), ANSL B31.1(15), ANSL B31(16), and Canadian gas association regulations 11 and 12. Gas to the engine was automatically shut down when the ignition was off. This was accomplished using solenoid valves in the fuel line adjacent to the engine and solenoid valves in the high pressure supply to the cylinder manifolds.

The fuel was delivered to the engine through a flexible hose and vibration-free connection.

Nonflammable nitrogen gas was used to flush the air out of the fuel lines prior to delivery of hydrogen.

Gas sensors were mounted on the ceiling to detect 25% of the lower flammability limit of hydrogen (1% hydrogen in air). When hydrogen was detected the sensor activated an alarm and cut the fuel delivery to the engine. A roof suction fan was also employed.

All piping connections were sealed to prevent leaks. High pressure material was used for the pipe material: CDA alloy 443 brass. Gas manifolds were manufactured by Rexarc and obtained from a gas welding company.

The fuel tank relief valve was set to open at 44.2 atm (4.46 MPa, 650 psi). The 2 cm (0.75 inch) vent pipe extended outside and rose 1.5 meters (5 ft.) above the roof level. **820p738**

Liquid hydrogen containers in many experiments are made of aluminum or stainless steel. These materials have *low temperature ductility*. They can stretch at low temperatures without cracking.

To meet the lack of safety codes written specifically for hydrogen, the Canadian Hydrogen Safety Committee was formed. It is a subcommittee of the Advisory Committee on Energy of the National Research Council. Its members include representatives of hydrogen producers and consumers, those involved in research and development, quality control and process safety specialists. It is in the process of drawing up long overdue guidelines for hydrogen safety.

SUMMARY

The safe use of hydrogen can be summarized as follows:

- Adequate ventilation
- Leak prevention
- Elimination of ignition sources

Chapter 10:
THE HYDROGEN ECONOMY

FUEL USE TRENDS

The Unmet Challenge

""**WITHOUT** *a supply of energy, in the right form, in the right place and at the right price, civilization as we know it today, would collapse."* **490p63**

Today we regard the term "energy" as synonomous with "petroleum". Morever, we regard our dependency upon foreign oil exports as the natural order of things. The prospect of our once great nation cringing in fear of any threatened disruption of the oil supply does not shame us. We in the West, particularly the United States, in making no more than feeble efforts to develop our own energy resources have failed to measure the full cost of our lethargy:

● 	In terms of our national *self respect.*
● 	In terms of *environmental* damage.
● 	In terms of the *risk of war.*

There can be no *military solution* to our energy dependency. Any serious use of force to keep the oil supply lines open, in opposition to any serious attempt to close them, would cost far more than what we are "saving" by not developing *our own energy resources.*

We remain dependent because we choose to be. In doing so, we ignore not only the present danger but the inevitable conversion to other forms of energy out of necessity.

The Technology Trap

Almost 75 percent of the world's known oil reserves are in the middle east. The Western Hemisphere has only 16 percent. New oil discoveries are increasing the percentage for the Middle East. The U.S. and Canada use twice as much oil per person than European countries. Two thirds of that is for transportation.

Despite the health hazards and costs of burning oil we are in a *technology trap.* This term is used by Roy McAlister of the American Hydrogen Association to describe the dilemma of sustaining our standard of living by burning the equivalent of 180 million barrels of oil every day at a cost of a billion dollars per week that the U.S. pays for oil. As of 1992 the U.S. uses 6.2 billion barrels of oil each year -- 58% of it is imported.

● 	It is risky and expensive for industry to supply an alternative fuel if they can't be sure that enough people want it and are ready to use it.
● 	The people don't want an alternate fuel unless it is widely available so they don't have to go out of their way or pay too high price to use it.

The deadlock can be broken if consumers would be willing to pay a higher price for energy alternatives until they can be produced in large enough numbers to bring the price down.

As an interim solution to both our dependency on imported oil and the problem of air pollution it is suggested that we run our vehicles on natural gas and increasingly substitute natural gas for oil. The supplies of natural gas in the U.S. have decreased since 1969. According to Charles Terrey of the Energy Information Administration, if new natural gas deposits are discovered at the same rate as in the past the U.S. will run out in about 18 years.

From Carbon to Hydrogen

Throughout history there has been an accelerating trend away from carbon, to hydrogen in fuels. Fuels having a high proportion of carbon are being gradually replaced with fuels with greater amounts of hydrogen. This is illustrated in **Exhibit 151.** Heavy oil, with 20 carbon atoms per molecule, represents one extreme. Methane, with one carbon atom per molecule is increasingly being used to place of fuel oil. Hydrogen can be seen to represent the future of combustible fuels. The ratio of hydrogen to carbon in the wood energy age was about 0.1. It is about 4.0 now. In the future hydrogen alone will be our main source of energy.

The increasing amounts of hydrogen in our fuels has lowered their *boiling points*. This is seen on the right hand vertical axis in **Exhibit 151.** The trend shown in the graph indicates the increasing use of liquefied gasses such as propane, liquefied natural gas and liquid hydrogen.

Despite these historical tendencies, hydrogen will not be widely used as a fuel before the year 2000. Until then, it will be used primarily in synthesizing chemicals, methanol production, and petroleum refining. It will be particularly valuable as a means of storing energy from electric power plants during hours when power demand is low. This keeps the electrical generating machinery running at a more even rate and reduces overall operating costs.

Nuclear energy now meets 10% of the world's electrical needs. By the year 2030 solar energy technology will assume another 10%. **370p501** *"Hydrogen, with its adaptability to solar energy and to other secondary energy carriers offers the possibility of promoting the introduction of renewable energy sources."* **670**

The Future of Coal

Consistent with the trend towards higher hydrogen/carbon ratios in fuel, **Exhibit 152** shows a declining use of coal as a solid fuel. The use of fossil fuels will peak between 2000 and 2020. Despite a declining overall trend, the use of coal for the production of liquid fuels will accelerate rapidly and peak for a short time around 2030. Coal will replace oil and natural gas *"in a few decades."* **580p349**

Exhibit 153 outlines major research and development goals of the West German government to implement hydrogen energy. **1010p544** In every case, there goals involve only modifications of *existing technology* and do not take into consideration major breakthroughs in technology that could accelerate hydrogen useage.

UTILIZATION EFFICIENCY OF HYDROGEN

Hydrogen has one-third the energy of an equal volume of hydrocarbons but three times the energy on an equal weight basis. An advantage of hydrogen is its *combustion efficiency*. When burned, the combustion of hydrogen with oxygen yields only water vapor.

Increasingly higher proportions of hydrogen are substituted for carbon.

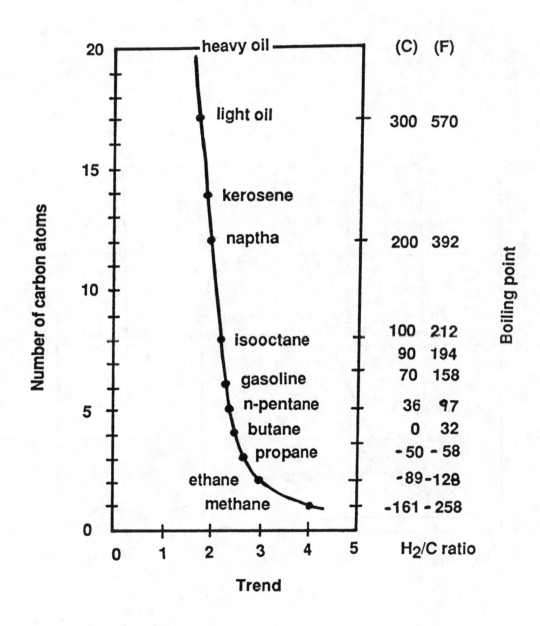

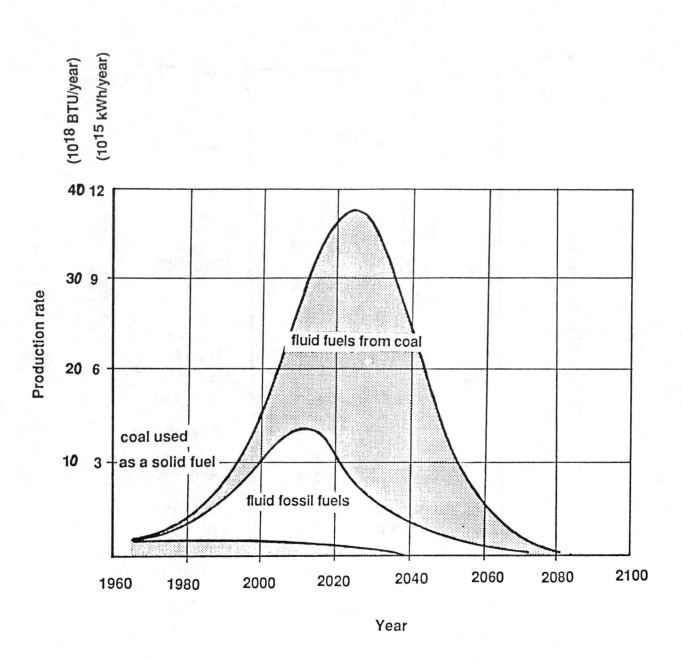

Goals	Means	Measured Results
Production of H_2 by decomposition of water	Improvement of Efficiency, economics and reliability of advanced electrolysis, SPE and vapor electrolysis.	$3.8 kWh/m^3$ of H_2
	Demonstration of electrolysis with high efficiency.	90% efficiency 5 - 10 yr. lifetime
	Demonstration and field test of electrolysis systems with intermittent primary energy sources.	Under $0.25/kW storage cost.
	Improvements of eff. of liquefiers, magnetocaloric refrigerators, refrigerators in orbit.	45 - 50% efficiency 8 - 10 kWh/kg LH_2 4 - 5 kWh/lb
Transport, storage and distribution	Developement of large scale compressors.	Turbomachinery instead of pistons.
	Demonstration of efficient large scale storage.	1 million kWh
	Large scale demonstration of usefulness of equipment for underground storage, pipelines, etc.	
Utilization	Specific end use technologies, field demonstration and upscaling for steam generators and catalytic burners, lower cost fuel cells.	Economic integration into existing systems, low NO_x (under 0.1 g/kWh (2.0×10^{-4} lb/kWh) $250/kWh
	H_2 auto engines.	Internal mixture form. lower NO_x under 10% 40% cycle effeciency.
	Modification of CH_2 systems for H_2 (burners, cogeneration, etc.).	
	Demonstration of safety and reliability.	Comparable to gasoline & natural gas.

Exhibit 154 was compiled by T. Nejat Veziroglu from a variety of sources. **670** It shows that hydrogen has a greater utilization efficiency than fossil fuels for transportation, industrial, commercial and residential purposes. Overall, it takes only 74% as much hydrogen to deliver the same energy as fossil fuels. The advantage is greatest for industrial uses.

AIR TRANSPORTATION

19% less energy is needed for liquid hydrogen fueled subsonic aircraft than with fossil fuel. For supersonic aircraft, the advantage is 38%. **610** Since hydrogen fuel is lighter, this reduces the weight of fully loaded aircraft and allows shorter wing spans. Smaller engines can be employed to take advantage of improved combustion efficiency as well as weight reduction. Increased range is also possible. Some researchers think that by 2040 all long range flights will be powered by hydrogen. **100**

Specifications for a proposed liquid hydrogen facility for one aircraft is given below. **900p5-22**

Flight schedule:	one per day.
	4,800 kilometers (3,000 miles).
Fuel on board:	25,000 kilograms (55,000 lb.)
Fueling times:	38 minutes.
Supply needed (including boil off and transfer losses):	3,000 kg/day (6,600 lb/day).
Plant output:	36,000 kg/day (80,000 lb/day).
Electric power needed:	40 MW.
Excess fuel storage needed:	14,000 cubic meters (494,000 ft^3).
Minimum stored:	10 days supply.
Means of transfer:	pipeline transfer to plane with cold gas recovery.
Boil off rate:	1,000 kilograms/hour (2,200 lb/hr).
Liquefaction rate:	1,000 kilograms/hour (2,200 lb/hr).

PRODUCTION COSTS

This book has covered a variety of methods of producing hydrogen but the most common methods are:

Petroleum reforming:	77% of world hydrogen production.
Coal gasification:	18% of world hydrogen production.
Electrolysis:	4% of world hydrogen production.

In 1986 500 billion cubic meters (17.6 trillion ft^3) of hydrogen were used. **350p39-46**

If the cost of coal falls below $20 per 1,000 kilograms ($20/ton) coal gasification can be competitive with petroleum reforming. **20p783-788** Coal at $45 is equivalent, on an energy basis, to the price of gasoline. **440** 65% of the

Energy Sector	Fossil Fuel Consumption (%)	Hydrogen Consumption (%)
TRANSPORT		
Road (Internal Combustion Engine)	12.0	9.9
Road (Fuel Cell)	2.5	1.1
Rail (Fuel Cell)	1.5	0.8
Sea (Internal Combustion Engine)	2.5	2.1
Sea (Fuel Cell)	1.5	0.8
Air (Subsonic)	2.5	2.1
Air (Supersonic)	2.5	1.8
Total	25.0	18.6
INDUSTRIAL		
Heat	25.0	14.5
Electricity (Fuel Cells)	5.0	6.5
Total	30.0	21.0
COMMERCIAL		
Heat	11.0	8.9
Electricity (Fuel Cells)	4.0	2.2
Total	15.0	11.1
RESIDENTIAL		
Heat	25.0	20.2
Electricity (Fuel Cells)	5.0	2.7
Total	30.0	22.9
GRAND TOTAL	100.0	73.6

energy of coal can be converted to hydrogen. For solar powered electrolysis the conversion rate is 10%. **940p3**

At Coolwater, California a coal gasification plant was built to employ the latest technology. Using this plant to determine costs, hydrogen can be produced at $0.04 per kilowatt hour ($0.012/1000 BTU). This is the equivalent of $0.36 per liter ($1.36/gallon) of gasoline. If the carbon dioxide could be sold, costs would be even lower. **60p2** *"This method (of producing hydrogen) is the cleanest and most effective method of utilizing Americas's large reserves of coal."* **250p825-828**

Hydrogen can be used as a means of extending our domestic fossil fuel supplies. The larger molecules of petroleum can be broken up into smaller molecules of hydrogen rich substances such as methane (synthetic natural gas). *"Hydrogen produced by water vapor electrolysis could be used for these purposes, thereby prolonging the use of the available (petroleum) resources."***280p294**

In the near future 10 times more hydrogen will be used in refining fossil fuels than in the chemical industry. To meet this demand the available electrolytic plant capacity must be doubled. In petroleum refining, electrolysis has two main advantages.

● Pure oxygen eliminates the need for an air separation plant to provide atmospheric oxygen to the reforming process.
● Pure hydrogen eliminates the shift conversion unit that produces hydrogen from coal.

The higher temperature electrolysis experiment - *HOT ELLY* - pioneered by the European companies Dornier and Lurgi in 1976 can produce hydrogen with 30 to 45% less electricity than conventional electrolysis. These and other improvements in electrolysis technology must be considered when assessing the economic costs of hydrogen production. *"Capital and operating costs have been tamed to the point that electrolytic hydrogen can now be made at power rates available in a number of locations for costs competitive with those of steam methane reforming."* **220p701**

PIPELINES

The cost of transmitting hydrogen by pipelines at 136 atm (13.8 MPa, 2,000 psi) pipeline pressure is 1.5 times the cost of an equal volume of natural gas. **580p94** Because of its low density, hydrogen gas requires *larger compressors with more power*. This can be offset by the *lower viscosity* of hydrogen, this allows a higher pressure to be used with hydrogen than with natural gas. **100** Natural gas can be piped in combination with 10% hydrogen with no modifications of the distribution system. **800**

It is possible to substitute hydrogen pipelines for electrical transmission lines. At the power station hydrogen is produced by electrolysis then sent through pipelines instead of electricity in high voltage lines. A 1,000 kilometer (622 mile), 1 meter (3.28 ft.) diameter pipeline at 98.7 atm (10 MPa, 1,450 psi) can replace two 400 kilovolt overhead lines. Underground hydrogen pipelines have several advantages.

● They are less obtrusive.
● Hydrogen energy can be stored in any quantity near the users, until needed.
● Hydrogen can provide electricity on-site in fuel cells or can be converted directly to heat by combustion.
● The gas can be used as a chemical feed stock for ammonia or methanol
● Large hydro plants now operating at 30 to 60% capacity, because of distribution problems, can operate at full output when producing hydrogen.

Hydrogen can be liquefied at various points on the pipeline with the boiloff used to maintain pressure, thereby replacing compressors. The fuel can also be stored in liquid form near to the users. A 100 meter (328 ft) sphere can provide 120 MW years of energy. **660p152** Several commercial pipelines are now in operation.

- Air Products and Chemicals, Inc. of Texas has 96 kilometer (60 mile) 10 to 30 cm (4 to 12 inch) diameter buried pipeline. No line compressors are used.
- Imperial Chemical Industries of Teesside, England operate a 16 kilometer (10 mile) above ground line.
- Chemische Huls, of Germany, and L'Air Liquide, of France, jointly own a 550 kilometer (342 mile) 10 to 30 cm (4 to 12 inch) line.

A study by the Institute of Gas Technology, in Illinois, found that hydrogen pipeline operating costs exceed the cost of natural gas by \$0.0004/kWh-km (\$0.0006/kWh-mile). This is mainly due to higher compression costs and leaks which are 3.5 to 30 times higher than with natural gas. In spite of this, it was found that *"The results indicate that the pipings and components used in natural gas home distribution systems should be adequate for hydrogen as well."* **670p111** Evan Orr concludes that *"Eventually, when fossil liquid fuels become uneconomic or unattractive for other reasons, the industrialized nations will probably transport energy by hydrogen pipeline."* **660p152**

During the Ninth World Energy Hydrogen Energy Conference in 1992 at Paris, France William Hoagland, manager of the Hydrogen Program at the National Renewable Energy Lab at Golden, Colorado described program for making the transition from natural gas to hydrogen using existing pipelines. Up to 15 percent by volume of hydrogen can be substituted for natural gas without significant modifications. Users will notice little difference but emissions of carbon dioxide and hydrocarbons will be reduced. Hydrogen and natural gas can be easily separated allowing users to selectively use either fuel. Liquefaction plants would supply aviation fuel, and later, be expanded to power ground transport. By the middle of the 21st century the pipeline grid will handle hydrogen exclusively.

UNDERGROUND STORAGE

For more than 50 years the petrochemical industry has stored natural gas in underground salt caverns and aquifers. Nature has stored natural gas underground for millions of years. Underground sites have been proposed for compressed air as a means of storing off-peak electrical power for utilities at a cost of about \$425/kW. Suitable sites are plentiful in about three fourths of North America. These sites have a projected life of 30 years. **569**

ENVIRONMENTAL COSTS

Much of the current discussion of alternative energy sources centers only on the cost of new fuels to business and ignores *environmental* costs. T.N. Veziroglu, President of the International Hydrogen Energy Association, has estimated the environmental "bottom line" cost of fossil fuels. Included in this assessment is the health cost, damage to water resources, treatment costs necessary to counteract these effects, the damage to the food supplies and the climate, acid rain, etc. **Exhibit 155** summarizes the damage costs for all fossil fuels. **670p107** The total is \$3.35 per 100 kilowatt hours or \$0.29/liter (\$1.13/gal.) gasoline).Burning fossil fuels spews forth 2.7×10^{13} kilograms (30 billion tons) of air pollution each year. The main components of air pollution are given below.

Type of Damage	Damage per Unit of Fossil Fuel Energy	
	($GJ)	($/100 kWh)
Effect on Humans (loss of work, medical costs, deaths)	3.89	1.4
Effect on Fresh Water Resources (loss of fish, damage to drinking water)	1.94	0.7
Treatment of Lakes (treatment by powdered lime)	0.06	0.02
Effect on Farm Produce, Plants, Forests (acid rain and ozone)	0.56	0.2
Effect on Animals (domesticated or wildlife)	0.56	0.2
Effect on Buildings (historical and residential)	0.83	0.3
Effect on Coasts and Beaches (oil spills, ballast discharge)	0.08	0.03
Effect of Ocean Rise (coastal protection measures)	0.28	0.1
Effect of Strip Mining (land reclamation)	0.11	0.4
Total Damage	9.31	3.35

- *Carbon monoxide:* this takes the place of oxygen in the red blood cells. In extreme cases it causes internal suffocation, cramps and heart attack.
- *Carbon dioxide:* is nontoxic but responsible for the *greenhouse effect.* This is caused by holding in more of the earth's heat than would otherwide escape into space. By 2050 earth's climate may increase 3 to 9°C (5.4 to 16.2°F). This will contribute to the spread of deserts and the melting of the polar caps sufficiently to raise the sea level 1 to 4 meters (3 to 13 ft). (Methanol is often suggested as an alternative fuel. With combustion it produces water vapor and carbon dioxide and far lower levels of other pollutants, compared with gasoline. Methanol has half the carbon as gasoline but also half the energy. Therefore, carbon dioxide emissions are the same as for gasoline to acomplish the same work.) **670p100**

- *Sulfur dioxide:* an irritant to the lungs, it can aggravate asthma and emphysema.
- *Nitrous oxide:* a major contributor to acid rain, a phenomena that destroys freshwater life and dissolves architectural masonry. Among other public monuments, Mt. Rushmore is a victim.
- *Unburned hydrocarbons:* the result of incomplete combustion. Many are toxic and in combination with nitrous oxides form another respiratory irritant.
- *Sulfuric acid:* another contributor to acid rain.
- *Particulates (soot):* this airbourne debris can block lung passages and cause cancer.
- *Lead:* increases blood pressure, causes permanent nerve damage and reduces bone marrow.

$526 billion is spent yearly in the U.S. to try and control air pollution with less than complete success. The total estimated environmental damage is $1,613 billion or one-eighth of all the world's production of goods and services. This figure ignores climatic changes due to carbon dioxide.

Exhibit 156 gives an estimate of the total costs of four synthetic fuels: synthetic natural gas, synthetic gasoline, gaseous hydrogen, and liquid hydrogen. In each case the cost is determined by the following relation:

$$(P + E) N_f / N_s.$$

Where:

P = production cost of fuel.
E = environmental cost of fuel.
N_f = fossil fuel utilization efficiency.
N_s = synthetic fuel utilization efficiency.

It is assumed that the environmental damage from synthetic natural gas is only two-thirds that of synthetic gasoline. The damage by hydrogen made from coal-fired steam reforming is only half that for synthetic natural gas. This is because the adverse effects on the environment occur only at the coal gasification plant, not at the user end.

Exhibit 156 shows that the total effective cost of synthetic gasoline is highest and hydrogen electrolysis from hydropower is lowest. Liquid hydrogen from coal has the lowest effective cost of the liquid fuels. Liquid hydrogen from hydropower is 40% of the cost of synthetic gasoline. **670p107**

Fuel	Production Cost		Environ. Damage		Util. Eff.	Effective Cost	
	$ GJ	$ 100kWh	$ GJ	$ 100kWh	%	$ GJ	$ 100kWh
Synthetic Natural Gas	7.42	2.67	5.51	1.98	1.00	12.94	4.66
Hydrogen from Coal	7.19	2.59	2.75	0.99	0.74	7.36	2.65
Hydrogen from Hydro	9.64	3.47	----	----	0.74	7.14	2.57
H_2 Other Processes	18.14	6.53	----	----	0.74	13.42	4.83
Synthetic Gasoline	14.47	5.21	8.25	2.97	1.00	22.72	8.18
LH_2 from Coal	9.00	3.24	2.75	0.99	0.74	8.70	3.13
LH_2 from Hydro	12.06	4.34	----	---	0.74	8.92	3.21
LH_2 Other Processes	22.7	8.16	----	---	0.74	16.78	6.04

THE LAST WORD

"In view of the fact that domestic petroleum will continue to be an increasingly scarce commodity, and that expanded reliance on imported petroleum by the United States is not feasible, alternatives to petroleum must be found and deployed."

Robert R. Adt, Jr.

"The question is no longer 'whether or not hydrogen?' but 'how fast' will hydrogen replace fossil fuels?"

T. Nejat Veziroglu,
President, International Association
of Hydrogen Energy

"National security, scientific contingency, and common sense make it clear that research on the production, storage and end use of hydrogen is required." **60p2**

John Appleby, Director
Texas A&M University
Center for Electrochemical Systems and Hydrogen Research

"The less desirable alternative of imported oil may require the United States to pay significant economic penalties and compromise our international political independence."
308

F.J. Salzano
Brookhaven National Lab

"The handwriting is on the wall. We are driving our energy economy with a depleting resource and are relying on foreign fuel sources of a most unstable nature. Our economy must unshackle itself by becoming energy independent through the use of renewable resources. Furthermore, we agree that the ultimate answer will include the production of hydrogen from these resources."

Frank W. Spillers
President, Industrial Fuel Cell Association

"The environmental defense industry can do well to follow the spirit of capitalism to bring about the Renewable Resources Revolution. The ultimate profit is prosperity without pollution." **568**

Roy E. McAlister, P.E.
President, American Hydrogen Association

Alternative Energy Engineering. Sells a variety of devices for producing electricity from photovoltaics and for energy savings.
- P.O. Box 339, Redway, CA 95560.

American Hydrogen Association. Sponsors annual energy exhibits and promotes its own research into using solar energy to generate hydrogen. Current research includes development of a "SMART" plug that promises to allow easier conversion of almost any car or truck engine to hydrogen combustion the development of an activated carbon hydrogen storage system that will hold more hydrogen per unit weight than hydride. Patent pending.
Publication: *Hydrogen Today,* a monthly publication.
Director: **Roy McAllister, P.E.**
Manager of Racing Program: **Demetri Wagner**
Manager Solar Development: **Irving R. Jorgenson**
Data Bank: Get updated hydrogen energy data can be by fax at 408-738-4014. Times: 12:00 noon to 6:00 am. pacific.
- 219 S. Siesta Lane, Suite 101, Tempe, AZ 85281.
- Phone: 602-921-0433 or 602-921-0433.

Home Power. The hands-on journal for energy self sufficiency. Typical issue includes topics such as: Solar cooding with parabolic reflectors, batch solar water heaters, case studies of photovoltaic applications, etc.
- P.O. Box 520, Ashland, OR 97520.
- Phone: 1-916-475-3179.

The Hydrogen Letter. monthly publication edited by Peter Hoffmann. He was a correspondent for major news organizations in Washington D.C. and a foreign correspondent in Germany and Italy. Newsletter covers major research and development in hydrogen energy, worldwide.
- 4104 Jefferson St. Hyattsville, MD 20781.
- Phone: 1-301-779-1561.

International Journal of Hydrogen Energy. Monthly publication of the International Association for Hydrogen Energy. Provides for exchange and dissemination of ideas on hydrogen energy between scientists and engineers worldwide.
- P.O. Box 248266, Coral Gables, FL 33124.

International Directory of Hydrogen Energy. Contains about 640 listings listed alphabetically. Includes individuals and entities by specialty (eg. storage, fuel cells). Available on disc (WordPerfect 5.1).
- The Hydrogen Letter Press, 4104 Jefferson St., Hyattsville, MD 20781, USA.

Solar Technology Institute. For over 10 years they've been teaching people from all over the world the practical use of renewable energy technologies. Workshops include using windpower, photovoltaics and passive solar for home and remote power applications.The hydrogen workshop includes, fundamental principles, safety, electrolyser construction and operation, fuel cells, and appliance conversion.
"STI offers the most comprehensive , intensive, and practicle training...STI is your best source for training." Richard Perez, Editor - Home Power Magazine
- P.O. Box 1115, Carbondale, CO 81623-1115.
- Phone: 1-303-963-0715.

SOURCES OF EQUIPMENT

See International Directory of Hydrogen Energy, above.
Butane-Propane News. Publishes a home study course in carburetion and propane conversion. May be found in libraries or purchased from the above address.
- P.O. Box 419, Arcadia, CA 91006.
California Air Resources Board. List of state approved liquid petroleum gas

conversion systems. Only these systems may be used on vehicles registered California.

- 9528 Telstar Ave., El Monte, CA 91731.

Hydrogen Wind, Inc. Has sold practical inexpensive electrolysers and building plans for wind-driven hydrogen generators since 1982.

o R.R. 2, Box 262, Lineville, IA 50147.

Impco Carburetion, Inc. Sells propane conversion kits and gas regulators.

- 16916 Gridley Plaza, Cerritos, CA 90701.

MPD Technology Corp. Manufactures "Hy-Stor" metal hydrides. Iron, nickle and magnesium based hydrides sold in 1 kg (1 quart), 10 kg (1 gallon), and larger quantities.

- 4 William Demarest Place, Waldwick, NJ 07463.

Manchester Tank. Sells California Highway Petrol regulation Title B, Article 2, Section 930-936 (revised 8-20-77). This document details the legal requirements for LPG conversions in California. Applicable to hydrogen, as well. Send a large self-addressed stamped envelope.

- 2880 Morton Ave., Lynwood, CA 90262.

National Fire Protection Association. Sells books about gaseous fuel safety standards. Inquire about prices.

- 60 Battery March St., Boston, MA 02110.

National Liquid Petroleum Gas Association. List of LP refilling stations, 5,300 locations nationwide, including safety tips. Write for information on prices. Send large self-addressed stamped envelope.

- 1301 West 22nd, Oakbrook, IL 60521.

Trans Energy Corporation. Currently engaged in research on retrofitting vehicles with PSI technology.

- 2026 West Campus Drive, Tempe, AZ 85282.

Tricomp Sensors, Inc. Manufacturers a hydrogen leak detector sensitive to 10 ppm at up to 150°C (300°F). It also detects hydrogen sulfide and ammonia.

- 2368 D Walsh Ave., Santa Clara, CA 95051.
- 408-988-6050

Windfall Energy Corp. Produces wind generator for generating hydrogen energy. Research in alternate sources of energy

- 2053 Electric Avenue. Buffalo, NY 14219.
- 716-826-6900

BIBLIOGRAPHY

ch. 1 -- Introduction

K. E. Cox, ed, *Hydrogen: Its Technology and Implications,* C.R.C. Press, Inc., 18901 Cranwood Parkway, Cleveland, OH 44128.

Peter Hoffman, *The Forever Fuel: The Story of Hydrogen,* Westview Press, Boulder, CO, 1981.

Davis A. Mathis, *Hydrogen Technology for Energy,* Noyes Data Corp., Noyes Data Corp., Noyes Bldg., Park Ridge, NJ, 07656.

T. Nejat Veziroglu, *Hydrogen Energy,* 2 Vols., Plenum Publishing Corp., 227 W. 17th Street, New York, NY, 10011.

L.O. Williams, *Hydrogen Power: An Introduction to Hydrogen Energy and Its Applications,* Pergammon Press, Inc., Maxwell House, Fairview Park, Elmsford, NY, 10523, 1980.

ch. 2 -- Electrolysis

A.F. Anderson and J.J. Reilly, *Hydrides for Energy Storage,* Pergammon Press, 1978.

James E. Bennethum, Thomas D. Laymac, (Detroit Diesel Corp.)

Lennart N. Johansson, Ted M. Godett, (Stirling Thermal Motors, Inc.), "Commercial Stirling Engine Development & Applications", SAE International, Future Transportation Technology Conference & Exposition, August 1991.

James E. Bennethum, "Stirling Engine Technology", Detroit Diesel Corp., October 1990.

E.F. Lindsley, "Storable, Renewable, Hydrogen Power ... Key to Unlocking Energy from Sun, Wind, and Tides", *Popular Science Monthly*, March 1975, p.88.

M.A.K. Lodhi, "Hydrogen Production from Renewable Sources of Energy", *Int. J. of Hyd. Energy*, Vol. 12, #7, pp. 461-468, 1987.

N.J. Maskalick, "Hydrogen Temperature Electrolysis Cell Performance Characterization", *Int. J. of Hyd. Energy*, Vol. 11, #9, pp. 563-570, 1986.

K. Tennakone, "Two Step Photochemical Reactions for Hydrogen Production", *Int. J. of Hyd. Energy*, Vol. 12, #2, pp.79-80, 1987.

A.Z. Ullman, et.al., "Methods of On-Board Generation of Hydrogen for Vehicular Use", in *Proceedings of the First World Hydrogen Energy Conference*, Miami, FL, 1976.

Ullman, "Hydrogen Production", *Hydrocarbon Processing*, April, 1984, p.103.

Ullman, "Optimizing Hydrogen Plant Design", *Chemical Engineering Progress*, Feb., 1983, p.37.

Ullman, *Perfluorinated Ion Exchange Membranes*, Plastics Dept., E.I. DuPont de Nemours & Co., Wilmington, DE, 1972.

Ullman, "Two Routes to Solar Hydrogen", *Science*, 5 Nov. 1982.

Ullman, "Water Splitting Claims Generate Controversy", *Chemical Engineering News*, 25 Oct. 1982.

"The Ultimate Fuel: Hydrogen on the Horizon", South Coast Air Quality Management District, El Monte, CA 91731.

Yu. I. Kharkats, "Hydrogen Production by Solar Energy: Optimization of the Solar Array & Electrolyser", *Int. J. of Hyd. Energy*, Vol. 11, #10, pp 617-621, 1988.

ch. 3 -- Chemical Hydrogen Production

Glendon M. Benson, et.al., "An Advanced 15 kW Solar-Powered Free-Piston Stirling Engine", *15th Intersociety Energy Conversion Engineering Conference, paper # 809-414*, American Inst. of Aeronautics and Astronautics, New York, NY, Aug. 1980.

J. O'M. Bockris, *Energy: The Solar-Hydrogen Alternative*, Australia & New Zealand Book Company, Sydney, Australia. 1975.

J. O'M. Bockris, *Real Economics and Solar Hydrogen Systems*, Halstead press, 1980.

M.S. Casper, *Hydrogen Manufacture by Electrolysis: Thermal Decomposition and Universal Techniques*, Noyes Data Corp., Noyes Bldg., Park Ridge, NJ 07656.

Charles R. Imbrecht, Chairman, "Energy Technology Status Report", California Energy Commission, June 1990.

John F. Kreiter, PhD, *Solar Energy Handbook*, McGraw Hill, Co.

Roy E. McAlister, "Renewable Electricity and Hydrogen Using Solar Thermal Processes", *Project Hydrogen Conference Technical Proceedings*, International Association for Hydrogen Energy, American Academy of Science, Sept. 1991. pp 45-57.

T. Ohta, *Solar Hydrogen Energy Systems*, Pergammon Press, Ltd., Headington Hill Hall, Oxford, OX3, OBW, U.K.

John C. Schaefer, Project Manager, "Performance of the Vanguard Solar Dish - Stirling Engine Module", Electric Power Research Institute AP-4608, Project 2003-5, July 1986.

L.W. Skelton, *The Solar-Hydrogen Energy Economy: Beyond the Age of Fire.* Van Nostrand Reinholt, NY, 1984.

Colin D. West, *Principles and Applications of Striling Engines* , 1972.

ch. 4 -- Fuel From Trash

R.E. Billings, *Hydrogen from Coal Gasification: Cost Estimation Handbook,* Billings Energy Research Corporation. 18600 E 37th Terrace, South Independence, MO 64057

ch. 5 -- Storing Hydrogen

A.F. Andresen, *Hydrides for Energy Storage,* Pergammon, NY, 1978.

"Energy Storage: How the New Options Stack Up", Electric Power Research Institute, 1989.

J.G. Finegold, et.al., *The U.C.L.A. Hydrogen Car: Design, Construction & Performance, Paper SAE 730507,* Society of Automotive Engineers, 1973.

K.C. Hoffman, et.al., "Metal Hydrides as a Source of Fuel for Vehicular Propulsion", SAE Transactions, Vol. 78, paper #690232, 1969.

M. Grall, et.al., "Heat and Mass Transfer Limitations in Metal Hydride Reaction Beds", *Int J. of Hyd. Energy,* Vol. 12, #2, pp 89-97, 1987.

L.W. Jones, "Liquid Hydrogen as a Fuel for the Future", *Science,* Vol. 174, p.367, 1971.

F.E. Lynch, et.al., "The Role of Metal Hydrides in Storage and Utilization", *Second World Hydrogen Energy Conf.,* Zurich, Switzerland, 21-24 August 1978.

J.J. Reilly, et.al., *Metal Hydrides,* Brookhaven National Lab Report # 50023, 1969.

J.J. Reilly, "Metal Hydrides as Hydrogen Storage Media and Their Applications", in *Hydrogen: Its Technology and Implications,* Vol. 2, CRC Press, 1977.

G.D. Sandrock, "Development of Low Cost Nickle-Rare Earth Hydrides for Hydrogen Storage", *Second World Hydrogen Energy Conference.*

G.D. Sandrock, "The Metallurgy and Production of Rechargeable Hydrides", *International Symposium on Hydrides for Energy Storage,* Geilo, Norway, 14-19 August 1978, Pergammon Press.

G.D. Sandrock, et.al., "Rechargeable Metal Hydrides: A New Concept in Hydrogen Storage, Processing and Handling", *ACS/CSJ Chemical Congress,* Honolulu, HI, 1-6 April 1979.

J.H.N. VanVucht, et.al., "Reversible Room-Temperature Absorption of Large Quantities of Hydrogen by Intermetallic Compounds", *Phillips Research Reports,* pp.130-140, 1970.

T. Nejat Veziroglu, *Metal Hydride Systems,* Pergammon Press.

W.P. Webb, et.al., "Metals for Hydrogen Service", *Chemical Engineering,* Vol. 91, pp. 113-114, 1 October 1984.

Saul Wolf, "Hydrogen Sponge Storage", in *U.S. Office of Naval Research, Naval Research Reviews,* Vol. 28, #3, pp.16-22, 3 March 1975.

Saul Wolf, "Compact Reactor for On-Board Hydrogen Generator", *Machine Design,* September 1980, p.50.

Saul Wolf, "How Metals Store Hydrogen", *Chemical Technology,* Dec. 1981, p.62.

Saul Wolf, "Hydrides: Theory and Uses", *Scientific American,* Vol. 242, #2, p.118, 1980.

Saul Wolf, "Hydrogen Liquefaction Flow Diagram", *Cryogenics,* Oct. 1980, p.605.

Saul Wolf, "Hydrogen Storage Metals", *Science,* 4 Oct. 1981, p.1081.

Saul Wolf, "Liquid Hydrogen as a Vehicular Fuel", *Mechanical Engineering,* September 1980, p.54.

Saul Wolf, "Metal Hydrides Make Hydrogen Accessible", *Chemical Technology,* December 1980, p.73.

Saul Wolf, "Magnesium Storage", *Light Metal Age,* Jan 1981, p.8.

Saul Wolf, "Methanol Reforming for On-Board Hydrogen Generation", *NASA* N 77-23256.

Saul Wolf, "Phillips Research Discoveries Could Lead to Safe Ways to Store Hydrogen, Unique Ways to Purify It, Compressors Without Moving Parts", *Inside R & D,* 14 June 1972.

ch. 6 -- Engine Modifications

R.R. Adt, et.al., "Hydrogen Engine Performance Analysis", *DOE Contract # EC-77-C-03-1212.* August 1978.

A.L. Austin, *Survey of Hydrogen's Potential as a Vehicular Fuel.* Lawrence Livermore Laboratory, Livermore, CA, 35 pp. June 1972.

M.A. DeLuchi, "Hydrogen Vehicles: An Evaluation of Fuel Storage, Performance, Safety, Environmental Impacts, and Costs", *Int. J. of Hyd. Energy,* Vol. 14, #2, 1989. pp. 81-130.

J.G. Finegold, et.al., "The UCLA Hydrogen Car: Design, Construction and Performance", *SAE Transactions,* paper # 730507, p. 1626. 1973

J.G. Finegold, "Converting a Gasoline Air-Cooled Engine to Propane", *Society of Automotive Engineers Paper # 740746.* 9-12 September 1974.

J.G. Finegold, "Effect of % Hydrogen in Fuel on Emissions", *Journal of Power Engineering,* October 1980, p.842.

J.G. Finegold, "Hydrogen as a Future Automotive Fuel", *Institute of Energy Journal,* September 1980.

J.G. Finegold, "Hydrogen as an Automotive Fuel", *Automotive Engineering,* August 1981, p.69.

J.G. Finegold, "L.P. Fuel: Does it Make Sense for Your Car?" *Popular Science,* Februrary 1986.

J.G. Finegold, *An Answer to the Air Pollution Problem,* Perris Smogless Automobile Association, First Annual Report. Perris, CA, 1971.

J.G. Finegold, "Piston Engine Hydrogen Fuel", *Mechanical Engineering,* September 1980, p.54.

S. Furuhama, "Hydrogen Engine Systems for Land Vehicles", *Int. J. of Hyd. Energy,* Vol. 14, #12, 1989. pp. 907-913.

Roy E. McAlister, "Direct Hydrogen Injection and Spark Ignition System for Internal Combustion Engines", *Project Hydrogen Conference Technical Proceedings,* International Association for Hydrogen Energy, American Academy of Science, Sept. 1991. pp. 139-147.

Roy E. McAlister, "Method and Apparatus for Fuel Injection-Spark Ignition for an Internal Combustion Engine", U.S. Patent 4,066,046, 1978.

W.D. VanVorst, *Studies Pertaining to hydrogen Car Development,* Technical Report #UCLA-ENG-7489, University of California, Los Angeles, CA, October 1974.

ch. 7 -- Fuel Cells

B.J. Crowe, *Fuel Cells: A Summary,* NASA Report SP-5115, 1973.

ch. 8 -- Stationary Applications

R.E. Billings, "Survey of Hydrogen Energy Application Projects", *11th IECED Conference,* State Line, Nevada, 12-17 September, 1976.

J.M. Burger, "An Energy Company's View of Hydrogen Energy", *Int. J. of Hyd. Energy,* Vol. 1, #1, pp.55-64, 1976.

W.J.D. Escher, et.al., *Hydrogen for Energy Distribution,* Institute for Gas Technology, 3424 South State Street, Chicago, IL 60616.

M.A. Fullenwider, *Hydrogen Entry and Action in Metals,* Pergammon Press, NY, 1986.

D.M. Gruen, et.al., "Solar Energy Storage Subsystems for Heating and Cooling of Buildings", *American Society of Heating, Refrigeration and Air Conditioning Engineers,* NSF-RA-N-75-841, 16-18 April 1975. Also, "A Thermodynamic Analysis of HYCSOS, a Hydrogen Conversion and Storage System", above.

K.C. Hoffman, *Economics of Hydrogen Energy Systems,* Upton, NY, Brookhaven National Laboratory, 14 pp. 1975.

K.C. Hoffman, et.al., *Hydrogen for Energy Transport and Storage in Solar Energy Systems,* Brookhaven National Lab., Upton, NY, 6pp. 1970.

K.C. Hoffman, et.al., "Metal Hydride Storage for Mobile and Stationary Applications", *Int. J. of Hyd. Energy,* Vol.1, #2, pp.133-151, 1976.

G.G. Libowitz, et.al., "An Evaluation of the Use of Metal Hydrides for Solar Thermal Energy Storage", *11th IECEC Conf.*

T. Ohto, *Solar Hydrogen Energy,* Pergammon Press, Ltd. 1979.

F.J. Salzano, et.al., *High Efficiency Power Cycles Using Metal Hydride Compressors,* Brookhaven National Lab. BNL 50447. 31 Jan. 1975.

Robert H. Williams, et.al., *Renewable Energy Sources for Fuel and Electricity,* Island Press, Washington, D.C., 1992.

ch. 9 -- Safety

A. Brown, et.al., "Hydrogen Induced Cracking in Pipeline Steels", *Corrosion,* Vol. 40, pp. 330-336. July 1984.

F.J. Eduskuty, et.al., *Liquified Hydrogen Safety,* PB-230845. Los Alamos Scientific Lab., New Mexico. 1968.

J. Hord, *Is Hydrogen Safe?,* Technical Note 690. U.S. Bureau of Standards. 1976.

R.E. Knowlton, "An Investigation of the Safety Aspects in the Use of Hydrogen as a Ground Transportation Fuel", *Int. J. of Hyd. Energy,* Vol. 9, #1, pp 129, 1984.

J.B. Porter, *Analysis of Hydrogen Explosion Hazards.* Du Pont de Nemours & Co., South Carolina. July 1972.

B. Rosen, et.al., *Hydrogen Leak and Fire Detection: A Survey,* NASA, Washington, D.C. 1970.

B. Rosen, et.al., *Hydrogen Safety Manual,* NASA-TM-52454. Lewis Research Center.

B. Rosen, *Safety Rules of the Liquefied Petroleum Gas Division,* Texas Railroad Commission, 611 W. Congress, Austin, TX 78711.

B. Rosen, "Summary of Hydrogen Safety Workshop Held at the Fifth World Hydrogen Energy Conference", *Int. J. of Hyd. Energy,* Vol. 11, #1, pp. 61-63. 1986.

ch. 10 -- The Hydrogen Economy

Walter H. Corson, editor, *The Global Ecology Handbook,* Beacon Press, Boston, MA. ISBN 0-8070-8501-4, 1990.

D.P. Gregory, "The Hydrogen Economy", *Scientific American,* pp. 13-21, Jan. 1973.

A.B. Hart, "Will Hydrogen Transmission Replace Electricity?", *Electronics and Power,* Vol. 27, pp.785-786. 1981.

Roy McAlister, "Prosperity Without Pollution", Am. Hyd. Assn. 1992

John O. Mingle, *An Engineering Assessment of the Hyd. Economy*, Report #CES-5. Center of Energy Studies, Kansas State University. 1974.

John O. Mingle, "Study of Hydrogen Energy Application Projects", *11th IECED Conference,* State Line, Nevada. 12-17 Sept. 1976.

John O. Mingle, *Hydrogen as an Aviation Fuel,* U.S. Government Printing Office, Washington, D.C. 26pages. 1974.

J. O'M. Bockris, *Energy Options: Real Economics and the Solar Hydrogen System, Technical Summary.*

D.S. Scott and W. Hafele, "The Coming Hydrogen Age: Preventing Climatic Disruption", *Int. J. of Hyd. Energy,* Vol. 15, #10, 1990. pp. 727-737.

REFERENCES CITED IN ALPHABETICAL ORDER

10.   **S. Abens**, et.al., *Development of 3 and 5 kW Fuel Cell Power Plants: Final Technical Report.* Energy Research Corp., Danbury, CT. AD-A 163603. Available from National Technical Information Service. Oct. 1979 - July 1985

20.   **Y.K. Ahn**, "Production of Hydrogen from Coal and Petroleum Coke: Technical and Economic Perspectives", *Int. J. of Hyd. Ener.* Vol. 11, #12. 1986

30.   **H.P. Alder**, "Hyd. in Air Transport.", *Int. J. of Hyd. Energy.* Vol. 12, #18. 1987

40.   **J.C. Anphletti**, et.al., "Hydrogen Production from the Catalytic Steam Reforming of Methanol", *Chemical Engineering.* Vol. 91, #107. Oct. 1984

50.   **M.J. Antal**, "Hydrogen and Food Production from Nuclear Heat and Municipal Wastes" in T. Nejat Veziroglu, *Hydrogen Energy.* Plenum Press. 1975

60.   **John Appleby**, cited in , *The Hydrogen Letter.* July 1987, p2.

70.   **G.E. Beghi**, "A Decade of Research on Thermochemical Hydrogen at the Joint Research Center at Ispra", *Int. J. of Hyd. Energy.* Vol. 11, #12. 1986

80.   **L. Peraldo Bicelli**, et.al., "Anodically Oxidized Titanium Films to be Used as Electrodes in Photoelectrolysis Solar Cells", *Int. J. Hyd. Energy.* Vol. 11, #10. 1986

90.   **L. Peraldo Bicelli**, "Photoelectrochemical Behavior and XPS Characterization of a (Ti,Al,V) O_2 Film Obtained by Nonconventional Anodic Oxydation of a Commercial TiAlV Alloy", *Int. J. of Hyd. Energ.* Vol. 12, #4. 1987

100.   **L.P. Bicelli**, "Hyd.:Clean Energy", *Int. J. of Hyd. Energy.* Vol. 11, #9. 1986

110.   **R.E. Billings**, "Hydrogen Storage for Automobiles", in *First World Hyd. Energy.*

120.   **R.E. Billings**, *Performance and Nitric Oxide Control Parameters of the Hydrogen Engine.* Billings Energy Research, Provo, UT. 1973.

130.   **J. O'M. Bockris**, et.al., "Electrochemical Recycling of Iron for Hydrogen Production", *Int. J. of Hyd. Energy.* Vol. 11, #2. 1986

140.   **J. O'M. Bockris**, *The Solar-Hydrogen Alternative.* John Wiley, NY.1975

150.   **E. Borgarello**, "Photochem. Water Splitting", *Chemtech.* Vol. 13, pp. Feb. 1983

160.   **Theodore A. Brabbs**, "Catalytic Decomposition of Methanol for On-Board Hydrogen Generation", *NASA TP-1247 (N78-23256/NSP).* Available from the National Technical Information Service, Springfield, VA 22161.

165.   **Harry Braun**, "Hydrogen Storage Systems", *Hydrogen: Journal of the American Hydrogen Association,* Summer 1991.

170.   **J.D. Canaday**, et.al., "A Polarization Model of Solid Electrolyte in Fuel Cells", *Int. J. of Hyd. Energy.* Vol. 12, #3. 198

180.   **C. Carpetis**, et.al., "Hydrogen Storage by Use of Cryoadsorbants", in *Seminar in Hyd. as an Energy Carrier.* Commission of the European Communities, Luxembourg. 197

190.   **R.L. Cohen and J.H. Wernick**, "Hydrogen Storage Materials: Properties and Possibilities", *Science.* Vol. 214. 4 Dec. 1981

200.   **K.E. Cox**, ed., *Hydrogen: Its Technology and Implications, Vol.I and II.* CRC Press, Inc., 1977. 18901 Cranwood Pkwy., Cleveland, OH 44128.

201.   **K.E. Cox**, Vol. II.

210.   **Kenneth E. Cox**, "Thermochemical Cycles: A New Method of Producing Hydrogen", Los Alamos Scientific Lab., 1980

220.   **G.A. Crawford**, et.al., "Advances in Water Electrolysers and Their Potential Use in Ammonia Production", *Int. J. of Hyd. Energy.* Vol. 11, #11,1986

230.   **G.A. Crawford**, et.al., "Electrolyser, Inc. Advanced Hydrogen Plant at Becancour, Quebec", *Int. J. of Hyd. Energy.* Vol. 12, #5. 1987

235. **Cummins Power Generation, Inc.**, Box 3005, Columbus, IN 47202, "Dish Sterling System", May 1990. Cited by McAlister **568.**

240. **R.P. Dahiya**, "Transition to Hyd.", *Int. J. of Hyd. Energy.* Vol. 11, #6. 1986

250. **P. Dantzer**, "Hydrogen...", *Int. J. of Hyd. Energy.* Vol. 11, #12, 1986.

260. **D. Davidson**, et.al., "Development of a Hydrogen-Fueled Farm Tractor", *Int. J. of Hyd. Energy.* Vol. 11, #1. 1986

270. **G. DeBeni**, "Thermochemical Processes for Hydrogen Production by Water Splitting", *Electrochemical Society Journal.* Vol. 129. Jan. 1982

280. **W. Donitz**, et.al., "High Temp. Electrolysis of Water Vapor: Status of Development and Perspectives for Applications", *Int. J. of Hyd. Energy.* Vol. 10, #5, 1986

290. **H. Eichert**, et.al., "Combustion Related Safety Aspects of Hydrogen in Energy Applications", *Int. J. of Hyd. Energy.* Vol. 11, #2. 1986

300. **H. Engles**, et.al., "Thermochemical Hydrogen Production", *Int. J. of Hyd. Energy.* Vol. 12, #5. 1987

319. **Joseph.G. Feingold**, et.al., "Crash Test of a Liquid Hydrogen Automobile", in *First World Hydrogen Energy Conf.,* 1976. Int. Assn. for Hyd. Energy.

320. **J.G. Feingold**, "Engine Performance With Hydrogen and Gasoline" in *First World Hydrogen Energy Conference.* Int. Assn. of Hyd. Energy. 1976

325. **J.G. Feingold**, et. al., "Methanol As a Consumable Hydride for Automobiles and Gas Turbines", *Hydrogen Progress,* 17 June 1982, pp.1359-1369.

330. **J.G. Feingold**, et.al., *The UCLA Hydrogen Car: Design, Construction and Performance.* Paper SAE 730507, Soc.of Auto. Engineers, NY. 1973.

335. **J.A. Fillo**, et.al., "Overview of the Hyfire Power Electrolysis Design",

340. **J. Fisher**, "Fundamentals and Technological Aspects of Medium Temperature Electrolysers", in *Seminar on Hydrogen Energy Vectors.* Commission of the European Community, Luxembourg. 1978

350. **M. Fisher**, et.al., "The Hydrogen Economy", *Int. J. of Hyd. Energy.* Vol. 12, #. 1987, *Vol. 4: Hydrogen Fuels Surface Transportation.*

360. **M. Fisher**, "Safety Aspects of Hydrogen Combustion in Hydrogen Energy Systems", *Int. J. of Hyd. Energy.* Vol. 11, #9, 1986

370. **M. Fisher**, "Review of Hydrogen Production With Photovoltaic Electrolysis Systems", *Int. J. of Hyd. Energy.* Vol. 11, #8. 1986

380. **S. Furuhama**, et.al., "Development of a Liquid Hydrogen Car", in *First World Hydrogen Energy Conference, 1976.* Int. Assn. for Hyd. Energy.

390. **S. Furuhama**, et.al., "High Output Hyd. Engine With High Pressure Fuel Injection, Hot Surface Ignition and Turbocharging", *Int. J. of Hyd. Energy.* Vol. 11, #6. 1986

400. **J. G. Geingold**, et.al., "Crash Test of Liquid Hydrogen Automobile", in *First World Hydrogen Energy Conference, 1976.* Int. Assn. for Hyd. Energy.

410. **O.G. Hancock**, Jr., "A Photovoltaic-Powered Water Electrolyser: Its Performance and Economics", *Int. J. of Hyd. Energy.* Vol. 11, #3, pp.153-160. 1986.

420. **K.J. Hartig**, et.al., "Production and Testing Methods of Different n-TiO_2 Photoanodes", *Int. J. of Hyd. Energy.* Vol. 11, #12. 1986

430. **Peter Hoffman**, *The Forever Fuel.* Int. Assn. for Hyd. Energy. 1980. and Westview Press, Boulder, CO, 1981.

434. **Peter Hoffman**, "Iron-Based Hydrogen System", *The Hydrogen Letter,* June, 1992.

435. **Peter Hoffman**, "Ovionics Wins Battery Contest", *The Hydrogen Letter,* June, 1992.

440. **Peter Hoffmann**, "Texas A&M Expands Program", *The Hyd. Letter.* July 1987.

441. **S.D. Huang**, et.al., "Hydrogen Production by Nonphotosynthetic Bacteria", *Int. J. of Hyd. Energy.* Vol. 10, #4. 1986. pp 227-231.

442. **Hydrogen Today.** June/July 1992.

460. **P. Jonville**, et.al., "Metal Hydrides and Propulsion", in *First World Hydrogen Energy Conference,* 1974.

470. **R.C. Kainthla & J. O'M. Bockris**, "Photoelectrolysis of H_2S Using a n-CdS Photoanode", *Int. J. of Hyd. Energy.* Vol. 12, #1. 1987.

480. **K. Katuta**, et.al., "Photo Assisted Hydrogen Production Using Visible Light and Coprecipitated ZnS.CdS Without a Noble Metal Catalyst", *Journal of Physical Chemistry,* Vol. 89. 28 Feb. 1985

485. **F.L. Kester**, et.al., "On-Board Steam-Reforming of Methanol to Fuel the Automotive Hydrogen Engine", *IECEC 1975 Record,* pp.1176-1183.

490. **A.T. Kuhn**, *Journal of Power Sources.* Vol. 11. 1984

500.   S.B. Lalvani, et.al., "Simultaneous Production of Hydrogen and Sulfuric Acid from Aqueous Sulfur Slurry", *Int. J. of Hyd. Energy.* Vol. 11, #9. 1986

510.   J. Lede, et.al., "Production of Hyd. by Simple Impingement of a Turbulent Jet Stream Upon a High-Temp. Zirconia Surface", *Int. J. of Hyd. Energy.* Vol. 12, #1. 1987.

520.   R.W. Leigh, et.al., "Photovoltaic-Electrolyser System Transient Simulation Results, Transactions of ASME", *J. of Solar Energy Engineering.* Vol. 108. May 1986

530.   R.W. Leigh, "Solar Hydrogen Aircraft", *Int. J. of Hyd. Energy.* Vol. 11, #3. 1986

540.   M.A. Liepa, et.al., "High Temperature Steam Electrolysis: Technical and Economic Evaluation of Alternative Process Designs", *Int. J. of Hyd. Energy.* Vol. 11, #7. 1986.

545.   Li Jing-Ding, et.al., "Improvements on the Combustion of a Hydrogen Fueled Engine", *Int. J. of Hyd. Energy.* Vol. 11, #10. 1986.

550.   L. Loy, et.al., "Photoinduced Hydrogen Evolution from Water in the Presence of EDTA and a Pt/TiO$_2$ Catalyst", *Solar Energy.* Vol. 32, #6. 1986

560.   F.E. Lynch, "Backfire Control Techniques", in T. Nejat Veziroglu, *Hydrogen Energy.* Plenum Press, NY. 1975

565.   Roy E. McAlister, "Alternatives Allowing Continued Use of Fossil Fuels", Trans Energy Corporation, Tempe, AZ, 1992.

566.   Roy E. McAlister, "Conversion of Automobiles to Air Cleaners", Trans Energy Corporation, 1992.

567.   Roy E. McAlister, "Hydrogen Mixed with Conventional Fuels for Improved Performance and Reduced Emissions", American Hyd. Assoc.,1992.

568.   Roy E. McAlister, "Prosperity Without Pollution", American Hyd. Ass'n" 1992

569.   Roy E. McAlister, "Renewable Electricity and Hydrogen Using Solar Thermal Processes", American Hydrogen Association, 1992.

570.   Donald B. McKay, "Hydride Tank Design", *First World Hyd. Energy Conf.,* 1976.

580.   David A. Mathis, *Hyd. Tech. for Energy.* Noyes Data Corp. Parkridge, NJ. 1976

590.   I. Maya, et.al., "A Thermochemical Hydrogen Production System Based on a High Temperature Fusion Reactor Blanket", *Nuclear Technology/Fusion.* pp. Sept. 1983

600.   J. Miyake, et.al., "Efficiency of Light Energy Conversion to Hydrogen by the Photosynthetic Bacterium", *Int. J. of Hyd. Energy.* Vol. 12, #3, 1987

610.   C. Marchetti, "Primary Energy Sources for Hydrogen Production", in T.Nejat Veziroglu, ed., *Intro. to Hyd.Energy.* Int. Association for Hydrogen Energy. 1975

620.   J.E. Nitsch, "Large Scale Solar Energy", *Int. J. of Hyd. Energy.* Vol. 11, #1. 1986

630.   T. Ohta, *The Solar-Hydrogen Energy System.* Pergammon Press, Ltd., 1979. Maxwell House, Fairview Park, Elmsford, NY 10523.

640.   S. Ono, et.al., "The Effect of CO$_2$, CH$_4$, H$_2$O, and N$_2$ on Mg-Ni Alloys as Hydrogen Transporting Media", *Int. J. of Hyd. Energy.* Vol. 11, #6. 1986

650.   S. Ono, "Hydrogen...", *Am. Institute of Chem.Eng. Journal.* Vol. 32. Nov. 1986

660.   Evan Orr, "Hydrogen Power Transmission for Remote Hydro Schemes", *Electronics and Power.* Vol. 31. Feb. 1985

670.   J. Pangborn, et.al., "Domestic Uses of Hydrogen", *1st World Hyd. Conf.*

680.   W. Peschka, "Cryogenic Storage Tank for a Passenger Car", in *First World Hydrogen Energy Conference, 1976.*

690.   W. Peschka, et.al., "Experience and Special Aspects on Mixture Formation of an Otto Engine Converted from Hyd. Operation", *Int.. J. of Hyd. Energy.* Vol. 11, #10. 1986

700.   W. Peschka, "Hydrogen for Future Tech.", *Int. J. of Hyd. Energy.* Vol. 12, #7. 1987

710.   W. Peschka, "Liquid Hydrogen Automotive Vehicles in Germany: Status and Development", *Int. J. of Hyd. Energy.* Vol. 11, #11. 1986

720.   E.J. Phillips, et.al., "Characterization and Optimization of Hydrogen Production of a Salt Water Blue-Green Algae...", *Int. J. of Hyd Energy.* Vol. 11, #2. 198

730.   G.P. Prabhukumar, "Water Induction Studies in a Hydrogen Diesel Fuel Engine", *Int. J. of Hyd. Energy.* Vol. 12, #3. 1987.pp. 177-176.

740.   K.H. Quandt, et.al., "Concept and Design of a 3.5 MW Pilot Plant for High Temperature Electrolysis of Water Vapor", *Int. J. of Hyd. Energy.* Vol. 11, #15. 1986 *Nuclear Technology/Fusion.* Sept. 1983.

750.   J.F. Reber, et.al., "Photochemical Production With Zinc Sulfate Suspensions", *Journal of Physical Chemistry.* Vol. 88. 22 Nov. 1984.

760.   J.J. Reilly, et.al., "Iron-Titanium as a Source of Hydrogen for Stationary and Automobile Applications", *Power Source Symposium.* Int. Assn. for Hyd. Energy.

770.   J.J. Reilly, "Metal Hydrides...", in K.E. Cox, above.

772.   **C.A. Rohrman** and J. Greenborg, "Large scale Hydrogen Production Utilizing Carbon in Renewable Resources", *Int. J. of Hyd. Energy*. Vol. 2, 1977, pp.31-40. Cited by McAlister **568**.

780.   **R. Rotenburg**, "The Musashi 7", *Int. J. of Hyd. En*. Vol. 12, #6. 1987

790.   **R. Rotenburg**, "Vibrational Effects on Boil-Off Rate from a Small Liquid Hydrogen Tank", *Int. J. of Hyd. Energy*. Vol. 11, #11. 1986

792.   **S. Roychowdhury**, et.al., "Production of Hydrogen by Microbial Fermentation", *Int. J. Hyd. Energy*. Vol. 13 #7. 1988. pp. 407-410

800.   **F.J. Salzano**, et.al., *Hydrogen Energy Assessment*. Brookhaven National Lab., Upton, NY. Sept. 1977

810.   **M.V.C. Sastri**, "Hydrogen Energy Research and Development in India: An Overview", *Int. J. of Hyd. Energy*. Vol. 12, #3. 1987.

815.   **Jennifer Sauve**, "LaserCel: A Fuel-Cell Car", *Hydrogen Today*, Apr.-May, 1992.

820.   **L. Selvam**, "Design of a Gaseous Hydrogen Fuel Supply ", *Int. J. of Hyd. Energy*. Vol. 11, #11. 1986.

830.   **S. Selvam**, "Magnesium Hydrides", *Int. J. of Hyd. Energy*. Vol. 11, #3. 1986.

840.   **F.B. Simpson**, et.al., "Modification Techniques and Performance Characteristics of Hyd. Powered Internal Combustion Engines", *First World Hydrogen Energy Conference*.

850.   **E. Smith**, "Improved Liquid Hydrogen Design", Patent # 4,530,744.

860.   **Frank Spillers**, cited in , *The Hydrogen Letter*. Sept. 1987.

870.   **S. Suda**, "Metal Hydrides", *Int. J. of Hyd. Energy*. Vol. 12, #4. 1987.

880.   **S. Suda**, "Transatmospheric Aircraft", *Int. J. of Hyd. Energy*. Vol. 11, #11. 1986.

890.   **S. Tanisho**, "Fermentation Hydrogen", *Int. J. of Hyd. Energy*. Vol. 12, #9. 1987.

900.   **J.B. Taylor**, et.al., "Tech. and Economic Assessment of Methods for the Storage of Large Quantities of Hydrogen", *Int. J. of Hyd. En*. Vol. 11, #1. 1986

910.   **H. Van Der Broeck**, et.al., "Status of Elenco's Alkaline Fuel Cell Development", *Int. J. of Hyd. Energy*. Vol. 11, #7. 1986

920.   **T. Nejat Veziroglu**, "Dawning of Hyd. Age", *Int. J. of Hyd. En*. Vol. 12, #1. 1987

930.   **T. Nejat Veziroglu**, cited in P. Hoffmann, *The Hydrogen Letter*. p.3. August 1987

940.   **T. Nejat Veziroglu**, "Hydrogen Technology for Energy Needs of Human Settlements", *Int. J. of Hyd. Energy*. Vol. 12, #2. 1987

950.   **M. Vincenzini**, "Hydrogen Production by Immobilized Cells III - Prolonged and Stable Hydrogen Photoevolution by Rhodopseudomonas Plaustris in Light-Dark Cycles", *Int. J. of Hyd. Energy*. Vol. 11, #10. 1986

960.   **J.W. Warner**, et.al., "Hydrogen Separation and the High-Temperature Splitting of Water", *Int. J. of Hyd. Energy*. Vol. 11,#2. 1986

970.   **K. Watanabe**, "Hydrogen...", *Automobile Industry*, Vol. 165. Aug.1985

980.   **M.F. Weber**, et.al., "Spitting Water With Photelectrodes", *Int. J. of Hyd. Energy*. Vol. 11, #4. 1986

990.   **W. Weinrich**, et.al., "Development of a Laboratory Cycle for a Thermochemical Water-Splitting Process (Me/MeH cycle)", *Int. J. of Hyd. Energy*. Vol. 11, #7. 1986

1000.   **Lawrence O. Williams**, *Hydrogen Power: An Introduction to Hydrogen Energy and Its Applications*. Pergammon Press, NY. 1980

1010.   **C.J. Winter**, "Hyd. Energy Breakthroughs", *Int. J. of Hyd. E*. Vol. 12, #8. 1987

1012.   **J.M. Woodwell**, "The Energy Cycle of the Biosphere", *Scientific American*. Vol. 223, #3. Sept. 1970. Cited by McAlister **568**.

1020.   **R.L. Wooley**, "Thermodynamic Considerations in the Production of Synthetic Fuels From Coal", Billings Energy Corp., Provo, Utah. 1977.

1030.   **R.L. Wooley**, "Water Injection in Hydrogen Powered Internal Combustion Engines", *First World Hydrogen Energy Conference*.

1040.   **B. Zaidman**, "Cars Can Run on Water and Fuel", *Mechanical Engineering*. Nov. 1976

1050.   **B. Zaidman**, *Carburetion Clinic: LPG Facts*. Propane Carburetion Co.

1060.   **J.B. Zaidman**, et.al., "Formate Salts as Chemical Carriers in Hydrogen Storage and Transportation", *Int. J. of Hyd. Energy*. Vol. 11, #5. 1986

1070.   **B. Zaidman**, "Water-Gas Engine", *Mechanical Engineering*. Jan. 1977.

1080.   **L.W. Zelly**, "Hydrogen as an Energy Storage Element", in T. Nejat Veziroglu, *Hydrogen Energy*. Plenum Press. 1975.

INDEX

absorption-desorpt. curves	112	carbon dioxide, absorption	14
acid electrolyte	17	carbon dioxide, emissions	184
acids in hydrogen prod.	15	carbon dioxide,heat storage	62
activation potential	187	carbon from waste	76-77
Adt, Robert R.	149-236	carbon monoxide	173
Advanced Battery Consort.	184-185	carbon storage, hyd., cost	140
air conditioning, hydride	134	carbon from pyrolysis	76-77
air pollution, hydrocarbons	164	catalyst, nickel	141-142
air pollution, hyd. in fuel	142,164,171-174	catalyst, ortho-para conv.	94
air pollution, nitrous oxides	164	catalyst, platinium	206
air pollution, utilities	184	catalyst, steel	66
aircraft, hydrogen	49,98,229	Carter,Jimmy,President	121
airport, specs for hyd.	229	cathode, fuel cell	185
algae, hydrogen production	55	cell voltage	22
alkaline electrolyte	17	centrifuging	58
alternat. current, fuel cell	190,194	Cherry, Paul	190
American Hyd. Association	59,62,87,140,616	Chevrolet, liquid hyd.	98
ammonia splitting	14-15	China	173
anode, fuel cell	185	chloroplasts	56
Appleby, John	236	circulation, electrolyte	32,36
Argonne National Lab	188	combustion temperature	166
Argosy bus	130	comparison, hydrides	114
asbestos separator	21	compression ratio, hyd.	164
autoignition, diesel	163	compression ratio, def.	163
		concentration polariz.	187
backfiring	169	condenser	142
batteries, lead acid	139	containment, CO2	141
battery charging	190	contaminants, hydride	114,116
Bernoulli Theorem	205	Cook, Newell C.	67
Bicelli, L.P.	67	coolant, liquid hydrogen	94,108,167
Billings Energy Corp.	14,68,121,125,130	cooling & heating,hydride	201-202
	150,163,206,216	corrosion of electrodes	17
Billings Hydrogen Home	121	corrosion, anode	29
Billings, Roger	149	corrosion, electrode	25
bismuth oxysulfate	65	corrosion, light	55
bismuth sulfate cycle	65	corrosion, separators	29
blue-green algae	56	cost, carbon hyd. storage	140
BMW car	154,174,178	cost, hydrogen, fuel cell	188
Bockris, J.O'M.	194	cost, fuel cells	194
boiloff reduction	92	cost, electrolyser	40
Braun, Harry	140	cost, electrolysis, fuels	51
Brayton Cycle	201	cost, environment, fuels	232-234
bromine-sulfur cycle	66	cost, hyd., comparisons	43-46,64
Brookhaven National Lab.	150	cost, hyd., thermochem.	25,64,67
burner port sizing	205	cost, hydrogen production	14
burner, fuel consumption	204	cost, hydrides	114
burner, fuel velocity	204	cost, hyd. vs fossil fuels	229,231
bus bars	32	cost, liquid hydrogen	92-234
bus fleet	139	cost, oil dependency	224
		Cummins Engine Co.	139
Cadillac, hydride	209,121	current density, electr.	22,32
cadmium nickel hydride	202	current requirements	32,41,43
cadmium sulfide electrode	54		
calcium hydride, hyd. prod.	16	Daimler Benz	202
cam shaft	161	Dandapani, B.	194
Canadian Hyd. Safety Comm.	223	Datsun, liquid hydrogen	101
carbon deposits	158	DeNora Company	40

dewar insulation	92	
dewar volume	94	
DFVLR	105,154	
diesel running on hyd.	171-174	
direct current,fuel cell	190-194	
direct injection	157	
Dodge Omni, hydride	121	
Dornier Company	231	
dual fuel car, specs	174	
dual fuel, gas and hyd.	134	
efficiency and pressure	28	
efficiency of liquefaction	92	
efficiency of liquid hyd.	108	
efficiency of combustion	225,229	
efficiency, electric motor	188	
efficiency, electrolysis	21,28,36,63	
efficiency, compress. ratio	163	
efficiency, exhaust temp.	166	
efficiency, fuel cell	190,194	
efficiency, heat engine	201	
efficiency, hyd. combustion	206	
efficiency, hyd. vs gasoline	150	
efficiency, magnetocaloric	92	
efficiency, meth. prod., hyd.	75	
efficiency, methane prod.	73-74	
efficiency, photovoltaic	47	
efficiency, thermal	166	
efficiency, thermochem.	63	
efficiency, voltage, electrol.	22	
electric motor, efficiency	188	
electrical resistance	17	
electricity costs vs hyd.	43	
Electrobus	188	
electrode area	47	
electrode corrosion	47	
electrode materials	17,54-55	
electrode, platinum	52	
electrolyser specifications	124	
electrolyser, materials	25	
electrolyser, solid polymer	212	
electrolyser, specs	31,36	
electrolyser, heat prod.	22	
electrolyser circulation	32,36	
electrolyte, solid, fuel cell	188	
electrolytes compared	41	
electrolytes, fuel cell	187	
electrothermochem process	63	
Elenco NV	190	
embrittlement	84,220	
endothermic reaction	71	
energy costs, liquefaction	92	
energy density, batteries	185	
energy of fuels, compared	215	
energy requirements, elec.	22,28,32,41,43	
Energy Research Corp.	190,194	
energy storage, hydride	132	
energy use, liquid hyd.	101	
energy, hyd. vs methane	204	
energy, wind vs water,hyd.	51	
engine exhaust for hydride	118	
engine control, electronic	158	
engine coolant for hydride	118,124	
engine electronic control	174-178	
engine load, equiv. ratio	158	
engine rpm, water inject.	166	
Environ. Protect. Agency	139	
equivalency ratio	158,166	
Ericsson, John	59	
Erren, Rudolph A.	149	
evaporation losses	78,87,105	
exhaust temp., efficiency	166	
exhaust valves, sodium	158	
exothermic reaction	68,71	
ferric oxide, electrode	54	
FeTi hydride, capacity	134	
Fillite (R)	141	
Fillo, J.A.	46	
Finegold R.J.	167	
flame speed, hydrogen	169	
flammability limits	152	
fluid wall, separator	57	
formula, Bernoulli	205	
formula, compression ratio	163	
formula, cooling water	112	
formula, cost syn. fuels	234	
formula, efficiency,electr.	21	
formula, effic., heat engine	201	
formula, effic.,thermochem	63	
formula, engine efficiency	163	
formula, equivalency ratio	158	
formula, Gibbs Function	70	
formula, iron, acid, voltage	194	
formula, therm. efficiency	166	
fuel cell cost	194	
fuel cell electrodes	187	
fuel cell electrolytes	187	
fuel cell output	187,190	
fuel cell range	190	
fuel cell efficiency	190,194	
fuel cell, solid electrolyte	188	
fuel consump., liquid hyd.	101	
fuel economy, PSI Tech.	180	
fuel igniter	105,164-165	
fuel injection, power gain	154	
fuel mixing sequence	154	
fuel pump	157	
fuel vaporizer	101,105	
fueling proceedure, hydride	121,132-134	
fueling proceedure, hyd.	101,105	
Furuhama, Shoichi	105	
Garrett Ceramics Corp.	188	
gas detector, hydrogen	101	
gas turbines using hyd.	181	
gasoline range	139	
General Elect., solid poly.	29	
General Motors solid poly.	29	
General Motors	188	

248

Gibbs Function	70,74	Illinois Institute of Tech.	149
		Impco gas mixer	84
H-Power Corp.	144-145	Indian Institute of Tech.	152,163
Hayden, Herb	180	infrared light	57
heat flow, hydride	125	injection pipe	161
heat loss, ortho-para conv.	94	Institute of Gas Tech.	206,232
heat of reaction	69-70	insulation, dewar	92
heat production, electrol.	22	insulation, quilted	94
heat pumps, hydride	201	internal heat exchanger	124
heat storage, chemical	62	iodine-sulfur cycle	66
heat transfer, hydride	112,118,134,202	ion exchange current	187
heat transfe, iron titanium	112	iron in fuel cells	194
heat, waste, hyd. prod.	46	iron in hydrogen prod.	15,53,144-145
hexachloroplatinate	56	iron titanium, water use	112
Hindenburg fire	219	isooctane	116
Hoagland, William	232		
Hoffman, Peter	12	Jeep, gaseous hydrogen	116
Hot Elly	40-41,44-45,231	Jorgenson, Irving	59
hybrid thermochem proc.	63		
hydride contaminates	114,116	kitty litter	140
hydride energy storage	132	Kordesch, Carl	188
hydride heat transfer	202		
hydride heating, cooling	201-202	Lake Mead	57
hydride in suspension	116	Lalvani, S.B.	52
hydride packing	116,125	lanthanum nickel Al	116
hydride range	130,184	lanthanum nickel hydride	202
hydride storage capacity	79,139	LaserCel 1	190
hydride storage safety	219	lean best torque setting	169
hydride tank	124	Liepa, M.A.	43,46
hydride tube bundles	120,125,130	Linde Div., Union Carbide	132
hydride volume	79	liquefaction costs	92
hydride vs liquid hyd.	183	liquefaction efficiency	92
hydride water coolant	132	liquid hydrogen car specs	108
hydride weight penalty	108	liquid hydrogen dewar vol.	108
hydride, range	139	liquid hydrogen as coolant	94
hydrides compared	114-116	liquid hyd. fueling proceed.	101,105
hydrides, general reaction	112	liquid hydrogen pump	101,105
hydrocarbons, steam ref.	14	liquid hydrogen range	87,139,184
hydrochloric acid electrol.	52	liquid hydrogen safety	101
hydrochloric acid, hyd.	15	liquid hydrogen vs hydride	183
hydrogen combustion	202,206	liquid hydrogen efficiency	108
Hydrogen Energy Lab.	124	liquid hyd. storage volume	98,101
hydrogen gas detector	101	Lorenzen, John	215
Hydrogen Homestead	125	Lurgi Company	231
hyd. output, biological	56	Lynch, F.E.	152
hydrogen production, NaOH	16		
hyd. production methods	229	magnesium nickel hydride	185
hydrogen production, U.S.	14,222	magnetic refrigeration	92
hydrogen purification	15	magnetic separation	58
Hydrogen Racing Program	178,180	manifold exhaust, types	161
hydrogen sulfide, electrol.	54-55	manifold, hyd. production	27,32-38
hydrogen added to fuel	171-174	Mazda RX-4, hydride	124
hydrogen tractor	209	McAlister, Roy	62,76,140,161,178
hydrogen stored, hydride	110		224,236
hydrogen vs natural gas	200-201	McCain, John, Senator	139
hydrogen, liquid, costs	234	McDonnell Douglas Corp.	59
hyd.-gasoline compared	146	Mercedes Benz car	174
hydroxyl ions	187	Mercedes Benz van	134
Hysolar Project	62	methane	225
Ideal Gas Law	83	methane production	62

methane, heat storage	62
methanol	68,71
methanol, steam reform.	144
mischmetal, hydride	114
monethylaine	14
Motronic microcomputer	178
Musashi Institute of Tech	105,161
Nafion (R)	41,54
National Bureau of Stds	92
National Fire Protec. Ass'n.	222
National Renewable Energy	232
natural gas vs hydrogen	200-201
natural gas, steam reform.	194
nickel catalyst	14,142
nickel hydride battery	185
nickel-oxy-hydroxide	185
Ninth World Hyd. Conf.	142,178,190,232
nitric acid	67
nitrosonium phosphate	67
nitrous oxides	121,133,147,157 164,166
nitrous oxides, burners	214
Nitsch, J.E.	51
nuclear energy	225
nuclear waste heat	46
off peak electric storage	139,232
Oklahoma State University	157,164
Oldsmobile, liquid hyd.	87
organic dyes	53
Orr, Evan	232
ortho-para conv. losses	94
ortho-para, catalyst	94
Oscillatoria sp. Miami	56
output, electrolysis	28
output, hyd. prod.,chemical	18
output, hyd., thermochem	66
over water collection	15,26,35
Ovionic Battery Company	185
palladium separators	58
parabolic solar dish	59
parallel-series, fuel cells	187
Penn. Depart. of Energy	190
perfluorinated sulfon. acid	29,41
photoanode	54-55
photocathode	54-55
photocorrosion	53-55
photoelectrodes	46,53
photosynthesis	55-56
pipelines	220,231-232
piston head shaving	163
platinum catalyst	206
platinum electrode	52,56
Podgorny, A.N.	161
Pontiac	163,169
Pontiac, hydride	121
poppet valve	161
potassium hydroxide elecl.	21
potassium, hyd. prod.	15,18
potassium titanite	41
power conditioning	47-49
power loss, hydride	125
Power Tower	59
Pratt and Whitney	181
pressure regulator	84
pressure, gas storage	83
propane,supplemental fuel	130,133
PSI Technology	178,180
pump, liquid hydrogen	101,105
pyrolysis, fuel cell	188
quenching, impingement	58
quenching, injection	58
quenching, water splitting	58
quilted insulation	94
race cars, hydride	124
racing cars, liquid hyd.	108
range, electric cars	184
range, electric fuel cell	190
range, gas storage	83
range, gasoline	139
range, hydride	130,139,184
range, liquid hydrogen	87,101-5,139,184
reactor	142
refrigeration, magnetic	92
regenerative breaking	183
Reilly, J.J.	121
relief valve, hydrogen	171
Rhodobacter sphaeroides	56
rotary engines	150
rpm and load, hyd. in fuel	171
safety, automatic control	18
safety, electrolyser	25-28
safety, hydride storage	219
safety, liquid hydrogen	101
Salzano, F.J.	236
Sasol process	64
Schaeppel, R.J.	164
separation	58
separator material	21
separator, fluid wall	57
Sievert's Law	110
silicone, electrode	54
smart plug	161
sodium bicarbonate	141
sodium formate	141
sodium hydrox., hyd. prod.	15,18
sodium, hyd. production	15,18
sodium sulfate	52
solar dish	59
solar energy	225
solar energy potential	46-47,57
solar thermal pyrolysis	77
solid electrolyte fuel cell	188
solid polymer electrolyser	212
Solvani, P.	110

Southern Calif. Edison	59	town gas	68
Southern Calif. Gas Co.	206	tracking the sun	59,62
spark plugs, low temp.	158	Trans Energy Corp.	178,180
spark plugs, smart plug	161	transatmospheric vehicle	98
specs, airport,hyd.	229	trimethylpentone	116
specifications, BMW	154	turbocharger	147
specifications, diesel, hyd.	150,152,173	turbocharger, hydrogen	152
specs, dual fuel car	174	turbocharging	108
specs, electrolyser	124-125		
specifications, engine, hyd.	171	U.S. Bureau of Mines	152
specifications, hydride bus	130-133	U.S. Department of Energy	139,141
specifications, hydride car	121-124	U.S. Department of Trans.	108
specs, hydride tractor	125	U.S.S.R.	161
specifications, Jeep	150	ultraviolet light	53
specs, liquid hyd. car	108	University of Arizona	142
specs, liquid hyd. engine	174	University of California	161
specs, mining vehicle	152	University of Miami	149
specs, photovolt. hyd. prod.	49	University of Texas	194
specs, solid polymer elect.	212	Urban Vehicle Competition	150
specs, spark ignit. engine	152		
specs, Suzuki diesel	161	vacuum	79
specs, VW fuel cell van	190	Van Vorst, W.W.	157
Spillers, Frank W.	236	vanadium separators	58
steam reform., fuel cells	194	vaporizer, fuel	101,105
steam ref., hydrocarbons	14,76-77	Vehicle Design Compet.	105
steam reforming methanol	144	vehicle specs, liquid hyd.	105
steam reforming, carbon	68	venting, combustion	216
steam refom., natural gas	194	venting, vehicle storage	101
steel, catalyst	66	Verne, Jules	2
Stirling engine, liquid hyd.	59,108	Veziroglu, T. Nejat	229,236
Stewart, W.F.	161	Volkswagen	142
storage plateau area	110	voltage efficiency, electro.	22
storage volume, dewar	94	voltage-current, fuel cell	190
stratified-charge	178,180	voltage input, elec.	32
sulfur dioxide, hyd. prod.	52-54,65-66	volume of hyd., hydride	110
sulfuric acid	65-66	volume of hyd.,in LH2	98,101-108
sulfuric acid electrolyte	19	VW van, fuel cell, specs	190
sulfuric acid, hyd. prod.	15,52,194		
sun motors, electr. output	59	Wagner, Demetri	87,108,178,180
supercharging	154	Watanabe, Kenji	124
superheater	142	water from combustion	209
supplemental hydrogen	142	water injection	121,133,147,166-7
Suzuki diesel, specs	161	water splitting, temp.	57-58
Swain, M.R.	149	Watson, H.C.	161
synjet fuel	98	weight penalty, hydride	108
synthesis gas	68,69,71	weight penalty, LH2	98
synthetic fuels, costs	234	Westinghouse Cycle	65
		wind energy vs water,hyd.	51
Teitel, Robert J. and Assoc.	141	wind potential, potential	51
Teledyne, electrolyser	29	Wooley, R.L.	68
Tempe, Arizona	139		
temperature, combustion	166	yttria-zirconium	41,188
temperature, water	47,57-58		
Texas Instruments	55	zinc, hydrogen production	15
thermocouple	142	zinc-chloride batteries	183
thermodynamic, laws of	69	Zweig, Robert	150
thermoneutral voltage	22,25,41		
thylakoid membrane	56		
timed port injection	147		
titanium dioxide electrode	54		